The Eskimo in the Net

The Eskimo in the Net

By
GERARD BEIRNE

MARION BOYARS
LONDON • NEW YORK

First published in Great Britain and the United States in 2003 by
MARION BOYARS PUBLISHERS LTD
24 Lacy Road, London SW15 1NL

www.marionboyars.co.uk

Distributed in Australia and New Zealand by Peribo Pty Ltd
58 Beaumont Road, Kuring-gai, NSW 2080

10 9 8 7 6 5 4 3 2

The publishers would like to thank the Arts Council of England for financial
assistance.

A CIP catalogue record for this book is available from the British Library.
A CIP catalog record for this book is available from the Library of Congress.

ISBN 0-7145-3093-X

Set in Garamond Elegant 10.5/13.
Printed and bound in England by Bookmarque Ltd, London

For Eilish

I am deeply indebted to John Keeble, a remarkable writer and instructor, who profoundly affected my approach and attitude to writing. Thank you, John.

Wayne, my gratitude for the many late-night discussions, spot-on advice, and cheap rides to Moscow (Idaho). Let me in!

Michael Murray. Stalwart. Thanks for the early heady days.

CHAPTER ONE

Everything started to go wrong the day we dragged the Eskimo up in the net off Malin Head. I wasn't long back from Alaska, and it seemed as if he must have followed me halfways around the world. My initial instinct was to pull his chewed-up corpse free from the mountain of fish and roll him overboard, to let him sink back into the depths of the ocean where he had first appeared from, to watch him slip beneath the waves as if he had never surfaced in the first place. Knucky even suggested as much.

'It's going to be a headache if we don't,' he said, 'a mountain of paperwork.'

But I didn't have the heart to do it. For all we knew someone could be out looking for him at that moment in time, searching this northern coastline for his remains. Or somewhere on the other side of the globe perhaps, clinging to some frail hope that he was still alive, still hanging on to the frayed edges of this world.

'We're going to have to take him in,' I said. 'It's our duty.'

'Fuck you and your sense of duty, Gallagher. This is going to cost us a full day's fishing.' Knucky cleared his throat of phlegm and spat into the sea. I watched it float there like spawn. Then a swirl of froth swept across it and took it from our sight. 'Let's just throw him overboard. It's where he belongs.'

'Knucky,' I protested, 'it's a human being we're talking about.'

'It's a corpse. A rotting corpse. It's probably been buried at sea. Now you don't want to start digging up the dead, do you?' Knucky walked back to the wheelhouse, his eyes on the buoys ahead.

'We don't know that,' I said. But all the same, Knucky had a point. There was a possibility that he, whoever he was, had died on board one of the vessels that fished these waters and had been buried in that time-honoured fashion. In fact, I had often thought myself that it would be the perfect way to go, to sink into the murky soul of the sea and be devoured by the marine life within, drifting forever in one form or another throughout the oceans of this world.

But what if that wasn't the case? What if he had fallen overboard during a squall, or if he had nothing to do with the sea whatsoever? If that was just where his remains had ended up?

A wave of spray washed over the boat, swept across my face like a light mist. I held onto the side and looked down at the black water he had emerged from. Its troubled surface swirled in a filthy froth, keeping its inner secrets to itself. 'If that's the case,' I said, 'if he's been buried, we'll find out.'

'It'll be too late then.' Knucky turned on the engine and let it idle. 'The body will have been disturbed.'

I listened to the low rumble of the hidden mechanical components, like a mumbling complaint. 'It's already been disturbed,' I said. The boat lurched, and instinctively I shifted my balance. The wooden deck groaned. I wasn't convinced by my own argument. Nevertheless, whatever way I weighed it up I knew we'd have to take the body in. My conscience wouldn't have allowed otherwise.

'It's my boat, Jim,' Knucky said. 'When you're out here you're following my orders. And don't you forget it.' The radio crackled next to him. A gull flew in low, stalled in its flight and landed on top of the wheelhouse.

It was a half-hearted attempt at asserting authority. It wasn't in Knucky's nature to be a boss of anything. Besides, that wasn't the way it worked between Knucky and I. I fished with him, and he paid me a wage. We helped each other out. We went back too far for it to be any other way.

I continued to insist, and Knucky had no option but to relent.

While Knucky turned the boat around I took another look at the body. It lay there in the net, swallowed up by a slimy wriggling mound of fish, crabs and seaweed. One half-eaten arm poked out through a covering of sea bass as if reaching towards me, begging to be saved. The putrid smell of the life of the sea mingled with the stench of his death. I swept seaweed and some carp and trout from his face to get a better look at him. His left ear was missing, and his skin and flesh were torn away in parts so that you could see right down to the bone.

It was like looking below the surface of your own body, seeing beyond the flesh into the hollowness of all you contained. His mouth was slightly open as if he was trying to say something but couldn't find the words to express it adequately. A small white crab the size of a ten pence piece crawled out of his mouth, across his lower lip and down his chin, then scuttled away to disappear into the scaly crevices of the stacked fish.

Although his body had started to decompose, I could still make out most of his features. And it was then I realized how far he had travelled.

'Christ!' I stepped back onto a small trout. I felt its firm body flapping beneath the sole of my boot. I raised my foot and kicked it away from me across the deck.

'What is it?' Knucky asked. 'What the hell is it now?'

The world swayed beneath my feet as we rocked on its shimmering surface. Knucky stared back at me through the door of the wheelhouse. He held on to the wheel lightly but firmly, like you would hold someone you love. Sometimes when I saw him like that it seemed to me as if he had always been at sea, as if he had been born somewhere out in the middle of the ocean, had been reared at its salty bosom and had never set foot on shore at all. I would watch the water swelling all around him like the rise and fall of his chest and hear it splash against the boat like the deep sigh of his breathing.

'What the hell, Jim?' he asked again when I didn't respond.

'Jesus, Knucky. It's an Eskimo.' I couldn't take my eyes off him, off the round dark features.

'Are you fucking crazy?' Knucky shouted. I heard him mutter to himself, 'Sweet Jesus.'

It was understandable that he didn't believe me. I felt a splash of water trickle down the back of my neck. I closed my eyes, breathed in the salty air. I opened them again and turned around to Knucky. He was watching me. He didn't look angry, more disappointed about something.

'I'm telling you, Knucky,' I said. 'I know. I worked with Eskimos for a while in the oil refinery at Prudhoe Bay. Whoever he is, he's an Eskimo all right.'

Knucky groaned, shook his head. 'That's all we fucking need.'

'Where do you think he came out of?'

I sat by the wheelhouse on an upturned plastic fish crate. The day was calm but cold. I pulled my jacket in tightly around me to keep out the wind. The boat slid along the backs of the waves. I looked up at the greying sky and the off-white clouds that streaked it like damp stains that would be difficult to remove. Knucky stood next to me, his jacket open, his dark black hair swept back across his head. He never seemed to notice the elements, whether it was cold or raining he always stood like this. As if he were beyond the elements, beyond weather itself.

'He came out of the fucking sea, Gallagher. That's where he came out of.' He looked over his shoulder as if viewing all the water this cursed corpse had caused him to leave behind. 'And that's where he should have gone back to.' He rubbed at the stubble on his chin and pulled at his nose as if he was about to blow it into his fingers. 'You're a softie, Jim. That's the real fucking problem here. Fishing is an altogether different sort of business.'

'We're all softies, Knucky,' I told him, gripping the sides of the crate with my fingers. 'Underneath it all we're nothing more than mush.'

Knucky swung his head across at me. He looked as if he was going to speak, but then he pushed his tongue through his lips and held it there with his teeth so it looked like a piece of someone else's flesh, a piece he had bitten off. And for one moment I could almost have believed that it was an ear.

'If you don't believe me,' I said nodding over my shoulder to the body, 'go ask the one down back.'

We sailed back up the narrow lough. Returning home almost before we had set out. Knucky gripped the wheel and steered, no longer speaking. I looked to the Northern Irish Coast to our left, the calm waters slipping across its borders, chipping them away. The loud boom of artillery from the army base resounded through the air as if paying its last respects to the dead on board. The prison camp next to it looked more bleak and hopeless than ever, and for the first time that I could remember I dreaded coming ashore.

We radioed our find ahead but said nothing about the body's origins. Tom Harte the harbour master, Sergeant Bonnar and Charlie Doherty, one of the local guards, were waiting to meet us as we docked.

I threw the rope to Tom and he secured it to the bollard. Knucky showed them on board.

'We hauled us in a big one,' he said, flinging his thumb in the direction of the nets. The Eskimo had sunk deeper into the fish with the movement of the boat. Up to his chin.

Knucky leaned up against the side of the boat and pulled out a pack of cigarettes. I went over and stood beside Tom and the others. They crouched in over the open net but straightened up quickly as though afraid they might lose their balance and fall in on top of him.

'Jesus, Jim,' Tom said. 'What the hell have you got there?'

'It's anybody's guess,' Knucky answered.

'He's not from around here, that's for sure.' Tom pulled at the collar of his shirt.

'He's an Eskimo, Tom. I've seen Eskimos before.'

Tom said nothing. He just stood there, clutching his shirt, looking down at the corpse as if wondering where all of this left him. The sergeant kicked at the fish at the edges of the mound, his hands buried deep in his pockets. Charlie Doherty looked away as though this were more than anyone had a right to see.

'Was anyone reported missing? From any of the factory ships or anything?' The ships had passed by on their way back up to the Baltics a couple of weeks previously. And for now it seemed the most likely explanation.

Tom wrinkled up his top lip and shook his head. 'Nothing,' he said. 'Nothing that would tie in.'

Knucky strolled over pulling on his cigarette with his thumb and forefinger. 'What have we got to do, Tom?' he drawled, tired of this whole business. He tossed back his head and blew a sharp plume of smoke high into the air, then flicked the butt overboard. 'Let's just get him out of here, sign whatever has to be signed, and get this show back on the road. I can do without this.'

Tom folded his arms in front of him and raised his shoulders, breathing inwards. 'We can all do without it,' he said, then cast his head towards the body. 'Him more than most.'

Charlie Doherty pushed past us, rushing to the side of the boat, and retched into the sea.

'Jesus!' Knucky blew out his cheeks.

Charlie retched again like the grating creak of the winch turning as it dragged in the nets. He leaned right over the side, in danger of falling overboard himself. When he came up again for air his dark blue uniform was splattered in the kelpy colours of vomit blown back in over him by the wind. His face was starkly pale as though, young as he was, death had suddenly caught up with him.

Despite Knucky's insistence, the *Lorna Doone* was going nowhere for the rest of that day. There were regulations to be followed, Tom said. Procedures to be carried out. He had contacted IMES, the Irish Marine Emergency Services, and was waiting for word back from them. An ambulance would be along later. In the meantime he wanted her left there tied up at the harbour.

Knucky climbed up on the edge of the boat and stepped out onto the pier. Charlie was already up there, standing against the wall for support. 'This is all your fault, Gallagher,' Knucky said. 'I want you to know that. I want you to know that I hold you personally responsible.' He spat back down into the water.

'It could be worse,' I said.

'What could be fucking worse?'

'It could be one of us over there, not him.'

'Don't you worry,' Knucky said. 'We'll have our fucking day.' He reached down and helped pull me up beside him. 'Oh Christ! Heaven protect us.'

I looked around to see what had caused Knucky's latest out-burst and saw Father Jack headed towards us, blowing into his cupped hands.

'Where is it?' he roared without offering any greeting.

'Over there,' I told him, pointing back down to the rear of the deck where Tom Harte and the sergeant were talking together.

He walked to the edge of the pier and stared down. 'Jesus!' he said.

Knucky and I looked to one another, and for the first time since we had brought the stranger up Knucky smiled.

Father Jack threw his arms up in the air as though waiting for an ascension. 'Hasn't anyone bothered to take him out of that shit? How the hell can I give him my blessing like that?'

CHAPTER TWO

After we had showered Knucky went off home. I suggested going for a pint but he said he didn't think so, that he wasn't in the humour. This whole Eskimo business had upset everything. But it wasn't just the fishing, or rather the lack of fishing, that had caused Knucky's foul humour. It was this brush with death. The whole ghastly putrid reality of it. There in his nets, on his deck.

Although we never talked about it, Knucky was doomed to a shorter life than the rest of us. Even though I had known him all my life, I didn't know much more about it than that he had a hole in his heart. He was born with it, Frances had told me, and had been lucky to survive in the first place. From the moment of his birth he was living on borrowed time, she said. That's just the way it was. I didn't ask anything more than this. It didn't seem as if I had any right to. A person's death was surely their own property. And yet that Eskimo we dragged up on board had failed to keep his death to himself.

I said goodbye to Knucky. I needed a drink even if he didn't. I also needed to see a friendly face, so I went across to The Porthole, where I knew Frances would be working the afternoon shift.

She was polishing glasses up at the counter when I walked in. At the sound of the door opening she looked up.

'Jim,' she said simply. She held the glass she had been shining up in the air to examine it as though looking for flaws. Not thumbprints or beer stains but imperfections in the glass itself, as if somehow she could shine them away. And if anyone could have, it would have been her.

The three of us, Frances, Knucky and I, had been friends together ever since childhood. Later on for a while Knucky and Frances had a thing together. Frances said it wasn't love, that neither she nor Knucky were capable of that. She said she didn't believe in it, but they did have

13

some good times together, some of the best. I was happy for them. They seemed good for one another. Frances seemed to fill in that hole in Knucky's heart somehow. And she filled in whatever holes riddled my body also.

'What has you in so soon?' she asked.

'Didn't you hear?' I pulled in a stool and sat up at the counter. The bar was empty except for the two of us. It seemed darker than usual. Colder, too, as if Frances hadn't been expecting anyone and was saving money on light and electricity. Though God knows why it'd be in her interest to do that. Orders from above perhaps, except that Frances was not a person you'd easily give orders to.

'Hear what?' She took a glass from beneath the counter and began pulling a Guinness.

'You didn't hear about the catch?'

'What catch? I haven't heard a thing. You're the first person in here since we opened.' She put the glass on the draining rack to let it settle.

'We hauled in a body this morning, Knucky and I. Caught in the nets.'

Frances shook her head slowly as though death never ceased to surprise her. 'Was it anyone we know?'

'No. Not as such.'

I told her all about it. About bringing him up in the nets and spilling his half-chewed up body out with the fish on the deck, looking at a loss to know what to do. Then I told her how he turned out to be Eskimo.

Frances looked at me sternly. I knew I had said something I shouldn't. 'Inuit,' she corrected me, 'isn't that the proper term now?'

Frances was sensitive to these things. The rest of us could live our lives as though separated from the outside world, but not her, not the world of the living or the dead. Apart from her I could not think of another person in these parts who would even have heard of the Inuit or be aware of their concerns. She knew as well as I did that around here he would remain an Eskimo forever, irrespective of his or anyone else's wishes.

She looked at me waiting on my answer.

'Not while I lived in Alaska,' I told her. 'The people there still called themselves Eskimos, but you're right, elsewhere it's different.'

'I was taught it was a derogatory term,' she said, not wanting to give up that easily, 'an insult.'

I shrugged. 'I guess some people don't see it that way.' I told her how I had even been to the World Eskimo Indian Olympics in Fairbanks. 'But he could easily be from somewhere else where that word isn't appropriate,' I said, seeking to appease her.

Frances looked disappointed, as though she had been let down somehow, as if something important she had put her trust in had proved to be of little substance in the end. 'I suppose it hardly matters to him now,' she said.

'Not much,' I agreed.

'What about Knucky?' she asked. 'How did he take it?'

'He was furious. Furious at losing a day's fishing. But I think it shook him up a bit, too, although he'd never admit it.'

Frances nodded. She went quiet, as though remembering some part of her life with Knucky that I had no knowledge of.

'Is he all right?' she finally asked.

'I think so,' I said. 'He wouldn't come for a pint. Said he was going home.'

She finished off pouring my drink and passed it out to me. I put my hand in my pocket for change but she shook her head. 'This one's on me. You deserve it.' She wiped a drop of Guinness from the counter. 'So where do you think he came from, this Eskimo of yours?'

She was still annoyed about it.

'Who knows,' I said. 'Maybe one of those big Russian factory ships. All I know is that he is here now, whether he likes it or not.'

'You think he fell overboard?'

'Your guess is as good as mine. But don't you think it's strange, here I am barely back six months from Arctic shores and now someone from there turns up dead virtually on my doorstep?'

'He's a long way from home, that's for certain,' Frances said. She didn't seem to know what to make of it any more than I did. 'So what happens now?'

'Oh, I'm sure the Department of the Marine or the Emergency Services will sort it all out,' I said. 'Tom Harte's taken command for the moment. Wouldn't let Knucky take his boat back out.'

'I bet Knucky was happy about that.' Frances laughed to herself.

I took a drink and wiped my mouth with my sleeve. 'Father Jack's none too happy either. Seems death was getting in the way of his living.'

'Gets in all our ways,' Frances said.

She had a deep respect for Father Jack. It was a respect for his faith, she told me once, his willingness to trust so completely in one person, someone you could not see, at that. It was more than she could manage. She could barely put her trust in the flesh and blood before her. Maybe that was the problem, I had said, maybe the upper hand God held was his invisibility. The way his faults could not be seen.

Frances told me that more than anything she wished to regain her faith. To have the belief in God that she'd had as a young girl. To be willing to put her body and mind into His hands. Some day, she said, hopefully before I die. But in the meantime, she smiled, I guess I'll continue to drop acid and hope for the best.

Frances was the only person I knew who took LSD in these parts. Drugs were not a common part of life here. And although I asked she never told me where she got it from. 'You don't want to know,' she said. 'You really don't.'

This was the way it was between Frances, Knucky and I. In some ways we knew each other as intimately as was possible, but in others we scarcely knew each other at all. As if there were parts within us we needed to keep to ourselves. Dark private ones only we were allowed go into, or perhaps ones even we didn't dare enter.

Frances leaned on the counter with her elbows. 'When do you get the boat back?'

'Later in the day, we hope,' I said. 'They're waiting on an ambulance now.'

'And what about the body? What will they do with that?'

'I don't really know.'

Again she went quiet, staring down between her hands as if they held something immensely important but impenetrable. She remained like this for a minute or two then slowly raised her head.

'I need to see it,' she said. 'Before they move it.'

She reached below the counter and took out a set of keys. 'Come on,' she said. 'I'll be back before the rush.'

We walked across the road to the pier. A large refrigerated truck drove out from the fisherman's Co-op past us. The driver nodded to us and swung out on the road. I expected to see a crowd gathered around the boat like it held some fairground freak show of old. But apart from the solitary figure of Charlie Doherty sitting on the steel bollard midway down the pier where it was tied up there was no one else around. It was early afternoon and everyone else was out fishing. The *Lorna Doone* tied up by herself looked as forlorn as Charlie. She tugged half-heartedly against her ropes as though she wished to be back out there where she belonged but realized the implausibility of it all. We watched her rise and fall gently on the small swell of the harboured waves.

Charlie looked up as we approached. His hat hung on one knee, and his chin rested in his hands. He still didn't look too good. He nodded at us both.

'You look as if you're suffering,' Frances said, kicking at one of the steel rings implanted in the concrete for tying up the boats. 'It must have been a rough night last night.'

Charlie glanced at me as if he expected me to say something smart about his vomiting earlier. Something that would let Frances know that his wretched appearance had nothing to do with a hangover. Something that would embarrass him. But I said nothing. I looked away beyond the pier out at the lough. A long yellow cargo ship moved slowly back out to sea. Undoubtedly word would get out. Maybe Tom Harte or Knucky or the sergeant would start off the laugh at his expense. But it didn't seem funny to me. What happened to Charlie is what should have happened to all of us. And if it had been someone we knew and not the Eskimo, it possibly would have.

I tried to smile in such a way as to let him know I was on his side but somehow it must have come out like a smirk or a sneer. He picked his hat up and put it on, then pushed himself up with one hand.

'What are you doing down here anyway?' he asked.

'I have to go to the boat,' I said. I had intended to tell him straight out that Frances wanted a look at the body, but something in his tone told me he was about to adopt the authority of his uniform.

'I'm sorry,' he said. 'No one's allowed through.'

'For God's sake, Charlie. I work on the boat. You know that. I just have to collect something.'

'I'm sorry, Jim, orders. No one's to go near the vessel.'

'Surely that doesn't include me?'

'You, Knucky, everyone. It's a no-go area. They don't want anyone interfering with the body.'

'Who's interfering with the body? I just want to pick something up I left behind in the confusion when we docked.'

'Look Jim, I'm just doing what I've been told. Surely it's in Knucky's and your interest. You don't want everyone swanning all over the boat.'

'Of course not. But it's not everyone. It's just me. You can make that distinction, can't you?'

'Come on, Charlie,' Frances said. 'Just let us past. This is ridiculous.'

'You too?' he said.

'Yeah, me too.'

'They could be here any moment. It wouldn't look good for me.'

'Who could be here?' I asked.

Charlie shook his head. 'Medical people, officials. I don't know. Whoever it is they are getting to deal with all of this.'

Charlie genuinely looked as if he didn't know what he was doing there. As if nothing about it made sense, but then again as if nothing about it had to. Frances had already walked past his blind side and had climbed on board. Charlie saw my gaze turn towards her and noticed what she had done.

'Hey!' he shouted.

'Some people!' I said and raised my eyebrows. 'What can you do?' I walked over and climbed down to join her.

Frances was down on her knees before the scattered mound of fish, almost as if she was praying. She leaned on a white plastic fish crate for support.

'It's hard to tell,' she whispered, 'if he's going down or coming up.'

The boat dipped slightly as Charlie jumped noisily down behind us. The fish or the body had moved again since I last saw it. The Eskimo's face was almost covered over completely now.

'I've got to see his face,' Frances said and looked back at Charlie for his approval.

'Don't touch anything,' he warned. 'This has gone too far as it is.'

'It's just a fish or two,' she said. 'Who on earth would know?'

Charlie rubbed at his eyes. He was losing control of the situation. He was unable to prevent it. 'Just don't touch the body.' Then he turned his face away. He stared up at the radio mast above the wheelhouse.

I couldn't tell if he didn't want to witness this breach of duty or if he simply couldn't bear to see the face of the Eskimo again.

Frances pulled the fish from around his head until it was exposed right down to the neck. She put her hand out and stroked his forehead. 'You poor thing,' she said. 'You are so alone.'

Then she bent down and kissed him on his cold and rotting lips that the crab had climbed over earlier.

'God help us,' Charlie whispered behind us. I saw him bless himself.

Frances raised herself up and placed her fingers to her lips and held them there. Her whole body began to shiver. 'Hold me, Jim,' she said.

I went over and put my arms around her, pulling her head into the crook of my neck. I shivered also, as though the tremor of her kiss had entered my body too.

'Come on,' Charlie said. 'We shouldn't be here.'

He climbed out. I held on to Frances, and we stayed there together until her trembling had ceased.

CHAPTER THREE

For the rest of the evening I sat in the corner and watched through the window of The Porthole. Charlie either sat on the bollards or paced the pier. People came and went, looking down at the boat, pointing out the body. From time to time some approached, but Charlie turned them away. At one point I thought I saw Knucky way in the distance, but something in the bar distracted me and when I looked again there was no sight of him to be had.

There were a half a dozen or more drinking now. Frances worked quietly away. Her tall frame moved through the bar with ease. Her surroundings, whatever and wherever they might be, seemed impelled to fit in with her, not the other way around. You could never imagine any uncertainty in her life, and yet that was not the case. 'I don't know where I'm going any more than the next person,' she told me just before I left for Alaska. 'It's all a lottery. If there is a God, you can bet He's got a gambling problem. And unfortunately for us we're His stake.'

What she felt when she kissed the Eskimo's lips I would never know. That was another part of her life I was not included in. And yet when she held me afterwards and those lips brushed my cheek in passing, it became a part of my life also. This was the way it went on. That kiss would permeate everything that Frances touched for ever. And everyone. It would linger on everybody's lips in one way or another.

Although Frances and I had known one another for almost thirty years I had never kissed her lips once, nor she mine. She would walk right up to a stranger and plonk one smack on his, but she carefully avoided mine. We would embrace, hold our bodies close, kiss cheeks or foreheads. We had even skinny-dipped together, disclosed our naked bodies to one another. But lips were out of bounds. This suited us both.

Although we never talked about it, we understood that this was as it was. That this was a defining feature of our relationship, like all relationships we needed one, and the boundaries of our lips were it.

When she and Knucky were together they would kiss all the time, as though that were the defining feature of their relationship. And maybe it was. But I was aware there were other definitions I knew nothing about. Ones that were around me all the time, but I could never notice. And maybe ones that I simply could not be present for.

I have often said it. When Knucky and Frances were together were some of the happiest times we had. Frances would say that it was a time of turmoil, a most unpleasant experience, and Knucky would laugh at this and agree. And it's true that their relationship was stormy and turbulent, but I had never felt so much at ease in their company before. It was as if we had found a way for the three of us to come together. As if their relationship was the defining feature of mine with them.

Frances came down and stood by my table, staring out through the window. 'There's warnings of a storm,' she said. 'Looks like it's going to get rough out there.' She put one knee up on the seat and leaned against the window sill with her hands.

'There must be someone somewhere looking for him,' I repeated for the umpteenth time. 'Someone somewhere wondering whatever became of the man they loved.'

Frances sighed deeply, as if ridding herself of the stale air in her lungs, and then sighed inwards. 'Do you ever wonder what would happen if you went missing, whether anyone would notice or not?'

'I don't think you need fear that your lack of presence would go unnoticed, Frances,' I laughed.

'I don't know,' she said. 'Maybe you, Knucky, but who else? And even you two, you'd give up the search eventually.'

'It's not like that, Frances. You don't get away that easily.'

'Ah, but you do, Jim. That's the point. People get away all the time.' She reached down and took a drink from my glass. 'Maybe that's what's so good about it all.' She finished off the last quarter of my Guinness. 'You need another drink,' she said.

After Frances and Knucky split and I decided to go to Alaska, Frances accused me of trying to disappear. She said all I was really doing was running away, but that she understood this and I was right to do it.

That if she had the nerve she would do the same. But you have to remember, she warned me, that it won't work, wherever you are you will still be present, still facing all that has gone before. The only one disappearing around here, she said, is Knucky. As fast as his little heart will let him.

Frances may well have been right. Maybe I was running away. I tried to tell myself that I was out to find new experiences, to discover a life I never knew I had. A cold bitter one we all held within ourselves. But if I was running away as she said, it wasn't from the past but the future. As Knucky and Frances and I had asked each other so many times throughout our lives, what future did we have in Donegal? What could it possibly hold for us? We had always talked about getting away. I reminded Frances of this then. But she said talk was just talk, and that underneath it was a foundation independent of words, and perhaps that was why we remained for so long.

If any one of us was to leave, Knucky and I had always said it would be Frances. But in the end it was me. Frances was right all along of course. Three years later I returned. I still didn't know why.

The grey overcast skies of the morning had crowded in on themselves and turned a nasty shade of burnt-out charcoal. The waters in the harbour curled sharply against the sides of the pier. My head spun in a similar manner. Frances suggested a number of times that I go home. But I told her I had already reached there. That this was as comfortable as it got.

'You're incorrigible, Gallagher,' she said.

I didn't know how to take this, but thanked her for her comment nevertheless.

The *Lorna Doone* dipped and rose. Charlie Doherty was still waiting beside her for someone to instruct him what to do next. I imagined his anxiety at the turn of events and the turn in the weather. He would be at a loss to know what to do. We all were. It seemed all we could do was wait until someone showed us who would take the Eskimo and this situation, whatever it was, off our hands.

The *Lorna Doone* lurched. I saw Charlie walk over to the edge and peer down into her. And in my mind's eye I saw the Eskimo reach upwards for the third and last time before slithering slowly beneath the sea of fish.

As the rain fell the boats began to return home one by one. They sailed in, docking next to each other. Charlie couldn't stop the fishermen from pouring over to view the body, but somehow he managed to prevent anyone from going on board.

I watched the forklifts from the Co-op driving back and forth, and the men unloading the boats. The afternoon's drinking took hold. And whether a mist or not existed one descended before my eyes. The men weaved in and out of it in their yellow oilskins. I felt the sway of the ground beneath me.

'It'll be dark soon.' Frances sat down next to me. 'I suppose he has nothing more to fear from darkness now.'

'Or everything,' I said.

Frances squeezed her lips together and nodded. 'Charlie was right,' she said. 'God help all of us.' She bit at the side of her mouth.

'I wonder what's keeping everyone. The ambulance ought to be here by now.' I reached for my glass and poured more alcohol into my body.

'There's a lot of dying going on out there,' Frances said.

'But I don't understand why they don't just take him off the boat,' I said. 'What possible harm could that do? It's not as if he hasn't already been disturbed. I pulled him from the bottom of the sea in our nets, for God's sake. I spilled him out on deck like an unsought-after species of marine life. A consequence of net size. What could be wrong with laying him on a slab indoors until this whole sorry mess is sorted out?'

'It's a waiting game,' Frances said. 'That's what we're all playing. It's what we signed up for.'

'I signed up for nothing. You just check,' I told her. 'That's not my signature at the bottom of the paper. It's a carefully transcribed forgery. Check out the hand of your God again.'

Frances put her hand on my shoulder. 'You're drunk, Jim.'

'I know.' I picked up my glass and swirled what was left around like it was a tiny turbulent ocean. 'Whose fault is that?'

Frances squeezed my shoulder gently. 'Who said it was a fault? I like you this way. You know that.'

And it was true, she did. We all liked each other drunk. We always had done. It was pathetic, we agreed, but that was the way we were.

'You're a good drunk, Gallagher. One of the best.' Frances got up, took the empty glass from my hand. 'Do you want to go, or do you want one for the road? Your choice.'

'Make it for me.' I leaned back on the seat strangely satisfied, as if something about my life was finally going to be sorted for me.

Frances smiled. 'I'll be back,' she said.

She drifted into the smoky dullness clearing tables as she went. Then from out of nowhere a nothingness took over.

'Hey, Jim. Move over.'

I was shook out of my sleep by Knucky. He put a pint down on the table beside me and drank from his own. I felt lousy. Not sick, just sluggish and drained.

'Compliments of Frances,' he said.

'How long have you been here?' I asked, ruffling my hand through my hair in some vague hope that this would somehow return me to normality. The bar was beginning to fill. The room shimmered in a haze of smoke.

Knucky looked at me as if I was in dire need of help. 'I've just arrived,' he said. 'What else?'

'What time is it?'

' Half past nine.'

This didn't help me at all. Time had long since lost its meaning for me. 'Have I been asleep long?'

'I told you, I just arrived.'

Knucky was getting impatient with me.

'Drink up,' he said. 'It'll make you feel better.'

I wondered about this and cautiously took a mouthful. Mingled with the taste of sleep in my mouth it almost made me retch. 'Don't ever let them bottle it,' I warned him.

Knucky smiled. He seemed to be taking pleasure in my discomfort.

'What's got you so happy?' I asked.

'She's free,' he said. 'The boat's been freed up. We can go out again tomorrow.'

This was not an encouraging prospect. But at least it meant that something had happened in my absence.

'What's been going on? Where's the body?'

Knucky shrugged. 'It's gone. Who cares? The guards may need us to make a statement at some point in the future but other than that we're just about done with it.'

I hated what I was hearing. I hated him showing this complete lack of regard for what once had been a living human being. I told him this.

'Well, hate me,' he said. 'It's a valid emotion.'

'You're incorrigible,' I told him, finally figuring out what Frances had meant. 'So who came? Who took over, removed the body and all that?'

'I really don't know,' Knucky said. 'Tom Harte rang me a little while ago to give me the all-clear on the boat, and that was all I needed to hear.'

'Then nothing's resolved,' I said. 'We're not the better of it yet.'

'What are you talking about?' he asked.

I turned my hands up the same way he did. 'I really don't know.'

'Frances was right. You're pretty steamed.'

The curtains had been pulled across the windows. Through the small gap where they didn't quite join I saw a line of pitch black. I disliked the shorter evenings. I felt cheated by them. Knucky often said they were his saving grace. He loved the bright early mornings. A clear indication of the possibilities of this world, he said. 'And the dark evenings?' I asked. The other side of the same coin.

'It's been a hell of a day.'

At least there was one thing we agreed on.

'Jim, I need to ask you,' Knucky put his pint down on the table and sucked his lips in to clear them of the froth from his Guinness, 'I know it's probably not the right time to ask, but do you want to give this up? The fishing, I mean. Don't feel you'd be letting me down.'

'Are you trying to get rid of me, Knucky?'

'No, no. God no. I just thought you might be getting fed up of it but might not have known how to say so.'

He seemed genuinely concerned. So I told him the truth. That I was fed up of it. Sick to the gills, if he'd pardon the pun. But all the same, I had no idea what else to do. So if he didn't mind, I told him, I'd like to stay on for the moment. Maybe for always. If that uncertainty was okay with him.

Knucky nodded. 'That's fine by me. You do all right out there. Not terrific, but at least we know where we stand.'

'Good,' I said. 'That's settled then.'

We drank to it knowing that nothing had been settled, that we had no real idea where we stood at all.

Since coming back from Alaska I didn't know what I wanted to do. Taking the job with Knucky was always meant to be a short-term thing, something to tide me over. It was decent of Knucky to have offered. He could get plenty of fishermen around here more experienced than me. His offer was a gesture. A gesture of all that had passed between us. I used to joke that all we'd need was Frances below deck cooking and we'd survive forever. That we could just head off into the wide unknown, the deep blue yonder. 'Wouldn't it be nice?' Knucky agreed. 'Wouldn't it be absolutely perfect?' And I often think he believed this. Frances hated the very notion that we should assume she would cook for the two of us. Of course we knew better than this, and she knew that also. But she'd tell us nevertheless how she'd make a better fisherman than the two of us put together. She was probably right. 'Surely you mean fisher-person,' Knucky said once. Although it seemed obvious to me that this was just a joke, Frances got angry. 'Don't you go giving me that feminist shit,' she said. Knucky went quiet. She truly seemed offended. 'It was just a joke,' Knucky said. But it was clear that he appreciated the inappropriateness of his remark. I stayed out of it. I had to. Whatever was going on between them did not include me. They were in territory now that I had no access to.

This, I often thought, was what going to Alaska was all about. About entering regions and territories I had never previously encountered. And coming back had an element of this in it also. Because whatever anyone else thought, what I had come back to was nothing like what I had gone away from. It was like mapping out a familiar land all over again only to discover that nothing was where you had thought it to be. That all the benchmarks had been erased, that the topography was so altered as to be unrecognizable, that even the monuments of the past seemed in danger of destruction. And none more so than Knucky and Frances.

The day I went Frances and Knucky came by my house to say their goodbyes. It was the first time I had seen them together since they had split. 'You'll come back a changed person,' Frances said. 'But you will come back.' Then she hugged me and pulled my head towards her. Knucky shook my hand. Then almost as an afterthought he embraced me too. 'Bon voyage,' he said. 'Let us know when you sight land.'

'Will you manage?' I asked them both together.

'Life goes on,' Frances said. 'In case you hadn't noticed. You're just one blip on a life-support machine.'

'And what about you?' Knucky wanted to know. 'Will you manage?'

'I've given myself no other choice,' I told him.

'Good on you,' Frances said. She seemed to savour the prospect of it. Then finally she turned to Knucky. 'Let's be off.'

Knucky and she left before our emotions took over completely.

I often wondered what they did after that. If they went home together or went their separate ways. If they went to Annie's, where we first started drinking together, and got drunk. If they ended up back in each other's arms in a way that was doomed to failure.

Knucky and I drank ourselves into oblivion. We were celebrating, Knucky said. Celebrating the return of his boat. The return of his life. I told him I was commiserating, offering my condolences to the dead. The other side of the same coin.

Frances called a taxi for us at the end of the night, to get rid of us, she said. But we knew she was really making sure that we got safely home.

CHAPTER FOUR

I spent the following morning throwing up over the side of the boat. Knucky was as fresh as a daisy, although he had absolutely no right to be. Even though I had drunk far more than him, he had not been lacking.

'I have webbed feet,' he said. 'The shifting surface beneath me goes unnoticed.'

Every time I threw up I couldn't help but think of Charlie Doherty and how death worked its way into his guts. And I wondered if that had anything to do with my illness. At the very least it was what drove me to the pub.

The fish had been cleared out and the deck scrubbed down. Nothing anywhere to indicate the lifeless corpse that had been spewed out with the catch yesterday. Belched up by the ocean. But I doubted if I could ever look at the *Lorna Doone* again without seeing it there. The Eskimo's presence would always be on board. No amount of scrubbing could rid us of it.

I sat up by the wheelhouse with my back against it, my eyes closed, clutching my stomach. Soon I'd have to be up and on my feet, dropping nets and pulling in the ones we had managed to drop the day before. We really could have done with another pair of hands but Knucky insisted it suited him better this way. Although he loved fishing, what Knucky loved more was being out on the sea. The two of us could only manage a small catch at best, but Knucky said that was adequate. Besides, he said, he paid me accordingly.

He loved the feel of the ocean. The God-awfulness of it and the loving touch of its waves. The smell of it, all around him. The taste of the salt on his tongue. The sound of it crashing or gurgling in his ears. The heart-rending sight of it stretching into infinity.

'I'll be truthful,' he once said, 'I must be the worst fisherman in the world on account of it.'

But it was this more than anything that kept me out there with him. There were times when he would get so enraptured by it he wouldn't even bother to drop the nets, but just sail or drift into the distance. And I never discouraged him from this. More than anything that morning I would have liked for him to do the same, but I didn't feel it within my capacity to suggest it. And Knucky, as much out of vindictiveness as anything else, I was convinced, pushed me as hard that morning as he ever had.

'That'll teach you,' he said as I threw up into the sea. He drank from a mug of tea.

'I doubt it.' I clung to the edge and tried not to look at the churning water. Thankful at least for the cold breeze. 'I don't think anything ever will.'

'You're probably right,' Knucky said. 'We never learn, do we? It's only a fool who thinks this life is about knowledge. It's about sea change. Ebbing and flowing. Drifting and being pulled. With the moon always at your back.' He set the wheel at automatic. 'Here, have some tea. It'll make you feel better.'

He came out and gave the mug to me. I took one mouthful and immediately threw it up.

'We'll soon be there,' Knucky said.

'I know,' I told him. 'I'll manage. I'll get up off my sick bed and walk.'

'No,' he said, his forehead narrowing into a frown. 'That's not what I mean. I mean we'll soon be there. Where we found him.'

And this is what it did mean. It no longer meant reaching the point where we pulled up the nets, it meant reaching the point where the Eskimo had been submerged.

'What do you think happened to him?' Knucky lay back against the wheelhouse with me, his hands behind his head, looking up at the clear blue sky. As if the darkness of yesterday had never existed. A passing squall. The gulls circled above us shrieking as though terrified of what was to come.

I pushed the mug of tea as far away from me as I could. Even the smell of it set my stomach retching.

'I thought you didn't care,' I said.

'I don't,' Knucky said, crossing his feet at the ankles. 'But all the same, you have to wonder. I mean if he was buried he'd have been weighted and dropped onto the rocks where he couldn't be dragged up. And if he fell overboard, surely it would have been reported.'

'That bothers me, too,' I said.

'Well,' Knucky said, 'I wouldn't go so far as to say it bothers me, but it poses some interesting questions. There must be a whole business to dying that we know nothing about.'

I looked over to see how Knucky appeared when he said this, to see if it might give some indication as to how he felt about his own death, his own process of dying. But he didn't have any particular look apparent. As if his own death might not be of any great importance at all.

I scoured the seas for a sign, anything that might give some clue as to what had happened. But nothing seemed any different than usual.

'What did you expect?' Knucky asked. 'A bottle with a note? His last will and testament? His dying words?'

I remembered his open mouth and the silence it had contained. The truth was I had expected nothing. But it would have seemed negligent not to have looked.

We reached our buoys. 'Come on,' Knucky said. 'Let's get to work. And promise me, no more fucking Eskimos.'

The smell of fish clings to you like a second skin. Gets in beneath your nails and into the strands of your hair, up your nostrils, between your fingers and toes, deep into the porous depths of flesh. It just won't let go. No matter how much you scrub.

Frances said this was the best part about Knucky. She said she loved to shed his clothes and touch the scaly skin of his body. She felt like a mermaid then. Or as close as she would ever get to being one. And not some lithe, demure beauty but a blubbery creature of strength.

'Not everyone is like you,' I told her. 'Most women hate the smell and hate you for it.'

'They have to hate you for something,' she said. 'It may as well be your aroma. Anyway, that's just your excuse for being alone.'

And maybe it was. Since coming back from Alaska I hadn't been with anyone. But this had more to do with my state of mind than anything else. I didn't feel up to anyone's company, male or female, other than Knucky's or Frances'. I couldn't bear to answer anyone's questions any more. I had asked them too often of myself, and I still didn't know where to begin. What I knew about Alaska or my time there had yet to find the appropriate words. Like the icebergs I had witnessed, most of it was still submerged.

Knucky would often ask about the women out in Alaska.

'What were they like?' he wanted to know. But where the roots of that question lay I had no idea. He said he met someone once in Killybegs who had spent six months out there who said the ratio of men to women was three to one. And when you examined the mathematics of that, it was not so good. But Frances said from her personal calculations it didn't seem so bad. And if ever there was a reason for her to get up and go, that would surely be it.

'Is that it?' Knucky asked. 'Is that why they go? For the men? Is it like a giant lonely-hearts wilderness?'

It seemed as good a description of Alaska as I could manage. But Knucky wanted more than this. He wanted to know what sort of woman would go to such a harsh and remote landscape. And how could they survive? They must be rugged, he said, built of sterner stuff.

I didn't know what to say. I couldn't even answer what sort of person I was to have gone.

'Did you meet someone?' Frances asked. 'Did you fall in love?' Frances laughed at my idea of love. My faith in it. But it was a nervous laugh, she told me. She was really just jealous of it.

'No,' I told her. 'I didn't meet anyone.'

I couldn't tell if she was pleased about this or not.

I had been with some women there but none of it was lasting or of any real consequence. This was a mutual thing. In the summer the students would come to work in the fish processing plants, and there relationships usually did flourish. There was nothing else to do. Nothing but handle fish, drink and make love in vast quantities. It was a dismal existence, and most didn't come back.

But at least in those circumstances everyone stank of fish. Like a horrific orgy of procreated stench. So you would wake up with the taste on your tongue and the warm wafts rising from beneath the covers.

Most of them were just girls though. Eighteen or nineteen-year-olds out to make money and broaden their horizons, who usually went home with vast uncertainties and a distant fear of the future.

Since finding the Eskimo the smell of fish seemed stronger than ever. It clung not just to my clothes and body but to every molecule of air. Like walking into a house where someone had recently died. Which of course they had.

I showered when I came in off the boat with Knucky, but as expected it did no good. And when I got home I opened all the windows in the house, but whether this was to let the air in or out I couldn't tell. In any case the smell grew denser. I still wasn't feeling too well. My stomach heaved continually like a choppy sea and my head pounded like the roar of surf.

Death was no stranger to this house. My mother died in childbirth in the room I now used as my own. We lost her and my baby sister at almost the same moment in time. And six years ago my father died in the same room. He collapsed getting out of bed and was dead before I could get to him. Some day I'd die there too, I told myself. In the vicinity of that big deathbed. It was my family duty. The least the sole remaining survivor could do.

At that moment in time I felt closer to death than I had for a long time. My steps were unsure, my body swayed as though still adrift on the open sea. I made my way through to the kitchen and pulled a bottle of whiskey from the cupboard beneath the sink. I kept it there with the oven cleaners and the bleach as if their job was one and the same. Right now I hoped it would clear my head. Either that or it would kill me outright. I twisted off the cap and took a drink straight from the bottle. I closed my eyes as it burned a hole through my throat and the lining of my stomach. Then I headed with the bottle into bed. Somewhere along the way I kicked off my shoes, and I fell into the bed in most probably the same manner my father fell out of it the morning of his death. And like something out of a bad movie my arm hung over the side with the bottle still gripped in my fingers.

The cold mist began to lift and the dampness infiltrated my body through my clothes. A light flickered above me as though signalling to someone off in the distance. My head thumped and my body swayed.

My stomach rose and fell with each motion. I put my hands down to raise the top half of my body up for a closer look and that was when I first felt the rubbery slime beneath me. I turned my head around, half in disgust and half in fear, to look at whatever it was I was lying on. Hundreds of small, round, beady pairs of eyes stared back up at me. For a moment I thought that was all that was supporting me. A rolling mountain of eyes prized from their sockets. Like a giant glob of roe. And then I saw how they were still intact in their bodies. In the slithering heap of fish wriggling out their last dying gasps. I turned over on one elbow and vomited.

A hand reached out of the mist towards me. Like the eyes it too seemed separated from its body. A severed hand floating through the dim light. Then as my eyes adjusted more I made out the fuzzy shape of a figure looming above me. Moving closer. Until I recognized the face of Frances. Smiling down at me. Drifting in closer still. As she came nearer I saw that the top half of her body was bare. I tried to speak but although my mouth opened no words came out. Frances put her finger to her lips and lay down on top of me. And I distinguished the same cold slime above me that I had felt below. The lower half of her body squirmed across me, flapped against my legs. I reached out tentatively with my hand and felt the scaly slippery surface of her skin. The solid mass of flesh tapering off into her tail.

She leaned her mouth in towards me and just as our lips were about to touch a small, scuttling crab passed from her mouth to mine.

I awoke drenched in sweat, a loud, coarse humming rang in my ears. I cautiously put my hands down to feel beneath me. The crumpled sheets were soaked through. But at least I was on solid ground. I pushed my head back into the pillow and ran my tongue across my lips, tasting the salt of my sweat. It took me a few moments to realize the phone was ringing. At first I decided to ignore it, to just lie there until it bled itself dry. But it refused to stop, until my whole body shuddered with its every ring. I swallowed and swung my legs over the edge of the bed. My swallow caught in my throat and I gagged. I squeezed my neck and throat with my fingers and it eventually passed through. I stood up and made my way stiffly out into the hall. But when I picked up the phone to answer it the line went dead.

Whether it had stopped ringing at that exact moment or whether someone had hung up on me I couldn't say. And for some extraordinary length of time I stood there looking at the receiver with no idea what I should do about it.

It was five minutes past eight according to the clock in the kitchen but I didn't know if this was morning or evening. 'This has got to stop,' I told myself aloud. 'Whatever it is. It has got to stop.'

I sat down in the armchair by the stove and fell back into a long, deep sleep.

The sun shone brightly through the kitchen window. Its strong rays warmed my drowsy body. I looked over at the clock again. It was still five minutes past eight. I rubbed deeply into the corners of my eyes with my forefinger and thumb. Time seemed to have given up on me. Ground to a standstill. It was not an unpleasant thought. When I awoke further I confirmed that the clock had stopped. I knew by the strength of the sun that I was late for work. I put the kettle on to boil and went for a shower. I was already late, I reasoned. There was no sense in rushing now. Then I dressed and made some coffee. And afterwards I walked down to the pier.

I looked in through the window of the newsagent on the way at the clock behind the counter. It was almost half past ten. I should have been there over four hours ago. Knucky would be raging. He'd most likely have gone out without me. But he would get little done on his own. And sure enough when I got there the harbour was empty.

I sat down on the end of the pier, looking out at the sea beyond the mouth of the lough. That's where I should have been. A distant dot on the horizon. Far off from the shore. Where little in this world mattered.

'We're a nomadic people at heart,' Knucky would say. 'All of us. But somehow we've got tied down. Rooted to one particular spot. It's the curse of our being. But it can never be like that on the sea. That's the true joy of it. Its exquisite nature. We should never have come in on land in the first instance. That was the single biggest mistake in our existence. We should never have forfeited our gills.'

Of course it was the sea which swept us up on land in the first place. But maybe this was a part of the exquisite nature Knucky talked about.

After Knucky split with Frances he would sometimes disappear to sea for weeks on end. I often worried that he would never come back, that he would do what he had often talked of doing, that he would just keep on going further and further into its lonely expanse. Frances said that maybe this would be the best thing he could do. That maybe that was Knucky's fate. And she said she would be happy for him if that was the case. But Knucky never failed to return. 'Thar she blows,' Frances would say when he finally turned up in The Porthole again.

'Don't you ever get lonely out there by yourself?' I asked him one of those times.

'Of course,' Knucky replied. 'Isn't that the point of everything about our lives? Is not that what we are after?'

Then he asked me if I wasn't lonely out in Alaska? If that wasn't a part of why I went there?

'I never thought of it that way,' I said.

'That's your problem, Gallagher,' he said, tapping the side of his head. 'You rely too much on up there and not enough on in here.' He beat solemnly at his chest.

It's true I was lonely in Alaska, setting out by myself, getting there and arriving on my own. I was lonely all the time I was there. And when I left I was lonelier still.

I had gone out on some vague promise of a job in the fisheries in Valdez. But at the time I needed that vagueness. Everything about my life had been too definite up until then. And still nothing had been clear other than that I was dissatisfied. Knucky and Frances parting seemed like the final straw. I really had a belief in their chances. But that petered out to nothing. 'Our relationship was as hollow as Knucky's heart,' Frances told me afterwards. 'We were lucky,' she said. 'It could take you a lifetime to figure that out. And I made the decision then not to wait that long.'

Other than travel arrangements I made no plans before leaving. My contact in Valdez was an English fisherman I had met here one summer. Frances and Knucky spent a lot of time by themselves so he and I drank together most evenings. Every so often after he left I'd get a card or a brief letter from him. The last time he wrote, which must have been eight months before I went out, he told me he was working in Valdez and could get me a job there if I wanted one. And that was what I headed off to. An almost illegible scrawl on one half of a postcard that was most probably written during a drunken binge.

He told me all about his life out there during our drinking sessions. He loved Alaska, he said. Although he hated the work. But then again you can't have everything, can you? Alaska was another world, he said. A world before this one. A freezing wilderness that was a part of all our histories. But the beer was bloody expensive. They had to import it. They had to import everything from the Lower Forty-Eight. That's what you're getting when you go out there. A world offering nothing but itself.

At the time he told me all about getting there. How you could fly straight to Anchorage and then on to Valdez by bus or plane. Or the other way he sometimes liked to go was through Seattle, getting the ferry at Bellingham all the way up the glacial contours of the Inside Passage right to the stinking heart of Valdez itself.

And when I went that was the way I chose. It would have seemed too much to simply alight from the skies into a new life like that. I needed some sense of adjustment. A coming to terms with what was lying before me and what I was leaving behind. Landing in Seattle would be shock enough in itself. The ferry journey would take the best part of a week. Everything would slowly slip past in a way that my eyes could measure.

Looking out at the lough now it struck me that in some ways you could easily imagine that you were in the Inside Passage and not the north eastern coast of Donegal; that with the snow on the hills in the winter little would be different. That all that really separated you from there was your imagination.

I heard a car pulling up behind me. Looking back I saw Tom Harte get out and make his way to his office. I got up and walked down the pier after him.

I got to the harbour master's office and knocked hard on the blue wooden door. It was slightly ajar and swung open. Tom sat at his desk looking over some paperwork. He glanced up and nodded over at me.

'Jim,' he said. 'What can I do for you?' He looked back down at his papers.

'Oh, nothing really,' I said and walked on in.

He pushed the papers away from him and looked up at me again. 'Have a seat.' He pointed at an old wooden chair by a filing cabinet. It didn't look secure to me at all. As if it would give out the moment you sat on it. Lose its sense of purpose.

'I'm okay,' I said. I walked over to the window and leaned up against the sill, looking out at the harbour. He had a good view of everything from here. All the comings and goings. I turned back and sat up against the sill. Tom leaned back in his chair with his hands behind his head. A framed map of the harbour hung above him. A brass porthole looking out to sea conveyed the impression of captaincy upon him. I felt sure it would not be an unwelcome one.

'I heard the guards might need a statement,' I said, rubbing my hands up and down the knees of my jeans.

'Oh, some such formality,' Tom said, and fell forward in his chair again. 'I'll let you know.' He picked up a pen off the desk and rolled it between his fingers like he was making a cigarette. 'Messy business all around.' He eyed me as if he expected me to say something more, to reveal what was really going on in my mind. And I wished I could have done that. To him, to anyone. To myself.

'What happened to him? Where's the body now?'

'The hospital, I suppose. Cold storage.'

'Will they do a post-mortem?'

'I'm not sure.' Tom seemed bothered by my questions. As though they were a waste of time.

But all of this uncertainty troubled me. I couldn't understand why people wouldn't want to know exactly what was going to happen to him. And what had happened to him. Everything about him. It seemed as if everyone considered it an inconvenience and nothing more.

I felt some loose flakes of paint under my hands and picked them off with my fingernail. 'Who's in charge now, Tom? Is it out of your hands?'

Tom looked at the pen between his fingers as if he had a strong urge to write something with it. Something he would file away and most probably forget.

'We all have our part to play,' he said. He must have seen something in my expression looking for more. Something indicating my anxiety. He put the pen down firmly on the desk. 'Look, Jim,' he said, 'it's not every day an Eskimo gets hauled up here.' And then he stood up as though that was it. As though that would satisfy me. As though our conversation had come to an end.

I levered myself up off the sill and stood there helplessly. 'I just want to make sure he ends up wherever it is he ought to end up,' I said. 'That's all. I owe him that. I'm the one who dragged him up, remember?' I needed to make this clear. I didn't want him to think I was interfering. Distrusting his ability or his office.

Tom closed his eyes briefly and nodded. 'We're all on your side. We're doing what we can. Everyone is looking into it. One way or another he'll rest in peace, Jim. Be assured.' He got up and stretched his arms behind him. Whatever business we had together was finished. He walked over to the door. He opened it wide and stood looking over at the Co-op. 'How come you're not with Knucky today?' he asked.

I walked over to him but didn't reply. He just scratched his head.

'Is it a fool's game?' I wondered, stepping out ahead of him into the weak sunlight.

Tom didn't seem to know which way to interpret this. But he finally said, 'You need your head set squarely on your shoulders.'

A gull swooped down and landed at his feet. He kicked at it shooing it away. It flapped its wings angrily and hobbled off a few yards from us.

'Leave it with us, Jim,' Tom said. Then he went back inside and closed the door.

I had the whole day ahead of me. I thought about going down to the station to see Charlie, to find out if he knew anything more, but decided against it. It was a long walk and there was no guarantee he was there. Besides, Tom was probably right. Everything would get sorted out. We'd hear all about it as and when we needed to. I headed off towards the Co-op without any real idea of where I was going. I had worked there for six months some years back. Driving a forklift. I never really could get the hang of it, though. I dropped more crates and pallets than the rest of the drivers in their entirety. I finally got let go for practically running down the plant manager. Reversing without due vigilance was how he put it. 'You crept up out of nowhere,' I protested unconvincingly. 'Go home, Gallagher,' he said. 'Before the rest of the staff start demanding danger money.'

I heard the noise of the refrigeration plant humming hoarsely as though suffering the effects of its own freezing temperatures. I exhaled into the mild air, but my breath remained invisible and formless.

In Alaska I came to love the sight of my own breath. Wavering on the air before me. Confirming the continuing functioning of my lungs. It was a reassurance I frequently needed.

The one thing she could not have coped with, Frances said, would have been the cold. I told her how it hadn't been bad all the time. How the summers had been very good, in fact. Better than here. Temperatures up in the seventies. The warmth and the clear crisp brightness of the sun.

'It doesn't make sense, does it?' Frances said. 'It's no wonder you went there.'

Knucky wanted to know why all the ice didn't melt away then. And I told him how it did all the time. How its whole existence was a process of melting and freezing. In the same way ours was about living and dying.

But even in the sunlight I remembered how a cold chill hovered at its extremities. Laden with the solid promise of glaciers and packed ice-fields. Untrodden territory.

I told them about climbing up on the ends of Sheridan's Glacier in a light cotton T-shirt. Traipsing over the mounds of rubble it had driven ahead of it to reach the visible edges of ice. And how I trudged across it for about half a mile. Fearful of slipping through melting ice into a crevice. Of breaking my leg or plunging deep into an ice hole. Still miles from the ice fields, where you could lose yourself forever.

'What about the winters?' Frances asked.

'You would have died,' I told her. 'Curled up and died.'

Weather was the same all over the world. It was never quite what it appeared to be. We mostly toyed at its edges. Even in Alaska. Toying at the edges of the Arctic. Its sub-tundra regions and its perma-frost. It required something more to give yourself up to it completely.

A reckless adventuring spirit, perhaps. Or, like the Eskimo, an accident of birth.

I stood at the gateway to the Co-op and looked back out at the sea. At the rough and tumbling waves in the distance. Where the edges of our weather ended and began.

CHAPTER FIVE

The roar of jet-skis cut through the clear air above the lough. I wandered across to the other side of the harbour for a better look. Somebody lay out in the water behind the jet-ski, revving it up. A man and a woman stood on the slipway unloading two more off the small trailers used to transport them down from the Portakabin they were kept in at the side of The Porthole. I could imagine Frances inside looking out the window. 'It's not natural,' she would be telling them. 'It's the most unnatural God forsaking act of all.'

She couldn't stand them. She hated their very existence and the existence of all who used them. 'There's such a thing as noise pollution,' she told me one time in The Porthole. I had slipped in for a quiet afternoon drink when they started up on the slipway outside. 'Just listen to their roar,' she said, raising her voice as much out of anger as the need to be heard above them. 'Like jets taking off outside your window. There ought to be a law against it if there isn't already. Look at them.' She stood up on the seats for a better view. 'Dressed in their wetsuits like slimy marine creatures. It used to be so quiet here. Nothing but the soothing natural sounds of our surroundings.' She turned and shook her head at me as if everything was lost.

Indeed, I shared many of her misgivings. But all the same a part of me would have loved to have given them a try.

All three lay flat out on the water now and revved their engines. Then they moved out in unison into the lough. And in a few quick deft movements they were standing upright, shouting across at one another. Though they were soon out of sight the noise of the engines persisted.

The jet-skis were a recent addition to the water life of our town. They would attract tourists from far and wide, we were told. Be an economic asset. And it was true that since their arrival a lot more people had been around during the weekends and holidays. 'Remind me again,' Frances would say, 'this is a good thing for all of us!' But it seemed to me that a few new faces around now and again wasn't such a bad thing. When Frances and Knucky and I were younger it almost drove us demented seeing the same old faces over and over again until we were all convinced that we needed to get out of there.

Frances cried when I left, and she cried the day I came back. Partly because she was pleased to see me, she said, and partly because I hadn't managed to stay away. 'Towns like this kill you one way or another in the end,' she said. 'You can't shed their skin no matter how you try. It's a travesty no one should have to endure.' Then she hugged me like she might never let me go.

Knucky said he was upset with me too. He had been planning to come out and join me. He had simply been awaiting the right opportunity.

'How do you think I feel?' I asked them. 'Where do you think this leaves me?'

Sometimes I thought I should go away again. But other times I thought that I should stay here forever. Await my demise placidly.

The noise of the jet-skis grew in volume as they returned. Emerging from the distance, charging out of the sea as if it could no longer contain them. For a moment I felt nothing but disgust. Frances was right. They should never have been allowed in the first place.

It was bound to happen. I ended up back in The Porthole.

'I haven't come here to drink,' I told Frances.

'Nobody does,' she said. 'What will you have?'

I ordered a Guinness.

'Knucky will be furious with you,' she said when she heard how I had slept in.

'I know.'

Frances smiled to herself. She seemed secretly pleased at his fury. Her long auburn hair was tied back with a carved wooden clip. She tugged at the ends of her hair with her closed fist. I saw her scalp move in response, and her eyes closed as though wincing with pain. Then she shrugged. 'Maybe he'll be glad of the excuse to be alone.' She pulled at her hair again, then wrenched the clip out of it altogether as if it had been annoying her for days. Her dark hair fell around her face. She looked to have receded into a tunnel. 'He hated me being on the boat with him,' she said. 'He absolutely hated it.' Her lips curled in on themselves, no longer capable of smiling nor certain what emotion they should reveal.

'But you were forever going off on voyages of one sort or another.' I had always thought that this was what they loved most.

'Voyages,' Frances repeated. 'That was it, wasn't it?' She folded her arms and stood upright in front of the cash register. The back of her head and upper body were reflected in the mirror behind the bar. 'They were all my suggestions. I wanted to see what it was like out there, out on the open sea. But Knucky had some vague notion that I was trying to spy on his life, to get an insight into his private world. He gave in grudgingly. We went no distance at all.' She came over and leaned in on the counter towards me. 'We'd stick to the coast. Drop anchor at some secluded bay and make believe we were shipwrecked. Which of course we were.' She took my hand and squeezed it hard, so that it hurt. And I could tell that she was trying to prevent herself from doing more. She would have dearly loved to hit me, commit some unspeakable act of violence against my presence, as though somehow I represented everything she hated in her relationship with Knucky. 'I wanted him to take me out to the edges of the ocean, to the edges of our visible world. But he refused, always. He said I would be unable to bear it. That I should never have to suffer all that he endured. As if somehow Knucky's suffering was a private privilege.' She squeezed my hand even harder. My eyes watered. 'Have you ever considered what it does to me when he takes you out each day? Out into the depths he would never allow me to go. You're as big a bastard as he is.' She let my hand go, cast it adrift as though it were something distasteful. Her breathing was ragged, and the flesh below her cheek bones quivered.

'Oh dear God,' she said, and swept in gently upon me, kissing the top of my head. 'I'm sorry,' she whispered. 'I didn't mean that.'

I placed my hands on her strong upper arms. 'It's okay,' I said. 'You're right. We are all bastards underneath it all.'

She breathed in hard and stood back from me. 'Now what will they make of that?' she asked, raising her eyes towards the others in the bar.

'It'll give them something to talk about,' I said.

Frances looked at me in a decisive way. She rubbed at the corner of her eye. 'You need to get yourself a woman,' she said. 'That's half your problem.'

Knucky came to the bar to look for me after he got in. My head was swaying once more in a sea of alcohol. A warm spray of redemption.

'There you fucking are,' he said. 'I knew I'd find you here. Propping up the fucking bar.'

The sickly smell of the ocean's rotten core hit me face-on. 'You stink. Didn't you even bother to shower?'

'Don't!' Knucky cautioned, pointing his finger down at me. Shaking it tiredly. 'Don't.'

He disappeared off. I stretched back in my chair and rubbed at my ribcage, strangely satisfied. I closed my eyes. Drifted away calmly. When I opened my eyes Knucky was sitting beside me again.

'I thought you had gone.' I really had. I had forgotten all about him. As if he was still out there on the sea.

'Fuck you, Gallagher,' he said, and drank thirstily. He banged the glass down on the table. The perfect pitch of its crystalline structure hitting the wood rang in my ears. 'I should fire you. I should fucking well kick your arse all the way back to Alaska. That's what I should do.'

'But…?' I said, knowing a 'but' was to follow. In the circumstances it was provocative and dangerous.

'You're a smart one, aren't you?' He wiped his mouth.

'But what?' I asked again.

'There's no point in talking to you,' he said. 'There's never any point in talking to you.'

I sat sharply upright and slapped his knee. 'Come on, Knucky. Drink up. Let's go get ourselves some women. Frances' orders.' I stumbled getting up and fell back down on the seat.

I woke up the next morning with my head completely clogged over. I felt as though I had been enclosed in a minute space all night long with the heating turned up full. My head, my eyes and especially my teeth hurt something awful. I extended my chest and felt a dull ache stretching the length of my spine. My own pungent odour hit back at me. I reeked of smoke and alcohol. I still felt drunk. I suddenly became aware of the strangeness of my surroundings. My feet hung out over the edge of someone's couch. I ran the tip of my tongue noxiously over my teeth and looked around for Knucky, vaguely remembering being with him the night before. But as far as I could make out I was alone.

I pushed myself up and swung my legs back over the couch. Then slouched back in a crumpled sitting position. For a moment I thought I was going to throw up. I closed my eyes as the insides of my head swirled. I waited for them to come to rest then opened my eyes again and got up.

The room looked like something out of a design catalogue. With dazzling white walls and perfect pine furniture.

'You're up!'

A woman's voice broke through one of the doorways. I looked around and for the first time noticed the door behind the couch. It was fully open. A young woman, pretty, as best as I could tell from where I was, was half-sitting up in bed with the sheets pulled up to her chin.

I was dumbfounded. This was not what I had expected at all.

'Hi,' she said and gave a little wave.

I rubbed at my chin and could feel a growth of stubble. I truly did not know what to do. It was not that I hadn't woken up in a strange woman's house before, but this was something altogether different. Although I had no idea why this should be.

'Hello.' I looked down at the ground. I felt awkward. I didn't know what to do with my hands.

'You look the worse for wear,' she said. 'There's coffee in the kitchen. Make me a cup while you're at it, won't you?'

'Sure,' I said. 'That would be nice.' I immediately realized how stupid that must have sounded. I squinted my eyes at her. 'Where's the kitchen?'

I found a bag of ground coffee and a glass plunger jug next to the cooker. I boiled the water and made a full jug. Then I took down two painted pottery mugs from a mug tree and filled them. 'I take it black,' she shouted in from the bedroom. I brought the mugs back in but stopped at the bedroom door. I felt as if I should knock. I stood there a moment as if looking for permission. She watched me, waiting for my next move. I went in and handed the mug with black coffee to her. There was nowhere to sit down so I just stood there away from the bed.

'Here,' she said, smoothing down the sheets beside her.

I took a drink of the coffee and grimaced. It was raw and strong. I went across and sat down. 'I hope it's not too strong for you.'

'I like it that way,' she said. She laughed in an embarrassed way as though she had been trying to say something assertive and dangerous but ended up sounding sluttish instead. She sipped at it and *hmm*ed her approval. 'You've no idea where you are, have you?' she said.

'Do I look so lost?' I asked. I felt uncomfortable sitting so close to her. She looked not to have any clothes on beneath that single white sheet. Her bare shoulders protruded over the rim.

'I'm afraid you do,' she said.

I slurped my coffee, burning the roof of my mouth.

'I suppose you'll want to know what happened last night?' Her eyes flickered mischievously as though she had no intention of telling me.

'No,' I said. 'I don't think I want to know.' I looked away from her. The window was slightly open and a light breeze fluttered through, ruffling the curtains. I stood up and walked over to it. Allowed the breeze to blow against my face. I could hardly believe it when I looked out. We seemed to be hanging over the edge of the ocean. Perched above it. All I could see was the sea. The white topped waves rushed beneath me.

'Isn't it about time for introductions?' She sat up higher in the bed now, holding the sheet in place above her breasts with her right arm.

'Didn't we get that far?' I pulled the window open further.

She shook her head. 'It didn't seem relevant at the time.'

'Jim Gallagher,' I said. My immediate reaction was to extend my hand for her to shake, but this seemed inappropriate. All the same I found myself walking back towards her with my hand held out in front of me.

'Lorna Doone,' she said and shook it.

'Very good,' I laughed. 'At least we got that far in our conversation.' Then it struck me what else must have followed. 'Did I tell you all about the Eskimo?'

She smiled resignedly. 'Yes. Many times.'

'I would have,' I said. 'I apologize.'

'No, don't. It seemed to matter to you greatly.'

I felt nauseous and asked for the bathroom. She directed me next door. I walked as quickly as I could while attempting to keep some decorum. I just made it to toilet bowl and threw up a number of times. I flushed the toilet clean and washed my face in cold water. I looked at myself in the mirror above the sink. I looked hellish. My hair was askew, and my eyes were bloodshot. Two large bags hung under them like wind-filled sails. This is going to have to stop, I told myself for the umpteenth time. One day you're going to have to grow up.

I went back into the bedroom and apologized again.

'It's perfectly all right,' she said. She seemed to mean it.

'You never did tell me your name.' I sat back down on the opposite side of the bed and put my empty mug down on the floor at my feet.

'Therese Doherty.' She smiled, and for the first time the full extent of her beauty became apparent. 'What's up?' she asked.

She must have witnessed whatever it was that registered on my face when I saw how beautiful she was. But I couldn't tell her this. 'Nothing,' I said. 'I was just feeling a little queasy.'

'You're not going to get sick again, are you?' She laughed.

Her laugh was far too sweet and kind. I hated this. I was making far too much of everything about her. She was attractive, I told myself. That was all. There was no point in going overboard.

I didn't know what I should do next. I was genuinely afraid I might be sick again. She looked as if she was going to stay in bed all day. I wasn't sure if it would seem rude to stay much longer or if it would be worse to get up and go.

'Oh Christ!' I suddenly remembered Knucky.

'What is it?' She looked alarmed.

'I'm supposed to be fishing,' I said. 'What time is it?'

'It's gone eleven, I'm afraid.'

I rubbed at my eyes with my fingers, trying to figure out what it was I had gone and done.

'Look,' Therese said, 'if it's your friend you're thinking about, I don't think he's going to be going too far today either.'

'Knucky was in a bad way?' I asked hopefully.

'As bad as you.'

'Oh, thank God for that.' Then I remembered those webbed feet he talked about. 'Of course that doesn't guarantee anything.' I kicked over the empty mug by accident and reached down to put it back upright. 'What happened to him?' I asked. 'Do you know?'

'That woman he was with called a taxi for themselves.'

'What woman?' I smiled to myself. Was Knucky in the exact same situation as I was?

'I don't remember her name,' Therese said. 'But you all came together.'

'Frances!' This was worse than I had imagined.

Therese nodded. 'Yes, that's her.'

'So Frances was there.' I felt deeply aggrieved now. I couldn't explain why, but I had not wanted Frances to know about any of this. If she was to find out, I wanted her to find out on my terms. But now it was all on hers. I felt foolish and let down.

'You really don't remember anything?' Therese reached over and stroked my face. Her fingers felt soft and warm and comforting on my skin. Something abominable was about to commence. I knew this. And I knew there would be nothing I could do about it. I was lost in a strange bedroom somewhere over the ocean. Totally out of my depth.

Therese was a generous and confident lover. I felt like a little boy in her hands. I felt depraved and warped. I could not relax. Every wave of emotion that washed over me reminded me that I should be on the sea with Knucky and not with this stranger. Letting him down once was bad enough, but twice in as many days! My only salvation was the possibility that he too was ill and had not woken up in time. But knowing Knucky no matter how late it was he might still come looking for me. Of course there was always the chance that Knucky was with Frances now, but I did not seriously want to contemplate this. It would set us all back years. They had avoided drinking together since they parted for fear that alcohol would return them to where they had come from. Neither could imagine anything more dreadful, they said. It had taken them long enough to dig themselves out of that mess.

Therese lay quietly by my side. She had one hand resting behind her head. The other lolled across my chest. I could hear the waves gently breaking outside the window as though hushing us, telling everyone to be quiet. A beam of sunlight splayed across the sheet at the end of the bed, pointing out through the open door.

As I listened I became aware of her breathing, barely distinguishable above the sound of the waves. I felt lulled by its deep soothing qualities. The tips of her fingers tapped lightly on my chest as though softly playing a piano.

'Where are we?' I asked.

Therese sighed. 'I wish I knew.'

A wisp of her hair blew across my face. I pushed it away with my finger.

'There are so many unanswered questions,' she said. 'Isn't that how we survive?'

'Do we survive?' I wondered how we knew this.

'Well, here we are,' she said. 'Is that not proof enough?'

'I doubt it,' I said. 'I would need more convincing than that.'

She grinned and pulled herself up above me. Her long, black, curly hair swooped low.

'Is that a fact?'

My stomach heaved, and I rushed quickly from the bed.

We ate later in her conservatory. Therese had prepared a light lunch of cheese and olives and pickles. Like her bedroom the conservatory had a sweeping view of the sea. I had since discovered that we were practically right on Malin Head itself. No more than a mile away to the east. From where I sat I could identify the exact spot the Eskimo was found. I thought about pointing it out to Therese but I was afraid she had heard too much about him from me already.

'Have you always lived here?' I asked. The cottage looked to have been recently renovated, with its newly painted white walls and deeply polished wood floors.

'In a way,' she said.

'I've never really noticed it here before, or if I have I haven't paid any heed to it.'

She bit an olive in half and pulled it into her mouth on her tongue. 'You wouldn't,' she said. 'It's hidden away.'

The way she said it you would think it had been hidden on purpose. As if houses were things you would possibly hide.

She walked over, placed her palms on the glass and leaned her forehead against her hands. She stared out at the sea beneath us. I followed down her long black dress to her ankles.

She stood in her bare feet on the cold tiles.

'It lay empty for years,' she said. 'Before I came back.'

I spat out the stone from an olive into my hands and looked for somewhere to put it. I hadn't seen what she had done with hers. In the end I simply put it in my pocket. 'Where were you?'

Before she gave her answer I already knew what it would be.

'Away.'

'You're a mysterious one,' I said, feeling the stone through the material of my trousers like you would feel a strange lump on your body.

She spun around on her heels and looked at me sternly. 'Not at all. Nothing could be further from the truth.' Then she smiled as though now I knew something about her that everything else could be gauged from.

Most of the night before was a blank to me. As we spoke certain moments and incidents would return to mind but in a distant, non-specific way as if our thoughts and actions were indefinite, pliable, as if everything could happen in any number of different ways.

It always scared me how alcohol affected my memory. How accountable it left me for things I knew nothing about. How others might know more about me than I did. How could I approach the future if I could not even claim the past?

But from my conversation with Therese and my own vague recollections an outline of the night emerged. It seemed after leaving The Porthole the three of us had gone on to The Grapevine, a local wine bar, where we proceeded to drink copious amounts of wine on top of all the Guinness we had previously consumed.

Somehow we ended up sitting at a table with Therese. She had been sitting with another man earlier. He was just a friend, she said. An old acquaintance. He left early for some reason, and Therese had stayed.

I tried to picture what the man looked like, but I couldn't. I could barely remember his presence at all other than cigar smoke. Even now I could smell the woody aroma. Beyond that I remembered knocking over a glass of wine at one point. On top of Frances, Therese told me. I remembered the singed yellow candlelight and the sound of Ella Fitzgerald imitating Louis Armstrong on 'Basin Street Blues'.

I told Therese all of this, and she said that was enough. That it was as much as anyone ought to remember.

'Was Frances drunk?' I asked her.

Therese's eyes and lips narrowed as she thought back. 'I really don't know,' she said. 'She was melancholy. I thought she might have been crying.'

It did not bode well.

It was mid-afternoon before I left. Therese drove me back. My head and stomach had eased off, but I still felt shaky. I asked her to drop me off down at the pier. She pulled in next to Tom Harte's office but left the engine running. Both of us sat there looking ahead through the windscreen. I don't know what Therese held in her vision, but I held nothing in mine. I waited for her to speak. She leaned over quickly and kissed me on the cheek.

'Take care of yourself,' she said.

It sounded final.

'I will.' I wanted to touch her one more time, but I knew it would be better not to. I knew she didn't want me to. 'From here?' I asked.

She closed her eyes and shook her head. 'I don't think so.'

I opened the door and swung one foot out. I hadn't expected it to end so quickly. I hadn't expected it to begin.

'Go on,' she whispered.

I got out and closed the door. She drove back up the hill and, turning around a slight bend in the road, was gone from sight.

CHAPTER SIX

I stood there for a moment after she had gone trying to get my bearings. The *Lorna Doone* was gone. Knucky was out there alone for a second day running. I felt lousy. I watched a small rowing boat coming back into the harbour with its stash of crab and lobster pots.

'Ah, Jim. The very man.' Tom Harte came up behind me and spoke over my shoulder.

'Tom.' I turned around to face him. He didn't look well. His usual sallow complexion had paled. His full face seemed to sag.

'The sergeant's just been on the phone. He's looking for statements. He mentioned he had been looking for you and Knucky.'

'Did anything turn up?' I asked. 'Did anyone find out who he is?'

'Not that I'm aware of.'

I would have hoped that Tom would be aware of everything. That if anyone was in a position to know it would be him.

'What will happen to him, Tom, if nothing is found to identify him?'

'Oh, don't you worry. I'm sure he'll be taken care of.'

Tom turned around and started back to his office. I watched after him. I had an uneasy feeling about all of this. I didn't understand why Tom couldn't be up front with the details. Why he couldn't just give me a straight answer. He seemed to be hiding something. As if he didn't want anyone else to know the workings of his office.

Charlie Doherty was on the desk when I got down to the station. He looked up from the newspaper and greeted me. I waited for him to say something to indicate why they had sent for me, but he continued looking at me as if waiting for me to tell him what I was doing there.

'Tom Harte told me I was needed here,' I said.

'First I knew of it.' He shrugged his shoulders. 'Let me go tell the sergeant you're here.'

He disappeared in through the door behind him. I looked at the walls with their posters warning of the dangers of bringing in animals from foreign countries, how to go about getting a passport, and even some 'wanted' posters with their unrecognizable identikit photos. Like some tattered fragment of the old Wild West holding its own. Charlie came back out a moment later.

'He'll be with you in a moment.'

'It must be that Eskimo,' I said.

Charlie professed not to know. 'I don't think it's anything serious,' he said. 'With good behaviour you should be out in no time at all.'

I feigned a laugh. Then I thought of something.

'Tell me, Charlie, have you got any relations out near Malin Head?'

'Any number of them,' he said. 'Why?'

'Do you know a Therese Doherty? Is she anything to you?'

Charlie thought a moment, then puckered his lips. 'Not as far as I know. But then again, I've got second cousins and third cousins and twenty-fifth cousins and great grand-aunts and on it goes.'

'I think she's just come back from somewhere,' I said. 'I've certainly never seen her before.'

'Like I say…' He puckered his lips again. 'Why do you ask?'

'Nosiness. Nothing else.'

Charlie grinned. 'She must be a looker.'

I smiled and lowered my eyes. 'You got me, I'm afraid.'

He nodded. 'I'll look into it.'

'That won't be necessary,' I said.

The door behind Charlie opened and the sergeant came out. 'Come on through.' He beamed over at me as if I had just won the jackpot.

Charlie opened the gate at the side of the counter and let me in. I didn't know the sergeant all that well. I knew him in so far as it was impossible not to know people in these parts.

'Thanks for taking the trouble to call,' he said. He sat down behind his desk and pointed with the flat of his palm to the chair across from him.

'You know what this is about?' He pulled at his tunic. Straightening it out. He was looking in my direction, but I doubted if he even saw me. The remains of a half-eaten sandwich lay on the desk beside him on top of a crumpled sheet of cling film. A mug of coffee steamed upwards. I had a strong suspicion that when I left I would know as little as I had previously.

'The Eskimo, I suppose.' I felt nervous though I didn't know why. I already felt as if I was being interrogated. As though I had something to hide. It was foolish.

The sergeant scratched the side of his head. 'I'll tell you something,' he said, slurping loudly from his coffee, 'I'll be glad to see the back of him. All due respect.' He beamed at me again as though we were conspirators in the same murky plot.

'What's to become of him?' I asked, fighting the odds.

He took a large bite out of his sandwich and shook the remain-ing piece towards the heavens.

'Up to the man above to decide on that.' He chewed as he spoke, barely comprehensible. 'Now,' he said swallowing, 'what I need you to do is tell me your side of the story.'

His choice of words made me feel guilty again.

'I pulled him up out of the water, that's all,' I said.

He looked at the piece of crust in his hand as though considering what to do with it. As if he had never liked crusts but felt bound to eat them. He made a sucking sound with his teeth and dropped it in his mouth as you would feed scraps to an animal.

'That's all I'm interested in.'

He pulled out a piece of paper from beneath the ancient blotting pad and took a pencil from the drawer. 'From the top,' he said, licking the lead.

'You could die from that,' I said.

He seemed confounded by my statement. Almost threatened.

'Lead poisoning,' I explained, although I knew it was really carbon.

He looked down at his pencil and then back at me. He parted his lips, and I knew he could taste the non-existent lead on his tongue.

'Is that a fact,' he said. He coughed hoarsely. 'There are a lot worse things to die from, don't you know.' He licked it again. Like some fearless hero. He twitched his nose at me indicating I should begin. And for the umpteenth time I recounted my story.

He scribbled down a few more sentences after I finished speaking, then stabbed the paper with the point of the pencil to mark out the final full stop. 'I'll get this typed up and have you sign it.' He scratched his jaw, looking over my statement. 'Right,' he said. 'Wait there.'

He went outside. I sat back in my chair and waited. This is what the Eskimo's life had been reduced to. Silence and badly scribbled words. Nothing to indicate the frozen landscape of his upbringing other than the cold stiffness of his dead body.

There was an obscure language absent. One that everyone was carefully avoiding. With the pretense that they could not speak it. Yet it was the one we all communicated in. One that could possibly translate the inevitability of our own deaths.

Sergeant Bonnar came back in. 'It won't take more than a few minutes,' he said. He seemed to think about sitting down, but instead he folded his arms and just stood there looking lost in his own office.

I sat forward in my chair again and placed my elbows on my knees, leaning in towards his desk, the space he had previously occupied. I looked down at the grey tiles under my feet.

'I have to confess,' I began. I immediately wished I had chosen a different set of words. The last thing I wanted was to confess to anything. To assume a sense of guilt. But what else could any of this be? I was caught in a purgatory of sorts. An uneasy transitional world with only a fluid surface as a base. Nothing you could stand solidly on. Where perpetual drunkenness seemed the order of the day. And when you came out the other side, assuming you ever did, all that lay before was exactly what had lain there in the past. In all its grotesque glory.

I realized the sergeant was waiting for me to continue.

'There's nothing I love more than a good confession,' he said. 'I've often suggested to Father Jack that we swap occupations. But he tells me, no. That the pension in his line of work may not be so good, but the long term security cannot be beaten.' He laughed at his words as if they were solely his and not Father Jack's at all.

I squeezed my eyes tightly between my fingers and felt their soft rubbery globes. When I opened them again my vision was blurred and scratched.

'What I mean is,' I said, trying to see through the haze, 'I am concerned for his well-being.'

Sergeant Bonnar looked at me, obviously concerned for mine.

'He's dead, Jim. There's no more we can do for him.'

'No, that is it exactly.' Although nothing here was exact. Nothing precise. Everything was wavering and undefined. 'There is more we can do for him. We can return him to his chosen place of rest. Wherever that is.'

The sergeant looked grim. He furrowed his brow. Something quite basic seemed to be missing between us. Something which confirmed how little we knew of each other. Despite the confinement of our small peninsula there were clearly things the sea could not hold back.

'Everyone is doing what they can,' he said. 'No one can do more than that.'

And still he was telling me nothing. Who was doing what they could? And where did the boundaries of what they could do lie?

'Has anyone located the ship he came off?' I decided to be more outright with him.

'It's being looked into.'

There was a knock on the door and Charlie Doherty entered. He held the typed up statement in his hand. Sergeant Bonnar took it from him and put it down in front of me. 'There you go,' he said.

'Do you know anything about him at all?'

Charlie stayed where he was. He seemed just as interested in the answer as I was. The sergeant looked at him, practically scowling. Charlie's lips spread in recognition and he turned around and went out. The sergeant handed me his pen.

'There's nothing to know.' He pointed down offhandedly at the paper. 'Now, it's busy here today. Let's have your signature and we'll move along.'

I didn't understand why everyone was taking this so personally. The questions I was asking were elementary. Yet no one was prepared to answer them. As if the answers did not exist or might reveal more than the questions demanded.

For a moment I thought about not signing. About holding out until further information was forthcoming. But this in turn might only blur the truth. Providing me with untrustworthy details. I started to read through it.

'Just there,' he said, pointing to a dotted line at the end of the page. 'It's just bumph. It mainly repeats what you told me.' He scratched his ear and waited for me to sign it.

'If you don't mind,' I said, 'I don't like putting my name to something I haven't read. That's how you end up in the Foreign Legion.'

The sergeant smiled quickly. He was impatient for this to be over with. I scanned down through it. He was right as far as I could tell. It was just a lot of details about the boat, who owned it, what its function was, etc. And a brief description of how I had found the body in the nets and had left it there undisturbed to be handed over to the authorities.

'Pretty harmless stuff, huh?' The sergeant raised his eyebrows. He was tiring of me.

For the most part it was harmless, but I was unhappy with the part that said I left the body undisturbed. How could you drag a body up from the depths of the ocean and leave it undisturbed? I had exposed him to the air once more, brought him back to the land of the living, where he was, no doubt, labelled, tagged by his toe, and left to rot in cold sterile surroundings. A distraught soul displaced in an unfamiliar world.

'Tell me you're doing all you can, Sergeant.' I held the pen aloft hoping for it or something else to take over, to do whatever had to be done.

'No stone left unturned, Jim.'

My hand moved down to the paper, and I signed my name. It was practically illegible.

The sergeant snapped the form back across the desk. 'There we go,' he said, slapping his hand down on top of it. 'Bingo.'

He put it into a tray on his desk and grinned up at me.

I felt duped. As if I truly had signed a life away.

It was still early evening. The light would begin to fade soon. And it would darken quickly. The sun continued to shine although it barely gave out any heat. I missed Therese already. It was at times like this I most despised myself. I hardly knew her. Truthfully, I didn't know her at all. And yet here she was holding on to a part of me. Taking it for her own.

I sat back on the bench on the green overlooking the lough and imagined her driving past the ocean with the windows of the car wound fully down and the radio playing. She would sing along. And her long black hair would splay in the breeze. It was sad how rooted in romance these thoughts were.

She had probably forgotten me by now. Was on her way to someone else. That man she had gone to the wine bar with the night before.

'You'll be swallowed up by romance,' Frances told me when I first learned that she and Knucky were going out with one another.

'But don't you think it's astonishing?' I had asked her. 'You and Knucky have known each other as friends for twenty-seven years, and now you suddenly discover that you are in love.'

'Who mentioned love?' she asked. 'You're incurable, Jim. And besides, what has been so sudden?'

I learned about it from Knucky first. I had to be told. They had been going out for almost six weeks when he mentioned it. I hadn't noticed anything different at all.

Ever since we were kids we had done everything together. All our growing up that far. We spent a lot of our time sitting down at the edge of the pier or out on the cliffs predicting our futures. In much the same way that we did now reviewing the past. The first time Frances was touched by a boy she came running right back to tell us. And Knucky and I revelled in every gory detail as if it had been one of us involved and not someone from another town. As we got older we continued to do everything together as much as we could. Often times, on the spur of the moment, we'd throw our tents and sleeping bags into the back of Frances' car and head off into the hills for days at a time. We'd lose ourselves from the world as if we were children again. As if all that existed revolved around us, and we were everything there was.

The only thing Frances kept from us was her trips on LSD. Even at the height of her relationship with Knucky she would not include him in those. She would never offer to, and neither he nor I would ever ask. In much the same way Knucky kept his hole in the heart to himself. I suppose I kept something back also. Something just as solitary and dangerous. Something I had yet to identify.

It was on one of those camping trips that Knucky told me about himself and Frances. We had driven up in the afternoon into the foothills of the Bluestack Mountains and parked the car in off the road. Then we trekked for miles along the indistinct trail of an old mountain road. All throughout the journey we had been joking and laughing, helped by a few pints along the way at Biddy's pub and later the hip flasks we all carried. Both Knucky and Frances were in as fine a humour as I'd ever seen them. But this didn't strike me as different, just right for the occasion. We had always loved these trips more than anything. They were our refuge, we said. Our survival.

We trekked up to a lake we knew and set up our tents beside it. Knucky gathered up some stones, made a ring out of them and prepared a fire. Frances had brought along three big slabs of steak which we fried up above it. I had the potatoes, already wrapped in tinfoil, and threw them in on the flames. Everyone had their own supply of beer. It was the heaviest burden of the whole journey, but it wouldn't have been complete without it.

We watched as the sun went down over the hills like a volcano being sucked back into itself. The burning orange and red light that had spewed out over the sky disappeared back into the earth leaving a pale grey backdrop that would continue to darken. Frances declared it the best sunset she had ever witnessed. And although I couldn't be as certain, it didn't stop me nodding my head in agreement. We got pleasantly drunk and sang every song we ever knew.

Later when the singing had died down we all lay back on the ground, resting our heads on the rolled-up sleeping bags. At first no one spoke. Then out of the silence Frances quietly asked, 'What else is there?' And indeed it seemed to us then that there was nothing else. That this was as far as it went. And that afterwards all there could ever be was disappointment.

We lay there in the open air talking and reminiscing until the damp chill of the night suggested it was time to retire. Knucky said he was going off for a pee, and I set off with him. We went about thirty yards away to a bush removed from the lake. We stood there together, listening to the hiss of our urine.

'This is just great,' I said. 'Sometimes I would have it no other way.'

Knucky said nothing. He zipped himself up and walked off a distance. He stared up at the stars coming and going in the night sky. He coughed and spoke quietly, as if speaking to the stars and not to me at all.

'There's something about the sleeping arrangements you ought to know,' he said.

I didn't know what he was talking about. We each had our own one-man tents. Sleeping arrangements were never a consideration.

'Are you drunk?' I asked, going over to join him. Although it was clear by now that all of us were.

'Jim.' He put his hand on my shoulder. 'What do you know of Frances and I?'

'I don't understand,' I said.

'That's what I'm afraid of.' He took his hand away from my shoulder and held it out by his side as if it contained something. Something he treasured. He began to walk back towards the dying fire. 'Frances and I will be sharing a tent tonight. That's all I wanted to say.' He began to walk a little more quickly. For all the world as though he were running away from me.

'Hold on,' I called after him. 'Wait a moment.' I wanted him to stop before he got back to Frances. I didn't want her presence here just yet. He stopped. I caught up with him and asked him what he was talking about.

'I'm talking about Frances and I,' he said.

At first when it dawned on me what he meant I felt all the coldness the alcohol had been keeping at bay. I felt strangely afraid. But as it sunk in more I could only smile.

'Good God of Almighty! Jumping Jesus!' I put my hands to the sides of my forehead as if to control my thoughts. It felt so good now. I couldn't explain it, but it felt as if everything I had waited for had finally come together.

I looked ahead at the three tents at the edge of the lake, outlined by the fire. Like three attics removed from their respective homes, storage places no one else would live in. And I thought of Frances moving into Knucky's. Or vice versa. I could see them covered in dust and cobwebs sifting through each other's pasts.

I ran ahead and threw my arms around Frances and began to cry. She looked over at Knucky. I couldn't see what look was exchanged between them. This would be a part of our future now, but somehow I felt relieved by this.

'You have my blessing.'

Frances took my shoulders and held me at arm's length.

'I'm sorry?' she said.

'No,' I said. 'No. There is nothing to be sorry for. I can think of nothing that could please me more.'

'You're weird, Gallagher. Have I ever told you that?'

Knucky came over and held her hand. And the three of us stood there in the near absolute darkness grinning foolishly to ourselves.

CHAPTER SEVEN

I went back to the harbour and waited there for the rest of the evening for Knucky's arrival. He was due that much. Despite the imp in my head I stayed clear of The Porthole. I sat down by the small pier where the jet-skis set off from. I was aware that Frances could easily be looking out at me. I turned my back. I couldn't bear to face her.

The water chugged against the walls and up the slipway. I looked over at the harbour master's office and saw Tom Harte's car outside. This Eskimo business was getting me down. If there was one thing I could undo in my life right now it would be snagging the Eskimo in our nets. Heaven knows what I had brought upon myself.

In actual fact it was simple. The Eskimo would be reported missing or buried at sea. This would come to light sooner or later. It was a matter of opening up the right channels of communication. IMES or the guards, or both, would access them eventually. The body would be identified and dealt with. How exactly I did not know.

But of course all of this could take some time. And no doubt Tom Harte and Sergeant Bonnar and whoever else was involved would do what they could. Were already doing so as they both had informed me.

It was clear. In fact, nothing could be clearer. Except that my brain was fuzzy these days, and nothing about the facts seemed actual.

It seemed to me as if I was being followed by this Eskimo. As if he had trailed me all the way from the Arctic Circle. From Point Barrow or Prudhoe Bay. Skating like an oil slick across the water, dispersing into our nets. Sticking to my skin like it would stick to feathers. Preventing me from making my escape.

There was no escape. This was abundantly clear. Alaska provided none and coming back would provide none either. Just as Knucky could not escape Frances, or Frances Knucky. Just as there was no escaping the hole in his heart.

When I set out from Bellingham in the ferry, up past the Queen Charlotte Islands in the Hegate Strait, I thought I was off and running. It was like nothing I had experienced on earth before. The texture of the air. The freedom it gave to my lungs. The striking whiteness of the Canadian glaciers etched along the coast. It was like catching a glimpse of the life you had yet to live. When we came upon our first pod of humpbacked whales blowing into the air like geysers, dipping their immense grey bodies through the clear blue water more gracefully than anything I had ever witnessed, I shuddered with the suspicion of all that we had forsaken.

I thought I had finally made it. Finally reached the point I had always been heading to, just as Knucky and Frances' coming together brought all three of us to the point we had always been headed to. It was as sacred and as sacrilegious as that. But in the end Alaska proved no better and no worse. It was another place to get drunk in. Another place to feel the cold.

I arrived in Skagway like any number of Irish had done in the past in search of my own fool's gold. From there it was by bus through the Yukon Territory into Alaska. The Last Frontier. To Anchorage. Back down to Whittier. Across the Prince William Sound by ferry to Valdez. With just my backpack on my back. Like some heroic frontier's man pushing back the boundaries.

For a while I almost believed it. Drifting past the icebergs of the Columbia Glacier I might even have been claiming the North Pole as my own.

I told all of this to Frances after I came back. I told her I felt like a fraud. And she said we were all frauds in one way or another. But she said that even if I hadn't pushed back any boundaries of my own, I had surely pushed them back for others. Knucky, herself and just about anyone in this town I cared to mention. Sometimes I tried to believe this too.

Frances said she was jealous as hell of me. She said she wished she had what it took to do what I did. If nothing else, you've seen some things few of us will ever see. But I told her she had it all wrong. That it was the other way around. That if anyone had broken ground, if anyone was to be envied, it was her.

It's funny how little we actually see of the mystery in ourselves. How seldom we look into the darkness. When I first looked upon an ice-field, stretching back into an infinity of distance and time, into the solid coldness of its core, it was like truly seeing inside myself for the first time. Seeing everything that had gone and all the possibilities to come. It was a beautiful and eerie thing.

'It's a day for walking on water, is it not?'

I recognized Father Jack's voice. He walked around me and looked out into the lough. 'I've often thought I'd love to try,' he said. He seemed in better humour today. Less tense.

'Nobody better qualified.' He looked over to the other shoreline as if choosing the best path, the best point of departure and arrival.

'No.' He squeezed out his lips and shook his head. 'I don't think so.'

'Is it possible if you had enough faith, do you think?'

'With enough faith everything is possible.' He squinted his eyes and took in a deep breath of fresh air.

'So why don't you then?'

'Faith like that is not easily come upon.' He smiled lightly at me. 'Do you swim?'

'Not very well.'

'Nor I. Not at all. You'd be surprised how few of the fishermen can swim. It's a wonderfully shocking statistic.'

He said this as if I knew nothing about fishing at all. And perhaps he was right. Even I would never refer to myself as a fisherman. I was casual help and that was about all. I could never forget that the sea was beneath my feet. I would be useless at walking on water. I would be sinking before I had even left the land.

'Perhaps they have acquired that elusive faith.'

'Perhaps they have,' he said 'Perhaps that's what it takes.'

'Jesus was a fisherman, was he not.' I meant it as a statement more than a question. Somehow it seemed to clarify our conversation for me. But Father Jack responded all the same.

'A fisher of men they say.'

'You've hooked your own fair share in your time, I dare say, Father.'

He laughed. His big hearty laugh. 'I suppose we'd all like to think so.' The light breeze ruffled through his greying hair. The fading strands tipped with white curling like waves. He was looking well. Tall and trim. As if he had been working out. I could easily imagine him astride one of those jet-skis soaring across the water, parting it as he raced along.

'You know,' he said, 'I've often thought I should have been a missionary. Setting out into a faithless country. Breaching its unbelieving borders. There would be so many souls to claim. Like a giant supermarket of lost souls. You couldn't go wrong, could you?' Another laugh roared free. He looked down into the water. I thought he was considering dipping his toes in. He rubbed his hands together. 'You're a missionary of sorts yourself.'

I was totally confused by what he meant by this. I didn't like to ask. He seemed to be looking inside some part of me that only he had proper access to. 'Alaska.' He sucked his top lip in behind his bottom one. 'A brave new world. You must tell me about it some time.'

'I will,' I told him. 'If that's what you want to hear.' He looked about to move on. 'Tell me, Father. Did you give that Eskimo your blessing?'

'I did.'

'Will he rest easy now?'

His shoulders rose slightly. 'I believe so.'

'My fear is that he is in torment. And that I might have had something to do with it. Do you understand that?'

He nodded. 'I do. But don't worry. You did what you had to. We could all learn from that.' He smiled pleasantly. 'Now I really should be off. But I mean it about Alaska. Pay me a visit some time.'

I looked at the water after he had gone. I could easily imagine his footprints embedded in its surface.

Frances confided once that she thought him very handsome. In a mature sort of way. I told her I was shocked, although little about Frances would shock me. 'I'm not alone in this,' she said. And then she said she heard he had many women friends. She raised her eyebrows knowingly. 'Idle gossip,' I warned. 'Now, Jim,' she said, 'you know there's nothing idle about gossip.'

If Father Jack did have women friends, as Frances put it, I wondered where that left the rest of us. Most probably, I thought, it left us exactly where we always were.

I had been told one time in Alaska about an Italian priest living with an Inuit woman in Hooper Bay. It was completely accepted by all. There's not a single priest untainted in these parts, I was told. And maybe this was so. The priest in Hooper Bay had worked wonders for the community. Built them a school, a church with a communal hall. He was the life and the soul of the area.

But it seemed more acceptable there somehow. Far away in the remote outreaches of civilization. Where the primitive urges were closer to the surface. Where to deny them would jeopardize survival.

For a moment the shocking image of Frances and Father Jack cohabiting along the desperate coastline of the Bering Sea came to mind. 'God forgive me,' I thought. And laughed nervously.

I was surprised at him asking me to visit. I had never called in on him before. Never considered it. But I thought now that I would. He was sincere about the invitation. It struck me he was lonely. And why would he not be? Trying to keep God's name alive all by himself. Listening to the sins of all and having to forgive them no matter how atrocious. Bearing our guilt for us. If anyone needed the companionship of a woman, it was surely him.

Whatever I might say or think, I knew that when the time came, when I lay buried in my mound of rotting fish, I would demand his face bearing down on me too.

The light was fading when one by one the boats returned. I was cold and hungry. I hadn't moved from my spot since I arrived. I tried to see if I could make out the shape of the *Lorna Doone*, but the sad fact was I couldn't recognize it from the others. I wasn't cut out for this. Maybe that's what the last couple of days had been telling me. Maybe if Knucky came ashore and told me he no longer wanted me around, it would be the best thing for me. But I didn't know what else I could do. I could go back to Alaska. It would not disappoint me greatly to have to. But I wasn't ready for that yet. On top of all that Therese had firmly cast her spanner in my works. Even if it didn't seem that anything more would come of that.

I wandered back over by the Co-op and watched the boats come in. There was little talk as the men tossed the ropes over the side and tied the boats securely on the pier. Some nodded or spoke a hello as they passed. I greeted John McAuley and asked if he had seen Knucky out there. He shook his head silently and passed on. I watched the catch being unloaded while I waited.

I could always try for a job again in the Co-op if it came down to it. But what I really needed, I thought, was to get away from the smell of fish altogether. There were other things a man could do with his life.

Darkness set in completely. The lights from the few remaining boats coming in for the night flickered at intervals along the lough. The outside lights of the Co-op lit up the pier. Their yellow glow diffused across the cold concrete and seemed to float a few feet above the water like a ghostly mist. The sharp screeches of machinery tore into wet air. Voices echoed as they bantered on about their work. I glanced across at The Porthole. The curtains had been pulled and other than the outside lights it could have been closed and empty. But inside I knew it would be noisy and warm and full. Frances would be trying to hear the orders above the noise. She would be snapping at those who wouldn't speak loudly enough or who looked in a different direction when they spoke. I would have loved a pint. I was even ready for where it could take me.

I walked up and down trying to keep warm. The low groan of the engines grew louder as the boats approached. I closed my eyes and had the impression that I was moving towards them and not the other way around. That like the yellow light I was floating above the surface of the water heading out to sea. I almost felt at peace.

There was no sign of the *Lorna Doone* amongst them. I scanned the lough, but other than the lights of the towns dotting the far coast there was nothing visible. I focused on the lights of the prison. All alone in the daylight, but now, in the darkness, from a distance, it seemed sandwiched in by living towns. Hemmed in as though it couldn't escape them if it tried.

I blew in my hands. My warm breath gathered in their palms then slipped away. It didn't look as if Knucky was coming back tonight. Damn him anyway. I still didn't know where I stood.

CHAPTER EIGHT

I had the good sense to go home early that night without stopping by The Porthole. I awoke bright and breezy the next morning. I made coffee and took a mug of it with me and walked down to the harbour. The *Lorna Doone* was still out.

The pale-blue early morning sky was cloudless and hid nothing. The water rippled calmly. Invitingly. Some of the boats were already out, and others were preparing to leave. I didn't want to have to talk to anyone, so I headed back up towards the town.

Knucky and I would settle this eventually. We always did. I just wanted to know what it was we had to settle. My coffee was cold. I threw what was left of it into the gutter as I walked and put the mug in my jacket pocket. I felt like a schoolboy playing truant. I felt childish and silly.

People regularly missed work in the canneries. Coming in late nursing hangovers or not coming in at all. The students who came out for the summer were the least able to take it. Running from the conveyor belt full of stinking fish to puke over the harbour wall or on occasions unable to make that short journey and spewing up all over the fish in front of them. But it was a different existence there. It was the underside of living. Feeling sick was a necessary part of it. With the gulls screeching out their callous enjoyment overhead, and the otters in the harbour on their backs with their paws folded across their chests like floating corpses.

If Knucky had made it out of here, no doubt this is where he would have ended up.

I stood in the square in town and wondered where to go. I had another whole day in front of me with nothing to do. It was like facing up to my life again, being given the chance to tackle it squarely head on. But I couldn't stomach it, it was too early in the morning for that. What I wanted was to see Therese again. To make another shoddy appearance into her life. I had a hunch that it would be a terrible mistake. The worst of its kind. But I had nothing better to do.

I headed out the Malin Road and began hitching as I walked. People were usually generous with lifts around here. They had little to fear and a lifetime of information to be gleaned. But only a couple of cars and a van passed. They indicated they were full or turning off soon, so I waved them on. It was early yet. No more than eight o'clock. Fragments of white cloud appeared on the horizon and slowly moved in. The sun threatened to spill across the sky at any moment. I walked off the road, on the grass verge. The cows chewed on their cud and watched me suspiciously. Some came right over and eyed me brazenly. I acknowledged their right to and carried on. Behind the flat fields the hills rose comfortably skywards. I wished I was out there somewhere with Therese. Trekking over the rough land and pushing through bramble or simply following some of the bog roads to their uncertain ends.

Frances told me she lost her virginity out there in those bogs up in the hills. It was a bitterly cold night, she said. With just enough moonlight to see what you were up to. It would have been better not to have seen anything at all. She told me how she felt the wiry spring of the dead beneath her. How she smelt their warm peaty aroma. She could almost hear them chiding her. 'It was as if I had sold my soul to the devil,' she said. 'Sometimes I think I'm still being paid back.'

I could never walk on the bogs now without thinking of that occasion. I wished I could have been there to stop it. But there was no stopping it. As Frances put it. We're all doomed in one way or another.

I knew that sometimes she went out there still, popped a tab of LSD beneath her tongue, and tried to redeem herself. Make peace with the ancestors, she would smile. She meant it too. It wasn't just a pretentious act of immaturity. Her intention was completely sincere. And I believe she sometimes thought she was winning the battle.

Knucky hated Frances' drug-taking. More than once he said it had destroyed their relationship. It was like a parallel life she had running alongside his rather than following in the same track. He said they would kill her in the end. That they were despicable things and that the law could not come down heavy enough on anyone dealing in them. But I think he probably hated how she left him out of it more than anything else.

I heard a car pull up beside me and looked around. A man dressed in a purple turtleneck leaned over and opened the door for me.

'Come on,' he said. 'Get in.'

Outside of his black clothing and white collar I would scarcely have recognized Father Jack. It seemed I couldn't get enough of him these days. But I was glad of the lift and sat in. As he put the car back into gear I couldn't miss seeing the bright blue leatherette glove on his left hand. His other one, casually guiding the wheel, was bare. I was stumped for a moment. With the window next to him rolled halfways down and the breeze blowing in across his hair he looked for all the world like an unreal character from an opulent soap opera world.

'Where are you headed?' he asked.

I wanted to ask him the same question. Ask him what he was doing dressed as he was. What particular aspect of his priestly duties he was carrying out now?

'Malin Head.' The crease of his cream flannel trousers peaked as sharp as the edge on the Sunday missalette. And it struck me that what he was doing was trying not to be a priest at all but an ordinary human being and had somehow got the balance wrong.

'I'll take you some of the way,' he said. The radio had been playing softly in the background, and he turned it off. 'A golf match in Buncrana.'

And finally it all made sense.

'A good day for golf,' I said.

'A perfect day.' He pushed a tape into the cassette player. Before it began to play I already knew instinctively it would be something classical. A strong and reassuring music filled the empty chambers of the car. His blue-gloved fingers beat time on the wheel.

'Are you a fan?'

I didn't know if he was asking about golf or classical music.

'So many people just don't care. Find it grating on the ears.' He laughed aloud sharply. 'Like my sermons, hah.' He seemed pleased about this.

'Well I know your sermons better than I know this music, that's for sure.'

He laughed sharply again. 'Shostakovich,' he said. 'Sometimes I think I should just shut up altogether and play this off the altar instead.'

'We'd miss your voice,' I told him. And we would have. It was a constant in our lives. Like the ringing of the Angelus bells. Whether you prayed along with them or not. 'We'd be lost without it.' Despite my uneasy view of religion, I believed this. It was like going to mass most Sundays still with no knowledge of why. It was a habit I was reluctant to break.

'You're a generous man, Jim. We might be better trading places.' He turned the volume up and sat back in the driving seat as if settling back for a shave.

I closed my eyes. The initial heat of the day magnified by the glass windscreen spread across my face. I shortly began to doze off. Faint details of being on board the *Lorna Doone* merged with the conscious rhythm of the car's motion. The Eskimo's body swayed before me and somewhere a piano slid hazily in the background, its internal workings rattling noisily. My head fell forward and I woke in my seat. Father Jack stared ahead absently. He didn't seem aware of my presence anymore. I noticed he wasn't wearing a safety belt. I wondered if he felt he had no need to. If he already had all the protection that was necessary. As I drifted off again I felt the front of my jacket, unable to remember if I had put my belt on or not. I needed all the help I could get.

The *Lorna Doone* lurched. I could hear the thud of a body falling and the sound of someone playing the piano. I looked for the Eskimo, but I couldn't see him anywhere.

'What's that?'

I opened my eyes. Father Jack was looking at me waiting on an answer. I tried to remember his question.

'Hmm?' I asked.

'I thought you said something.' He turned the music down again.

'No. Nothing.'

I looked to see where we were. We were almost at the turn for Malin Head where I would have to get out. I started to thank him for the lift.

'Not at all,' he said. He slowed down and pulled in just opposite the turn. 'You should get a lift most of the way from here.'

I nodded. I opened the door and got out. 'Good luck with the golf.'

'I'll need it,' he said. I was still woozy from having dozed off. Shostakovich rang in my ears. My feet curved over each roll of wave. I closed the door and walked behind the car to cross the road. He pulled the window down further and stuck his head out.

'Jim.'

I looked back.

'I've been asked to bury him properly. Your Eskimo friend. I just thought you'd like to know.' He smiled, waved goodbye and pulled away.

I stood alone in the middle of the road. Stranded. There were so many questions I wanted to ask him. So much more I needed to know. But he was gone. Soaring down the road.

I sat down at the side of the road and tried to think clearly. If they were burying him locally, they must not have located his family or have found out anything about him at all. Unless there were some legalities preventing them returning his body. Whoever *they* were.

And what did burying him properly mean? Incarcerating his body in such a way that it could never break free again, at least not into this world?

Perhaps it was the best they could do. But it just didn't seem right. What did Father Jack know of Eskimo death or rebirth? For all he knew he could be entombing him into this material world for all eternity. I tried to remember what little I knew of Eskimo culture, what I had heard about death. But nothing would come. My mind went a complete blank. It had ceased to exist. I felt as if I had ceased to exist also. It wasn't warm or black like sleep. It was empty like a faint recognition of loneliness. Like I had nothing to believe in.

A cold shiver ran through me and I jumped to my feet. I needed to keep moving. For unknown reasons I was beginning to panic. It descended on me like fog. Blinding me to all that surrounded me. Something terrible was happening and I was caught up somewhere in the middle of it. Terrible in that the events were disconnected and unknown. My life and the Eskimo's death.

I felt like running. Running all the way to Malin Head. All the way to the edge of the ocean. To the edge of the physical world. Where looming out of the fog Therese's face was beckoning. Like a siren.

Luring me forwards step by step.

I thanked the two strangers, waving after them as they disappeared around the bend. German tourists. A man and a woman. But their relationship was unclear. They looked like brother and sister, but they seemed more intimate with each other than that. Although I didn't see them touch I could believe they understood each other's physicality.

They picked me up about a mile down the road from where Father Jack had dropped me off. The man told me that from a distance they had thought I was in training. Then he asked if I was late for something. I told them he was right. That I might even be too late, but that I appreciated their stopping all the same. They looked in their mid-twenties. I didn't feel any older than them. Younger if anything. The man did all the talking. The woman turned around and nodded whenever I said anything. As if I was making the utmost of sense, speaking of things she could not figure out for herself. But most probably, I thought, she did not understand what I was saying. His English was broken but coherent.

He told me they had come up from Galway, where they had spent the last two weeks, and were touring around the Peninsula for a few days. He asked if I lived here. I told him sometimes, but that sometimes I thought I was just touring too. He seemed puzzled by this. The woman nodded as if she could appreciate what I was saying.

Then he asked if there was anything I would recommend them seeing. He said he had heard there were many monuments here, High Crosses and Stone Circles. But what I wanted to tell them was to go see the Eskimo. If I only knew where he was. That if it was historical sights they were after, or sights of outstanding natural beauty, that was where it all began. Instead I answered, 'Alaska. Glacier Bay. You could do worse than that.'

He looked across at the woman, nodding intently. He didn't ask me anything else after that and seemed relieved when I asked to be let out. I pointed out Banba's Crown on the top of Malin Head in the distance and indicated they should head in that direction. I told them how you could still make out where EIRE had been spelled out in stones by the Irish during the war to prevent their fellow countrymen from confusing its coastline with England's. 'It's quite an attraction,'

I told them. 'You really shouldn't miss it.'

After they had gone I headed east in the general direction of Therese's cottage. I only hoped I could find it. I hadn't really taken too much notice of my surroundings the day before. I remembered something about the remains of a stone wall at the end of the lane which brought you up to where it was hidden behind the trees. For all I knew it could be miles yet.

It had turned out to be a beautiful morning. I took my jacket off and swung it over my shoulder. I could feel the mug in the pocket hitting against my back as I walked. I was dressed for a day out on the open sea, not for a casual walk along the back roads. I was already sweating beneath my thick wool jumper. I should have taken that off too, but I didn't. Either from laziness or as penance.

Over the fields I could make out the shoreline. Despite the sunny weather the waves continued to crash in across the rocks. The white turmoil of the water was visible from here. Spraying up into the air and dissipating. Knucky could be anywhere out there. Coursing over the waves in anger or with deep exhilaration.

It seemed ages since I had last seen him and Frances although it had only been two nights earlier. But that night was not real at all. A drunken mirage. Maybe Frances was even out on the water with Knucky. Together again.

I was losing them. This had been apparent since my return. And perhaps long before. Losing them, not necessarily to each other but to the distances I needed to explore.

I saw the Germans' hire car winding around a turn in the road. It moved uphill like a small crawling insect with a mind of its own. I could imagine them inside it talking in their own language. Sorry for ever having picked me up. I envied their relationship, whatever it was. At once familiar and intent. In a way it reminded me of how mine had been with Frances before the balance of it had shifted. I regretted now telling them about the stones. It had been unnecessary.

I came across the laneway about a mile and a half up the road. I recognized it at once despite my concerns. I stopped at the end of it and questioned my sanity. I should not have come out here, but I hadn't known what else to do. I thought about going back home but instead started to walk up the lane.

Therese might not be here anyway. She could be anywhere, doing whatever it was she did with her life. She was like the Eskimo. She seemed to have come up out of the depths of nowhere. To have followed me from a foreign country. Alone and unclaimed.

I saw her car at the side of the cottage. My chest constricted. The sun glared off the whitewash. I shielded my eyes with my hand and approached the door. Like the whitewash its bright red paint had obviously been recently applied. I took hold of the ring knocker and held it. It felt as if I was holding on to a bull. I knocked weakly at first, then again more loudly. I listened for her step but could only hear the insides of my ears clicking, like typewriter keys. I knocked again. Maybe I would be all right yet. Maybe she would be somewhere else. The door opened suddenly, catching me unawares.

Therese stood there in a white towelling robe. She didn't seem to have anything else on. Her feet were bare, which was probably why I hadn't heard her approach. I made a number of attempts to stand naturally before her, but slumped each time into an ungainly and awkward posture.

'Jim.' She sounded curt. Angry.

I tried to smile. But my lips just assumed a pained expression.

'What are you doing here?' She tightened the belt on her robe as though afraid it might fall off her at any moment.

I didn't know how to answer her. What could I tell her? That I had nowhere else to go?

I couldn't stop thinking about her bare feet. How cold they must be on the flagstone floor. She folded her arms and waited on my answer.

'I was just passing,' I said foolishly.

'Don't.' She ran her hand through the back of her hair. She had no intention of inviting me in.

'You must be cold.' I couldn't find any words that would make sense of this. I felt like nodding, as the German woman had done, in the hope of deciphering something. Anything comprehensible.

'You shouldn't have come.' She started to close the door. 'Why did you have to do this?'

'I needed to see you, Therese.' I didn't want her to close the door. It seemed important to keep talking at any cost to keep it open.

'Go away,' she said. Not angrily, but with concern.

She pulled the left collar of her robe over the right then closed the door further.

'Can't we talk? For just a moment?'

'No.' She shook her head. 'Go home.' She finished closing the door.

I stood there staring at the thick red paint. Picturing the large flakes that would scrape away in years to come. If I had stopped to think of it for any length of time, I would never have come.

CHAPTER NINE

Frances called by my house a few days later. I had been up and down to the harbour frequently, but the *Lorna Doone* hadn't shown up. Frances wanted to know where I had been, why I had deserted her. I brought her into the kitchen and offered her tea or coffee.

'Nothing for me,' she said.

I wasn't long out of bed and had yet to wake up fully. I put the kettle on for tea for myself. Frances pushed herself up on the cupboards and sat on the worktop. She wore a white T-shirt with the words *The Porthole Bar* emblazoned above a picture of a porthole. She saw me looking at it.

'Tacky, huh?'

I shrugged.

'I tried to tell him. But there was no talking to him. Seems to think it'll pull the tourists in. Is convinced he'll sell a bundle.' She smiled.

Her boss, Eddie, had bought the bar a few years previously. Something to do with his days after he retired from fishing. He had no sons to follow in his footsteps, so he had sold the whole fishing operation. He was gruff, had earned the right to be, he told Frances once, having struggled against the sea for nearly forty years. But he was okay, she said, if you knew how to deal with him. Frances knew how to deal with everyone.

'So where have you been?' She smiled again and clacked her front teeth together. I knew exactly what she was thinking.

'Nowhere.' I heard the kettle turn itself off and went over to make a pot of tea. 'Have you seen Knucky?' I put a couple of slices of bread in the toaster and waited on her answer.

'Not a sign,' she said. 'But you know Knucky. He's on one of his little journeys. Seeking satori.'

'Are you sure you won't have some?' I poured out a mug of tea for myself. Frances shook her head.

'So come on,' she said, 'out with it.' She sat on her hands and banged her heels against the cupboard doors.

'There's nothing to come out with.'

'You've been missing for days.'

'I've been here. I've just been keeping to myself.'

Frances didn't seem convinced.

'Really. I have.' The toast popped up. Frances leaned over and took it out, tearing off half of one slice for herself and tossing the rest over to me at the table. She began to eat it dry. 'I know I went home with her. But that was it. She dropped me back in town the following day.'

'God, you were drunk!' She laughed with immense pleasure.

'I know,' I said. 'I don't know what came over me.'

'So, come on. You can do better than that. Who was she?'

'She was no one, Frances. No one at all. That's the truth of it.'

'But you spent the night with her, right?'

'I slept on the couch. You said yourself how drunk I was.'

She slid down off the worktop and wiped the crumbs off her hands on her jeans. 'And that was it?'

'That was it.' I didn't know why, but I didn't want her to know anything more than this.

'You must be losing it,' she said.

'Getting sense,' I told her.

'Now wouldn't that be a turn up for the books.'

I wanted to ask her about herself and Knucky, but I didn't know how to. It was one of those things I had no right to know unless they decided to tell me. All the same I tried approaching it in a round about way.

'Was Knucky in a bad way?'

'He was funny,' she said. 'You both were.' She took a drink from my mug then handed it back to me. 'Did you even ask her name?'

'Therese Doherty.' I wished I didn't have to tell her.

'I can't remember ever seeing her before.'

'I don't know,' I said. 'I think she must have moved away when she was younger. America or somewhere. I really don't know.'

'I see.' She looked out the window into my yard, trying to piece all these bits of information together. 'So is that it?' She glanced over her shoulder.

'That's it.' I refilled my mug. 'Do you know if Knucky is mad with me?'

'Why should he be?' She turned around. She looked confused.

'Well, I didn't turn up for work the next day. And I had already missed that day's fishing.'

'I haven't seen him since.' She raised her eyebrows in a form of shrug. But what or when she hadn't seen him since she didn't say.

'Look, it's my day off,' she said. 'Do you want to do something?'

I could think of nothing I would have preferred more.

We took a drive over the hills and down to Kinnagoe Bay. As we drove over, Frances pulled in just at that point on the hills where the ocean looms up before you. Up to that point, the bogs and hills seem to stretch into infinity. In a vast array of tufted shades of oranges and browns. A mellow ferrous glow. A world that has you held in its grip and might never let you go. Where the horizon seems to get further away the more you approach it. And then, as if out of nowhere, the ocean surfaces, and the immenseness of the world's possibilities are laid bare.

Frances loved to stop here. It was a point where everything in this life interacted, she said. Things solid and viscous. Real and unreal. Corporeal and ethereal. She loved to get out and walk back and forth on the rough road watching the ocean come and go. Sometimes she would do so in her bare feet. So that her flesh made contact with the earth.

There were points all over this peninsula, she told me, energy points that contained our life source. A series of points that connected and intersected. Stretching over the landscape and focusing themselves around ancient sites of ceremony and burial. And if you discovered them and made one with them, it was possible that they would bring you through. It was better than drugs, she said. And all for free.

'Do you think that's him?' Frances leaned on the steering wheel and pointed through the windscreen. I looked to where her finger directed. I could make out the dark blotch of a boat far out to sea, northwest of us.

'Who knows?' It was too far away to make a reasonable guess at.

'It is him. I can tell.' Her eyes were closed, and she smiled lightly to herself. 'It's him.'

From this distance it could have been anything floating aimlessly.

Something with no control. Yielding completely to the pull of the tides.

'Don't you find it strange to be sitting here? Not to be out there with him.' Frances pushed some strands of hair from her eyes and looked at me over her elbows. 'Isn't it like an out of body experience?'

'No.' But I knew what she was asking. And there was some truth to it. Looking out at what might be Knucky floating alone on his boat was like looking at yourself from a great distance. Not being rocked by the vagaries of the sea's motion, the incalculable complexities of its fluidity, but sitting solidly on land. It was like seeing another part of yourself you had only suspected existed up to that point. A part everything else depended on.

'Ever since we split up it's been like that for me.' She furrowed her brow as if it made no sense. 'Every time I see him it's like looking at him from up here. Seeing the vastness of the ocean around him like an energy field, but one born out of loneliness.'

I wanted to reach for her, to put my arms around her as I had when she looked at the Eskimo, to share in her loneliness, but it was like walking, unasked, onto private property.

'What do you talk about out there?'

There was no easy answer to this. As Frances had told me herself it bothered her that Knucky and I had been fishing together since I came back. Not in a disapproving way. But as if the distance between us was increasing with each journey we took. As if every time we returned we did so a little further up the coast from her.

I had never felt it this way when Frances and Knucky were together. I had always recalled it as the best times we ever had. Maybe I should have.

I could never have asked them, either, what they talked about when I was not there. Whether they mentioned me at all. Yet when Frances asked me it seemed perfectly proper. As if she was incapable of trespassing. As if she understood that this was a shared land-scape, one beyond possession.

'We talk about work a great deal,' I said. 'I know so little about fishing. Knucky has to inform and harangue me all the time.' I noticed that the windscreen in front of Frances began to cloud over with the proximity of her breathing. She stared ahead as if it made no difference.

'But when you're not working. When you're just lost to the pleasure of the sea?'

'It's hard to get Knucky to speak at those moments,' I told her. Aware that she already knew.

'You know, the three of us have never been on his boat together. Don't you think that strange?'

I hadn't thought about it before. But it was true.

'It's not a deliberate thing, I'm sure,' I said.

'Of course not.' Frances took this for granted. 'It is just the way we are. The way our lives relate to one another. We're not the stuff of liquid at all, flowing into one another, merging completely in a viscous pool. We're more like planets, don't you think? With our own attractive and repulsive forces. Trying to strike a balance.'

'You're probably right.'

Frances had a way of looking at our lives that was usually correct. She seemed to have a vantage point that no one else had yet discovered.

'Knucky's out of control.' She said it as though she were a newscaster recounting disaster. 'In the way a meteorite appears out of control to us as it comes crashing towards our earth. And he's on course for collision. Mark my words.'

I wanted to know exactly what she meant by this, but I knew I had reached another point of no entry. She started up the car and drove down the steep, winding road to the bay.

Down on the shore we couldn't see the boat at all. We made no mention of this, but both of us looked for it. We walked along the tide-line. For a while I walked with one foot on the wet sand and the other on the dry. Frances kicked at the thick yellow foam that washed in. It was cold on the open beach, and both of us kept our hands in our pockets. The day was overcast. A damp grey.

Frances stopped and pointed back up the beach towards the lifebelt posts spread along it.

'Look. Some have disappeared completely.'

The shifting sands brought in by the tides and wind had drifted in mounds around them. The top half of one of the red and white rings stuck out of the sand directly in front of us as if it too was in danger of drowning.

'I wouldn't like to be depending on them,' she said. She burrowed the toe of her boot into the wet sand beneath her. 'Have you ever known Knucky to wear a lifejacket?' Although the connection was obvious, the question seemed to come out of nowhere.

'Too cumbersome,' I said. 'You know that.'

'I know.' She kicked her toe free, scattering sand over the bottoms of her jeans.

We walked to the end of the beach and climbed over the rocks into the next small inlet. I always felt that I should be examining everything about me. The seaweed, the shellfish, whatever. It was like a complete breakdown in my morality not to. Yet I rarely did. The bother of it seemed overwhelming. And it wasn't as if I inherently knew everything there was. Despite growing up by the sea I was almost completely ignorant of it. Frances sat down on a rock and pulled her legs right up against her. I sat down beside her. The spray off the waves landed in mist upon us, but I knew Frances was savouring this so I said nothing. She closed her eyes, allowing it to coat her lids.

'Whatever happened to that Eskimo of yours?' A fine mist of water, like gauze, covered her face.

'I've been meaning to talk to you about that.' The water slurped in the crevices at the base of the rocks. 'I'm not sure what's happening exactly, but I know they've asked Father Jack to bury him.'

'I see.'

I thought it possible that she did. That she saw more in this than I could. 'I'm not happy about it,' I told her.

'I know.'

A line of cormorants flew in a low line just above the water. With her eyes closed, Frances missed seeing them.

'What else can they do, I suppose?'

'No one will tell me anything. I'm not sure they're doing their best.'

'Who have you spoken to?'

'Tom Harte. The sergeant. Charlie Doherty. But Charlie doesn't seem to know anything either. It doesn't seem to bother him, though.'

'He can't concern himself with everything.'

'This is different. It can't get much more different than this.'

Frances opened her mouth and pushed her tongue out flat, awaiting another wave of spray. 'Maybe you should talk to Father Jack.' She opened her eyes and pulled her hair back behind her ears. She wore a thick dark-blue Aran jumper over her T-shirt. The sleeves were rolled up to her elbows, revealing her strong freckled arms.

'I intend to. But I think he just sees it as a job, nothing more. No one seems interested. It's as though it's all an inconvenience to everybody. Like something washed in on the beach no one wishes to claim. But I can't help thinking how it would be if it was one of us that was found drowned in some remote part of the world. Would we be happy to be filed away as Persons Unknown? To be disposed of in whatever way was deemed fit?'

'You feel responsible, don't you?'

'I am responsible. I sometimes think I should have stayed in Alaska. I should never have come back. So much has been a mistake.'

'Well do something then.' Frances jumped down off the rock. The soles of her walking boots sank in the wet sand. She began to walk further down the beach, picking up stones and skimming them along the surface of the water. I looked at the ridged imprints of her boots like topography. Like two mini versions of almost identical countries. She turned around and walked backwards. 'If I can do anything to help.'

I got down and followed after her.

'As long as they've really tried their best to identify him. I'd be happy then. And if they bury him with some thought of who he is.'

'An Eskimo.'

'As Knucky would say, a fucking Eskimo. Jesus, Frances, it's like a little part of my life in Alaska coming back to catch up with me. That's how deep it goes. It's scary. Downright so.'

'Talk to Father Jack. He may have some answers.' She said this as though she knew authoritatively that he had. As if he could be depended on to have access to this information.

'What have they been saying in the pub? What's the talk? I've been avoiding everyone as much as possible.'

'Oh, the usual. There's been a run of dead Eskimo jokes. Some of them funny. All terrible. A Russian factory ship. That's their deduction.'

A lone kittiwake landed about forty yards in front of us. Like the lost soul of the Eskimo begging up at me.

'It has to be. Anything else would be too much to contemplate.' Although that was all I had been contemplating since I'd found him. I'd been searching in the furthest extremities of reason. As if real sense always lay in its outreaches.

'It's a sign. You know that much?'

'What is?'

'Finding the Eskimo. You have to assess it in relation to your life so far. That's what it's all about. Things like this don't just happen.'

Frances seemed to think this was a positive thing. She beamed broadly with pleasure. 'I wish I had found him.'

'Well, I wish so too.'

Frances dropped down on her hunkers and scratched at the wet sand with her nails. She looked out in the direction of the boat we had seen earlier. 'What way do you want to die?' she asked.

'I've never really thought about it.'

Frances looked up in surprise. 'Honestly?'

'Truth to tell.'

'I think about it all the time. I thought everyone did.' She looked genuinely taken aback. Embarrassed also as though caught in the middle of an act she should not have been committing. She began writing her name in the sand with her finger with sharp, fluid motions. 'I asked Knucky once how he wanted to go, and he said in his own time.' She smiled at this. She finished off the 's' of her name and then waited for the water to wash in and sweep it away.

'So what have you decided?'

She stood up and wiped the sand off her fingers. 'Nothing. It's not an easy decision.'

She began to walk back up the beach. I looked to have offended her, but I didn't know how.

'We should get back,' she said. She climbed over the rocks towards the first beach. Halfways over she stopped and looked back. She held her arms out from her sides for balance. 'I can't believe you've never thought about it,' she said.

I shrugged.

She stepped backwards without looking, finding a rock behind her and placing her foot carefully on top of it.

'It's irresponsible. That's what it is.'

She lowered her arms and turned her back on me.

On the way back into town in the car she hardly spoke a word at all. I wished I knew what I had done. I had let her down. Lowered her estimation of me. Ignored the signs all around me.

We drove over the hills and joined up with the main road into town again. She paused at the intersection to make sure the way was clear. But even though it was she didn't move off. She remained stationary at the white line, revving the engine gently. She put her hand on my arm and gripped it tightly.

'It wasn't easy without you being here.'

I felt her fingers digging into me. Hurting me again like that time in the bar.

'It wasn't easy being around Knucky.' She took her hand off my arm and put it back on the wheel. 'It still isn't,' she said, pulling out into the road.

I sat there silently. My hands resting on my knees. I knew little of what they had gone through. To do so I would have had to imagine myself in their situation, and that was not something I wanted to do. Like contemplating my own death, I avoided it. When we were camping nothing could give me more pleasure than seeing them head off at night into their tent together. I never tried to understand this. I just accepted it.

Sometimes I'd hear them whispering or one of them might giggle, and I'd wonder what they were talking about or what was going on between them. And sometimes I'd hear the sounds of what could have been their lovemaking. I never knew anything for certain, and I preferred it that way. I treated them as I did the other sounds of the night. I revelled in them. In the strangeness of their purity. Their confirmation of my unique place in this. For if they were making love, was it not true that they were making it for all of us?

When they split up I never fully understood the depth of their feelings. Neither of them would talk about it. I didn't know where my own fitted into it. I felt let down. Disappointed. Not with Frances or Knucky, but the way it turned out. The way my faith had been misplaced. Disappointed with myself.

When they were together I didn't know what happened between them when I wasn't there, but I had no need to. And they had no need to talk about it. But now Frances had broken the silence about their time apart during my absence. I didn't feel ready for it yet.

'There's so much we don't know.' Frances pulled up in front of my house. She put her hand on my forehead and trailed her fingers across it. I felt uncomfortable. I understood nothing of her touch. Frances had her own set of boundaries. I felt right at the edge of my own, but I didn't know where she stood in relation to hers.

I thought I might panic at any moment. She held her fingers lightly to my brow as though reading my thoughts through their tips.

'I slept with Knucky again.' She took her fingers away and put them to her lips. She looked petrified. She waited for me to speak. But again this was something I was not ready for. Although I had thought it possible that it might happen, I was not prepared to cope with it.

We sat there waiting for each other to speak. Frances sniffed quietly and bit at the sides of her fingers.

'When?' It was all I could think to say, although I already knew the answer.

'The other night.' She breathed in heavily. 'After The Grapevine.'

The leatherette creaked as I moved uncomfortably in the seat. 'I don't know what to say. I feel completely useless here.'

Frances smiled resignedly. 'I don't know what to say either. This world is inherently corrupt. We're all a party to it. I don't think there is anything else we can do.'

I looked at the radio and wished I could turn it on.

'Where does it leave you and Knucky?' It was another unnecessary question.

'Adrift.' Frances tapped her fingers on her jeans along her upper thigh. 'We both lay awake for hours early the following morning without speaking. Unable to. Then Knucky slipped out of bed, dressed and left. He may not have known I was awake.'

Frances looked frightened and sad. I was not accustomed to seeing her this way. But it suited her. I liked seeing this other side of her nature. It didn't make her weaker in any way. Stronger if anything.

'It's killing him, you know that?'

I didn't know if she was talking about his heart now or the end of their relationship. It may well have been both.

'Sometime he's going to go off in that boat of his and never come back.' She smiled as though this would be the most perfect thing imaginable. 'It's finding my own boat that's the problem.' She laughed. 'Landlubbers. Ahoy.'

'I'm sorry it worked out this way,' I said.

She shrugged. 'What else can we do?'

I looked at the clock on the dashboard. It was a quarter to three. She saw me looking and asked, 'What now?'

'We could go and get drunk,' I suggested.

'Maybe I'll just go back.'

'It's probably best,' I agreed. I thanked her for the drive and got out. I waited for her to start up the car to start up and drive back to her flat above The Porthole, but she just sat there. I looked out the window of my front room twenty minutes later and she was still there. When I looked again ten minutes later she was gone.

CHAPTER TEN

I was caught off my guard when Father Jack opened the door of the presbytery himself. I had expected his housekeeper, Mrs Gillen, to answer it. I mumbled something that came out like an apology.

'Jim. Come in.' He seemed pleased to see me. His black shirt was open at the collar, and his sleeves were rolled up.

'I hope I haven't called at a bad time,' I said.

'No. Not at all.'

I stepped into the hall. I had never been in the presbytery before. It was not at all as I expected. I had imagined something more church-like. Something more hollow and cold. But it seemed quite ordinary. Like a large house. Which of course was what it was. Apart from a small crucifix attached to the wall there were no religious artifacts that I could make out at all.

A grey overcoat hung on the tall wooden coat-stand, and some letters and loose change lay on the hall table. Across from it a tall grandfather clock ticked loudly. Its brass pendulums swung evenly. I checked my watch against it. It was exactly two minutes past eight on both.

Father Jack led me across the tiled hallway and into the front room. 'Can I take your coat?' He held his hand out to receive it. I hoped he would put it on the coat-stand. I liked the thought of it hanging there. But he left it folded over the arm of the chair at the writing desk.

'Have a seat.' He pointed towards the big leather armchairs either side of the fireplace. A large woven rug of maroon and black wool was spread across the floor. A coal fire burned warmly in the grate. A folded newspaper lay across one of the chairs and a glass of red wine rested on the arm. I sat down in the empty seat.

'You'll join me in a drink?' He walked over to the mantelpiece and took a bottle of wine down off it. 'Wine? Or would you prefer something stronger?'

'Wine's great.'

He went over to a cabinet against the far wall to get a glass. The room was full of clocks. I had seen at least three on the mantelpiece before I sat down. There were two more hanging on the walls. And I counted another five on top of tables and cabinets and bookcases. They all looked like antiques. The two on the walls had pendulums also. The room was filled with their ticking. But none of it was synchronized. As if it were possible for time to be out of synch.

'Beautiful, aren't they?' He smiled appreciatively around the room. 'I collect them. You're seeing only a small selection of them here. Too many of the damn things, to be honest.'

He filled a large glass for me and topped up his own. I wondered about his fascination for clocks. Why would a man of the cloth, who surely believed in eternity, be interested in time? But maybe it could only be someone like that who would be so interested. Maybe time had more meaning for those who had no need for it.

He raised his glass to his lips and took a sip of his wine. He held it in his mouth. Then swallowed. Although he was seated in front of his fire, it was like watching him on the altar during the Consecration. I imagined him tasting the blood of Christ, running it around on his tongue enjoying the aftertaste.

'A robust one, don't you think? Woody and fruity.' He nodded. Pleased with his own choice. 'Do you know anything about wines?'

'I have to plead ignorance, I'm afraid. White and red. That's as much as I can distinguish. And only with my eyes open.'

'I know very little myself,' he said. 'But I'm learning. By trial and error.'

I looked at the bottle down on the hearth and read its Spanish name. I would have liked to ask him what wine he used on the altar. If he ever varied it. Treating himself on special occasions. His own secret world of blood and wine.

He was waiting on me to take a drink from mine. To see how I reacted. I took a drink but found it bitter. It dried my palate and tongue uncomfortably.

'It's good,' I said, as if I knew about these things.

'I thought you'd like it.' He stretched back and crossed his feet at the ankles. 'I'm glad you called. I was afraid you wouldn't bother.' He seemed to fit his chair exactly. He lounged in it with authority. I felt swallowed up by mine. 'You still go to mass, don't you? I see you there.'

I had been afraid this was the way the conversation would turn. It was this fear, if anything, that would have kept me away.

'Don't get me wrong,' he said. 'This is not an inquisition. It just intrigues me why you would bother.'

I had no way of answering this. I wished I hadn't come. He held his glass out by the light of the fire and looked at the wine through it. It glowed in a translucent way. A number of clocks chimed at once, on the quarter hour. Individually the sounds may have been pleasant, but together they were difficult to take. Grating on the ears. Father Jack didn't seem to notice.

'I don't mean to pry.' He waved his previous comments away with a flutter of his hand.

'It's okay,' I said. 'Habit, a lot of it, if I'm being honest.'

'For all of us, Jim. But habit is important.' He sucked at his lips through his teeth. 'Young people are very direct nowadays. I go around the schools sometimes, and they more or less tell me I am redundant. They have no time for religion. Too busy growing up.' He raised his eyebrows. 'I can see their point.'

I went to take a drink from my glass and realized it was all gone. I must have been drinking it unawares to myself. Nerves, perhaps. Father Jack leaned over and filled it up again. The heat from the fire was strong. My face felt very flushed. I was already beginning to feel drowsy.

'The truth is, Father, we'd be lost without you. Whatever way we look at it.'

'Kind of you to say so, Jim. My trust is that there is some element of truth there. Anyway. That's not what we're here to talk about. Tell me all about Alaska. Now that must have been something else.' The leather creaked as he sat back further in his chair.

'I'm not sorry I went,' I said, trying to stifle a yawn.

He made me begin from the moment I left Ireland. I had to tell him all about my jobs and what every place looked like. He asked me if I had any photographs. When I said I had he told me I should have brought them with me, that he'd have to see them sometime. Somewhere in the middle of it he got up and opened another bottle of wine. I didn't see where it came from but held out my glass nevertheless.

'You'll find this a little less mature, I think,' he said as he poured it. I didn't find it one way or another, I just kept swallowing it down. Although I was sleepy I was enjoying myself. Feeling good from the wine and the warmth of the fire. Happy looking on my journey from a distance, where the finer parts could be splendidly recalled and the harsh ones kept safely at one steps remove.

'I wish I had your courage,' he said when I finished. 'I've never been further than England myself.'

'It had little to do with courage if the truth be known,' I told him. 'More to do with fear.'

He didn't ask me what I meant by this, and I was grateful for him for not doing so.

'Speaking of fear,' he said. 'When you went alone on your trips into the wilderness, were you not constantly afraid?'

'I suppose so. It just wasn't the most important thing. If you prepare well, you can eliminate most of the dangers. Enough food. The right clothing. Maps. That sort of thing.'

'And what about bears?'

'Again, there are some basic precautions you take. They want to be left alone as much as you do.'

'Did you carry a gun?'

'No. I think I'd have been in more danger from my own handling of one of those than from all the bears in Alaska.'

Father Jack growled with laughter, the bear in him clearly apparent.

What I had found with my trips into the wilderness was that the further I went in the less fear I felt, the more conscious I became of my own position in the wilderness, and the less concerned I became for my own survival. I had always imagined that was how religion would be too. That Father Jack would travel so far into the landscape of his belief that all uncertainty would cease to exist. That the desire to re-emerge would disappear forever, survival no longer a consequence.

I remembered travelling by boat into a sea of icebergs, cutting the engine and allowing ourselves to drift amongst them. Feeling the chill off their icy mass on our exposed hands and faces. Their towering crisp, blue whiteness, as if the sky itself was frozen within their bulk, reflected through the sharpness of the still air. Gliding past great bobbing mountains of frozen time. And I remembered thinking how I had witnessed a little piece of eternity. A small fragment of my infinite future. If there was a God, he would surely come from the far north.

'Tell me, Jim, did you ever meet any priests out there?'

We were at the end of the second bottle. Father Jack looked as flushed as I felt.

'Not personally. I did hear of some from time to time, but I had no contact with them.'

There had been Catholic churches around me in many of the places I lived in, but I never went to mass there. I didn't feel the need to. It wasn't a part of that life of mine. The space it occupied back here was already filled by something else.

'And where would they be living?'

'Some in the towns and cities like Juneau or Anchorage, but I heard of others scattered throughout the interior and the less accessible coastlines of the Arctic Ocean or the Bering Sea.'

'How would they have got there?' He held his empty glass against his chin.

'I suppose they were flown in and dropped off.'

Father Jack looked impressed but disconsolate.

'We don't know the half of it.' He reached for the bottle and poured himself out the last few drops. 'You know, people often ask me how I cope with the remoteness up here. And it is true we are cut off on our peninsula, but it's nothing is it? It pales in comparison.' He held the empty bottle in his hand. He looked angry with it, with its lack of wine. Then he stabbed himself with his forefinger in the side of his head, his glass in hand. 'It's all up here anyway. This is where the real remoteness lies.'

I listened to the loud ticking of the clocks. I wanted to put my glass down on the floor, but I didn't feel like I could at this point in time. His humour had changed. It reminded me of how he was when Knucky and I met him down at the harbour when he came down to give the Eskimo his blessing.

'A man could get lost up here and never find his way out.' He continued tapping at his head. 'Did it never drive you demented?'

he snapped at me. 'Did you never feel as if you were going mad? When you were out there by yourself for days on end with nothing but the natural world for company?'

'Cabin fever. It was not unknown.'

'Cabin fever.' He considered the phrase. Seemed to like it. A smile came back over his darkened face. 'Forgive me,' he said.

He stood up and went over and put the bottle and glass down on the writing desk. He opened a drawer in it and searched around through loose sheets of paper.

'Is that where you write your sermons?' I asked. In ordinary circumstances I would never have dared ask a question of that nature. I would not have pried into the sanctity of his life. But these were no ordinary circumstances. It wasn't just the effects of the wine that made it so. It was as if we shared something. Some common understanding of the vagaries of human existence. The sheer vast emptiness of it all.

He slapped his palm down on the polished surface of the table. 'This is where it all comes to pass.' Then he pointed to an overflowing wastepaper basket by the side of the desk. 'The rejects. The ones that failed to express the message. The ones the devil had his hand in. Now, where is it?' He rooted through the papers again. The light from the flames flickered on the wall beside him, throwing his distorted shadow across it. I looked back down at the roaring fire. His own little piece of Hell. 'Aha!' He pulled a sheet of paper out and held it in front of him triumphantly. 'What do you make of this?' he came over, shaking the paper at me.

I reached out and took it. I began reading it but realized after a few lines that I had taken nothing of it in. It was hard to concentrate my mind. I started again but still couldn't grasp what I was reading. I squeezed my eyes together tightly and allowed them to refocus. I began reading once more.

The distance you have come is nothing. The journey is what counts. And though there is little we know of that journey we appreciate the size of the waves and the drag and pull of the undercurrents. That you made it here is what counts. That the tides have finally abated. The seas have rolled away from you revealing the spirit and not the flesh. The last great Ice Age awaits. A land you are familiar with and comfortable in.

The rest of the lines were scribbled over so that I couldn't make them out. I looked at him to see what he wanted me to make of this. It must have been an extract from a sermon or prayer. His expression gave nothing away. He stood there with his large bare arms folded. Holding his ground. He was waiting for a response.

I tried to remember what had led to this. Where it fitted in with our conversation. I was just about to ask him what he meant by it when suddenly it all seemed so obvious. This was clearly written for the Eskimo.

'Did you bury him?'

He nodded.

'Where? Can you tell?' There seemed no earthly reason why he shouldn't be able to. But everything else so far had been so secretive.

'I'm not sure if I should,' he said. He let his hands drop by his sides. He seemed to be thinking about the implications of telling.

I didn't feel in any position to encourage him to. Burial was his business. Between him and his God, and my God too if I had one. I had no right that I was aware of to interfere.

'You understand,' he said. 'It may not be good for people to know.'

I appreciated this. But I didn't see myself as just people. I was the one who found him. If I did seek out his place of burial, it would not be to gawp.

'So it's finished then.' The words were my own, but I barely recognized them. Nor was I convinced of their truth. I heard the rattle of paper. I saw the sheet he had given me shaking in my hand. I read the words again. 'It's very fine,' I told him and handed it back.

'It's inadequate,' he said. He moved back from my chair towards his own, but he didn't sit down. He stood next to it as if he had no recall of its function. 'It contains what I meant. But in the end I simply wished him Godspeed.' He screwed the paper up into a ball and threw it on the fire. We both watched the flames ignite at its edges and then erupt. A quick burst into a charred remains.

My relationship to all of this was faltering. It was no longer clear what Father Jack's role was. His emotions had come into play. And this was not something I was accustomed to. He looked sad. As though he had let himself down.

He walked behind his chair and leaned on the back of it. The black leather creaked again. The clocks chimed. It was eleven o'clock. He looked back over his shoulder to the one on the wall behind him.

'It's getting late.'

It felt as if it could end here. That I would have to agree and suggest that I would go. But I didn't want to go. Nothing was finished. Father Jack had more to tell. Had almost been about to do so. I sat upright in my chair. I rubbed my hands together beneath my chin. I looked at them, not him.

'Something feels wrong, Father.' I felt as if I were in confession. Hidden behind a screen in the dark about to disclose the blackest secrets of my soul. How he lived with those secrets was beyond me. There would hardly be a voice in this parish he would not have recognized. Not a wrongdoing he was not a party to. 'From the start, something has felt wrong here.'

I heard him push himself up off the back of the chair. 'There are wrongs all right. It's not always clear where they emanate from however. Whether they are wrongs of your own or those of other people.'

I picked at my nails. 'It's like I killed him. Sometimes it feels that bad.' I lifted my head up. Looked into his eyes.

'You most probably saved him,' he said.

I watched the bronze second hand of the clock behind him jig forward one step at a time before returning to where it had started from. He dug his hands into his pockets and walked back out across the rug into the centre of the room. The polished wood of the floor skirted its edges. He looked nervous. Another emotion to add to the growing list of those he had displayed before me tonight.

'What do you know of death, Jim?'

The immensity of the question made it impossible to answer. I struggled for any words.

'I don't know what I know. My parents. That's really all.'

He rubbed his index finger lengthways between his lips. 'I see it every day of the week. Any moment now that phone could ring, and I'll see it again.' He breathed in and out hard. 'I thrive on it.' His large chest rising and falling. 'But what I know of it…' He tugged at the belt of his trousers. 'You're right. There's something wrong.'

He stared sharply at me. He had told me what he had not wanted to tell. Then he sat back down as though he needed to. As though the weight of what he had just done necessitated it. A confidence, it seemed, had been broken. And a new one shared. But the former perhaps with a deity and the latter with a mere mortal.

'God help us all.' He poked at the fire stirring up the coals that had died down.

I waited for him to tell me more.

'He's at rest now. I feel happy about that.'

'What did you mean?' I had to ask. 'What's wrong?'

'Your guess is as good as mine.'

'No,' I said. 'No it's not. What is it?'

'A troubled soul. I buried a troubled soul. I could feel it.'

'Troubled by what?'

He clattered the poker down on the hearth. He was getting exasperated with me. I was pushing it too far. And yet I had to. What was the sense in his holding back now? Whatever trust he felt had been broken was just that, broken now. There was no going back on it.

'Jim, I'm a priest. Nothing more than that.'

He wanted me gone. Out of there. He wanted the solitude of his room back for himself . It was like somebody stumbling into your camp when trekking alone in the wilderness. I had become as intrusive as that.

I looked for a way out. A way to slip back in the wide open expanse unnoticed.

'I appreciate your candour, Father. I hope I haven't offended you.'

He smiled and stood up with me. 'I invited you. I've had a good evening.'

He walked me to the front door. We stood on the step outside and looked across at the full moon glowing above the lough. Its yellow reflection shimmered on the rippled surface as though the water was lit from underneath. The orange streetlights led out of town into the barely visible countryside.

'It must have been quite a country,' he said.

I couldn't tell if he was talking about Ireland in the past or my tales of Alaska. Or even death itself. He held out his hand, and I shook it.

'Safe home. Don't be a stranger.'

CHAPTER ELEVEN

There was still no sign of Knucky. He had been gone for almost two weeks now. I hoped his heart hadn't given up on him. Or he on it. This was the longest I had known him to be away, but Frances told me he had been out to sea for almost a month shortly after I had gone to Alaska.

'Doesn't it worry you?' I asked her. 'Aren't you afraid he might never come back?'

'That would be his decision,' she said. 'And who would we be to interfere in that?'

'His friends. We're everything he has.'

'Knucky has his hole. A vacuum inside of himself. We're not a part of it, and we should never try to take that away from him. That's where he is now. Exploring the boundaries of that hole. Sailing right up to its edges and peering over the sides. If you want to know the truth, I envy him.'

She meant it. What Frances wanted more than anything was a hole in her life. A hole that even drugs could not take her out of. 'It's there in all of us,' she said. 'We just don't know the way in.' She felt certain that Father Jack held the map to it. 'Call it organized religion, call it Zen enlightenment, call it what you like. It's all the same in one way or another. You have to recognize the structures and then see beyond them. You have to worm your way in deep. The sad thing is that I'm really too lazy for it all.' Her eyebrows shrugged upwards as though the recognition of her failings was the saddest part of all.

She was pleased when I told her that I had called in to see him.

'Did he tell you anything?' We were sitting at the harbour, outside The Porthole, our legs dangling over the sweep of the water. The day was overcast again. The sky an even spread of grey. The far coast looked dull and dismal. More like a secluded island than a stretch of coastline. A cold, unwelcoming refuge, as though it had grown out of the prison built upon it and not the other way around.

'Nothing I didn't already know.' I kicked my heels against the stubbled concrete. The dampness seeped into the seat of my pants. 'He confirmed my need for concern. That's all.'

'Maybe that's enough.' Frances' hair had come undone. Some was still tied back behind her head, but loose, bushy bunches straggled around the sides of her face. I couldn't remember ever seeing it fully tied back. It was like a lifelong struggle to maintain control of it. Every time she managed to capture some strands others seemed to break free. I remembered how she used to let it down when we were camping. When we skinny-dipped beneath the moonlight. Its red tint crackled as though charged with electricity.

'I have decided I have to get to the bottom of it. I won't be able to rest easy otherwise.'

'And perhaps not even then.'

'That's a chance I have to take.'

A car drove down behind us. The loose stones cracked beneath its wheels. On the water ahead of us the orange pilot boat swooped beside the long low coal ship making its way back up the lough. Empty.

'They're bringing the liners back, did you hear? Passenger ships.'

I hadn't. Although I often liked to imagine that's what those ships were that travelled up and down the lough, carrying not freight but people. I frequently had to fight the urge to wave.

'What will you do?' Frances asked.

'I'd like to see some of the reports. To see exactly what has been going on so far.'

'And you think they would tell you that?' Frances had little faith in the written word. With good reason.

'No. But they might give some indication.'

'Why don't you just ask Tom Harte straight out?'

It was the obvious solution. But although I'd had no reason in the past to doubt his word on anything I was no longer so sure of this. However open to misinterpretation the written word might be, I had more faith in it now than the spoken one. Neither Tom nor the sergeant seemed keen on giving straight answers to me. I was not official enough.

'He won't tell. This is the whole problem. A distortion of the truth is emerging. It can only get worse. I need to get at the facts.'

'But how?'

'Charlie Doherty might be able to help. I just don't know if he'll want to. Anyway, one way or another I'm determined to see those reports. Also there must be the results of a post-mortem somewhere. After that I want to visit his grave. Father Jack might lead me to that.'

Frances pulled her legs in beneath her and got up excitedly. 'Leave it with me,' she said. 'I bet I can find it for you. I bet I can pinpoint it exactly.'

Without so much as a goodbye she headed back across the road to The Porthole and went inside.

I knew what she was thinking. She was thinking about those energy lines she believed in. Lines that ran all over the Inishowen Peninsula, she said. Connecting ancient sites and relics. Frances believed that the lines predated the sites themselves; that they determined the sites and not the other way around. Nevertheless, these sites were like a source of energy, and that energy flowed between them. She had a whole range of Ordnance Survey maps marked with a purple felt-tipped pen indicating the ones she had discovered so far. Someone she met in The Porthole had told her all about them. He had been living in Cornwall with a band of New Age Travellers and understood that sort of thing. But he had come alone to Donegal to clear his head. To get his psyche back into order. But from the moment he arrived those energy lines shot through his body like bolts of lightening. He felt them beneath his feet wherever he walked. Inishowen was a charged place, he said. A high voltage self-generator.

Frances was overwhelmed by all he told her. She just had to feel that energy for herself. She begged him to take her with him and show her how this was possible. He reluctantly agreed. It was the drink that made him do it, he told her later. But he was never so grateful for anything else because what he discovered was that Frances herself was the greatest source of power for his own personal supply. She was like a megalithic tomb, a Stone Circle and a High Cross all wrapped up in one.

She moved in with him into a rundown cottage he claimed to be renting overlooking Kinnegoe Bay while all this power was surging. It was better than all the LSD in the world put together,

Frances said. Even when he disappeared as suddenly as he had appeared she didn't hold that against him. She was more than grateful for all that he had taught her.

She would go out with her maps seeking out old ruins and derelict ancient sites and wander around leaving her body completely open to the acceptance of whatever energy might be flowing in the area. Like a divining rod seeking water. And when she discovered it she would follow it as far as she was physically able to. Then later she would mark it on her map, picking out the other primitive sites in its path. And if there were none marked on her map, that only proved they had yet to be discovered or reclaimed. The Eskimo, I knew she would believe, would lie on one of the lines.

Despite my cynicism, I sometimes wanted to believe in them as much as Frances did. If nothing else this belief gave her some respite in what she termed her otherwise unsatisfactory life.

I thought about Therese. I recalled our morning and afternoon together and wished I hadn't met her. I didn't know what to make of my feelings towards her. I had felt like this before, but when I was much younger. In my teens and early twenties. And no matter how serious it had seemed at the time, I had learned that it was simply a transitory emotion. But I had assumed that with age, with maturity, any similar feelings would have greater import, would indicate something more permanent. And while I'd had many short relationships with women since then all of them had had a jaunty air of lightness about them. Nothing that needed to be taken too seriously. But Therese was different. Something dark was in play.

I didn't like being reminded of my childhood like this. I had to believe in the intervening years.

But what now? Therese made it clear I wasn't welcome around. I had caused a disturbance by my uninvited arrival. But I didn't know how. There may have been a man involved. Or I may have disturbed her state of mind. Or simply a set of basic plans. Perhaps I had woken her from her sleep. There were no reports to be had on this anywhere.

Fortunately Charlie was on the desk when I got to the station. He looked glad to see me. Since the discovery of the body we were being drawn in together. Our casual relationship was being redefined.

'I've got something for you.' A sly look slipped across his face. For a moment I thought he must have read my mind. Already had a copy of the report stashed away beneath the desk. But he didn't reach for anything. Whatever he had for me was contained in the spoken word. 'I tracked her down.' He grinned in a way that removed all authority from his uniform. 'I imagine we are related, in a distant sort of way.'

We were talking about Therese now. I was standing in a police station discussing a woman I had slept with once. A woman I did not know and who did not want to know me. It seemed to criminalize the act somehow. Make it sordid.

I didn't want to encourage him in this, but all the same I wanted to know what he had found out. He waited for me to ask him for more. I stood there like a dummy. More often these days I was becoming paralysed. Unable to make a move in any direction.

'Are you okay?' Charlie looked confused.

'I'm fine.' It was all I could manage to say. My body felt stiff. Unable to comply with the demands of my brain.

Charlie continued to look at me worriedly. 'You don't look well. Do you want to sit down.'

He was afraid something would happen to me in front of him. But I was feeling fine. Powerless, but fine.

'I'm okay.' I managed to move forward towards the counter. I placed my hands down on its edge and rested on my palms. 'You were saying?'

Charlie was not convinced. He looked about him as though he hoped to find someone else in the room who could tell him what to do. But he found no one there. And that was when my legs gave way. A light blinded me. And I felt the beginning of a long fall.

When I came around I was lying on a hard couch staring up at a brown, damp-stained ceiling. A blur of faces crowded in over me. For a while they zoomed in and out of focus but gradually they emerged with clarity. I made out the sergeant and Dr Brennan. And in the background Charlie, standing by the wall moving from foot to foot like a bird with a broken wing.

'Welcome back.' The doctor let go of my wrist. He looked as if he had just finished a major operation on me. He smiled. Happy with the results. The sergeant stared at me without making any form of real human contact. As if intent on committing each facial feature to memory to assist with a identikit picture later.

'I suppose I fainted.' I stated the obvious.

'That's about it,' the doctor said. 'You'll live.' He almost seemed to wish he hadn't said that, as though he had been saying it all his life and wished he could give it up. 'You're still living on your own?' While it sounded like a question it was stated with the assuredness that he knew the answer. There was no need to respond. I wondered what information had passed between them all, right there in my presence when I was unconscious, that I had not heard, what they had said about me that might have revealed to me something of worth.

I tried to sit up. A wave of dizziness washed over me, and I had to take my weight on my elbows to prevent myself from falling back down.

'Take it slowly.' Dr Brennan put his arm in under the crook of my elbow and helped me up. I sat on the edge of the couch holding on for dear life. 'You're not taking care of yourself, that's what it comes down to.' I squeezed my eyes shut and listened to these judgements on my life. 'You need to eat better, more regularly.'

He was right of course. I ate in a terrible way, cooking only when I thought of it. Living off sandwiches and cereals.

'Can someone take him home?'

He looked to the sergeant who looked to Charlie. Charlie nodded.

I got down off the couch slowly. Lowering myself onto my feet and testing their ability to support me before putting all my weight on them. Both the doctor and the sergeant stood there ready to catch me if I fell. I appreciated the security.

'You need rest, Jim. Take it easy.' The doctor closed up his bag. 'Drop in one of these days, why don't you?'

I told him I would. He seemed to know more than he was letting on. Someone else who was now involved. This situation was growing. At some point everyone would be touched by it if I couldn't get it under control.

I looked around at the room I had woken in. The walls were painted a miserable blue. Apart from the red leatherette couch, a table and two chairs, one each side of it, stood over by the far wall. There was nothing else in the room. I wondered about its use. If it was an interrogation room. I had never imagined that our police station would possess one; I had supposed that outside of the movies they did not exist at all. But it was now possible that they did. That this indeed was one. I looked at Charlie and the sergeant. Good cop, bad cop. One way or another I imagined some heads being cracked here. It was a violent moment in my thoughts.

Charlie had the door open. The doctor left. I followed him. I passed the sergeant on the way out.

'Sorry for the disturbance,' I said.

He cocked his head to one side. Either unconvinced that I was sorry or that a disturbance had been caused. I walked out into the reception area, behind the counter where Charlie had been standing.

'Jim.' The sergeant called after me in a quiet manner. He used my first name with apparent sincerity. I stopped and looked back. The doctor and Charlie carried on walking. 'It is finished. With the Eskimo. You heard.'

He must have known that Father Jack had spoken to me.

'Yes, I heard.'

'Good.' It now sounded as if he had been checking that I had been told. As if confirming that his instructions had been carried out. But I couldn't believe that Father Jack had been involved in this way.

His look seemed to suggest that everything had been taken care of. That there was nothing more anyone needed to know. That the burial had seen to that. Was a completion in itself.

'Aha,' I said. Without any understanding of what it was I meant.

'You're looking a bit better.' Charlie glanced across from the driver's seat. He had opened the door to let me into the back of the car, perhaps out of habit. I asked if I could sit up front. It would have made me feel even more criminal than I already did to sit behind.

'I don't know what happened.' I was feeling embarrassed about it now. Nothing like this had ever happened to me before.

'Like he says, you probably just need to rest up.'

I looked out along the lough, half hoping to catch sight of Knucky returning home. Apart from two people out on jet-skis it was completely empty. Not a ship or boat to be seen anywhere.

Charlie began to whistle. He looked young. Twenty-five or twenty-six. But even that could be considered old compared to some of the guards. It was a ridiculous age to have to bear that responsibility. He stopped whistling as abruptly as he had begun.

'Don't you want to know about her? Maybe you're not feeling up to it now.'

He was right. I wasn't feeling up to any thoughts of Therese. She had played her own role in my collapse. But I did want to know. I wanted to know everything.

'Go ahead,' I told him.

He was eager to oblige. As keen to tell it as I was to hear.

'Okay.' He coughed. Cleared his throat. 'She's the daughter of John and Elizabeth Doherty from Malin, an only child. They left in the early seventies. Sold up and moved to the States. The house belonged to her grandparents. They both died shortly after the family left. The house remained empty until early this year when renovation work began on it. An outside contractor. No one knew what was happening until about six weeks ago when Therese Doherty returned and began to live in it. I've heard she's an interior designer, but I can't be certain of that.'

Charlie spoke clearly, concisely. Reporting the facts as he knew them.

'And the man?'

Charlie looked over. 'What man?' He seemed genuinely surprised.

'The man she's with?'

Charlie shook his head. 'No man. No mention of any man.'

'There is a man.' I only had a vague memory of him from my drunken haze in The Grapevine. But his presence was all around.

'You're sure about that?' Charlie was disappointed. His sources had let him down. His investigative powers were in doubt.

I nodded.

'We'll have to see about that. Leave it with me.' He glanced in his rear-view mirror then back at me. 'So you've competition?' He didn't smile although he wanted to.

The insides of my head began to tighten. Shrink in on themselves. I could feel a monumental headache coming on. I stuck my first finger and thumb into the sockets of my eyes and rubbed hard. 'I'm not sure what he is. I don't know how they're connected.' I didn't know how we were connected either. What I was to her or she to me.

I felt guilty discussing this with Charlie. It was like having my own personal private investigator. It didn't seem right. She was entitled to live her life as she wanted without anyone snooping around. My head pounded. Pulsed like an endangered heartbeat. But all Charlie would have done was to talk to people around. This went on every day of everyone's life around here. We all lived in some surreal world of private investigation. A murky undertow of deciphered information. With no one to assess its correctness or incorrectness. Or its use at all.

What would I do with what I had found out? How would I best handle the details? My eyes ached, and my jaw hurt. This was only the beginning. I had yet to ask Charlie what he now knew about the Eskimo. And worse than that, for a sneak look at his sergeant's report. It wouldn't be appropriate for me to ask him this, and I doubted he would oblige. It was out of his jurisdiction. Although the Eskimo and now Therese were pulling us in the same direction there was no reason for Charlie to take the risks involved. He owed me nothing. If I did ask, he would have every right, and every obligation, to inform his sergeant of my request.

He pulled up outside my house.

'Will you be okay from here?'

I needed to ask him now. If I let it go, it might be impossible to come back to. He kept the engine ticking over. His left hand shaking the gear-stick over and back into neutral. I thought I should probably arrange to meet him when he was off duty. Out of uniform. Perhaps then my request would be less compromising. But again it seemed sneaky. Underhand. I was slipping deeper into a world of intrigue.

'Charlie, I need a favour.' I came right out with it.

Some inner working of my ear clicked repeatedly. I was getting used to it.

Charlie ran his right hand around the plastic coating of the steering wheel. 'I told you, I'll find out who he is.'

'No, not that. I need to know about the Eskimo.' I pulled at the lobes of my ears. They burned between my fingers and thumbs.

'You still worrying about that?' His face loosened, indicating I had no need for worry.

'I just want to know what happened. I would have thought I was due that.'

The skin above Charlie's nose pinched and wrinkled. 'Don't you know? I thought everybody knew. It's all anyone's been talking about.'

I didn't know. I didn't even know anyone was talking about it. It was all happening somewhere out of my reach. I was being left behind. That Eskimo had followed me all the way across continents and oceans, caught up with me, and finally passed me by.

'I don't know anything.'

Charlie raised his eyebrows in surprise. 'He's an unknown soldier. Nothing could be found out about him. He's been buried. Sent on his way.'

This was a deliberate skimping on the facts. This may have been what everyone knew, but I wanted to know more. I wanted to know what only the few were privy to. I wanted the hidden details. Those that were contained in the reports and those that didn't make it that far.

'There has to be more. I need you to tell me, Charlie.'

Charlie sat back. He didn't try to avoid me.

'There is no more. Well, there's where he is buried. Out of respect they've been trying to keep it quiet, but it's no great secret really. I suppose I could let you know if you promised to keep it to yourself.'

It wasn't the information that was easy to hand out that I wanted anymore. In the beginning this would have satisfied me. It would have been more than enough. But it hadn't been forthcoming then. This was part of what troubled me. If the simple facts could not even be divulged, it seemed to suggest they were part of a greater complexity. And that's what I needed to understand now.

But when Charlie said there was no more, I knew he believed it. He was being excluded also. To a different degree than I. A slightly lesser degree. There was a chain of command here. A conveyance of information. And Charlie was towards the end of this chain. I was hanging on beneath him. But it was by no means clear that the further up the chain you went the greater the degree of information or inclusion you received. There was a point somewhere that exclusion recommenced. So that those at the top were as badly off as those at the bottom. The middle ground was where the answers lay.

'I understand your concern. It was a terrible thing to happen.'

I recalled Charlie's vomiting. He was thinking about it also. His face reddened. 'It's awful that he couldn't be identified. There's no question of that. But everything possible was done. It was, Jim.'

He sought to reassure me. And perhaps himself too.

'I don't understand it, Charlie. He must have come off one of the Russian factory ships. Surely someone would have reported him missing or buried at sea. It can't be that difficult.'

'It's not that easy. Not all these ships keep as good records as they should. We're dealing with foreign countries here. Foreign methods. It doesn't always correlate. It's shoddy, but there you are.'

I couldn't accept it that easily. I wanted to make certain that the shoddiness didn't originate in the land he was dragged up on.

My head was splitting. I thought I might pass out again. I rubbed my forehead with the ball of my hand and lowered the window. The cold damp air blew through with a minor soothing effect.

'I'd love to see the reports.' I didn't look at Charlie at all. There was a long silence. 'I suppose it's out of the question?' The base of my hand rested on the bridge of my nose. I looked through my fingers at him. He was staring straight ahead, his tongue licking at his upper lip, both hands on the wheel. He looked as if he was still driving. In a resolute fashion. As though he wanted to get out of where he was as quickly and safely as possible.

'There's nothing different in them. Trust me, Jim.'

I did trust him. I just didn't trust his knowledge or the direction of his vision.

'You've seen them?'

'Of course.' He was upset that I doubted he would have. And then as though to reassure me further: 'I typed them up myself.' He put his hand on my shoulder. 'You're making too much of this. When you're feeling better it won't seem so bad.'

I looked down at his hand on my shoulder. I felt like I truly was being arrested. I opened the door and got out. There was no more to be said. Maybe I had been wrong about Charlie. Maybe he was less on the outskirts than I had previously imagined.

My legs felt shaky. I didn't trust my body. I leaned on the top of the car and pushed my head back inside.

'One more favour, Charlie. Will you drop by The Porthole. Tell Frances I'm not feeling so good.'

Charlie smiled. 'Sure. Anything. Do you want me to go in with you?'

'It's okay.' I pulled the top-half of my body back out of the car and steadied myself before letting go. My legs held. I closed the door behind me and waved back at Charlie over my shoulder without turning around. He waited until I had the door open and was gone inside before driving away.

I dropped down on the bed and fell back in a prone position. The room began to spin. Another bad bout of dreaming lay ahead.

I sat in the back of the church and watched the coffin float up the centre aisle to the altar. The church was crowded. It was filled with Eskimos, loggers I had drunk with, women from the fisheries I'd had drunken encounters with and long since forgotten. I made out Frances in the front seat between a long line of Eskimo men and women and children. And elsewhere, scattered around, Tom Harte, Charlie Doherty and the sergeant. Father Jack stood in his soutane with his arms outstretched. Drawing the coffin towards him. For a while it looked as if the coffin wouldn't stop but would hit up against him. I tried to shout a warning but nothing came out. Just at the last moment Father Jack lowered his hands and the coffin halted. My legs started to give way and I sank to my knees. When I looked again he was standing behind the altar with a chalice held aloft in one hand and a bottle of red wine in the other. He prayed in a language I couldn't comprehend and then raised the chalice to his lips and drank from it. Blood dripped from his open mouth onto the white cloth covering the altar. A green sludge began to seep from the lid of the coffin. Flowing over the side. A slimy seaweed mixture. Rising rapidly until the lid of the coffin fell away revealing Knucky inside with a large gaping hole in his chest effusing the putrid green slime.

I felt someone grasping my hand tightly.

'It's okay. It's okay, Jim.' A woman's voice kept repeating this over and over again. I tried to open my eyes, but they wouldn't budge.

'Frances, is that you?' But the words came out mumbled. The coffin floated somewhere unattainable above me.

'It's okay.'

But nothing was okay. I couldn't speak. I couldn't open my eyes. I couldn't wake up.

All I wanted was to open my eyes and see Frances there.

Comforting me. But the more I tried the harder it seemed to get. The base of the coffin hung over me like a door.

'Frances.' Her name formed in a crude manner. The flesh of her hand warmed through my whole body. My eyelids were finally prized apart. It wasn't Frances who sat on the bed next to me but Therese. Before she floated off into that unattainable space.

I opened my eyes but could see nothing at all. I thought it was happening again. That I was going to be confined to my dream world forever. But gradually my pupils adapted to the darkness, and my sight returned. The curtains were pulled apart slightly and the moonlight filtered through.

A woman stood next to the window with her back to me. I couldn't tell if it was Frances or Therese. In the near darkness they could have been one and the same. I didn't know whose name to call. I shifted in the bed, pulling the pillow up behind my head. The base of the bed creaked. And the woman turned around.

'You're awake,' she said.

And still I couldn't make out who it was. Then her face caught in the moonlight.

'Frances.'

'You had me worried.' She came over and stood looking down at me. She did look very worried. The skin around her mouth and eyes was taut and tense.

'I was just asleep.' My headache was almost gone. I pulled myself further up in the bed and put one hand behind my head. I saw my clothes folded neatly on the chair beside the bed. Frances must have undressed me and pulled the covers over me. She had left my boxer shorts and a T-shirt on me.

'You were in another world,' she said.

'Sit down.' I patted the bed beside me. I could hear the rain beat against the window like thousands of little feet running in all directions. The wind gusted in loud exhalations. Frances stayed standing.

'You two will be the death of me.' She pushed her hair out of her eyes and pulled at her upper arms as if she was cold. She walked back over to the window. Drifted back into that world of silhouettes. 'It's a bad night,' she said.

'These are bad days all round.' Something in our lives had taken a turn for the worse. It was hard to fathom. I felt like I was on the outskirts of something terrible. Something I was being pulled into head first. And when I got to the centre of it I had the awful suspicion that I would find myself already there. Waiting.

'What happened to you?' Frances was half-coated in the pale-grey moonlight. The pallor of death. It didn't suit her.

'I don't rightly know. Dr Brennan seems to think I'm a bit run down. Not taking care of myself enough.'

'He's right there.'

'Which one of us is?'

'You need to find yourself someone. You need to get out of this mess. What the hell did you come back for?' Frances was crying. Tears spilled down her cheeks. 'Damn you, Jim. You were the only one to get away.'

This side of Frances always shocked me. It was possible to believe that she was beyond tears. That like love she would not believe in them. And yet it was reassuring to see her this way. It made my own weaknesses bearable.

She leaned her forehead in against the glass, and placed her palms either side of her. Like she was pressed up against the transparent limits of her existence looking out on the unsavoury climate that lay beyond.

'Knucky's caught up in that. It'll be much worse before morning.'

That's what the winds amounted to. And the rains and the pull of the tides. And the lack of light. They all added up to a threat on Knucky's life. A threat on all of us.

I listened to what Frances had been listening to all evening. I felt the full force of it.

'Gale warnings. Force ten.' Frances pulled back from the window. She shivered.

'You're cold.' She was feeling the elements.

She hugged herself tightly. 'You have no idea.'

Then she kicked off her shoes. I watched as she pulled her jumper over her head and unzipped her jeans and took them off. She wore a white cotton T-shirt down to her hips. The tip of her white pants showed beneath its hem. 'Move over. ' She came across and got in next to me. The cold flesh of her thighs rubbed against mine as I pushed across. She snuggled in close. 'Hold me, Jim. Make me warm.'

I put my arm in under her neck and held her upper arm. She turned on her side and pulled in close. Her right arm drew over my chest. Her head rested beneath my shoulder. Her hair scratched lightly against the side of my face.

'There's no one else,' she whispered. 'There's the three of us, and then there's no one else.'

'Shh.' I stroked her head for comfort. Until we both dropped off to sleep.

When I awoke we were still in the same position. My arm felt numb from where she was lying on it, but I was afraid to move it in case I would waken her. She was like a little girl. Knucky would have known this. He would have awoken to it many times.

The wind howled lamentably outside, and I hoped to God he had taken shelter. The rain beat without mercy. Through the slight parting of the curtains small slivers of the moon were visible, shining through the black rain-sodden clouds. I tried to look at my watch without disturbing Frances. I twisted my body upwards and peered over her body at my wrist. The luminous dial slipped in and out of view. It was ten minutes past two. As far as I could remember, I hadn't dreamt at all this time. I was grateful for that. Small mercies.

Frances tossed in her sleep and groaned. She threw her right leg across my lower body. The side of her knee rested on my groin. A niggling doubt of wrongdoing persisted. Like siblings carelessly wrapped in intimacy. I knew Frances wouldn't feel this way. For her it would be the most natural thing in the world for friends to do.

The numbness in my arm developed into a cramp. I would have to move it. I eased it out from under her as gently as I could. Her head dropped lightly back against the pillow. Her eyes flickered open. She saw me and smiled.

'You're a trooper,' she muttered sleepily. Then she started and sat up abruptly in the bed. Remembering Knucky. 'What time is it?'

'Ten past two.' I bent my arm up and down renewing the circulation.

She pulled the sheets and blankets up around her. Her face was creased from lying on my chest. She listened to the storm outside. On cue a streak of lightening lit up the sky. 'Jesus! She joined her hands across her nose and mouth and jaw. The tips of her fingers dug into the corners of her eyes. I chanced putting my arm around her again. The muscles immediately seized. I tried to swallow the sound of my pain. It growled in my throat. I wrenched my arm back.

'What is it?'

'Cramp.' I bent it up and down again. Frances reached over and began to massage it.

'This should get the blood flowing.'

A bolt of thunder rocketed through the night. We both jumped.

'We're losing touch,' I said.

Frances' fingers dug deep into my arm. 'He'll make it through, won't he?'

I placed my hand on top of hers. Felt its movements beneath it. 'To one side or the other.' I could hear her breathing. And my own alongside. Her face looked up at me, our lips nearly touching, not by desire but by the sheer location of our bodies. We watched each other. The she pulled the blankets back off her and got out. She went over to the window where she had dropped her jeans, bent down, and reached into the pocket of them. I saw the taut curve of her spine through her stretched T-shirt like a bow poised. Her toes bent taking her weight, and the pale soles of her feet gleamed beneath her taut haunches. She pulled something out of her pocket and came back to bed. She was cold again and shivered more intently. She curled in against me.

'I have something here that might help us.' She smiled a resigned pitiful smile. She held out her hand, cupped and closed, as if she was about to make something appear or disappear. I knew what was in it but not what to do about it.

Frances had never offered to share her drugs with any of us before. But until it comes down to it who knows what any of us will really do? Who knows what we are capable of? It's the most frightening truth of all.

Frances unfolded her fingers. Two tabs of acid lay in her hand. I was reminded of those thin plastic fish you got in Christmas crackers that curled on your palms determining your future. Frances was offering me a part of herself. It was the most generous gift of all. I had no business refusing it.

I felt the need to swallow. My throat contracted.

'Go ahead,' Frances said.

Who knew what this might do to Knucky? And yet surely Frances had considered that. 'I've never done this before.'

Frances smiled broadly. 'Then you're in for a treat.' She rubbed my cheek lightly with her fingers. 'Trust me. We'll mind each other.' She stuck out her tongue, placed one tab on it like a communion host and drew it back into her mouth. She held the other out to me. I looked at Frances and saw her as I had never seen her before. She was radiant. A perfect act of God. I closed my eyes, extended my tongue outwards, and received her offering.

We lay in the darkness holding one another. I felt unafraid. Secure in the sanctuary of her body. For a moment almost glorious. And then the dark sky shattered and splintered in an explosion of unforetold light.

CHAPTER TWELVE

Knucky turned up safe and sound two days later. Frances was cleaning up the bar after the night before when she saw the blue and red sides of the *Lorna Doone* gliding past the window like a flag. He didn't contact either of us for a day after that. And we left him alone.

The storm had continued right throughout that night and most of the next day. Going off the boil around mid-afternoon, then simmering and dying away. Knucky didn't make radio contact with anyone. But Knucky never did when he went off by himself. We had hoped he would feel a responsibility to do so during the storm, but he had lived with storms all of his life and he didn't see them in the same way we did. He didn't recognize the same dangers.

In a similar situation some years before I had even called Tom Harte to see if there was anything that could be done. But Tom was reluctant.

'He can't have it both ways,' he said. 'Our resources are stretched as it is. Knucky can't just keep coming and going as he pleases.'

All the same he said if I was requesting assistance, he wouldn't be the one to refuse it. In the end we decided to ask the other boats to keep an eye out for him and take it from there. They agreed to assist. But then of his own volition, he sauntered home.

The three of us sat in Annie's at our usual table in the back. Knucky and I either side of Frances. Knucky didn't mention anything about his time away. I didn't like to ask, and I knew Frances never would. Our pints of Guinness were barely touched.

Knucky had called on me a few hours earlier. Casually dropped in as if he had never been away. He suggested meeting for drinks later. Said maybe I'd mention it to Frances. He was testing the water. I told him I would.

We needed to get the drinks in faster. The conversation was stilted. Knucky and Frances didn't know where they stood anymore. Their recent night together had thrown everything in the air. I supposed his journey was intended to provide some solutions to that, but if it had, it was not evident. I no longer knew where I stood either. I probably never had. What I wanted to do was go back to The Grapevine in the hope of seeing Therese again. But that was where this had all begun anew. I didn't dare suggest it.

For the want of something to say Frances began to fill Knucky in on what I had learned about the Eskimo. Although Knucky indicated all along that he couldn't care less about him other than as an inconvenience, Frances and I knew him better than that. He drank and listened without interrupting.

'Well he's off our hands. That's the main thing,' he said when Frances finished.

'In a manner of speaking.' I traced a figure eight in spilt beer on the Formica table top. The television sang in the background. Some political discussion. A panel of people arguing over taxation.

'I'm going to get to the bottom of this. It's my intention.'

'You're wasting your time,' Knucky said. 'There is no bottom to it. It goes on forever.'

There was truth in what Knucky said. I could go into this and never re-emerge.

'I just want to satisfy myself that everything was done that could be done. There's a body out there that I'm responsible for.'

'It's your call. But be warned.' Knucky crossed his legs and caught the bottom of the table. We all reached for our glasses to steady them. He apologized and looked out through the open doorway into the small bar. The usual people were lined up at the counter talking, with their eyes raised to the television. A few sat around the tables provided. Knucky held on to the leg he had just crossed with both hands.

'Isn't this pitiful?' He looked at a loss for more concrete words that could describe how he truly felt.

'We're not completely without hope.'

I could not see a way that any of us could function in this town if the three of us were not friends still. When Knucky and Frances began to go out together, I think we all knew the possible consequences.

But at the time, it seemed a risk worth taking. And for a while we all believed we had got away with it. Somehow we had found something new here, discovered a way to move forward. Even when they split up it seemed that, too, had possibilities. As if that was their uncertain trip to Alaska. A place to go to and come back from to help make sense of the here and now. Maybe this is what I meant by not being completely without hope, at least now, confused as we were, we had a measure to gauge our lives against. The fog would lift sooner or later. The clarity of light unique to this region would creep across the horizon. But we needed each other for that.

Knucky got up to go to the toilet. Frances stretched her legs beneath the table.

'You have to wonder,' she said. She stared ahead into the bar.

'Wonder what?' I asked.

'Oh, don't mind me,' she said.

She was obviously thinking about herself and Knucky. Seeking to calibrate that measure.

She looked at me hard. Puzzling something out for herself. 'Are you going to go back fishing with him?'

I drank from my Guinness. 'Should I?' I asked, wiping my mouth with my hand.

'Most definitely,' Frances answered.

'Despite what goes on between us on the boat?' I was thinking of her comments the other day on the beach.

'On account of that,' she said. 'That's the very reason you must go back.' She took a drink, placed her glass squarely in front of her. 'You should know by now not to pay much heed to half the things I say. I blame it on the moon myself.'

But the truth was I listened to everything Frances said. I always had done. She never failed to tell it as it really was.

Knucky came back. He stood for a moment at the side of the table looking down at Frances and me. He looked to be sizing us up. He nodded a confirmation of his assessment whatever that was. Then he sat down.

Frances looked uneasy. She looked down at the tiled floor. She was right. I needed to go back fishing. I needed something regular in my life other than alcohol. I didn't want to say anything about it to

Knucky now. I was afraid it would laden down the atmosphere even more. I'd just turn up at the harbour the next morning. Be waiting for him when he arrived.

We sat and drank in silence. The barman came in after a while to clear away any empty glasses. I ordered another round. After he left Knucky cleared his throat.

'So,' he said. He looked at Frances and me. 'Like old times.'

We laughed as best we could. Knucky sighed.

Frances tossed her hair back, looked from Knucky to me. 'We're not part of the fixtures yet,' she said.

'Too damn right!' I lifted my glass. 'Down the hatch.'

Knucky and Frances lifted theirs in turn.

'One, two, three.' And down they went as fast as we were able. Knucky finished first as ever, Frances second, and me last. Frances laughed loudly. Even Knucky seemed pleased. This was how it used to be.

'Okay,' Frances said wagging her finger. 'What's it to be?'

'What do you suppose?' I asked. 'Whiskey and Guinness chasers.'

Frances stood up between us. 'Excuse me, boys,' she said.

Knucky and I stood to let her out. She was posed with a dilemma. In the olden days it wouldn't have mattered. She shuffled past Knucky and went to the bar. It was a wise decision.

'The hell with it,' Knucky said.

'The hell with what, Knucky?'

'This,' he said. 'And everything else.'

'I don't understand.'

'Sure you do.' He inhaled deeply. 'There was a time after you left when I didn't know if I could face it here anymore. Face Frances. I had a strange notion, a ridiculously strange notion of sailing all the way up to Alaska. I really thought about it seriously. Got out the maps and charts, looked at what I'd have to undergo. The currents, the winds, the sea changes. And although I knew it couldn't be done, not in the *Lorna Doone*, I wondered if I should do it anyway. Go as far as it was possible. As far as I was allowed.'

I could see him out there. Alone on the seas with no intention of returning to shore. 'What stopped you?'

Knucky sneered. 'I told you, it was a ridiculous notion.'

Knucky hadn't said anything about Therese. I suspected he was afraid of where it might lead, what it might force him to disclose about himself and Frances.

Frances came back with the drinks. On the count of three again we knocked back the whiskeys. Then started in on the pints. The bulb above us flickered then dulled as though it was about to blow. Frances and I looked up at it swinging lightly from the nicotined ceiling. Knucky didn't seem to notice.

'Do you remember the first time we drank here?' Frances smiled to herself.

We couldn't have been more than fifteen or sixteen. We sat in more or less same spot as we were sitting now. I couldn't remember who bought the drinks, but I remembered how awful I thought it tasted.

Frances laughed. 'God, Jim, you were so drunk. We all were, I suppose.'

'We've come a long way, haven't we?' Knucky sounded grim.

It was then I told them what I had decided. I lowered my voice. 'I'm going into Tom Harte's office tonight. I'm going to take a look through his files.'

Frances and Knucky said nothing at first. Knucky pushed his chair back to uncross his leg. The chair scraped across the tiles. 'Don't be a fool,' he said. 'You don't need this.'

'I'd be happier if you came along.' I looked to him.

'Ah shit, Gallagher. Don't do this to me.' Knucky shook his head in despair.

It wasn't a refusal.

We had a few more drinks to steady our nerves. Frances suggested coming along to act as lookout. I hadn't wanted to involve her in this way, but her presence might be useful. The Harbour Master's office was perched at the corner of the entrance to the harbour across from the side door of The Porthole. Further along, at right angles to it, leading onto the pier stood the Co-op. Frances suggested leaving it to the early hours of the morning to avoid being seen by anyone. But I knew if I didn't do it now I never would. Breaking and entering did not come as second nature to me.

'You're asking for trouble,' she warned.

And maybe I was. Maybe that was exactly what I was looking for.

It was almost eleven. We had a half an hour until closing time. Then everyone would start to pile out onto the road. We needed to be out of there by then. We agreed that Knucky and Frances would sit on the wall by The Porthole where they could see all comings and goings. No one would pay the slightest bit of heed to them there. It was the most natural thing in the world. I was going to look for a way in. If anyone came in the meantime, Frances would simply cough loudly twice. The sound would carry easily on the night air. And if anyone came along when I was in there, she'd just walk on over as if taking a stroll to view the still waters of the harbour and knock on the window in passing.

It seemed too easy. Not underhand enough by half. Perhaps all illegal behaviour was like that once you were engaged in it. Perhaps it was the most natural thing in the world.

Frances' car was parked outside The Porthole. She kept a torch under the front seat for emergencies. We had one on our hands right now, I told her. She also gave me a screwdriver she kept in a tool kit in the boot.

I walked over to the edge of the harbour by the side of the office. Despite the beer my heart beat irregularly. I looked at the two small side windows on the way. They were both closed. I walked around the back. My best bet lay there where I couldn't be seen by anyone other than someone on the pier or in the boats. Muffled voices carried over from the Co-op. An engine whirred behind its closed doors. An almost full moon, its top edge closely shaved away, shone brightly down. Streaks of cloud splattered its gleaming surface. The boats rattled on the eddying water like dull cowbells. The three windows along the back wall looked shut also. I looked all around the pier and along the tied-up boats but couldn't see anyone. It was no guarantee that there was no one there. That someone wasn't hidden from view watching my every move. Recognizing my features.

I took a deep breath and stepped back to the wall. I looked once more but still couldn't see anyone. To hell with it, I thought and turned around and tried each of the windows in turn. Although none of them pulled open the middle one felt loose. I placed the torch on the ground beside me, took the screwdriver out of my back pocket, and pried it in at the side. I forced about a quarter of an inch gap. I looked through the pane at the catch. By moving the window in and out with the screwdriver I managed to move it slightly to the side. Despite the cool night air, my hands were sweating. It seemed that it might just work. A waft of fish odour caught on a sudden breeze and blew into my face bringing back memories of those early days of finding the Eskimo. I felt nauseous but continued to work at the window. The side catch suddenly freed and the window snapped outwards. It caught on the bottom catch and sprung back. The frame banged loudly rattling the glass. I heard Frances' double cough and froze. I could hear the footsteps now, rasping on the gravel. I had been so caught up in my actions that I had lost all outer auditory sense. All I had heard were the inner workings of my body. I quickly pushed the screwdriver back in my pocket and stood against the wall with my hand on the zip of my jeans as if I was relieving myself.

I listened to the footsteps approach until they were directly in line with my hearing. I placed one arm on the wall and rested up against it. I thought I might collapse if I didn't hold on to something. The footsteps moved on. Began to fade into the distance. I continued to listen. A burst of din escaped from the pub and then went quiet again. The water flapped against the harbour wall. I looked down and almost expected to see it rising around my feet.

I pulled at the window again. The catch had slipped back down when it slammed, although not fully this time. I took the screwdriver out and began again. I was ready for it this time when it freed and held it between my fingers to prevent it slamming shut. Then I pushed the screwdriver in through the gap at the bottom to release the bottom catch and opened the window. I took another look around. A yellow forklift lit up by its own light slapped its way through the thick rubber door of the Co-op. It turned in a complete circle as though unsure what to do next, then drove off towards the pier. I could just make out the dark hunched shape of the driver. He was looking away. I picked up the torch and placed it and the screwdriver on the sill inside the window. Then I pushed myself up with my arms, put my left knee in over the frame, and climbed through. Jumping as lightly as possible to the ground. I blew out sharply and pulled the window shut behind me. I was in.

I stood just inside the window and let my eyes adjust to the darkness.

Enough light slid through from the cloud-covered moon to allow me to move around at my ease without turning on the torch. My armpits were drenched in sweat. My hands shook. I was caught up in a situation nothing in my life had prepared me for. And, despite my apprehension, I was starting to enjoy it.

The room, although familiar to me in daylight hours, looked different now. Felt different. I walked around by its four walls, examining everything, to get my bearings. The same maps of the harbour and coastline hung on the wall. The same charts. But the land and seas they detailed seemed foreign. As though the maps and charts could not be depended on. Were rough early circumnavigable estimates of recently discovered portions of the world. The room itself resembled a tract of uncharted territory whose mysteries I had been sent to unfold.

A brass porthole from some ship of old had been built into the wall and antique flare guns hung above it as though all who entered there remained at sea. A lifebelt rested against a cardboard box. A Certificate of Fire Equipment Maintenance Record was framed next to a green beige covered board bearing an assortment of keys. Half empty shelves clung to the wall next to the filing cabinet. I leafed through a large dust covered book, *Manual of Navigation Volume 1*, and a *Report of Review Group on Air/Sea Rescue Service*.

I sat down at the desk. Grateful for the support of the chair. From where I was I could see Frances and Knucky sitting together. Knucky rested both hands over the edges of the wall and banged his heels against it rocking the top of his body over and back slowly. Frances sat cross-legged as though meditating, calling on some oriental deity to replenish our inner strength. I put my hands down on the desk in front of me. I looked at them. At the veins bulging through like tributaries. I was leaving fingerprints all over the place. Exhibiting complete disregard for the seriousness of my actions. My intention was simply to look. To remove nothing physical. To absorb and then to depart as though I had never been present. Even if Tom Harte sensed the intrusion, he would be unable to pinpoint it exactly.

I looked over everything on the desk. I used the torch to give better visibility, shielding it with one hand. There were a few marine magazines still in their cellophane wrappers. A copy of the

Marine Times. Some paperwork I could make head nor tail of. And a manual for a piece of sonar equipment. Other than that just some pencils and rubber bands and paperclips. I opened the drawers and looked through their contents. More folded up charts and lists of specifications for trawlers. A copy of the tides timetable. A small bottle of tablets for headaches. And a short piece of redundant electric cable. Nothing of interest. I closed them and looked to the grey filing cabinet in the corner. This was where I had been headed all along. Whatever I wanted would be in there somewhere. If I could only recognize it. If it existed at all.

The second drawer from the bottom was slightly open, so I started there. It was not the right approach. I knew that. I needed more order to my search. It was not enough to plunge, gropingly, into the unknown hoping to find something to grasp onto. I needed points of departure and arrival. Bench marks to read everything from. But for now this was as good as it got. I didn't know what I was doing, what order there was to follow. I would have to learn by experience. This was only the beginning of my search. The harbour master's office was a single location in an altogether larger landmass.

The files bulged with paper. Creased sheets stuck out at angles. I flicked quickly through them reading off their titles with the torch. *Fire Regulations*, *Income/Expenditure*, *Harbour Maintenance*. Nothing that seemed of any use to me. I closed the drawer over to exactly the point it had been open at and tried the top one next. The filing system was not clear. It looked as if it might have been in alphabetical order at some point in its existence, but now everything was all over the place. But perhaps there was a sense to it if I could only decipher it. Maybe then it would lead me directly to what I was seeking.

My fingers ground to a halt at a file called *Accidents and Deaths*. I hadn't noticed how my body had resumed normal circulation until I held the file in my hands and my pulse shot off on its own ragged rhythm once more. A rhythm that seemed to match the disarray of the files. It was too much to hope for that what I was looking for was here. Too simple. Too overt. Nothing about the Eskimo was this much in the open. Everything was shrouded in a secrecy of gestures and language. Where words had a diversionary tactic attached to their meaning. Where ambiguity thrived. *Accidents and Deaths* could only contain the information I was after if nothing was accidental and death was not absolute. I put the file aside of the desk and searched through the rest of the drawers. No longer trusting titles I scanned through some of the contents but could find nothing awry. It would take all night and maybe longer to look through every page of every single file. I stood back from the cabinet and looked down at the file on the desk. I looked out at Frances and Knucky. Knucky was now standing in front of her. He was holding her shoulders. I couldn't see her face to make out her expression. They could just as easily be arguing as touching tenderly. I hoped they were still watching out for me.

I sat back down behind the desk and flipped open the file. It was thick. Full of forms and reports going back to the seventies. I turned it over and started from the end. The *Lorna Doone* stared out at me. It was Tom Harte's report on the incident. I leafed back through the pages dealing with it.

Tom merely outlined the details of how Knucky and I had found the body and brought it back to shore. How he had contacted IMES and the guards, and how an investigation was currently underway to identify the deceased and the cause of death. IMES were contacting their relevant counterparts around the world to see if anyone was reported missing or had been buried at sea. He finished by stating his belief that most probably the Eskimo had fallen overboard from a Russian factory ship on its way back to the Baltics and that IMES were pursuing that as their first line of inquiry.

That was all. I don't know what I imagined I might find in his files; perhaps a result of sorts. An indication how the inquiry was going. But Tom didn't seem interested in results. No one did. They all seemed more interested in pursuing a direct sequence of events whether it lead to an outcome or not. I thought about looking through the rest of the file, at the other deaths that had occurred over the years, but I couldn't bring myself to do it. To desecrate their memory. I closed over the file and replaced it in the cabinet.

There was no way of telling if the information I had read and held was all Tom Harte's office had to disclose. I could be missing vital pieces. What I had seen might be nothing more than a distraction. But it was as much as I was capable of discovering for now. I didn't know how to proceed any further.

I looked around the office to make sure nothing looked out of place, turned off the torch, and retrieved the screwdriver. I opened the window slightly and listened at it but could hear no one. I pushed it open more and looked through, then climbed out. Landing softly on my feet. I managed to close the bottom catch and by jiggling the window caught the side one enough to hold it in place. I walked back out into the open. Into the combined light of the town streetlamps, the bar, the Co-op and the moon. Almost at once the door to The Porthole opened, and groups of people came out laughing and talking loudly. I looked to the wall. Frances and Knucky were gone.

CHAPTER THIRTEEN

The yellow glare of the mast light glowed beyond the harbour wall, moving out into the lough like a guiding star. Where, if you were to follow it, you would be led to the birth and death of everything. I watched it glide away. With Knucky and Frances in tow.

I felt like running down the pier to shout obscenities after them. They had endangered me. Left me without a lookout. Resumed something of their relationship.

Frances' car was open, so I put the torch and screwdriver under the front seat and strode up the hill. I thought about heading home but walked defiantly to The Grapevine. At the very least a few more drinks were necessary.

Louis Armstrong's 'St James' Infirmary' wailed through the open door as I entered. A foreign but familiar anguish. Cigarette smoke whirled maliciously in the air above the tables. I coughed. It would stick in my clothes for days afterwards, sickeningly. Most of the tables were full. Mainly after-pub customers looking for more alcohol. Food was wasted on the majority.

It neither surprised me nor was it wholly expected when I saw Therese at one of the far tables, half-turned away from me. Her profile was sharply defined and glorious. She spoke vibrantly across at the man opposite her, making grand gestures with her hands. Although my recollections of my last night here were vague at their best, I recognized him from before.

He wore a checked jacket and open-necked shirt. His style matched Therese's. It had to be said, they looked good together. They stood out in a place such as this. They always would. Would probably be grateful for that.

If I stood at the doorway long enough, they would notice me. Were bound to turn in my direction. I saw an empty table in the opposite corner and made for it. A waitress approached with a menu. She held it out to me. I waved indicating I'd pass on it and ordered a bottle of house white. She came back after a few minutes with a bottle and opened it before me. I wondered what Father Jack would make of it. It tasted sweet and cheap to me. A wine list was balanced between a salt and pepper set and an empty wine bottle which now acted as a candle holder. I looked it over. It had a selection of wines from France, Germany, Italy and the New World. Wherever that was. It sounded like a place I would like to start over in. Like a marketing ploy offering false hope from alcohol.

In a way the whole idea of a wine bar here in Inishowen was a similar ploy. An incongruous notion. As if a New World existed somewhere beneath its peaty surface. One you could drink yourself into. And many had tried.

A couple at the next table were getting over-amorous. Kissing passionately in full view of everyone. A bemusing and unsavoury spectacle. No one knew what to do about it. The manageress watched from behind the cash register as if taking notes while wondering how to put a stop to it. If it was within the realms of her power. If she had any rights over their sensual behaviour? She stood on the same choppy surface that I did with Frances and Knucky. I sympathized with her. From either side there were rights that needed to be upheld.

I drank down half of the glass and looked over at Therese again. She was engrossed in conversation. She held her cigarette aloft above her head like a small lighthouse. A warning beacon. The light that told you there was danger all around, but drew you to it all the same. A monument to safety in the middle of impending disaster. The sad reality of all safety equipment was that without the surrounding danger its existence would be unnecessary. She pulled from her cigarette and flicked her head back to expel the turbulent stream of smoke. Her black hair shook in waves. The wine tweaked at the backs of my eyes. Therese's face slid in and out of focus. I debated whether I should go over and say something or stay out of view. I couldn't trust what words might come out.

I felt an unreasonable fear of the man. Not a physical fear, but a fear over the security of his relationship to her. He was on home territory, whereas it was completely unpredictable how she would react to me. I filled my glass and held it before the flame of the candle. It shimmered. A pale yellow.

The woman at the table next to me ran her fingers in clawing circular motions through the man's hair. His hands were all over the back of her blouse. The manageress's shoulders twitched nervously. She pulled at her fingers. I almost leaned over to ask them to stop. For the manageress's sake. People were beginning to stare at them from every table. I saw the man opposite Therese say something, and she looked around. From where I was sitting, behind the couple, I was directly in her line of vision. She seemed to be staring straight at me. She may well have been. I raised my glass in greeting just in case. Therese raised her eyebrows and tilted her head towards the man, her lips edging towards a smile as if something was both sad and funny at once.

Satchmo sang 'Black and Blue'. The register bell rang, and a man settled his bill. The manageress seemed relieved to be able to look away. Frances and Knucky would be out on the open sea by now. Trying to resolve, in one fashion or another, the difficulties that had arisen between them. The no-mans land they were floundering in. Like all great explorers they had paid no heed to the boundaries that confined them. They stepped over them, but now found there was no way back. I didn't envy them their difficult and dangerous journey.

Frances told me once that it didn't matter that she was sleeping with Knucky. That it was a consequence, not a cause of anything. That it in itself was an end result, and nothing had changed because of it. She meant that as much about the three of us as about herself and Knucky. But if that was so, then we were all caught up in consequences and left with no room for choice. It was an achingly sad thought. 'We all have to live with it,' Frances said. 'We could start by learning from Knucky.' She beat her chest above her heart. She looked like someone seeking absolution.

'Jim.' Therese leaned one hand on the edge of my table and supported herself on it. She was bent towards me. Her cheekbones gleamed, catching the light as she smiled. It looked like I was on safe ground, but I still didn't know where.

'It's good to see you.'

'You too.' I held the stem of my glass far too tightly. I waited for it to snap but couldn't loosen my grip. I glanced inadvertently over her shoulder to her table. He sat back, gazing at the ceiling, sipping red wine with no apparent interest. She noticed this.

'Listen, I'm sorry about the other day. You just caught me at a bad time. I find unexpected visitors make me edgy. I don't know why. My problem.'

'It's okay.' It wasn't yet, but I was feeling better that she had apologized. Something approaching normality could now return.

'Look, why don't you join us?' She pointed with her eyes to her table. The couple beside us had disengaged and were sitting back drinking. They had the air of strangers about them. As if at any moment one or other of them might wonder aloud what they were doing there and get up and leave.

'I don't think so,' I said shaking my head.

'It's okay,' she said. 'He's just a friend.' She touched my hand momentarily. 'I'd like you to.'

I felt confused. I had drunk half a bottle of wine without noticing. Decisions were becoming more difficult than ever. I looked across again. I caught him looking at me. But neither of us acknowledged this.

'I'm not good with strangers,' I said.

'Don't give me that. Alaska was hardly a home from home.'

'It wasn't much else.'

She was still smiling. I looked to my instincts for guidance. But in her presence they had deserted me. She grabbed the neck of my wine bottle and swung it off the table.

'It's decided.' She started back with it.

Consequences. I had no other option.

I followed after her.

'Hal, I'd like you to meet Jim. Jim Gallagher.'

He reached out his hand to be shaken while I groped at the table behind me for the empty chair I had seen on the way over. I caught the back of the chair and shook his hand with my free one at the same time.

'Good to meet you, Jim.'

He had a strong American accent. I was glad of this. I had been fearful of hearing an Irish one. The space between us was easier to contemplate.

'Hal's visiting. Helping me get settled.' Therese fed me this information.

I was still holding onto his hand. I knew I should let it go. I tried to grin and released my grip. My palm was sweaty. I could feel my own dirt. I waited for him to wipe his palm on his trouser leg or somewhere on his chair, but he left it there resting in front of him on the table.

Therese's words finally sunk in. 'It's a long way to come,' I observed.

Hal blinked his eyes slowly brushing his generosity off.

'Any excuse for a vacation.' He smiled his practiced smile. But that didn't make him any the less likeable. And so far he was likeable.

'Are you two old friends?' he asked. 'Go way back to your childhood?'

I fought a smile. Therese loosed hers.

'We only met the last time you and I were here,' she told him. 'After you left.' Her tone held little back. Nothing evasive in it at all.

Hal laughed. 'Big world.'

'Did you bring your glass?' Therese held out my bottle.

I had forgotten to bring it. It was like another time altogether. A different night. Hal signalled the waitress and asked her to bring another over. I had to thank him.

'Jim's a fisherman,' Therese explained.

'Was,' I said.

'Was?'

'Was. I haven't been out since...' I almost said it. '... well, weeks ago.'

Therese understood. 'You're not going back?' She looked unhappy about this. Guilty almost.

I hadn't thought about it much in recent times even though Frances had told me that night in Annie's that I should go back. I couldn't when Knucky was away, and since he had returned he hadn't been out fishing himself. He hadn't suggested it, and we didn't talk about it. It was just the way it was. It all seemed perfectly natural.

'I don't know.' I twisted my glass around the table top. 'I think not.'

Therese seemed to be trying to digest this last piece of information. As if somehow it interrupted her plans. Plans that concerned her and me in some capacity.

'Is that wise?' she asked.

'You've got me on that one. I'm not sure I know what wise is.'

Hal spoke again. He seemed keen to reconcile whatever my words had broken down. 'Wise is living here.' He wagged his head in awe. 'This is one of the most beautiful places I have ever seen. We did just about the whole of that Inishowen 100 the other day, and I'll tell you what, it would do your heart good.'

The Inishowen 100 was a drive right around the peninsula of one hundred miles, even. As Knucky would say, the length of the peninsula's circumference was the only convenient thing about it.

'It is beautiful. You're right. Even when you have to live here.' I began to hum along to 'Stardust' aloud. I heard myself humming and stopped myself. I must have been getting very drunk indeed. I wished I could be more sober for Therese's sake. I wanted to remember everything about this meeting. Particularly the outcome. I breathed in and held it, tried to get my mind back in order. To put some logic on my tongue.

'So what do you do?' I hoped my question hadn't come out offensively.

Hal gave no indication if it had. 'Real estate.'

I nodded as though I understood everything clearly now.

'He deals in islands.' Therese bit at the edge of her glass. Held it between her white teeth.

'Islands?' I wasn't sure if I had heard her properly.

'Yes.' She released the glass from her bite. She looked pleased with herself. 'Hal buys and sells islands.'

'Somebody has to.' Hal appeared to shrug it off, but it was obvious he was proud of what he did.

'What sort of islands? I mean how big?'

'I'm not fussy. I'd buy Ireland if it was up for grabs.' He grinned out of his drink.

'I'm not so sure you'd be able to sell it again.' I tried to warn him off it.

'Never failed to make a sale yet. I guarantee there's a world of people who'd be willing.' He was very serious.

'It's not a world I'm familiar with.' My bottle was empty. I thought about ordering another, the pros and cons of that particular piece of commerce.

'We all live in different worlds,' Therese said. 'That's what's so nice about us.'

'A collision of continents.' I put one hand up to call the waitress and immediately sought to retract it. But she had already seen me.

'Actually I deal mainly in remote islands. Private ones.' Hal nodded along to his explanation.

I tried to get a grasp on what he was talking about. How islands were held in ownership.

'Where are these islands?'

'All over the world. In the middle of the great oceans.'

The waitress came over and stood by the table. I intended to tell her that I had called her by mistake, that it was okay, that I had everything I needed. Instead I ordered another bottle of house wine.

'Are there many? I mean how many of these islands can there be?' I asked turning back to Therese and Hal.

'Hundreds of thousands actually.'

My head could not consider these figures. This treatment of the world's surface.

'Of course very many of them are not for sale. Yet. It's my job to alter that situation.'

'But don't they belong to governments? Isn't that how it works?'

'Some do. Many are held in private ownership. But even governments can be persuaded to sell. If the price is right.'

This was moving into a realm far out of my reach.

'But who would buy them?'

'People like me.' Therese tapped a cigarette off the table and lit it up.

'You mean you bought one. You bought an island?'

'I most certainly did.' She flicked her match into the ashtray.

I sought to understand the implications of this. The waitress put the opened bottle down in front of me. I filled my glass by reflex.

'Where?'

Therese inhaled and blew smoke through her nostrils. 'In the Pacific. I've forgotten the coordinates. Oh it's only a little one. A few square miles.'

'But it's an island. Your own island.'

'Isn't that something?'

A part of me agreed with her, but a larger part held deep reservations. 'What's it like?' I pictured a tropical paradise.

'Well I've only ever seen pictures, but it seems very beautiful.'

It was all clearly above my head now. 'What do you mean only pictures? You've never been there?'

She shook her very pretty head. 'This is the island that just about defines remote. It's quite inaccessible. It would take a lot of effort, money and time to get there. But one day...'

She seemed happy about this. As if she really didn't mind if she ever got there or not. As if the possession of it was enough. It was like signing up to one of those schemes to buy your own star.

'Do you want one?' Hal looked serious again. Making a pitch.

'I don't think so,' I said. 'I wouldn't have the money.'

'That's where you're wrong,' He shook his finger at me like I was being naughty. 'I've got islands to suit every bank account. Name your price.'

I was downing the wine at an enormous rate now. I needed it to hold on to for stability. I could barely hear the music. A grating howl. Hal and Therese began to merge.

'Are you all right?'

One of them asked me this. I couldn't tell who replied.

The manageress shook me awake.

'Your taxi's here.'

I struggled to put her in perspective. 'What taxi?'

'Your friends ordered you one before they left. Now go home. We're closed.'

Therese and Hal were gone. I was deserted again. Completely alone.

CHAPTER FOURTEEN

A sharp deep pain split through the crown of my head. My mouth and saliva tasted sickly sweet. The chorus of 'Black and Blue' spun behind my forehead. Endlessly. I needed to open a window.

I had blown it big time. Passed out in front of her. She was unlikely to be impressed. I remembered her island. I felt sick. I pulled the covers off me and got out of bed. I held onto it for support then stood up. When I felt steady enough I went out to the bathroom. I gripped the sink, closed my eyes, and let everything rush by. Slip past. I opened them again and brushed my teeth trying not to look at myself in the mirror. I was shaky and weak. Close to tears.

Something from the past welled up inside of me. Like a child missing his parents. I didn't want to think about them. Not now. I showered and got dressed.

I went for a walk to clear my head. Away from town. Out towards the bay. The wind blew in off the lough and across the fields to the road. Although cloudy it was another bright morning. The road wound ahead between the hedges towards the sea. The top of the lighthouse was visible in the distance. I felt a little better out in the open. I tried hard not to think of the night before.

I was nearing the golf club when Charlie Doherty pulled in beside me. He lowered the window. 'Can I give you a lift somewhere?'

I needed to walk more, but I didn't want to pass up the opportunity to talk to him.

'I'd be grateful,' I said and got in.

'Where to?'

I shrugged. 'The beach, White Strand. Wherever.'

He indicated and pulled back out onto the road.

'You play, don't you?' I nodded in the direction of the golf club.

A man and woman walked up the fairway together pulling their caddy cars behind them.

'As much as I can. You've never bothered?'

'A couple of times when I was younger. Could never get the hang of it.'

'That doesn't stop most,' Charlie said.

'What about Father Jack, is he handy?' It seemed like a way in to the conversation I desired.

'He never plays here. He plays all the time over at Ballyliffin. A much better course. I hear he's okay. Blesses his putter approaching the green. It's a bit of an unfair advantage really.'

I looked out ahead at the lighthouse. I thought of Therese holding her cigarette.

'Is she really related to you?' The question came out of the blue, but Charlie seemed to understand it perfectly.

He allowed himself to smile. 'Not that you're interested, right?'

'Not that I am.'

'It's far out,' Charlie said. 'Cousins of a cousin of a cousin. That type of thing.' He looked over to watch someone hitting off the tee. 'Terrible swing. I don't know where that's gone, but it can't be where he wants it.'

It looked fine to me. There was obviously so much I didn't understand. I told him about Hal.

'You want me to check him out? I've been meaning to.'

'No, no. I was just filling you in, that's all.'

But that wasn't all. By mentioning him I was opening up that possibility. Charlie took a sudden right turn and drove in off the road past the golf club down to a short tract of beach and dunes. I said nothing. He stopped the car on the sand. Held the wheel a moment longer then swung open the door and got out. He leaned on the open door looking out across the water at the long sweep of hill outlining the horizon on the other side. The guns boomed across the water. A jet-ski roared past.

'I don't know which is worse.' I closed the door and rested my back against it, listening to the receding noise.

Charlie looked at me as if he didn't know what I was talking about.

'What is it you really want to know?' He began to walk down the beach. He knew where we were headed. I followed after him a pace or two behind. He went up onto the dunes. I climbed up through the sand and the long brown prickly grass.

'The truth. That's all I'm after.'

'There have been no lies.'

He looked down our length of coast now. Past the caravan park to the mouth of the lough. A coal ship came into view. The jet-ski turned and headed back up towards the harbour.

'What happened after the boat was taken off our hands, when you were put on guard?'

'The coroner was called. He gave a quick inspection of the body and requested the pathologist to carry out a post-mortem at the hospital.' Charlie pulled at the bridge of his nose. Cocked his head towards me. 'Didn't you know that?'

'I guessed as much. But no, I didn't know. No one told me. This is what I am talking about. Even the most ordinary pieces of information are not being offered.'

Charlie looked perplexed. 'Everybody is aware of it.'

'I'm not. Somehow I am missing out on all of this. Somehow these details are evading me.'

Charlie shuffled his foot in the dry strands of grass. I knew he was thinking that the fault was mine. That if I simply opened my eyes and ears, I'd know as much as anyone. And maybe he was right. Maybe I was looking in all the wrong places. Or maybe I was no longer a part of the circulation of common knowledge.

'Standard procedures.' He shrugged.

But Charlie knew the standard procedures, I did not. These procedures were not a part of my world. Were not standardized for me in any way.

'I'd like to know the results of the post-mortem.' I was upfront with him. There was no other way to handle it.

He opened his tunic and put his hands in his trouser pockets.

'Can you tell me?'

Something clumped down in the grass behind us. I jumped involuntarily.

'Stray ball,' Charlie said turning around to look for it. 'Out of bounds.'

'The ball or the results?'

Charlie gave up as soon as he began. 'It's a lost cause.' He crouched down on his hunkers as though hiding from sight. As if someone might come to look for the ball and catch him there in some sort of compromising situation. 'There's nothing to tell.'

But this was clearly not true. Carelessly or otherwise people were manipulating the facts. And the facts were that the post-mortem had much to tell.

'How did he die?'

'Naturally.' He looked directly at me to reassure me on this point.

'So he didn't drown?'

'Look, Jim, I'm going to be straight with you. I don't know the details. I didn't see the pathologist's report. He spoke with the coroner, and in passing he relayed the gist of it to me.'

'What did he say?'

'He simply said that his death was of natural causes, one less area we had to concern ourselves with.'

'And that was it?'

'That was it, Jim.'

'You didn't ask anything more?'

Charlie sighed. 'No, I didn't. If there was more to be told, he would have told me.'

'Is that how it works?' I couldn't believe that Charlie would not want to know everything, would be content to let it lie there.

'That's how it is.' He pulled a tall piece of grass from the dune and chewed on it.

'So you don't know how he died?'

'I told you, natural causes.' He sounded angry.

I was irritated. 'What does that mean? What does natural causes mean? That could be anything.'

'It means that there is no need to go making more of this than should be made of it.'

'Did he fall overboard? Could that be considered natural causes? Did he have a heart attack? Did his liver fail? How did he end up in the sea? Come on, Charlie, where does this leave us?'

'It leaves me exactly where I ought to be. Getting on with a hundred other things just as pressing. There's no point running around in circles, Jim. The report doesn't alter the enquiry in any way. It's all steam ahead. It has been. It still is.'

'So you don't care about the specific details?'

'That's between the pathologist, the coroner and the sergeant. That's why they are in the positions they are in. We all can't be involved in every single aspect. Otherwise nothing would get done.'

'On a personal level, don't you care?'

'On a personal level, that's my business.' Charlie spat a chewed up glob of grass onto the sand. I had pushed him too far. 'Jim, back off a bit. That's all I'm saying. Maybe you are getting too personally involved.' He folded his uniformed arms in front of him. 'Look, the details of the report, I'll learn more about them in time. It was a passing comment from the sergeant. More will emerge, not that it makes any difference.'

I asked him the same question Knucky had asked of me. 'If it was a sea burial, Charlie, how come his body came free?'

Charlie grimaced and shook his head. 'Who knows, Jim? Sea burials are often crude. It's being looked into. Everything in its own time.' He rubbed his finger along the bridge of his nose and smiled. 'I heard a story one time about a woman over on the east coast who instructed in her will that she be buried at sea. So her relatives dressed her in a white gown, put her in the coffin, loaded it up with stones, and hired a boat to bring them out to sea. They said a few prayers and heaved the coffin over. Then solemnly watched it sink to the bottom of the ocean. The ripples settling on the surface. They had just turned around to go back when they heard this almighty splash and looking around they saw the woman come flying out of the water high up into the air, her white gown billowing around her. Like a manic angel headed for heaven.' Charlie laughed loudly. 'The sea pressure was too great, propelled her back into this world.' He laughed again but more quietly. 'Jim, you ought to know, it's a question of international waters too. Here we're on solid ground but out there it's very often a no-man's land.' He nodded out towards the ocean. 'There are limits to our control.' He shrugged and said he'd have to be getting back. 'I'm glad I caught up with you though. I feel better now.'

'You were looking for me?'

'Yes, I'd been to your house.'

'How did you find me?'

He tapped the side of his nose. 'Good detective work.' The artillery boomed out again. Charlie re-buttoned his tunic, looked directly at me. 'You should know by now that there's nothing you can do around here without someone knowing.'

It sounded like a warning.

I stayed on the beach after Charlie left. Letting the details sift and merge. My head was still clogged with the alcohol from the night before. My whole system in fact. But I felt better able to cope with it. The banging continued from across the water. I wondered how the people over there lived with it. It must have been substantially worse for them. And the prisoners? It must have served as a constant reminder of their ultimate doom, the limitations of their own control.

A helicopter took off from the base like the giant insect it was designed to resemble and hovered tantilizingly in the air. Then it turned through one hundred and eighty degrees and disappeared up the coast. Sticking to its side of the line.

When I got back home Therese's car was parked outside the house. I saw it from a distance and felt my legs stiffen. I walked slowly towards it trying to see if anyone was inside. I was afraid that Hal would be sitting in it with her, but as I got nearer I saw she was on her own.

She saw me coming but didn't react in any way. I walked over and knocked on the window. She pressed a button next to the gear stick, and the window rolled down.

'Hi.' I made an effort to smile.

Therese rubbed her thumbs on the steering wheel. 'Can we just drive?'

It was my day for getting lifts it seemed. My day for being sought after. I went around to the passenger door, heard the lock pop open, and climbed in. She started up the engine, revved it far too hard, and sped quickly out onto the road. She headed back out the way I had just come from. She didn't say anything, and I took my guidance from her. We passed the golf course at over fifty miles an hour, which was far too fast for these roads. Therese maintained that speed until we got to the lighthouse where the road turned sharply to the left at White Strand. A few cars were parked at the beach. Therese slowed to turn then picked up speed again. At the top of the incline she veered off to the right up a badly surfaced back road to the top of the headland. We had to drive through someone's farmyard to get there. Although we had a right of way it felt wrong. As if were intruding on someone else's property and life.

Therese slowed to a more suitable pace. We bumped over the rugged road avoiding potholes.

'Why do you drink so much?' She looked out at the ocean as if it had some bearing on her question.

'I don't really,' I said. 'You just caught me on my bad nights. That's not usual.'

'It looked usual. You looked like you were doing something you had done many times before.'

I wished she'd look back at the road. It was a steep drop from there to the rocks below. But she was on auto-pilot now.

'You can't expect me to endure it.'

The sun slipped free of cloud cover and sparkled brightly over the choppy surface. Like molten gold.

'I don't know what to expect from you,' I said shielding my eyes from the glare

Therese swung around. 'Well, what do you expect *of* me?'

'I have no expectations. I thought we got along. I hoped it could continue.' Her bare legs curved gracefully from beneath her print skirt. It was the most inappropriate time to notice them. I averted my eyes.

'You passed out. Right on the table in front of us. What is that?'

'I don't know. I really don't.' The sheer cliffs hung to the right of us while on the left the russet grasses of the bog land stretched like the sun-invested sea to the horizon. A multi-coloured layer of browns, tans, yellows and sudden deep maroons blending naturally to perfection. I felt tearful again. Just as I had that morning. Saddened by my own frailty.

'I don't know what to make of you.'

'It's a common complaint.' I looked to my right, out at the red buoys dotting the sea in patches. Like groups of remote islands. The dust off the road blew up past the side windows.

'Where to from here?' I asked.

'There's no map. Nothing to point us in the right direction. All we

137

can do is keep moving forwards.'

'We could end up anywhere.'

'We could drive right off the cliffs.'

It was not a reassuring thought.

At the top of the headland Therese pulled in off the road and parked the car. We both got out and instinctively walked over the tough grasses to the edge of the cliff. I looked between my feet at the brown crumbling peat that showed through. Centuries of death and decay. Therese pulled her light grey cardigan in around her and wrapped her arms over it. Hugging herself. Her cotton skirt flapped in the breeze. Her long dark curly hair blew back off her face and trailed behind her. The climate suited her well.

'Do you ever think about jumping?' She stepped right up to the very edge. Completely fearless. It was a foolish act. A gust of wind could easily blow her over, the edge could easily give way, any slight loss of balance at all. I wanted to pull her back, but the sudden movement could send her on her way.

'That's dangerous, Therese.' I spoke softly. Fearful that a raised voice could do untold damage.

'I suppose it is.' An arctic tern swooped low in front of her. A pure white splinter of ice. 'Thinking is always dangerous.' She twisted her head over her shoulder and looked at me accusingly. She looked down then stepped back to safety.

The rush of the sea and the smack of its waves filled the air again. I tasted the salt on my tongue. My own salt.

'I've only recently realized what I've been missing all these years.' She stood with her back to the sea. Arranged it about her as backdrop. I wondered if I was included in her realization or not. Most probably I wasn't. 'Come stand with me.'

I went over and stood shoulder to shoulder. I longed to take her hand in mine.

'What do you see?' she asked.

I looked out at the unending expanse of grass-tufted bog stretching in front of us. Its eternal autumnal melancholy. Like nicotine-stained fingers.

'I see the tundra. A familiar sub-arctic landscape. We could be someplace else in the world. If we didn't know better.'

'Do you wish you were?'

I was close enough to feel the warmth off her body. 'No.' Not at that moment in time.

'Well then, you have it made.' She put her arm through mine and pulled me around to the sea. 'One last look.'

We bent our heads over and watched the surf being torn apart on the rocks at the base of the cliffs, and the rocks being torn apart in turn. Vast grasping hands of spray reached vainly towards us. To the side I noticed the sheer winding path Father Jack led a local prayer group down as pilgrimage once a year to the sheltered inlet below. Putting their trust completely in the hands of their God.

'I think about being elsewhere all the time.' Therese clung tightly to my arm. It made it all worthwhile.

Therese lay across my chest. Her chin resting on her arms. I stroked her hair and stared up at her ceiling. I wondered about Hal. Where he was. But I didn't want to interrupt the communion between us.

'Has your Eskimo re-submerged then?' Her breath trickled across the underside of my chin.

'Have you heard something?'

'I've heard nothing, that's why I've asked.'

'He's been buried. On land. So that he can't get away again.'

'Does that make it better?'

'In some ways it makes it worse.'

'I'm sorry.' She kissed the depression above my sternum. 'Did you say you lived among Eskimo people?'

My fingers caught in her hair, and I prized them free gently. 'No. I worked with them a while. And I visited some of their villages.'

'What were they like? Or are we all the same?'

'More or less,' I said. 'There's an Eskimo at the heart of us all. But we've walked them into a blizzard, and now we can't find our way back to them.' I cupped the back of her neck. Felt her bones beneath my fingers. I wondered about their uses when her life had passed out of her.

Therese was right, we were all the same, each as remote from the other, as exotic in our own ordinary way.

I remembered a marine scientist I had met in Point Barrow who spoke of his life being spent slowly moving through ice floes at the southern edge of the polar pack in the Chukchi Sea. How he often felt that those large chunks of drifting ice were the segments of his life floating inextricably about him. Too dangerous to get too close to. And too vast to grasp. While the ink black water churned perilously beneath him pushing him in unknown directions.

'We've got to learn to live with the ice-field surrounding us. Not to try to change it for our needs.'

'You're changing me,' Therese said. 'Whose needs are being satisfied by that?' She freed her arms from beneath her and held my face with her hands. 'Explore me. Tell me everything you find. Map out my life in its most primaeval state.' She turned over and pulled me down on top of her.

Therese lit two kerosene lamps, and we sat out in the conservatory and watched the falling night descending on the sea. I lounged back in the large cushioned wicker chair. She filled two gin and tonics in the kitchen and brought them in.

'What was the cottage like before?' I asked.

'From the outside the same, but inside nothing you would recognize. It's a luxury now. Not a shelter.' She sucked on a slice of lemon. 'To be honest I don't remember much about it. Vague recollections of something cold and dismal. I sent on the plans from New York. Most of the work was done by the time I got here.'

'What about Hal? Does he stay here too?' My curiosity got the better of me. I felt reassured by our day together. I could manage his company now in conversation.

'Are you asking if I sleep with him too?'

I drank my gin down too fast and it caught in my throat. I coughed and beat at my chest. Therese stared at me like she had spotted a weakness in my character. My resolve fractured.

'No. Not at all. I simply wondered where he lived while he was here?'

'Don't you think you have the right to know if I am sleeping with him?'

She kept staring at me, trying to force me to move in a

wayward direction. She pulled the lemon through her teeth by its rind. 'Well, don't you?'

I knew that if I said I did, that she would say I didn't. That I had no rights over her whatsoever.

'Are you sleeping with Frances?' She stood up before I could answer. 'I don't want to know.'

She walked over to the far corner. The sky and sea were barely distinguishable. 'Hal stays here sometimes.' She left it at that. I didn't ask anymore. She put her hands behind her and leaned up against the glass. 'If you're wondering where he is now, he's somewhere on the periphery of this country looking for islands to buy.'

I resented this. Resented his purchasing power. And his gall. But there was no buying without selling involved. He couldn't bear all the responsibility.

'He's been a great help. I couldn't have done this without him.'

Whatever that was.

She turned up the wick on both of the lamps. 'Do you want to stay the night?'

It was a kind offer, and I took her up on it.

CHAPTER FIFTEEN

Therese dropped me home early the following morning. She said she had to meet someone in Buncrana for something to do with business. She was trying to set herself up in Interior Design. I told her I wasn't sure there'd be many opportunities for that around here. But she said I'd be surprised. That opportunities existed everywhere. It was just a matter of digging them out. Hal was helping her with that.

'Here, ring me.' She gave me her business card.

'Well, you're on the ball,' I said.

'You have to start somewhere.'

'Be careful,' she said as she let me out.

'Depend on it,' I told her.

During the early hours of the morning I had told her about breaking in to the Harbour Master's office. I wanted her to know this about me. I wanted her to know that I was capable of such a thing. It was a new revelation to me. And in return I wanted to hear something from her. For some sort of trade to occur between us. She told me nothing directly. She just said that she worried about my activities. For the moment that was enough.

After she left I walked back into town. I could have got her to let me out there, but for some reason I didn't. As if I didn't want her to know what I was doing. I didn't know myself.

A quick glance at the harbour told me the *Lorna Doone* was still out. Knucky and Frances had been set adrift again.

I thought back on what Charlie had told me and what I had read in Tom Harte's files. I needed more information than this. There were ways of obtaining it other than going through official channels.

Other equally or more trustworthy ways. There was a shared knowledge of events on the sea circulating about us. Drifting in on the tides. Waiting to be beach-combed.

I walked down the hill past The Porthole following my steps from the other night around the back of Tom Harte's office. I saw him moving about inside. I looked over the edge of the harbour into the still water. I could see right to the bottom. The pink-tinged edges of a jelly fish quivered upwards like the rim of a rare tropical flower opening to the sun. A couple of row boats were tied at the side, sliding easily over the slurping water slapping up against the harbour walls. I followed the white splatter of gull droppings along the wall like a trail to an ultimate secret destination.

I stopped across from the Co-op. I tried to put the location, the ongoing series of events and my position within it all together. To seek out a logic that would determine my next move. However I arrived at it, I found myself pushing my way through the flaps on one of the side entrances to the Co-op. Forklifts trundled past carrying their fishy loads aloft, high in the air with pride. Loud voices mixed with the metallic banging and clanking of machinery. The smack of hard plastic and rubber. The ongoing roar of busy engines. And two radios blaring out in tandem gave a tinny stereophonic effect. Andy Williams singing 'Moon River'. The concentrated smell of fish clammed up the air.

I spotted Frank Bonnar over by the stairs leading up to the office, talking to one of the forklift drivers. Frank checked the fish in and out. He knew all the comings and goings. He held a clipboard under one arm like an injured appendage. I waited in the background until they were finished.

'Frank, how's it going?' I came up behind him. He turned around casually like a man who had spent the best part of his life with people creeping up on him.

'Jim.' He smiled. He didn't look too good. Like all of us he had gotten older, but he wasn't carrying his years well. His full face was flabby and sagging. His white hair thinning rapidly. I hadn't seen him since I had come back from Alaska. 'Good to see you. I heard a rumour you were back in town.'

'I've been back a while.'

'I don't get out much anymore,' he said. 'Just as well.' And he laughed a short sad laugh. Someone shouted something at him from across the floor. I couldn't make out a word of it. Frank made a few waving gestures and everything was settled.

'Maybe you're too busy, but I could do with a word?'

Frank looked about him. Assessing the situation. He wrinkled his nose and forehead. 'I can take a few minutes. Let's get the hell out of here.'

He led me out the back through an exit marked *Emergency Only*. The sting of the fresh salt air was a marked glorious relief. A paved path led around the side of the building. We crossed over it and climbed down a grassy ledge to the rocks. Frank knew exactly where he was going. He sat down on a large flat one and pulled out a cigarette.

'Smoke?'

I refused with a polite negative wave.

'Me neither.' He took a large deep pull. 'Not officially.' He groaned out of pleasure or pain. He cleared his throat roughly and spat at his feet. 'It doesn't get easier,' he said. He scratched at his ear. 'You hated it, didn't you?' he nodded back at the Co-op.

'Pretty much.'

'It's not so bad.' He didn't sound convinced. He coughed again. 'You don't want to know this, but I'm on the way out.'

It was a sudden comment. One he had probably not intended making. He squeezed his eyes tightly shut and grunted. 'I'm sorry, that wasn't for your ears.'

I wasn't sure if he meant he was on the way out from life or the Co-op. If there was any real difference. I was afraid to ask.

'I don't know what to say,' I told him.

'Don't say anything. That's the only way.'

A wave splashed across the rocks just below our feet. Its spray blew in on our faces.

'You've got a friend on the way out too, don't you?'

I presumed he was talking about Knucky.

'Knucky.'

'That's the one. Some sort of heart condition.'

I didn't like to talk about it. It didn't feel right to.

'We don't talk about it much,' I said.

'Why would you?' He dragged more smoke down into his lungs. 'All the same, it's a wicked shame.'

'You take what you get, I suppose.'

'No other option.' He tossed the butt of his cigarette into a pool of water gathered between the rocks. 'So, what is it? What can I do you for?'

I felt a dampness in the seat of my pants. I repositioned myself on the rock. 'You heard all about the Eskimo, I suppose?'

'Almost forgot about that. It was you pulled him in. Strangest thing.' He lit up another cigarette. 'I don't envy you.' He quenched the match with his fingers and flicked it away. 'They buried him out by Malin I hear.'

This was more than I knew. Frank blew a cloud of smoke out in front of us. It hung there like the aftermath of an explosion.

'What have you heard, Frank?'

'About the Eskimo?'

'Yeah.'

'Not much.' He rolled the cigarette with his fingers between his lips. 'All I heard was he fell off a ship. One of those Russian ones. No one seems to know. These things happen all the time. Ships that disappear. Bodies that get swept in on the tides. Fishermen that never return. Debris that cannot be traced.' He tipped the ash into the sea. 'It's the story of our life.'

The butt of his last cigarette bobbed haplessly in the rock-pool.

'An uncle of mine was lost overboard in the waters off the Bloody Foreland. Did you know that?'

I recalled my father saying something about it.

Frank pulled on the cigarette and exhaled. 'He was never found. That must be all of thirty years ago now. Even yet when I hear of a body being found I have the impossible notion that it might be him. The thing is you don't know, his bones could yet float our way. Stranger things have happened. They found an arm on a beach somewhere in the southeast last month. Belonged to a Welsh fisherman. Came all the way in on the Irish Sea.'

'At least they found out whose it was. And yet here I am with full body in tow.'

Frank coughed. 'This is what I am saying. You find a distant Eskimo. I lose a close relative. An arm surfaces. A whole body disappears. It's part of the struggle isn't it?' He coughed again and spat. 'One thing I did hear, George Fleming said something about bruising on the Eskimo's body.'

Frank and I turned to one another at the same time. He shook his head. 'I wouldn't go making too much of it. If you hit water the wrong way, it's like hitting solid ground.'

'Why did George mention it then?' I asked.

Frank shrugged. 'Who can say? Maybe he was just relating what he had been told. Then again George likes to stir things up.'

'Where did he hear this from?'

'Who knows?' Frank stubbed out his cigarette and put what was left of it into the top pocket of his overalls. 'You could always talk to George. He's due in tomorrow. You'll catch him anytime after that in The Porthole. I'll keep my ears open for you.' He stood up. 'I better get back.' He stared out at the water. 'What I said earlier, I haven't been telling anyone.'

'I understand.'

We walked back to the Co-op. I left him at the emergency exit. I promised him a pint sometime. He smiled as though the promise of it was as much as he could hope for.

My whole body shook as I walked back up towards the town. I was in need of a drink. I held one hand out in front of me and watched the quivering movements I could not control. I thought of the fisherman's arm being carried by the currents it had no say over.

Frank was right about the bruising, it was to be expected. I wondered where George had heard about this though. It had either initially come from someone who had seen the body when it was being removed from the boat, or it was information from the post-mortem. If nothing else, I wanted to establish which of these it was. To discover another source of information.

I went into the hotel in the square in town for a coffee. I looked at the waitress. She was a daughter of someone I had gone to school with. It was despicable I knew, but I found her attractive. There was a depravity in this world we were all susceptible to. At the last minute I changed my mind and ordered a pint. I looked at the clock. It was a quarter to twelve. Not yet noon.

I thought of Father Jack. I realized I didn't know where he was from. He had moved here when I was a child. A part of us, but an outsider. I had seen another side to him the other night. There was another side to all of us, but we rarely got to see it.

The waitress came back with my pint. She smiled in recognition of who I was. She could only have been about sixteen. I recalled Frances at that age. Precocious. Indestructible. She still was. Of the three of us she was the one most likely to survive.

I held my pint up to the young girl. 'Your health,' I said. She smiled again, hurried away.

The door to the dining room opposite me was open. It was like something from another era. White tablecloths and candles. Tall wooden fireplaces and thick framed imposing pictures of people who looked important. Their health too, I thought.

My father's family had settled here in the early eighteen-hundreds. My mother's in the later part of that century. Outsiders all of them, too. You had to start somewhere. Neither had ever left. My mother almost went to America, she told me. Had planned to. Had saved enough for the ticket. Then she started going out with my father and that, as she said, put paid to that. It's a cruel world, she told me. She had winked at my father as she said this. I remember him grinning.

After my first pint I ordered a second. This was logic, I thought. One pint leading to another.

Later that afternoon I stumbled out. A row of buses were parked in the square. An aeroplane trailed through the sky. I walked home to my bed. It was still early in the day.

CHAPTER SIXTEEN

The following morning I rang the number on Therese's card. She answered herself. She sounded sleepy.

'Did I waken you?' I wished I hadn't rung.

'It's okay,' she said. 'I should have been up by now.' She sounded like she was trying not to be cross. I couldn't think what to say to her. I should have thought more before dialling her number. 'What is it?'

It was nothing. I just wanted to ring her. To hear her voice. I thought I heard someone in the background. A low voice. The receiver shook in my hand. I felt panicky.

'Who's there?' It came out before I could stop myself.

'What?' She was clearly angry now.

'I'm sorry. I thought I heard someone.'

'I've got a radio on, Jim. A radio alarm to wake me up. What's wrong with you? What difference would it make?'

It would have made all the difference in the world.

'None. I didn't mean it the way it sounded.'

'Well what way did you mean it?'

'I didn't mean it at all.'

I had dug myself into this.

'Jim, what is this about?'

I looked at her business card in my hand. I felt the receiver pressing into my ear.

'Business,' I said. 'It's about business. I want to hire you.'

'I'm not for hire, Jim.'

I was digging myself in deeper all the time.

'I want you to decorate my house, redesign it, whatever it is you do.'

'Stop, Jim. I really can do without this.'

'I'm serious, Therese. It's a business proposition, nothing more than that.'

There was a long silence from the other end of the phone. She seemed to be contemplating it. Or about to lose her composure completely.

'You can't afford me.'

'I can. I have money.' My parents had left me sufficient in their wills.

Again there was silence. I could hear her rustling in the bed. I tried to imagine her there. But all I could see was someone else lying beside her. Hal.

'Jim, I don't need charity. I can do this on my own. I ran a very successful business back in New York.'

'I'm sure you did. I'm not doing this for you. I'm doing it for me. I can't cope with this house anymore. With its pathetic memories. I want to put it all behind me. I'm tired of living amongst the dead.'

Although I hadn't come on the phone to say this, although it just came out, it was the truth. And the more I thought about it, the more I liked the idea. It would be like starting out again.

'Do you mean this?'

'Yes. Please, Therese.' I was pleading with her now.

Therese sighed. As though her will had been broken down. 'Okay.'

'You'll do it?'

'Business.'

'Yes. Of course. Business.'

'It's a deal.' She laughed. She even sounded pleased. 'I'll ring you back later. We can talk about it then.' She hung up. I held onto the receiver.

Therese rang back about an hour later. She suggested meeting two days later to discuss what I wanted done. I invited her for dinner. With my culinary skills, it was a foolish invitation. She accepted with pleasure.

That night I went down to The Porthole to look for George Fleming. He knew more about the Eskimo than he ought to, possessed information he would not be expected to have. It was possible he knew even more than Frank had told me. I needed to find this out. I also needed to know how he had found out all of this, how he had attained access to areas I was being excluded from.

A low mist had slipped in across the lough earlier in the evening and hung above it. It was too dark to see now, but I felt it lick upon my face. Bright yellow lights lit up the other side of the lough like warning fires. The red tail light of a helicopter whizzed like a flare through the night. I stopped at the door of The Porthole and looked back. There was still no sign of the *Lorna Doone*. I pushed open the door and went in.

Strong laughter and snatches of drunken conversation were pitched against one another. Smoke filled the air as though the mist had moved indoors also. Most of the tables were taken, and people stood around in clusters. I squeezed through and went to the bar. A few lines of people thronged at the counter looking to be served. Frances' boss, Eddie, and one other member of staff did their best to serve them. I stood on my tiptoes and looked around, but I couldn't see George yet. Eventually someone got served in front of me, and I made it through to the bar. I looked up and down the counter, but he wasn't there either.

'Where the hell's Frances?' Eddie leaned in on the palms of his hands. He took his frustration out on me.

'Your guess is as good as mine, Eddie.'

A line of sweat gathered above his lip. His cheeks burned bright red.

'Well when you see her, you can tell her from me she's through.'

'Do your own dirty work. This is none of my business. All I'm doing here is looking for a drink.'

Eddie began to pull a pint of Guinness.

'She's out with Knucky again, isn't she? They're off on one of their half-baked trips. An ocean cruise. Well she's way off course this time.' He released the tap and put the pint aside to settle. He took orders from beside me and from over my head. I watched the door for George. 'Her ship's going down, and she can't depend on me to throw her a lifebelt again.'

He topped off my pint and put it in front of me. 'Knucky's to her what the iceberg was to the Titanic.'

I let him go at it. In a way I didn't blame him.

'Have you seen George Fleming?' I asked when he stopped to draw his breath. He cracked his knuckles slowly in his large chubby fingers and went off to serve someone else.

I met a member of George's crew on the way down and asked him if he knew where George was. He pointed him out to me half-hidden at a table in the corner.

A woman and two men I barely knew sat at the table with him. I went over and excused myself.

'George, do you have a moment?'

'Jim Gallagher, isn't it?'

'That's right.'

'I thought you were in fucking Iceland or somewhere.'

'I'm back.'

'I can tell,' George said. He sucked air down into his throat through his nose. He rasped out a cough as though about to spit.

'Do you mind?' I pointed at an empty chair at their table.

'Go right ahead.'

I sat down with my drink. I dived straight in.

'I was talking to Frank Bonnar. About that Eskimo. He said you might know something.'

'Of course,' George knocked back the rest of his pint, spilling some along his chin, 'you're the one pulled the fucker in. Brought him back from Iceland as a fucking souvenir, did ya?' He laughed and wiped at his face. 'So what's Bonnar being saying?'

'He said you mentioned something about bruising on his body, that sort of thing. I was just wondering.'

He grunted in his throat again and swallowed his phlegm. 'I don't know what the hell I said. I was probably drunk.' He laughed loudly.

I laughed too. A strange loud high-pitched nervous laugh. Everyone at the table turned to look. I thought George was going to hit me. My heart turned over.

'So you don't know anything about him?'

George drank, looking out at me over the rim of his glass. He put his glass down. 'He fell overboard, didn't he? I heard that.'

'And the bruising?' I was risking a bruising of my own.

'Jesus Christ! What is this, the Spanish Inquisition? There was some fucking mention of bruising all right. I think one of the ambulance drivers might have said something. Somebody probably beat him to fucking death with a fish.'

He turned to the people he was with and roared laughing. 'I'll tell you something, Gallagher. If you fell overboard, you'd be fucking bruised.'

'You're right,' I said. 'You're fucking right. Thanks, George. I owe you one.'

'You can owe me that fucking one.' He took my untouched pint from me. I let him have it gladly.

I found an empty table and drank myself stupid. I had some sort of recollection of seeing the *Lorna Doone* on my way out of the pub. But, as George might have said, I could have been hallucin-fucking-ating.

CHAPTER SEVENTEEN

Frances was on my doorstep bright and early the next morning. She looked as if she had been crying.

'You stink of booze.' She wrinkled her nose in disgust.

'Have a little bit of sympathy. At least you don't have to live with it.' I brought her in and made coffee.

'Have you talked to Eddie?'

She shook her head. 'I don't think I want to see him.'

'You lost your job.' I told her as gently as I could.

She folded her arms and straightened her back. 'That figures.' I brought her over a cup of coffee. 'It's not all I lost.'

I hated what was about to unfold. I wanted no part of it. The last time I got out before the worst of it. But this time I was right here with no plans to go anywhere.

'He's one sorry bastard.' She chewed the side of her mouth.

I sat in at the kitchen table opposite her. 'It didn't work out?'

'It was never meant to. We both know that. I don't know why we tried.' She unfolded her arms and looked at her fingers. As if she had seen something about them that was not quite right, something she had never noticed before. 'He thinks we slept together. You and I.'

I rubbed my hand across my eyes. Suddenly tired of everything. 'This is getting ridiculous.'

She shrugged. 'It's the way it goes. You should know that by now.'

'What did you tell him?'

'I told him nothing. I told him it would make no difference if I had.'

Frances believed this. She had a faith comparable to none.

'So what happens now?'

'It's anyone's guess. He says he's leaving. But we've heard that before.'

I couldn't bear this. These were my two closest friends. The only real friends I ever had. 'What are we doing to one another?'

'Killing each other, of course. Isn't that how it is?'

'I should never have taken that acid with you.' I had tried to block it out of my mind since, but I had known it would be the death of us. There were some things we were never meant to share. As far as Knucky was concerned I may as well have slept with her.

'It was a good trip.' She tossed out a smile.

'It was hell on earth.' I had never known anything like it.

'It was Judgement Day.' She got up. Stood in the centre of the kitchen as though lost. Unsure where to go next. She rested the knuckles of one hand on her hip and rubbed at the back of her neck.

'Do you want to sleep with me?'

'Aw Jesus, Frances.' She couldn't take it back now. There was no way out of this.

She put her other hand on her hip. 'Well do you? I need to know.'

It was like taking your whole life as you knew it and throwing it up in the air to scatter aimlessly to the ground. I turned my head away.

'Look at me, Jim. Do you want to sleep with me?'

I didn't want to look at her. I didn't want to notice her body. To see the shape of her breasts beneath her T-shirt. Or the round curves of her hips. Her questions were forcing this.

'You're looking to walk on water, Frances. Be careful we all don't drown.'

'I never thought about this before. I never thought that you would think about it. Did you think about it?'

'Frances.' I needed the full depth of her name.

'Did you? Did you ever wonder what it would be like to sleep with me?'

'Frances.'

'Did Knucky ever discuss it with you?'

'Please.'

'Did he? Did you?'

'Of course, he didn't. What do you take us for?'

'I'm sorry.' She sat back down and put her head in her hands. It was the only gesture left to her.

The moment had passed. The moment where I was bound to be completely honest with myself and her. The moment, when despite all of my better judgements, it could possibly have happened. That Frances and I could have slept together. I was relieved and disappointed. It was a sorry mix.

'Where's Knucky now?'

'Somewhere far off.'

'You look tired,' I told her. 'Get some rest.'

'I am tired,' she said. 'I didn't sleep last night.' She looked up from her hands. Her fingers stretched the skin around her eyes. It made her look older than was ever imaginable. 'Can I stay here?' she asked. 'I don't want to go back there again just yet.'

'Of course you can.' She waited for me to tell her where she could lie down. 'Take whatever room you want.'

Frances smiled at my diplomacy. 'You're a good man, Jim,' she said. 'I'll see you later.'

I watched her go upstairs.

I went up after a while to check on her. The door to the spare room was ajar. I looked in. Frances was fast asleep.

While she was sleeping I went downtown to Dr Brennan's surgery. The waiting room was full. I thought about going to Annie's until it quietened down a bit. But I thought better of it. I didn't want to go in reeking of alcohol. I sat down and waited my turn.

He was going to ask me what I was doing there, and I didn't have an answer for him. I was there about the Eskimo, the bruising on him, the decomposition of his body, his waterlogged lungs. And I was there for myself, my own deteriorating condition.

I listened to the talk around me. The medical tales of woe. The local gossip. In this way the story of the Eskimo would have come out. The known details, the embellishments, the unreliable sources of information.

Dr Brennan finally called me in.

'Jim, it's good to see you.' Giving me all of his attention as if I was the first person he had dealt with in months. As if he did not have a roomful of patients day after day. 'I wondered if you'd show. How are you feeling now?'

'I'm much the same,' I told him.

He looked at me kindly. Behind him his bookcase of medical books loomed over his shoulder. I heard the noise from the street. A car pulled up outside.

'Let me just check you over,' he said. He took my pulse, listened to my heart, and checked my blood pressure. 'Still getting those dizzy spells?'

I told him I was.

'Looking after yourself any better? Have you altered your routine any?'

It struck me that he too would have heard the local tales about me. How I was drinking all the time now. How I was no longer working. And as much as anything, that would inform his diagnosis.

'Am I a wreck?' I asked.

'No, I wouldn't say that.' He smiled. 'We won't be going diving for you just yet.'

'I'm drinking far too much.' There was no point in hiding what he already knew. He nodded waited for me to say more. 'I'm still not eating great. My sleep is very disturbed.'

He nodded again. Took advantage of silence. Two women passed by the window. They laughed, then one told a child to be quiet.

'It's the Eskimo,' I said. 'And it's more than that.'

'In what way?'

'That, I don't know. I need to know things. I need to know about the condition of the Eskimo. In that way I can find out about my own condition. Do you understand that?'

'Explain it to me.'

'There's a pathologist's report out there. There's rumour of bruising on the Eskimo's body. It may or may not be suspicious. There's a question of how long he was in the water. What the cause of death actually was. What specifically happens when you drown. How long a body can be kept in a morgue. Whether the word of an ambulance driver is worth more than the word of a policeman. Whether the pub or the pathology lab reveals the greater truth. And this is only the start of it.'

I looked at the shelves along the wall full of supplies, swabs, syringes, medicines. 'Everything I say here is confidential, isn't it?'

'Of course.' He looked at me with interest.

'Can you tell me anything? In the interests of my medical condition, can you give me the treatment I need? You must know what is in the report. You must know what the bruising means. You must have heard.' I stopped myself. 'I'm sorry.' I wanted his confidence, and yet I was asking him to break other confidences.

He looked at his watch. 'Jim, we need to talk more. I'd like you to come back. There are a lot of people waiting now. Let me arrange an appointment where we can have sufficient time to discuss this fully.'

I told him that made sense. I thanked him.

'I mean it,' he said. 'This has been useful.' He said to talk to the receptionist on the way out. To tell her to arrange a half-hour appointment.

I stood up. He got up and came with me to the door. 'I haven't seen the report,' he said. 'Even if I had, it would be confidential. You understand that?'

'I know.'

He stopped and folded his arms in front of him. 'Something I did hear, no more than the next man, I heard his heart gave way on him.'

He seemed to be telling me something I could hear for myself, something I probably soon would. But he was doing more than this. He was stamping it with his professional approval. As if, despite not having seen the pathologist's report, he nevertheless knew something about it.

'One other thing. From what I know of decomposition he couldn't have been in the water more than a few days. Four or five at the most.'

I thanked him for this.

'Be careful, Jim,' he said as I left. 'You're a young man yet.'

It was all I seemed to hear these days, warnings and forewarnings.

I sat on the bench in the square in front of the doctor's surgery and tried to pull together what I knew of the situation this far. I knew that the Eskimo had probably died of a heart attack. I knew he had probably been buried at sea. If Doctor Brennan was right about the decomposition, he would have been in the water for too short a time to have swept in from somewhere else. I also knew that no record of his death or sea-burial had, as of yet, emerged. But his absence from the ship would be documented somewhere, would be known. The details of his burial here would surely get passed on. His next of kin, assuming there were any, would eventually get told. What more did I need to know?

I knew that Frances was asleep in my house. That I had fallen for Therese. That Knucky was far off. That my days as a fisherman were over. And that, although I was falling apart, at least I knew it.

I went back home and looked in on Frances. She was still sound asleep.

Frances finally surfaced at half past five that evening. She came into the living room where I was sitting in front of the fire. She smiled over at me from the doorway.

I smiled back. 'The dead arose and appeared to many.'

It was no smiling matter.

'How are you feeling?' I asked.

'I'm good. Thank you.' She came over and sat down in the armchair across from me. The chairs my parents had once possessed. 'And you?'

'So-so.'

Frances watched me closely.

'I went to see Dr Brennan.'

'Good,' she said. 'I'm glad to hear it. What's the verdict?'

I shrugged. 'Nothing serious. Same old story, not taking good enough care of myself.'

'I know that story,' Frances said. Knucky was still preying on her mind.

'Look,' I said, 'you can stay here a while if you want to. If Eddie's serious about giving you the sack, you might lose the flat anyway.' I had been thinking about this offer all evening. It seemed the least I could do, but I was only too aware of how it might look and what it might lead to.

Frances thought about it. She tapped her fingers on the worn arms of the chair. She shook her head. 'He won't sack me. He wouldn't dare.'

'It would take a braver man,' I agreed.

'But you know, it's a kind offer, and maybe I will take you up on it for a while. I don't think I'm ready to go back just yet. Another few days aren't going to make a difference now.'

'That's settled then.' I was relieved and frightened at the prospect.

'It's not a wise decision though, is it?' asked Frances.

'No,' I said truthfully. 'It could easily be misconstrued. Considering the way Knucky is thinking.'

'But we can't live our lives for him, can we?' Frances pulled at the skin at the sides of her nails.

I didn't answer.

'I was thinking of taking a trip to Killybegs tomorrow,' I told her. 'Do you want to come along? The truth is I could use your car.'

Frances grinned. 'Sure,' she said. 'That'd be fun.'

'I'm not so certain about that,' I said. 'I'm going to see if I can find out anything about the Eskimo.'

'Like what?'

'I really don't know. It seems increasingly likely that he came off one of the ships. Maybe somebody there knows something about him.'

Frances nodded. 'We're a pair of lost souls,' she said. 'That's the truth of it.'

'We're not lost yet,' I told her. 'If we cling to one another a while, we may yet pull through.'

'First things first,' Frances said. 'I'm going to make you some dinner. Get some proper food into you for a change.'

Things were already looking brighter.

CHAPTER EIGHTEEN

Frances prepared a cooked breakfast of scrambled eggs and tomatoes early the next morning, and we headed off. With everything that had occurred I forgot all about my date with Therese. I had been so concerned about what Knucky might think about Frances moving in with me I hadn't considered what she might think about it.

The sun threatened to break through all the way there but never quite managed it. It edged through the gaps in the clouds and disappeared again. Frances was at the wheel and drove with no great urgency. I knew this was one of her favourite drives. Down through Barnsmore Gap with the mountains sloping outwards on both sides and the river running along the edge of the road. The rusty orange glow glimmering off the grasses and the yellow tainted fleece of the mountain sheep.

She couldn't get enough of it.

We had often camped up in those mountains together. They brought back fond memories to us both.

I told her what I had heard from Frank Bonnar and George Fleming.

'So what are you looking for now?'

'Confirmation. See if anyone else remembers the Eskimo.'

'Even if they do, how can you guarantee it's your Eskimo?'

'I can't. But I have to start somewhere.'

Frances shifted gear. She reached across me to the glove compartment and searched around for a tape. 'As long as you know what you're doing.' She found a tape and pushed it into the cassette player.

'What do you mean? What am I doing?'

The music began to play. It was an old country compilation tape we used to listen to all the time. 'You're getting involved in the next world.

You're getting in deep.' She began singing along with Hank Snow. 'I Heard That Lonesome Whistle Blow'.

I thought about what she said for a few moments but didn't know what to make of it. Then I joined in singing with her.

We got into Killybegs around lunchtime. We parked and entered the nearest bar. Both of us ordered a basket of chicken and chips along with a pint of Guinness.

'Where do you begin?' Frances licked the grease off her fingers.

'Right here, I suppose.' Someone dropped money in the cigarette machine behind us and yanked the drawer open then slammed it shut. The lighting was awful. If you didn't know the time, you wouldn't know if it was morning or night. It would be easy to have a few pints there and have no idea what had become of you. A couple of men who looked to be in their seventies or eighties sat at the counter with half-pint glasses and bottles of Guinness. Chain-smoking as if they were keen to hurry their lives to an end. Two other tables were taken up with people eating food. The barman stood behind the counter reading the paper. The television above his head behind him was switched to a satellite sports channel. An ice-hockey match no one had any interest in played itself out.

I went up to the counter and ordered more drinks. While the barman poured them I tried to formulate a sentence that wouldn't sound too out of place. He put one pint up on the draining rack. The thick liquid sunk and rose within itself as it settled.

'I'm curious,' I said. 'I heard an Eskimo came in on one of the factory ships last time around. You know anything about that? I used to work with them in Alaska. I'd be interested.'

I felt awkward. It came out worse than I imagined.

'No. We got a rule. No Eskimos served in this bar.' He poured the second pint. 'No Red Indians either.' He should have smiled, but he didn't. He put that pint up on the rack also and turned back to his paper.

I was left there waiting. I looked up at the television and watched the hockey game. When the drinks had settled he topped them up and handed them to me, the creamy heads pouring over the sides. I paid for the drinks and food and went back to Frances. She had heard it all.

'Good start,' she said.

'I wish I hadn't got these now.' I motioned to the pints.

'We could always leave them behind.'

'We could.' But we didn't. We drank them down quickly and got up to go. One of the old men at the counter turned around. He held his glass out as though toasting us.

'I was in Alaska once,' he said. It sounded spiteful.

'When was that?' I asked.

'Oh, I don't know, the fifties sometime.' He looked at me accusingly. 'I didn't meet any Eskimos.'

'All depends where you were.'

'I hated the place. It was one big shit-hole.' He squeezed his eyes up tight as though each terrible memory had come back to him all at once. 'Instead of building more prisons they should ship every last one of those criminals out there. That's what I'd do.'

I took Frances' elbow, indicated we should go.

'I never saw an Eskimo in this town either.'

'Well, there probably never was one then.' I smiled a thank you and made to leave.

'Were you ever in the Philippines?'

I shook my head.

'There you go,' he said and turned back to his friend at the counter.

I could see the barman watching us from just over his paper as we left.

We trotted around from pub to pub all afternoon. I don't know what I hoped to achieve by it. It was all I could think to do. I didn't want to get too drunk, so we ordered coffees or cokes in most of them. I tried a different approach in each, but every time it came out sounding strange and suspicious. People seemed reluctant to answer. There had to be a better approach, but I couldn't come up with it. Frances said she could try asking if I thought it might help. But I refused. I told her it was my shout.

'It's as if there's a moratorium on talking about it. Doesn't it strike you as strange?'

We sat at a bench down at the harbour. The smell of fish from the boats and the factories surrounding the harbour was rich and pungent. As sickeningly odorous as the first whiff of Valdez. It was hard to believe how you could become accustomed to it, until you no longer noticed it. Until the overwhelming stench of your life was no longer discernible. Frances looked intently at a crane winching boxes of fish off one of the trawlers.

'There's probably nothing to talk about. Either he wasn't here or they don't remember.'

'You think it's that simple?'

She smoothed out the creases in the leg of her jeans. 'What else?'

I ran my hands across the top of my head. Dragged my hair backwards. Felt it pull at its roots. 'I don't know. I just keep feeling that people are hiding something from me. That nothing is as straightforward as it seems.'

'Maybe that's just the way you want it to feel.' She didn't sound fed up or angry with me. Indifferent almost.

A car drove down in front of us. Past the sign that said no unauthorized people should proceed beyond that point. The crane creaked noisily. I listened to the squawk of the gulls fighting over scraps.

'Is that what I'm at,' I asked nodding towards them, 'fighting with myself over scraps of information?'

'It's indicative of us all,' Frances said. She squinted her eyes as though blinded by the sun still hidden by the clouds. 'I know where he's buried.' She pushed her tongue through her lips and ran it along her top one.

'Who told you?'

'No one. I felt it in those energy lines. They drew me to him.'

Frances wouldn't lie to me.

'It's common knowledge. Frank Bonnar told me.' She was greatly disappointed. I probably shouldn't have said that. 'He just told me the general area. He didn't seem to know any more than that.'

'I have it pinpointed exactly.' She smiled as though she thought it was possible she held all the answers and all she had to do was look.

If she even got it in the vicinity of Malin, I would be impressed. 'Well, go on then.' I was glad to be able to test her. To see just how much of this energy business I should take seriously.

She shook her head. 'We'll find it together. He's your Eskimo. I've only worked off maps so far. We'll go out on the land itself.'

I jumped to my feet. 'Help me find him here. That'd be a start.'

'Foreign soil,' she said. 'You'll have to guide me.'

We went back to the pubs.

Frances was in a drinking humour. It had something to do with Knucky. Forgetting all about him. Neither of us could stomach any more coffee or coke, so we went back on the Guinness. We drifted from pub to pub with no great plan in mind other than to visit each and every one. Some more than once. 'We've been here before,' Frances would say. We'd pretend it didn't matter.

It began to rain hard outside. The sound of tyres on wet roads sloshed in my eardrums. Interrupted only by the synthesized music of slot machines.

At first we talked to anyone who would listen. Buying drinks on the off-chance. Speaking freely now with the alcohol. Keeping nothing hidden. We heard about a lot of ships and a lot of foreign fishermen. But no Eskimos. Finally we gave up on others and immersed ourselves in our own company.

'It's not looking good,' I said. 'We must have been to every pub and still no sign of him.'

Frances looked at me as though she felt pity and as though she felt saddened by this. 'He might not have come ashore. Is that possible?'

'I suppose.'

She shrugged. 'There you go.' She placed her hand on the back of mine. 'Whatever it is, you are eliminating possibilities. It's as much as you can do.'

I felt the warmth of her palm on my flesh. I hadn't known what I expected to find out by coming here. It was one port of call amongst many. Perhaps I had hoped that he would be well known around here, around the pubs. In the way that many others off the factory ships were. A home from home. That people would know his name. That even if there were a number of Eskimos on board the ships this one particular one would stand out in a way that would clearly identify him. But this was unrealistic. Charlie had already said the guards were looking into it here. They would have elicited this information too by now. And it was simply too large a chunk to keep to themselves. What I hoped for was something less explicit. I hoped to stumble on something. Something outside of the sequence of official procedures. Something random that would explain everything. Something as random as Frances placing her hand on top of mine.

I saw her smiling at me. 'I'm glad we came,' she said.

'Good.' My own feelings were less clear.

'Our trips were always the pinnacle.' She tightened her hold on my hand. Knucky's absence was as great as the Eskimo's. 'I'm sorry about the drinking.' Her words had a noticeable slur. 'Am I dragging you into the mire instead of leading you out?'

'No. Not at all.' I needed to reassure her on this. 'Whatever is in front of me is of my own making.'

I looked up as the barman approached. 'Didn't you hear me?' He leaned in on the table. His broad muscular arms divided the space between Frances and me. His rough face loomed in front of us. The smell of tobacco clung like a rough aura around him.

Frances looked at me. Neither of us had heard him.

'Time to go,' he said. He pointed to the clock behind the bar. It was ten minutes to twelve. The night had slunk away.

I noticed that no one else was leaving. Someone laughed heartily in the corner. 'Couldn't we have just one more?' It was a foolish and inappropriate question.

He stood upright taking hold of my elbow without any apparent movement in my direction. I stood up and tried to shrug free of him, but he gripped tighter still. Digging his fingers and thumb in hard in the spaces above my joint. An excruciating pain shot through my arm to the tips of my fingers. People turned to look. The barman forced me along. Frances stood up and intercepted. She put her hand on top of his.

'There's no need for that,' she said.

He looked at her sternly and then let go. 'I've been calling time for the last twenty minutes,' he said.

'That may be so,' Frances nodded. She slipped her arm in under mine and walked me out.

It had started to rain. We stood in the doorway and sheltered from it. A hazy ring of moon was visible behind the buildings.

'Now what?' Headlights spun past us in both directions. The drink hit me all of a sudden. I had difficulty standing.

Frances gazed out at the wet street. 'I'm in no fit state to drive.'

'Me neither.'

She grabbed my hand. 'Come on. My treat.'

She walked me back up the street without explanation. I tried to understand why the barman had turned so nasty. I remembered his face from earlier in the day when we had been in asking about the Eskimo. I must have upset him somehow then. Although Frances' hand felt cold, for the first time in ages I felt secure. With someone else to look out for me.

We stopped at the hotel. A stream of rainwater poured across the pavement out onto the road.

'Welcome to the great outdoors,' Frances said pulling me in after her through the hotel doors. She went up to reception and rang the bell. We waited there still holding hands.

The receptionist came out and Frances asked about rooms.

'Single or double?'

I closed my eyes and waited for her answer. I was afraid she would feel my hand shaking within hers. She took a long time in responding. And then I heard her voice speaking with great deliberation.

'A double with two single beds.'

It was the perfect compromise.

'I couldn't afford two single rooms,' she apologized as we went upstairs. It was hard to tell how serious she was.

She pushed the key into the lock, opened the door, and turned on the light. She raised her eyebrows with satisfaction and threw the key on one of the beds. Then pushed her head through the bathroom door.

'That's what I need right now. A long hot bath.'

Everything about the room was exact. The beds were perfectly made up. The bedspreads smooth across them without a single crease. The cups and saucers stacked evenly beside the electric kettle, and the packages of tea, coffee, sugar and milk dispersed neatly in a bowl. The television was positioned above the spotless mirror, its screen without a single thumbprint. And the bathroom a gleaming expanse of tile, enamel and mirror. I was almost afraid to touch anything.

I sat on the edge of one of the beds, the one Frances hadn't claimed with her keys. The mattress barely sank on its firm springs.

Frances began to take her clothes off. She threw her coat across the back of a chair and pulled her jumper over her head. She stooped to undo her laces and yanked her walking boots off. Then went into the bathroom and turned the bath on. I hoped she would stay in there. Finish the rest of her undressing in private. But Frances had no inhibitions. Years of camping together had made this clear. But that was when there were three of us. When numbers took the edge off it. And when she was with Knucky it was another thing altogether. But now it was just the two of us in a hotel bedroom together with all those recent events behind us and our conversation earlier that morning.

She came back out. She carried her socks in her hand and threw them under the chair. Her hands crossed and took hold of the ends of her T-shirt. I got up and began taking my wet coat off. I moved conspicuously around the room avoiding her. I heard the creak of her zip and the soft swish of her damp jeans against her legs. I threw my coat across the bottom of the bed. I got the remote control for the television aware of her standing in her underwear. Then she was gone. Back in to check the bath. I kicked off my shoes, lay up on the bed, and turned the television on. The steam drifted through the open door. The strong flow of the water gushed like a spring stream. The taps were turned off. I heard the splash as she lowered herself down into the bath.

'Aha! This is the real Mc Coy, Jim. Mmmh!'

I shouted something pointless back and flicked through the channels. Then switched it off altogether. I wished we had more alcohol.

'Do you want something to drink?' I shouted into her from the bed. 'I'll get something from the bar.'

'Uh huh. '

'What do you want?'

'Whatever you're having.'

I slipped my shoes on and got money from my coat. I took the key off her bed and closed the door gently behind me.

The bar was closed by the time I got back down. The aluminium shutters were pulled down tight. A man and a woman sat by the window finishing off their drinks, and four men sat a few tables behind them with three drinks lined up in front of each of them. They were just settling in. I went back out to the lobby. Reception was closed. I was just about to head back upstairs when I saw a man in a uniform coming in from the hallway. The night porter. We were residents. That had its concessions. He could get us some drinks. I wandered over, told him the room number we were staying at and showed him the key. I was desperate to convince him.

'No problem,' he said. 'What'll you have?'

'Two Jamesons.'

He nodded.

'You better make them doubles.' I decided to make the most of it.

He disappeared off. I went over and hung around the door of the bar. After a short while I saw him moving about behind the shutters. The man and woman got up to leave. The men threw back their heads and howled with exaggerated laughter at something one of them had just said. They turned around to watch the woman. Their gaze took in her whole body. Then they turned back to one another and laughed again.

Although my eyes were still tired and heavy and my head woozy I was sobering up. It wasn't pleasant. The couple walked past me. They went up the stairs together, their hands touching each other's rears. I heard the door close behind the bar and went back out to wait for the porter.

'Here you go.' The porter held the drinks out to me.

I told him to put it on our account and thanked him. I didn't want to go upstairs just yet. I didn't want to walk behind the couple, watch them together. 'Can I ask you something?' It came out without contemplation.

The porter widened his eyes waiting for me to continue. His permission granted.

'Do you mind if we sit down? Is that okay.' I didn't know if he'd be allowed to or not. If it would be considered a neglection of his duties.

'I make the rules,' he said and went over to the couch at the side of the stairs. 'You're in the night hours now.' He smiled quickly. Slyly. 'So. What is it?'

I asked him about the Eskimo. If he knew anything about one. He folded his arms and crouched in on them. He asked why I needed to know. So I told him how I had pulled him up in the nets.

'Jesus,' he said. 'You're the lucky one.'

'That's right.' I took a drink of whiskey. Enjoyed the strength it gave me.

He nodded slowly. 'I already told the guards,' he said. He paused and looked up at me. The logic of the words began to sink in, the low level of his stare, where this was all leading to. He did know something about the Eskimo. My hand began to tremble. The whiskey ebbed in the glass. He continued to speak. 'I heard something about an Eskimo one time. But like I told them, I have no way of knowing if it was the same one or not.'

I could barely take in what I was hearing. Proof of an Eskimo's existence was being offered. The first indication of a time before his death.

'Some of the Russian crew had been drinking in here one night. They come in from time to time when the ships are in. I can't remember the details but one of them had his nose broken, and I overheard some story afterwards about how someone on board, an Eskimo, had smacked him with his fist from out of nowhere. Seems he got mean with drink and hit him for no real reason. To be honest, there's nothing new in that, and I wouldn't have paid much heed to it except for the mention of an Eskimo. We get all sorts coming through, but I never heard tell of an Eskimo before.'

'When was this?'

'A couple of seasons back. Maybe more.'

'Can't you be more specific?'

'Afraid not. The guards already pushed me on that one. Two or three seasons back, that's as close as I can get.'

'So you told the guards this?'

'Yeah. Well I knew they were asking around.' He pulled at the bridge of his nose.

'What did they say?'

'Not much. They asked if I knew what ship he was off. And I told them, not a chance. They just said they'd look into it.'

'And have they come back to you?'

He drew his breath. 'What'd be the point? There's nothing more I can tell them.' He looked directly at me confirming there was nothing more he could tell me either. He pulled at a button on his cuff. 'How did he end up in the water?'

I finished off my whiskey, looked at Frances'. 'Heart attack, it seems.'

He grinned. 'You believe that?' He raised his eyebrows.

'I believe what I have to.'

He nodded. 'I'd say he got his desserts.' He looked down the length of the lobby as though he owned it. The darkness of night blacked out the glass on the doors. 'I told the guards that too.'

'And?' I needed to know their response. It could help inform mine.

'They said they were keeping an open mind.'

I started on Frances' whiskey without noticing. I couldn't think what else to ask him. Here was the first person willing to talk about the Eskimo in any real way, and it seemed there was nothing to ask. Of course it was still possible that it was another Eskimo altogether, that there could be any number of them working on the boats, but it didn't seem to matter somehow. It felt as if any Eskimo would do. In my own way I was as unconcerned as the rest of them.

The porter said he had things to be doing and went off. I thought about asking him for another whiskey but didn't.

I went back upstairs to Frances. I expected her to be in bed watching the television, but the beds were empty. The bathroom door was ajar and the light still on.

I called in through the open door. 'Frances.' But there was no response. I began to wonder if she had gone out somewhere. She might even have gone down to look for me. We could easily have missed one another. 'Frances.' I knocked on the door. It pushed open a little. I could see her reflected in the mirror, lying in the bath with her head back, her eyes shut. 'Frances.' I pushed the door open further. She still didn't respond. Something irrational inside of me worried that she might have collapsed or even have died. I walked on in. I was just about to shake her when I noticed her chest softly rise and fall. She groaned from her throat, and her left leg lightly moved sending gentle ripples through the water.

I stood at the side of the bath, looking down at her naked body, shimmering beneath the stirring water. Asleep like that she could easily have drowned, have slipped beneath the water never to come back up.

I drank down the rest of her whiskey. What could I have done to save her?

Even when I dragged her out of the bath and dried her off she didn't wake up. She partially supported herself, but didn't respond to anything I said. She seemed halfways in and out of life. It seemed like a good place to be. I brought her over and put her to bed.

It was then I remembered Therese and the meal I had promised her. It had something to do with the lie of Frances' body in the bed, the way her head crooked to one side.

'Oh shit!'

Frances coughed in her sleep. It was too late to ring Therese now. Even in my drunken state I knew this. But still I went and did it. I dialled her number knowing how foolish I was being.

Therese answered. 'Yes?' She sounded nervous.

I looked at my watch. It was five minutes to one.

'Yes? Who is it?'

I was unable to find the words. I sat down on the edge of Frances' bed.

'Is that you Jim? IS IT?'

I thought about putting the phone down while I still had a chance of getting out of this.

'Is it, Jim? Is it you?'

I held the receiver to my ear and listened to her frightened voice.

'Don't do this, Jim. Please don't do this.'

But I didn't know what else to do.

'Please, Jim. Tell me it's you. Tell me.'

I could never have imagined Therese panicking before. I could never have imagined myself bringing her to this state.

'Is it you?'

'Yes. It's me.'

'Goddamnit Jim!' I listened to her unmitigated anger. 'Goddamnit. How can you do this? Have you no idea what you are doing?'

That was it, I thought. I did not know, I simply did not know what I was doing. The answer was as straightforward as that, and yet I could not even say this much. Instead I tried to explain.

'I want to explain,' I told her. But I couldn't. I wanted to tell her how much this showed I cared for her, but I couldn't find the words.

'You're drunk, aren't you?'

'No.' It was a careless lie.

'Leave me alone, Jim.' She sounded like she might cry. 'Put the phone down and let me be.'

She could have cut me off, but she didn't. She was waiting for me to put the phone down on her. I listened to Therese's breathing and looked down at Frances asleep beside me then carefully replaced the receiver. It was the least I could do.

I checked that the key was in my pocket, took the car keys from Frances' coat, and turned out the lights. The porter was elsewhere, and there was no one to see me leave. I went back to where we had parked the car, got the torch and screwdriver, and went back down to the harbour. I moved cautiously and calmly as though following a plan. Except that there never had been a plan. I had no way of knowing what I was capable of doing next.

CHAPTER NINETEEN

I told Frances about it over breakfast. She dipped her toast in her coffee and chewed it. I was whispering. I didn't want anyone to hear. The couple from the bar the night before sat at the far end of the room eating their breakfast in silence. They looked like they had made a mistake and knew it. Like it would come back to haunt them for the rest of their lives.

A piece of crust hung out of Frances' mouth like a cigarette. She nibbled it in. 'I've got to hand it to you,' she said. 'So what did you find out?'

'I'm not sure. I got a list of the ships that were anchored here before the Eskimo's body was found.'

I found the diary with the shipping schedules straightaway on the harbour master's desk. There were twenty-nine factory ships and six reefers.

Frances refilled both our cups. 'You're sure no one saw you?'

'I don't think so.' I took a drink of coffee, swirled it in my mouth, and held it there like I was checking its vintage. It tasted sour. I swallowed it down quickly. 'I had to break a window.'

There had been no gap between the windows to slip the screwdriver through like the last time. Whether it was the drink or just the need for further excitement I hadn't wasted any time. I broke the window with the back of the torch. The glass shattered noisily to the floor. I stood back and waited but no one came to investigate. I put my hand through and opened the catch from the inside. A part of me had wanted someone to come, had wanted me to be caught in the act. But I wasn't. I got in, searched his office, and left. I rang the bell for the night porter to let me back in. He didn't seem in the least bit surprised to see me again. 'Sleep well,' he said as I went upstairs.

'Jesus, Jim, you're going to have to be careful. I don't want to end up seeing you on visiting days only.' Frances sounded concerned, but she was enjoying every moment of it, I could tell. 'They'll have found the broken window by now.' She chewed it over.

'I know.' I played with the coffee spoon. Spun it in circles on the table with my finger.

She hadn't said anything about the night before. About me putting her to bed. And I couldn't say anything about it without her asking me to.

'Are we finished here?'

'For now.'

Frances wiped her mouth with her napkin. It was an odd thing to watch.

'Napkins suit you. It's another life altogether.'

She looked at the white cloth in her hand. I thought she was going to fold it up and take it with her. She wrung it between her hands.

'What do you mean for now?'

'The ships will be back. The season starts up again in a few months time. I intend to be here.'

There'd be ships coming and going for the three months it usually lasted here before they moved on down the southwest coast.

'It's a date,' she said. She leaned in over the table with the napkin and wiped my mouth. 'There.'

We took the long way back through Glenveigh National Park on Frances' suggestion. It was a relief to be back out in the fresh smelling air.

'It's like a holiday,' she said. She drove with one arm resting on the open window. The sun struggled with the grey clouds. Patches of yellow light shone across the open brown fields. She slowed at every sign warning of deer crossing.

'I always hope to see one,' she said. 'I never do.'

She played the same tape as the day before. Skeeter Davis sang 'The End of the World'. Frances joined in. 'Don't say no, it's the end of the world. It ended when you said goodbye.'

I thought about Therese. Strangely I felt like laughing. A shocking tragic laugh. I almost told Frances everything.

'I know I've asked you before,' Frances said, 'but did you see many bears in Alaska?'

Frances was forever asking me this, but each time she made it sound as if this time she would finally grasp the answer.

'Quite a few.'

'That must have been something.' She knew rightfully it was.

'It was always a cause for excitement,' I said.

Frances bit at the nail of her little finger. We both looked over at Mount Errigal at the same time. Its silvery-white side of stone turned away from us like distant glacial ice.

'Were you scared?'

'All the time.' I had never got used to their presence. The knowledge that they could be anywhere where you might disturb them unintentionally. It was a fear to be savoured. 'The thing to do is talk to them at all times. Even when they cannot be seen. Let them know you're there.' This was the part she liked to hear.

I told her again how they just weren't interested in you. Not if they could help it. How the worst thing you could do was get between a mother and her cubs, which was easy to do on a trail, how I sang songs to ward them off. Kris Kristofferson or Leonard Cohen.

I recalled the time I had hiked all day across rough sub-tundra terrain. Not all that different in some regards from what stretched all around us in Glenveigh. I was wet, tired, hungry and fit to drop. Finally I came upon what looked like the perfect spot to make camp. An open flat patch of ground down at the bottom of a steep hill right next to a glacial river. I climbed down carefully, unbuckled my rucksack and let it slip from my aching shoulders. Then I untied my hiking boots and pulled them and my thick woollen socks off my swollen feet. I released my tent from the frame of the rucksack, and had just started to open it out when I looked up and saw the bear. No more than a hundred yards away. Ambling straight at me. I had been warned about making no sudden movements, and absolutely no running away.

Frances smiled to herself as I told her again. She was very proud of this tale. You could almost have imagined she had been there herself.

I told her how I pushed my bare feet into my boots and stuffed my tent into my rucksack talking loudly to the bear all the time. Making it aware of my presence. But still it came towards me. I threw my rucksack over one shoulder and slowly backed away. Trying to walk calmly downstream, my heart on edge. Chatting amicably. 'Now be a good bear. You just be on your way. Otherwise I'm going to have to start singing to you.' And so on. But it never let up. It seemed to be in no great hurry, but with its generous strides it was getting closer all the time. Then I began to wonder if I wasn't in its way, if I wasn't walking in a bear path all along. But the river was too fast and too cold to cross, and the climb back up the bank was still too steep and covered in brush. If I took that route and the bear followed, it would catch up with me in no time. I continued downriver for another five minutes with it following in my every footstep. Eventually I decided I had to take the chance, and began the climb uphill. I didn't dare look back. But about halfways up I had to stop from exhaustion. I looked down behind me. The bear was gone. Then I saw it way across the other side of the river heading into the distance. I got my breath back and climbed the rest of the way to the top. A huge elk stood a few hundred yards in front of me, defiantly proud, surveying its territory. I barely glanced at it. Just dropped my pack and counted my blessings.

I had never been in any real danger, I told Frances. I had just been in the way.

'Story of our life,' she said. 'Still and all. It's a question of survival. One wrong move. But you did what you were supposed to. That's what got you through.'

'He could just as easily have followed me up the hill.'

Frances drummed her fingers on the wheel. 'But he didn't.'

Then she asked me again about hanging my food up out of reach away from the camp, or burying it in the ground when there was nothing to hang it from. How I couldn't even keep toothpaste in my tent. And how menstrual blood had a way of attracting them. She wanted to know what I would do if she was with me, and she got her period.

'I'd hang you from a tree,' I told her. 'Or bury you in the ground. What else?'

It began to rain heavily. Lumps of hail beat against the windscreen. Frances rolled her window up and put the wipers on full. I could hardly see anything through the thick hail. Suddenly the car slammed to a halt as Frances jammed on the brakes. I was thrown forward towards the dashboard, and held back from serious damage only by my seatbelt.

'What the hell, Frances?'

She opened her door and jumped out. A large deer bounded off the road in the direction of Errigal.

'Can you believe that?' She shouted from outside.

I pulled down my window and looked after it. Frances laughed, almost hysterically. The hail caught in her hair like sequins.

'You'd have to believe in something, wouldn't you?' she said. 'You'd have to be convinced of something other than the two of us.' She grinned in at me.

'You'll get drenched. Get back in the car.'

But Frances ignored me. She sat up on the bonnet and lay back. Her hands stretched behind her, her fingers touching the windscreen. Her legs draped over the edge.

'Drive,' she shouted. 'James, take me home.'

CHAPTER TWENTY

Every time I thought of Therese now I panicked. I couldn't believe how recklessly I had behaved with her. It was as if I was intent on throwing everything away. But I was too far in to turn back. I didn't seem capable of ordinary behaviour anymore. I should have called her to apologize, but I didn't. I was at a loss to know what to do.

I was glad of Frances' company but fearful of it at the same time. Afraid of how it might be interpreted, by others and by myself.

She avoided going out for fear of meeting Knucky, and I too was afraid of who I might meet. And so for the next week we stayed put in my house only going to the nearby shop for provisions when absolutely necessary. Holed up together as though battening down for the winter.

'What have you got there?' Frances asked. She stood behind me looking over my shoulder. The lamp cast her shadow across the paper I was looking at.

'The list of ships. That's all.'

Frances placed her hand on my shoulder, leaned in on me. 'It's a start.' She spoke quietly as if trying not to disturb someone.

I didn't know what I hoped to achieve by looking at it, reading the names. It was almost as though I hoped one name would jump out at me, let me know somehow that this was the Eskimo's ship.

'Maybe I should get you to run your hands across it. See if you can home in on one in particular.'

Frances squeezed my shoulder eagerly. 'I'd certainly be willing to give it a try.'

I had only been half-serious when I said it, but what, if anything, had I to lose? I handed her the list. She laid it on the table and closed her eyes then held her right hand above it, the tips of her fingers dipped downwards. She moved her hand over and back as if reading braille. That's what I was after all, blind, unable to see what was right in front of me.

She stood like this for a few minutes then took her hand away. She opened her eyes and handed me back the list. She shook her head. She looked sad, disappointed.

'It's okay,' I said. 'Maybe it means he was never from one of these ships in the first place.'

'Maybe,' she said quietly, but I could tell this altered nothing. She had let herself down somehow.

We hadn't had a drink since returning from Killybegs. I had felt reassured by this. But I wanted one now. I asked Frances.

The clock on the mantelpiece ticked loudly. A floorboard creaked. Frances looked down at her fingers.

'You go alone,' she said. 'I'm not ready for it just yet.'

She smiled and went out of the room. Something had given. It was hard to know what. I heard her climbing the stairs. I missed her already. I put my jacket on and went to Annie's.

I drank far too much and wondered what to do about Therese. I had no answers. I needed to see her again. I needed her company. I remembered Frances' hand on my shoulder. And I recalled Therese. I recalled the softness of her mouth on mine. I finished my drink and without sufficient contemplation left the pub and hitched out to her cottage.

It took me three lifts to get there. I tried to talk as little as possible. Sitting quietly as if headed nowhere in particular. The lifts came in quick succession as if to ensure there was no turning back. I asked to be dropped off about a half mile up from her laneway and walked the rest of the way. It was late and dark. I could hardly see a thing. In the absence of light the Atlantic disappeared completely off the headland. I watched the red taillights of the car that had dropped me off trail luminously up the hill. I reached the entrance and turned up the lane to her cottage. I could make out the lights ahead flickering through the gaps in the trees. Now that I was there I wondered how I should proceed. I couldn't go up to her door again unannounced. But otherwise what was the point of being there?

I saw two cars parked out front. Her own and someone else's. I wondered if it was Hal's. I crept up the last few yards keeping close to the edge of the lane and sheltered behind the trees. I felt like a fugitive. On the run. Under threat of being trapped. It felt good.

The light in her front room, the dining room, showed through the curtains. I tiptoed over and peered through the chink in them. I knew that this was what I had come here to do. To spy. To watch her life from a secret distance. From a hitherto unknown angle.

I half-expected someone to be standing inside looking out. Looking right into my narrowed eyes. But the room was empty. The remains of a meal were spread on the table. The empty plates and discarded cutlery. A wine bottle stood off to the centre, but the glasses were missing. I knew she would be around the back in the conservatory with her dinner guest. I looked at the second car on the way around. I recognized it, but still I couldn't place it. The door was open, and the keys were in the ignition. I thought about getting in and driving away. It might be the best thing I could do. It couldn't be any worse than what was about to occur if I stayed. I put my hand on the handle and pressed it open. The soft click resounded in the stillness. The door opened a fraction then caught again, neither opened nor closed. The hinge creaked loudly. I immediately released the handle and slipped into the darkness around the side of the cottage.

I heard the waves sliding up the beach and over the rocks at the base of the cliffs. The light from the conservatory lit up the ground ahead of me. I moved along as quietly as possible. I got to the corner and clung there trying to build up my nerve. I held onto the whitewashed wall and inched my head out into the open. The curtains were only partially drawn. Therese was sitting inside with her back to me. A man I couldn't yet make out sat the opposite side of the glass-topped coffee table. Another bottle of wine stood on the table between them. They each held a half empty glass in their hands. I got down on my hands and knees and crawled over to the bushes at the side where I was less likely to be seen. The cold damp grass pressed into my palms. The sharp edge of a stone cut into the cushion at the base of my right thumb. The skin tore and blood rushed to the gash. I licked it away and hurried into the bushes. I crouched amongst them like a garden ornament. Therese and her man friend were obviously talking. There was little to observe. I searched the sky, but I couldn't find a single star. And then all at once it seemed to fill with them. Twinkling on and off. Until one by one they were doused again.

Ten or fifteen minutes must have passed. My right leg began to seize, contract into a cramp. I stretched it out in front of me and rubbed at it, balancing against the ground with my left hand. I pointed my toes away from me as far as possible. But it only made matters worse. My leg seized up more. Through the window I saw the man lean over for the wine bottle. The side of his face came into view. I lost my balance and slipped backwards into the branches. I looked up quickly, afraid they might have heard. But they did not appear to. Therese sat with her back to me. The man was partially out of sight again. I hadn't got a proper look at him, but it wasn't Hal. That much I was certain of. He was too broad for him, older too.

I examined the large hole my fall had made in the bush. Therese would see it over the next few days and most probably blame it on an animal. She wouldn't be far wrong. That was if I wasn't caught before then. I got up and walked brazenly around the garden trying to rid myself of the cramp. If one of them stood up, I would easily be seen. I felt a strong urge to walk to the end of the garden to the edge of the cliff. Whether it was Therese's talk out on the headland those few days previous or not, it would not have surprised me if I had jumped. It was getting cold, and I began to shiver. I walked about the garden where I knew I couldn't be seen to try and keep warm. I had lost all track of time. Twenty minutes might have passed or maybe an hour. I was a sad spectacle, if there was anyone to notice.

When I looked in again both Therese and the man were standing up. I pushed back into the safety of the bushes. Therese walked around the table and embraced him. His large hands were clasped around her back. Her head pushed into his shoulder. They separated and moved away until I could no longer see them from where I stood. I couldn't control my shaking. It might have been the cold or whatever it was I had witnessed. I heard the front door open and crept back around to the front of the house. I kept to the bushes again. Therese stood in the doorway and kissed him on his cheek. He said something I couldn't hear and squeezed her hand. Then he broke away.

'Until the next time,' he said, his voice carrying high into the night air this time. Therese stepped back inside and closed the door. He walked back to the car. I was prepared for it to be anyone, anyone except who it actually was. Father Jack looked up as he pulled on the car door handle I had opened until I was certain he must have seen me.

I stayed back in the bushes long after he had driven away. I held onto them with my hands as though I was impaled upon them. My night vision was blurred. I no longer knew what it was I was seeing, or what I had seen.

The conservatory light went out, and a short while later a light went on upstairs. Therese's bedroom light. I saw her walk past the window. She came back, I assumed to pull the curtains, but instead she stood there looking out into the night. She held a half glass of red wine in her hand. She raised it to her lips and sipped from it. I felt its warm fruity richness slither down my throat. I began to shake again. My whole body convulsed. I tried to stop it but was unable. My legs weakened until I thought I would fall. I became aware of my own breathing gasping loudly. I inhaled as hard as I could and held it for as long as I was able. I looked back at Therese's creamy face paled by her jet black hair. It was hard to tell how she was feeling. I wanted to call out to her. She drank down the rest of her wine and moved away.

I waited until the light in her bedroom went out. Then I walked back to the main road. I watched for car lights to hitch home. But there were none. It was quarter to six in the morning before I got home. I stumbled through the front door and passed out in the hallway.

CHAPTER TWENTY-ONE

Frances made a passing reference to my early morning but did not ask about it. I don't know what she thought had happened, but I was in no position to explain. Therese and I were navigating a different course. It was not one Frances would willingly have taken.

I recalled Frances' comments about Father Jack's girlfriends. I could hardly believe Therese would have been one of them. But then I could hardly believe anything about my life right now. In some ways I was just drifting along much as I always had done, but in others I was being pulled by the undertow, being sucked under.

There were moments in Alaska amidst all the excess of loneliness, drink, sex, ice and wilderness when a sense of understanding emerged. Solitary moments standing amongst a vast primitive landscape when I experienced a feeling of truly belonging. But they were short-lived and could not sustain me. And there were moments here too. Moments spent with Frances and Knucky. And moments with and without Therese.

Over the next few days I tried to pull together all the pieces I had. The scraps of information from Charlie, Dr Brennan, Frank, all of the sources. The list of ships, the details from the reports. It was perhaps just a matter of getting my thoughts in order. I wrote everything I knew about the Eskimo out and came at it from every angle. But still I needed more. It had yet to add up.

Frances listened patiently when I needed her to. I liked her presence about the house. It made it more alive than it had been for a very long time.

'What have you decided?' she asked me one night. We had taken to staying up late at night and rising very late in the afternoon.

'The more I know of it the less I understand.' I leaned back in my chair at the table.

Frances sat by the fire. She pushed her hair behind her ear. Her fingers trailed down the back of her neck. 'Nothing changes,' she said.

'Have you found me my ship yet?' I knew she had borrowed the list again earlier, had not given up on herself entirely.

'There's something not quite right with the atmosphere here,' she said, holding her neck now as if for support. 'I still can't get any feeling whatsoever.'

'Are you unhappy here?' I asked.

Frances looked surprised. 'No, not at all. That's not what I meant.'

I smiled weakly. 'Good.'

Frances rubbed at the base of her skull. 'Was it always like this?' she asked.

'What?'

'Me, you, and Knucky.' Her chair creaked as she sat back. 'Did we just not notice it before?'

'I don't know, Frances.' I heard her soft breathing.

'I remember the three of us in the back row of the cinema. Holding hands. Purely out of friendship, but with that feeling of something more illicit. Surrounded by snogging couples. All wondering what was going on between us. Back then I could imagine nothing more thrilling.'

'I remember that too. I always felt as if we were the most important people in the world.'

Frances smiled, bit at her lip. 'The first time a boy touched me I ran all the way back to tell you and Knucky. Every sordid detail. I remember thinking you would be so glad, and I remember the look of horror on both of your faces.' She looked around the room. At my papers on the table, the dust and ash covering all of the furniture. 'God but you're filthy. This house is a disgrace.'

'I'm not a well man,' I said. 'You know that.'

Frances laughed. 'That's about the height of it,' she said. Something had changed. She no longer wanted to talk about us.

I thought about ringing Therese. I had tried a few times during the week, but there was no reply. The phone rang out. It was the worst response I could have imagined. I was afraid of Frances overhearing the call, but she was here now on my invitation, and it was something I would just have to endure. If she was to find out about Therese, there was nothing I could do about it. I excused myself and went out to the hall to ring.

I listened to the ringing tone afraid of who, if anyone, might answer the phone. I thought it was going to ring out again, but finally I heard the receiver being picked up. I heard Therese say hello.

'Therese.'

'I don't want to talk to you, Jim,' she said when she heard who it was. She hung up. I stood in the hallway shaking, the phone still in my hand. I instinctively reached out and dialled her number again.

'Don't make a nuisance of yourself,' she warned me. 'Don't drag us both down.' Then she hung up again.

I inhaled deeply to try and steady my breathing and replaced the receiver. I went back in to Frances. She glanced up.

'You know,' I said, 'we don't do half enough drinking in this house anymore.'

I awoke around noon with a familiar headache. Frances and I had polished off a bottle of whiskey the night before. We ran through all the usual ground once more. Frances', Knucky's, and mine. I very nearly told her all about Therese, but I couldn't. We were stalled here. There was nothing it would do her any good to hear.

I lay in bed for a while trying to get back to sleep, but I wasn't able. I eventually got up and showered. There was no sound from Frances' room. I had coffee and decided to go back down to see Frank. Just talking to him the last time seemed to help.

I walked into town and turned down towards the Co-op. From the top of the hill I saw the *Lorna Doone* tied up at the pier. Knucky was on board dressed in a pair of old overalls washing the deck down. I didn't want him to see me just yet. I waited until he had his back turned to me and went past.

I walked on down to the Co-op. Frank saw me coming through the doors and indicated to go out back. He disappeared up the stairs into the office. I went back out and around the side of the building and climbed down onto the rocks we had been to the time before. I watched the water splashing in and out between them, coming and going at once. It was how I felt.

Frank came out about ten minutes later. A cigarette still burning between his lips. He came over and sat down beside me. He ran his hand through his hair and pulled at the bridge of his nose. He took his cigarette from his mouth and turned the lighted end towards him. He held it up like he was examining a component he was trying to identify, wondering what precisely its use was, where it fitted in.

'It's closing in on me,' he said. He put the cigarette back in his mouth and drew hard on it. He exhaled a grey cloud of smoke and spoke out of it. 'I suppose that's its nature.'

'It's all our nature,' I added.

Frank nodded and spat into the water. 'Did you ever track down that Eskimo of yours?' he asked.

'Not yet,' I said. A discarded buoy floated past. A wispy string of blue cord floated behind it.

'That's what I want to talk to you about.'

Frank lit up a new cigarette off the butt of his old one. 'Fire away.'

I told him what the porter had said. How there was at least one Eskimo on board the ships. And I told him about the list of ship's names. He didn't ask where I got it from, and I didn't say. I told him I needed to narrow the list down.

Frank puffed on his cigarette and nodded. 'What can I do?'

'Advise me.'

'I don't know,' he said. 'If the guards couldn't find out anything, I don't know what I can do. They'll have got that list of names too. They'll have contacted them.'

'Nothing's showing up,' I said. 'Charlie Doherty told me. It's all lost in bureaucracy, the limits of their jurisdictions.'

Frank thought about it for a moment then said to leave it with him. 'I'll see what I can do. I know some of the agents who deal with these ships, sort out their arrivals and departures, what ever problems they have. Fuel, money, ice, that sort of thing. I'll look into it.'

I thanked him.

'I'd better be getting back,' he said. He looked pale and drawn. 'You take care of yourself.' He stood up and slapped my back.

I watched him walk back to the Co-op and wondered who should be taking care of whom.

I walked down along the pier and stepped on board the *Lorna Doone*.

Knucky wore a small set of headphones and didn't hear me come on board. He sang to himself as he scrubbed hard.

'Hey Knucky!' I tried to shout above the music. But he didn't respond. I tapped him on the shoulder, and he jumped.

'Fuck it, Gallagher!' He pulled the headphones down off his head onto his neck.

'Sorry.' This apology went further than my startling him.

He stood there not knowing what to do about this. He had no doubt intended to be angry when he next saw me. But I had caught him with his guard down.

'You going out again?' I had never seen the boat looking so tidy or clean.

'She's going to fall apart if I don't do something with her. It's time she got a painting.' He looked to the tins stacked in the corner of the wheel house. 'I was just about to start.'

It was long overdue. We had been talking about it for months now but had never got around to it.

'You need a hand?'

Knucky looked away and thought about it. He walked across the deck and emptied the bucket of dirty water overboard. Then he came over and put the empty bucket at my feet. He looked like he could hit me. I would not have been surprised.

'It makes no difference,' he finally said.

I tried not to smile. 'What colours did you get?'

'Blue and red.'

The same as before.

We both stood there avoiding each other's eyes.

'Well, what are you waiting for,' he finally said. 'Grab a fucking bucket.'

Knucky put his earphones back on so he didn't have to speak. We worked through the afternoon washing down the deck and wheelhouse. Then spent the rest of the day bringing her up on dry land. There was little time for idle talk, which suited both of us fine. The harbour had recently acquired a syncro-lift for lifting boats out of the water. Knucky had arranged with Tom Harte to get use of it. John Cavanagh, the charge hand, and one of his young workers helped us bring the *Lorna Doone* in. Knucky and I sailed her into position.

We got her secured on the cradles, then John started the lift up, and we watched her rise like the proverbial phoenix. Something mystical, beyond our belief, ascending from out of the waters to perch high above its surface like the Ark after the floods. John hitched her to the back of a tractor and dragged her along the tracks into the boatyard. Tom watched from the door of his office, beaming with the sheer pleasure of all that he controlled.

Knucky sighed. 'That's enough for one fucking day.' He nodded his thanks to John and went over to talk to Tom. I was left there standing by myself. I watched him and Tom for a while, talking and laughing as though they were engaged in some great conspiracy together. I shouted over to Knucky that I'd see him in the morning. He scarcely glanced my way.

Frances was still in bed when I got back. We were going from bad to worse.

I turned up at seven the next morning. Knucky was already there scraping the paint and barnacles off the sides. He handed me an old shovel to use then went around the far side of the boat, his music playing again. And this was the way it went on for the rest of the morning. Keeping our distance. Working in silence. I had brought sandwiches along for lunch and stopped around midday to eat. I went around and offered Knucky one. He just shook his head. I ate them on the pier while Knucky kept working.

When I got back I found a ladder resting against the side of the boat for me and next to it a few tins of paint, a tray and a roller. He had already started painting his side. I finished off the scraping and began painting too.

Knucky came around my side later on that evening and surveyed the work I had done. He nodded a reluctant approval.

'Will I see you tomorrow?' he asked.

'Of course,' I said. I started down the ladder. Our day's work was done it seemed. Knucky turned and headed home.

I told Frances all about it when I got back.

'That's Knucky for you,' she said. 'That's about the cut of him.' She leaned up against the kitchen wall. 'Did you tell him about me?' She rested her hands flat against the plaster.

'Do you think I'd still be working with him if I had?'

Frances laughed. 'I don't suppose.' She tilted her head back and stared aimlessly ahead. 'He must be wondering where I am.'

'I'm sure he is. I'm sure he has his suspicions.'

She pushed away from the wall. 'Well at least you're back working with him. That's got to account for something.'

Frances was angry. She walked out and went to her room. I didn't see her for the rest of the night.

We finished painting the outside of the boat a few days later and started up on deck. It was harder to avoid one another there. We got down on our knees and began scraping the loose paint off the wood. Keeping our distance. At first Knucky kept his head down and his earphones on. But after a while I heard him pulling them off and tossing them aside. 'Fucking batteries,' he muttered. Then he stood up and arched his back stretching his arms above him. I rested back on my heels. The fumes from the recent paintwork drifted lightly in my head.

'Were you talking to Frances recently?' He made it sound such an ordinary question. As though our silences had never existed.

I didn't know how much I should tell him. The truth was I hadn't been talking to Frances much. She kept to herself a lot these days. I looked at Knucky. I didn't know what he wanted to hear. I told him about our trip to Killybegs, but I didn't say anything about her staying over.

'So you're still chasing up that Eskimo?' He bent down and began scraping again.

'I can't seem to let him go. Or he won't let me go. It's one way or the other.'

He didn't say anything for a while. I began to wonder if that was it. If our conversation had come to an end again. I listened to the gulls overhead. A lorry came down the hill carrying kegs of beer for The Porthole. It pulled up at the side. Two men got out and started to unload.

'I've been out,' Knucky said, 'out to where they buried him.'

The kegs rattled noisily across the uneven concrete as the men rolled them along. I wiped the edge of the scraper against my jeans to get rid of the loose flakes of paint that were stuck to it. I turned around on my knees. Knucky was stooped over scraping into the corner.

'I thought you didn't care,' I said.

'I don't. I just wanted to make sure they had him weighed down enough. Didn't want him interrupting my livelihood again.' He sat back up on his hunkers and stretched his back once more. 'You been out?' His voice was strained as he stretched.

'No. Not yet. I'm still not sure exactly where he is. Frances says we'll find him together. She has it all worked out with her charts and things.'

'Hah. She's going to lose it completely one of these days.'

He pushed into the small of his back with his hand and groaned. 'You know, she really believes all that stuff.'

'Maybe there's something to it.'

'Not you fucking too.' He gave me a bitter look. I knew he was thinking about me and Frances together. It was time to put an end to it.

'Nothing ever happened between us.'

He pretended he didn't hear. He bent his back into his work again.

'I swear to God, Knucky. Not a thing.'

He slapped his scraper hard against the side of the boat. 'Fuck you, Gallagher. You don't know when to let go, do you?' He shook the sharp edge of the scraper at me. 'She's staying with you now, isn't she?' He sounded calmer as though this thought could somehow soothe him.

'She needed a place for a while. That's all. Eddie's on her back about disappearing off without a word. It'll blow over.'

Knucky just nodded. 'You're a good friend,' he said unconvincingly.

'What do you want from me, Knucky? What do you want from Frances? Have you any idea?' I was tired of it all. I didn't know what had brought it to this.

Knucky stayed on his knees. 'No. I don't,' he said. 'I don't have the slightest idea. What do you make of that?'

I looked out at the other boats tied beside us. At their tall masts swaying with the water's undulations. I felt trapped behind them. A gull nose-dived into the water in front of us.

I didn't answer him. The hollowness of an empty keg hitting the ground reverberated back into itself.

'Help me get the fucking boat back into shape. Let's begin there.' He sounded tired too.

I was having a nightcap when Frances came in. I asked her if she'd join me. I didn't know if I should tell her that Knucky knew she was staying here. It might only make matters worse.

Frances said she would, that she needed one. I was glad she accepted my offer. I felt bad about the way we were hardly talking anymore. I had been unprepared for that. I know she was upset about me renewing my relationship with Knucky, or perhaps more upset with the fact that this bothered her. But I hadn't expected that it would come to this.

I got her a glass and poured her a whiskey. She sat down in the armchair opposite.

'I went to see Eddie today,' she said. She looked across at me as though I should understand everything else from there. And I believed I did.

'So when are you going back?'

She took a drink. 'I can start back any time I want.'

It didn't surprise me. They would be lost without her.

'Do me one favour, don't leave too suddenly.' I meant it. I would need time to adjust.

Frances smiled. 'I'm sorry the way things worked out.'

I wondered if this was how it was with her and Knucky when they decided to part the first time.

'Did I leave you in a worse state than I found you?' She was being serious.

'No. I don't think so.' I was eating better than I had been. And, despite the whiskey in my hand, drinking less. 'I may be on the mend.'

'Me too,' she said.

A swirl of wind got trapped in the chimney blowing down smoke. We both heard its sad gusting.

'Could it have been any different?'

I wondered if she meant if we had slept together.

'We did all we could.' I tried to sound reassuring.

'I'm sure you're right,' she said.

But she didn't sound certain at all.

We drank a few more whiskeys and Frances told bar stories until we both felt better.

CHAPTER TWENTY-TWO

It took us another week to get the painting finished. I threw myself wholeheartedly into it. Arriving most mornings before Knucky. It helped keep my mind off the Eskimo and Frances. Knucky and I talked on and off during the day but he made no more mention of her. I wondered if I ought to tell him about her recent decision to move out. But in the end I decided to let Knucky find out for himself, just as he had found out about her moving in.

And as it happened we both found out together. We looked up one day from the boat and saw Frances standing at the door of The Porthole watching us. Neither of us said anything. She had been in bed that morning when I left. Although I knew she was leaving, it still came as a surprise to see her there.

Knucky said nothing, but he was clearly more relaxed after that. Easier company to be around.

'We ought to wrap it up tomorrow,' Knucky said before I went home that evening, 'if we get one last good day's work done.'

He was right. I was sorry about this. I had enjoyed giving her a new lease of life.

The following day we went at it with great energy eager to meet our deadline. A couple of times I saw Frances looking over our way. I was tempted to wave, but it didn't seem appropriate.

We put the finishing touches on around seven that evening. Knucky washed his hands with white spirits.

'We did well,' he said. It was the closest thing to a thank you I had got all that time. 'What do you say we get a pint?'

I didn't think it was a good idea at all. It wouldn't do for either of us to get drunk.

'I don't know,' I said.

'Oh come on. We deserve it. The *Lorna Doone*'s never looked so good.' He wiped his hands on an old rag.

She did look well. Like she was starting out all over again. The blue and red paint shone brightly. The name was painted on anew in white lettering. Knucky looked at her proudly.

'It's almost enough to make you believe in love,' he said and smiled over at me.

It was not what I wanted to hear.

'So?'

'Well, just the one then.' I thought it would be worse to refuse.

Knucky tapped a finger towards me. 'Just the one.'

I suggested Annie's, but Knucky was intent on The Porthole. He had something to prove. And maybe he was right. We would all have to face up to each other sometime.

There were a dozen or more people seated around. Tom Harte was sitting at the counter with one of the pilots. Frances was placing a couple of fresh pints in front of them. Her lips moved into a greeting when she saw us. But it wasn't a smile. Knucky pulled a stool over to the counter and sat up. I did likewise.

'Pints, Frances,' he said as though nothing had ever happened.

She poured us a Guinness each. 'You've been working hard,' she said looking intently at what she was doing.

'You've been watching.'

Frances ignored him. 'She's looking well.'

I knew the moment she said it what was coming.

'Almost enough to make you believe in love is what I say.'

Frances sucked in her bottom lip and bit it. She fiddled with the taps. There was a bad air about Knucky. This had not been a good idea. He tapped his fingers on the counter top. I turned a beer mat between mine. For once I wished Frances would hurry with the pints.

Tom Harte slid his elbow along the counter and leaned in over the stool separating us.

'Tom.' I acknowledged him.

He looked like he had something on his mind. He seemed to be searching for the right way of putting whatever it was he had to say.

He pulled back slightly, and I thought he had changed his mind.

'I heard you were in Killybegs.' He squinted into my face.

I didn't bother to say anything in response. This was all up to him now. He stretched his mouth back into his cheeks. He spoke low so only I could hear. 'I don't know what you're after, Jim, but you're just making trouble for yourself.' He burped silently to himself. 'Can't you leave well enough alone?'

'What are you talking about, Tom?'

He shook his finger. He pulled back further, then leaned in again. 'I also heard about a break-in in my counterpart's office. Now you wouldn't know anything about that, would you?' He grinned in spite of himself.

'I'm not sure I want to hear this, Tom.'

'I bet you don't, ' he said. 'But you'll hear it, and a whole lot more.'

'Threat, Tom?'

'I'm simply saying that you're treading in dangerous water. Poking around for something that never was there. Something of your own making. You're up to your neck in your own distrust. Get a grip of yourself before it's too late.' He pulled away. 'Frances.'

She looked over at him.

'Watch that fellow,' he said. 'Keep him on the straight and narrow.'

Frances looked at me, confused.

'Never mind,' I told her.

Someone asked for change for the cigarette machine, and she went to the till to get it.

'What are you doing?' I asked Knucky when she was gone.

'What are you talking about, Jim?'

'You know damn well.'

Knucky looked over at the bottles of spirits lining the shelves at the back of the bar as though making a conscious effort to read each label individually. He arched his head slowly towards me.

'You've got your own life, Jim, to take care of. And it's more than you can handle.' He looked back to the bottles. He seemed to be trying to make up his mind which one to start on. 'You fucked her didn't you?'

'Oh Christ, Knucky.' This was turning for the worse more quickly than I imagined.

'Ah you did, Jim. Don't I know it?'

'Knucky, Knucky, Knucky.'

'Where's the fucking pints, Frances?' He raised his voice loudly enough to be heard the length of the bar.

'With you in a minute.' Frances looked at me apprehensively from the other end where she was finishing an order for somebody else.

'With you in a minute.' He mimicked her. 'That's how it's always been. ' He closed his eyes and rubbed at them harshly with the palms of his hands.

'I swear to God, Knucky, nothing happened.'

'It's okay.' He peered out from the sides of his palms. 'It's okay, Jim. I fucked her. You fucked her. We're evens. It's okay.'

'Don't talk like that, Knucky. Don't do this.' I couldn't bear to hear it. This was Frances we were talking about. Knucky's crude words were transforming her into something else. Something cheap and disposable.

'What am I doing? I'm telling it as it is, that's all.' He smiled across at me in a forcefully strained way. 'We do what we have to do. No hard feelings.' He stuck his hand out to prove his point.

'I don't want to talk about this, Knucky.'

He pushed his hand closer.

I turned back to the counter. Looked to see where Frances was. She was still serving others further down the bar.

'You don't want to shake it. You don't want to shake my hand?' Knucky furrowed his brow in a dramatic puzzled way.

'Stop it, Knucky.'

'What? I just want to shake hands. Don't you want to shake it?'

'No. No I don't want to shake it.'

'You don't want to shake it.' This was what he had been waiting for, and he was playing it to full effect.

'There's nothing to shake hands over, Knucky.'

'So you're not going to shake my hand?'

'Knucky!'

'You fuck Frances on me, but you won't shake my hand.' He was working himself up into the anger he so desperately needed. I had to diffuse this somehow.

'Sorry about the delay.' Frances put a pint down in front of each of us and smiled, but her eyes showed the worry she felt.

Knucky withdrew his hand. He looked down at his fingernails.

He picked at a daub of paint on the knuckle of his right thumb.

'He wouldn't shake my hand, Frances. What do you think about that?'

'Maybe he wants you to wash it first.' She made a laughing sound, but it was a clumsy joke. More likely to offend than placate.

'Your health.' He raised his pint then tipped it back into his mouth. He drank over half of it down. He grunted with pleasure and wiped his mouth with his sleeve. 'Set us up two more, Frances, and get me a whiskey.'

I hadn't even begun to drink. 'I'm okay,' I said to her quietly.

'Is my drink not good enough for you.' He grabbed my arm above the wrist and squeezed it tightly.

'Enough's enough.' Frances pulled his face around to her and held it in one hand. She spoke straight at him. 'You're out of order, Knucky. Cut your losses and get the hell out of here.'

She made it clear that she was in no mood for any nonsense. Knucky leered at her like he wanted to hurt her badly but knew of no way other than violence. But Knucky did not want to be violent with her. He wanted to be violent with me instead. 'Get out, Knucky. Get the fuck out.' She practically slapped his face away.

Knucky let my arm go. He got off his stool, picked up his glass, and finished the rest of his pint. 'You're in this together,' he said. 'Don't think I don't know that.'

I thought he was going to throw his empty glass, smash it against something, but instead he placed it very gently down on the counter and left.

We watched after him until the door closed behind him. I swung back on my stool to the counter. Tom Harte and the pilot were watching it all. Frances leaned over, held the sides of my head, and kissed me on the forehead. She pulled away and smiled sadly at me.

'Back to business,' she said. She went over to the dishwasher and loaded it with dirty glasses.

'Here.' I pushed my untouched pint across to Tom. 'On account of your concern.' I left through the side door to avoid meeting Knucky.

I sat down at the edge of the small pier. The water splashed beneath the soles of my shoes. The lough was dotted with light all the way to its mouth with the returning boats. The chug of their engines drifted in and out on the winds competing with the hum of the Co-op. Things were going from bad to worse.

I lay down flat on my back and looked up at the sky. It too was dotted in light as though it were filled with boats also. Not ones returning but ones getting away.

I stared hard up at them, concentrating on their burning cores, until the sky was streaked with their movement as they expanded and contracted whirling like furious tornadoes of light reaching out to touch me.

The night I took LSD with Frances I gave myself up to them completely, soaking up their energy until I could whirl in their midst, shooting defiantly into their infinity. But now I clung to the ground and squeezed my eyes tightly shut. I didn't want to let go ever again. I didn't want to go that far out and still have to come back.

'How did you do?' Frances asked me when the effects wore off. She lay beside me holding my hand. 'Wasn't it incredible?'

It had been but in the most terrifying way possible. It was like catching a glimpse of Heaven from the gates of Hell and knowing there was no way out. But Frances said that was all that kept her going. The knowledge that another world did exist, one infinitely more appealing than this, a world that one day we might reach forever.

'Say a prayer for me,' she had whispered as she left.

I opened my eyes and sat up on the pier. My hands were trembling. The rumble of a helicopter came in from the hills on the other side. Its red lights burned a hole in the night sky. It hovered above the prison for what seemed like an eternity then veered off to the landing pad at the army camp. The red lights clung to the air, then sank to the ground and died.

CHAPTER TWENTY-THREE

Frank rang the following morning. The shrillness of the phone's tone convinced me it was Therese. I was almost afraid to answer it. Although I wanted desperately to talk to Therese I was relieved to hear Frank's voice. He told me he hadn't time to talk, but he had some news for me. I told him I'd buy him that pint we had talked about if he liked. He said he'd like that a lot. We arranged to meet that evening in The Porthole.

I held onto the receiver after Frank had put the phone down his end. I squeezed it in my fist and thought of Therese. I ought to ring her. Try to explain. Instead I replaced it carefully on the hook. No good was going to come of this.

For the want of something to do I walked into town. I saw Therese's car parked in the square and stopped to take stock of it. It was hard to know if it was God or the devil at work. I felt weak. I thought about turning around and heading back the way I had come, but instead I walked towards it. The window was half-open. The keys in the ignition. She couldn't be too far away. I looked around and saw her a few minutes later in the butchers. She was pointing in through the glass counter at a large slab of meat. I waited outside until she had finished. It was like spying on her all over again. This was the worst thing I could do. I felt nervous and uncomfortable. I decided that when she came out I'd make it seem as if I just happened to be passing by.

She stepped out onto the pavement and saw me immediately. It was obvious that I was waiting for her. The sweat ran in the curves of my palms. She looked at me then glanced away as though she were going to pass me by. Ignore me. But she looked back as if something she would live to regret had got the better of her. She came over.

'I don't usually approve of strong language,' she said, 'but you are a bastard.' Her slim fingers whitened as she dug into the red meat in the white plastic bag in her hands.

'I don't usually approve of being called one,' I told her, 'but in this case it's more than deserved.'

We stood there unsure what was to happen next. She folded her arms across her body, still holding the meat tightly in her right hand. Her eyes lost contact with me. She seemed to be deciding on something.

'I can't talk to you,' she said.

'We don't have to talk.' I felt awkward and clumsy. I didn't know where to put any part of my body.

'Oh, Christ, we do.' Her face turned in on itself. 'We have a lot of talking to do. If there is anything left to do.'

'Hold out for me,' I pleaded.

Therese looked around her as though suddenly afraid we might be noticed together. 'Give me more time,' she said. 'Then ring me.' She turned and went back to her car.

I looked down to the harbour from the top of the hill by the Allied Irish Bank. I hadn't expected to see the *Lorna Doone*. Once more I thought Knucky would have headed off to his own refuge. But she floated there ducking and weaving the waves and currents. Her new coat of paint gleamed in the morning light. Knucky was dressed in overalls and moved about her deck. He looked to be making a few last repairs. I'd have loved to set out in her then, into the wide open ocean, starting out afresh.

I walked down the hill across the green at the back of the hotel to the shore path. The path went all the way along the coast out to the open sea. If you weren't careful, you could walk right out into it. I walked down past the playground and the crazy golf course which was closed until the summer. Young mothers passed me by pushing babies in buggies. Elderly men and women strolled along the path enjoying the fresh sea air as though tasting the last of their breaths. A lone jet-ski cut through the water slicing its surface apart like a gash.

I walked around the path at the bottom of the cliff and back out onto the open fields. A row of bungalows lined the top of one of them. I hated to see them there almost as much as Frances did. But I had to admit it was the perfect spot for a site, and if I was offered one, I have no doubt I would have taken it.

I stepped down off the path across the sand. I tried not to think of Therese. I would ring her as she suggested. What else could be done?

The orange pilot boat sped back up the lough alone. The stray dog that continually roamed the shore ran up panting at my heels. I patted his head and regretted it immediately. It would be impossible to get rid of him now. He followed after me across the rocks and back up into the small hills and dunes. The larger houses were situated further up there. Set back into the hills overlooking all. Their white walls reflected back the light. Large anchors and other marine accoutrements adorned their expansive lawns. One had a small deer farm attached to the side. Some deer would eat at the grass while the others lay down or ran in their enclosure. Although Frances could have seen all the deer she ever wanted to right there, she said she always closed her eyes when she came to that part, that it was more than she could bear to witness.

I crossed over the right of way onto the front lawn of one of the houses. Like the road through the farmyard leading up onto the headland I could never get used to doing this. Usually I clung to the edges keeping out of sight as much as possible. But this time I strode right across the middle of the lawn with the dog yapping behind me. Intruding where I wasn't welcome seemed to have become a comfortable way of life.

Knucky told Frances and me that there was a small cottage hidden behind the trees up a laneway at the back of the house. If you didn't have someone like Knucky to tell you, you would never be aware of its existence. Frances and Knucky and I used to say we'd buy it when we could afford to. Make the owners an offer they couldn't refuse. And we'd live out our lives there, hidden from the rest of the world as though we could manage without it. We even drove across to the other side of the lough one time and climbed up into the hills with a pair of binoculars. We could see clear along the coast right out to the lighthouse and beyond, and although we could distinctly make out the town and all of our houses, the cottage was not visible at all. We focused the glasses right on the spot were Knucky knew it to be, but all we could see were the trees and shrubs surrounding it.

'Can't you imagine it?' Frances said. 'Can't you just imagine it?'

I walked out through the gap in the wall and climbed down onto the green slime-coated rocks. I stepped carefully across their slippery surface and over the sea pools between them. I tried to shoo the dog away, but he ran in circles around me, threatening to knock me over. I made my way back down onto the beach and sat down against one of the rocks. I threw stones for the dog to chase after, far out into the water. I looked at the square concrete block of the prison across the way. The loud reports from the firing range echoed again in the air above the lough.

That day we had driven across to the other side we had passed by the prison on our way to the pub down at the Point. The road led straight past its gates. Large barbed wire fences ran along the side of the road leading up to and away from it. It was surrounded from the back and sides by the firing range and by the water in front. A few cars were parked in the car park beside it. Some women and children waited at the gates. Directly across from the gates, on the grass leading down to the shore, was a row of picnic tables.

'Can you believe it?' Frances asked. She was furious. 'There are some seriously perverse people in this world. It's them that ought to be locked up instead.'

I suspected that Knucky, like me, would have liked to stop, to sit down at the tables, eat some sandwiches, and pull open a few cans of beer. I was worse than any of them. I should have told Frances that. We drove past the prison, about a mile down the road to the pub. We stopped and parked out front. Frances got out and slammed the door behind her. She walked over to the litter bin and leaned on it looking down at the beach. A group of children were gathered around a middle-aged man examining something. They looked to be on a school outing. Frances shook her head with despair. A man and woman dressed in lurid pink and green dry-suits dragged two windsurf boards out into the water.

'Looks like they're making a break for it,' I said. Frances just scowled. I was dying for a drink but didn't dare suggest it now. Knucky eventually took the decision.

'Well, I don't know about the rest of you,' he said, 'but I could drown a pint.'

He headed off towards the pub. Frances stared after him. Then she looked at me. I shrugged and followed after Knucky. Frances came and joined us a few minutes later.

'Will we damn ourselves for this?' she asked.

'Most probably,' I said and drank to it. It's what we had been doing all of our lives together. It was the one thing we couldn't seem to change.

The dog came running back up out of the water and shook itself all over me. I wiped the spray from my face and heard the jet-ski roar past. Then the engine cut and died. I looked up and saw it bobbing in the water. About twenty yards away somebody splashed wildly as they swam after it. I thought of the Eskimo, of his body sinking down with no thought of ever coming up.

When I looked around the beach for the dog again he was gone. Vanished without a trace.

Frank turned up after work. I was already mid-ways through my second pint.

'It's been an age,' he said sitting down. He tipped the side of my glass with his pint. 'Your health.' Then he sat back to enjoy the sour creamy taste. He licked his lips and wiped them with his hand. 'You've been busy. I was watching you and Knucky.'

All eyes in these parts were on everyone else. Always had been. It was worth remembering. 'Just knocking the *Lorna Doone* into shape.'

'She's looking well.'

I agreed.

He put his glass down. 'I've made some inquiries. I may have something for you.'

'What is it?' I asked. This was the first piece of information that was willingly being offered.

'I made contact with a few different people. There's an agent operating from out of Ramelton that seems to know something. I don't know him personally. In fact, he's not too well liked in these parts. Blew in about twelve years ago. Stole a lot of business. A friend of mine fishing out of there spoke to him for me. He was very coy about it all. But he's probably worth speaking to.'

I thanked Frank and told him I'd do just that. Frank looked quickly around the room. He nodded briefly at someone in the far corner.

Then pulled in close to me and spoke quietly.

'Just be careful,' he said. 'I've heard a lot of rumours about him over the years. Smuggling and the likes. Contraband.'

He put a special emphasis on this last word as though he loved the sound and feel of it. But he looked serious all the same.

'What's his name?' I would most likely have heard of him.

'Mullen. David Mullen.'

The name rang a bell.

Frank shrugged. 'He may be harmless, but it's best to know.'

'You're right,' I said. 'Better safe.'

Frank coughed harshly. He pushed his pint away from him. 'This is the worst of it. I'm losing my taste.' He sucked on his tongue. He looked sad. I didn't know what to say to him. He stood up. 'I'd better go.' He put a hand on my shoulder. 'You can ring him any time you want.'

I nodded.

'Just there,' he said, 'just for that moment you reminded me of your old man.' He winked and walked out slowly.

That was all I needed.

CHAPTER TWENTY-FOUR

I should have gone home after Frank left. I should have finished my pint and followed out after him, but I stayed. I thought about Mullen, the agent, the information he might have. And I thought about Therese. What might happen between us. I was optimistic about neither.

I stayed in the pub until closing then started home. I felt the urge for more alcohol. I knew I should fight it. Regain some control. Instead I turned back for The Grapevine.

I looked around on entering, but fortunately Therese was not there. I saw an empty table, sat down and ordered a bottle of white wine. I would learn some time, I told myself. It would not always have to be like this. The waitress came back, poured me a glass of wine and left the bottle on the table. I smiled as though she had just done me a favour. I wondered if I had the nerve to get up and leave.

'Jim, my old buddy. My partner in crime.' Charlie Doherty slapped me hard on the back almost knocking the glass from my hand.

'Charlie.' I smiled up at him. He was obviously the worse for wear. Sheila Donnelly stood at his side. She smiled sweetly, hiccoughed, and put her fingers to her lips in mock surprise.

'Oh, pardon me.' She was well on also. One touch and she could fall over. I got up and held a chair out for her. Charlie pulled one out for himself, turned it around, and sat on it cowboy fashion.

I hadn't seen Sheila for a long time. I had gone out with her sister, Andrea, for a few months when I was sixteen. She taught me all about love. All the nitty gritty parts. She got a job in Dublin after she left school, and I had hardly seen her since. I probably wouldn't have recognized her if I had.

'So what's up?' Charlie leaned his elbows on the back of the chair and rested his chin on the back of his hands. 'Didn't expect to find you here on your own.'

'Oh, you know how it goes.'

Sheila reached across for my glass. 'Do you mind?' she asked and took a drink before I could reply.

'Do you know each other?' Charlie asked.

'Oh, we most certainly do.' Sheila grinned. 'Jim and Andrea went out together. Oh years and years ago now. ' She laughed seductively. 'I learned everything I know from watching them.'

Charlie winked over at me. 'I got to hand it to you.'

Sheila took the bottle by the neck and poured it liberally into the glass. 'Did you know that? Did you know I used to watch you together.'

'Of course I knew, ' I lied. 'Why do you think we used to put on such a show.'

Charlie grinned inanely and brought us right back to the present. 'So where is she? Where's the looker?'

'Your guess is as good as mine, Charlie.'

'Like that, huh?'

'Like that.' I called over the waitress and asked her to bring two more glasses.

'And we'll have one more of whatever that was,' Charlie said pointing at the bottle.

'I was just thinking about leaving,' I told him.

'You stay where you are, Gallagher. I'm putting you under house arrest.'

Another waitress brought a tray full of food to the table beside us. Dishes of pasta covered in a ripe red tomato sauce. The smell of garlic wafted in waves over us.

'My God, that's making me hungry.' Charlie rubbed his stomach.

'You've just got the munchies,' Sheila said laughing a little too loudly.

'Well whatever it is I got, I know I need some of that to cure it. ' He leaned back and grabbed the waitress by the arm as she brought the empty tray away. He looked down at the food on the table again, his gaze finally settling on a plate of garlic bread. 'Could you bring me some garlic bread? Anyone else?' He looked back at us.

I shook my head. Sheila put her hand on her stomach.

'I don't think I could,' she said.

'Charlie,' I suggested. 'Maybe you should turn your chair around. You're not up at the OK Coral with Sheriff Bonnar now.'

Charlie looked a little offended, then seemed to think better of it. He turned his chair in properly. The waitress arrived with the bottle and the glasses. Charlie filled them for us. '*Slainte*,' he said and held his glass up. We all tipped glasses and took a drink. Charlie looked around at everyone as though my mention of his place of work had instilled a sense of duty in him again.

The waitress returned shortly with his bread. She placed it down in front of him.

'You're my saviour,' he said and dove into it. He sucked his fingers. Melted garlic butter dripped down his chin. He licked at it with his tongue.

Sheila began to hum along to the music. Fats Waller's 'Honeysuckle Rose'.

'She's got the sweetest voice,' Charlie said smiling over at her. Sheila stopped humming and looked bashful. She stifled another hiccough.

Smoke drifted from somewhere and stung my eyes. I could feel the wine beginning to take effect. Charlie filled the glasses again. Drained off the second bottle. He held it aloft after he emptied it. He seemed to ponder something, then came to some sort of decision he was prepared to live with. He moved closer to me, leaned away from Sheila. She began to hum again.

'Here's something I shouldn't say. Proceed with caution.' He bit at his upper lip and looked for a way to say what was coming next. It seemed important to him to make everything he said come out in a cryptic fashion as if this avoided any real compromising of his position. 'Watch yourself, that's all.'

'What are you talking about, Charlie?'

'You know what I'm talking about, Jim.' His words were slurred. He spoke with extreme care.

'I wish to God I did.'

Charlie tapped the bottom of his glass against the table in an infuriating way. 'Let's just say Breaking and Entering is a serious charge.'

'What are you saying, Charlie?'

'Just what I said.' He looked into the remains of the wine in the glass, swirled it around, and finished it off.

'You got something, Charlie. You charge me with it.'

'You're tempting fate, Jim. Just be careful, that's all I'm saying. I'm on your side. I don't want trouble coming your way.'

'What trouble?'

'Whatever trouble you're thinking of self-inflicting. That's what trouble.'

Charlie pushed the empty glass away from him and put his arm around Sheila. He wanted this conversation to come to an end. Sheila rubbed his cheek with the backs of her fingers.

'Let's go dancing,' she said.

'I, for one, don't think I'm up to it,' I said. 'That second bottle of wine has finished me off completely.'

'Oh come on. Don't be such a spoilsport. What do you say Charlie?'

Charlie was eating and didn't seem to hear her. Suddenly her eyes widened like she had just thought of something quite brilliant. 'I know, Andrea's home for a few days. I'll give her a ring.' She grinned at me. 'Now there's an offer you can't refuse.'

'Let's just leave it.' Despite the effects of the wine I recognized how bad a decision that would be.

'Come on. I'm sure she'd love to see you. She's not going out with anyone at the moment. I bet she'd be only too delighted. You two could pick up where you left off from.'

'Believe me, Sheila, it would not be a good idea.'

'Course it would.' She looked like she was going to get up and phone.

'Sheila.' This time I put my hand out and placed it on her arm, to stop her. She put her other hand down on top of mine and held it warmly.

'Hey, what's going on here?' Charlie grinned but looked genuinely perplexed. He wiped his lips with his sleeve. I took my hand away again.

'I just want to go dancing.' Sheila put her arms around Charlie's neck. 'Pleassse,' she pleaded in a mock small-girlish voice. She flicked her tongue in his ear.

Charlie shrugged at me. 'What can you do?'

'I don't know,' I said. 'What can you do?'

Sheila smiled to herself. Glad for the lack of answers. She excused herself and went off towards the Ladies. The other bottle of wine was taking charge. My vision blurred and came back. I widened my eyes as much as I could, but this only seemed to make things worse. Charlie suddenly stood up. He looked terrible.

'Excuse me,' he said. He moved swiftly across the floor to the toilets. He was about to get sick.

I saw Sheila standing by reception talking to someone on the phone. It had to be Andrea. My own stomach lurched. What could you do?

Sheila had a taxi waiting outside. Andrea sat in the back. It surprised me how little she had changed. I told her this when I got in.

'What did you expect?' she asked.

'I had no expectations whatsoever other than some sort of alteration.' It had been almost fifteen years since we had gone out together. Since she had moved to Dublin, I had only seen her a couple of times that I could recall. And none of them recently.

'Fate,' Sheila said smiling back in at us from the front seat.

Charlie sat the other side of Andrea. He had the window half-down and kept his face turned to the breeze.

'How are you doing over there?' I asked.

'Never better,' he lied in a half-hearted fashion.

I remembered the last time I had seen him when he got sick, the day we brought the Eskimo in. It seemed like an eternity ago.

'Where are we going?' I lay back and closed my eyes. I wished I was going home. I felt unsafe. Particularly with myself. My chest tensed, tightened in on me. I blew out hard.

'Are you okay?' Andrea had a very concerned look on her face when I opened my eyes.

'Tired,' I said. 'That's all.' I knew she was feeling awkward. Probably wishing she hadn't allowed Sheila to talk her into this. 'I just hope someone knows where we are going.'

'The White Strand Hotel,' she said. 'That ought to bring back some memories.'

I didn't know who chose the venue or if it was being done on purpose, but that was where we had split up all those years ago. I had arranged to meet her there, but she was dancing with someone else when I arrived, and I had taken it personally. She said she felt obliged to. That it would have been rude to have refused him. She was afraid, she said, of hurting his feelings. What about my feelings? I had asked.

Was she not afraid of hurting them? Things got very dramatic then in an adolescent sort of way. The sort of way you hope to grow out of and never do. And that was it. We both stormed off in opposite directions.

'Were we stupid?'

Andrea shook her head. 'No. You were stupid.' She touched her bottom lip with her finger, pulled it lightly with its tip and released it, then pulled at it again. 'Is there any hope you've changed?'

I laughed loudly and fell against her shoulder. She didn't push me away. I listened to Sheila chat incessantly to the taxi driver. Approaching headlights lit up the darkness outside. The greyness of night.

I must have nodded off. At some point I woke and realized I was holding Andrea's hand. I tried to picture her but was unable to. The next time I awoke we had arrived.

'Are you sure you're up to this?' Andrea helped me out of the car.

'Just give me a moment,' I said. 'I'll be right as rain.'

Andrea looked to Sheila like she was looking for advice, advice she knew a younger sister wouldn't have. 'It's a man thing,' Sheila said casting her eyes towards Charlie. He was paying the driver. He still did not look well.

Once inside Charlie made for the bar and came back with a tray of drinks. I began to feel better at once. Andrea drank her gin and tonic down quickly. She had a lot of catching up to do. It had been years since I had been at a disco. The horror of it all came back to me. The pounding dance beat shuddered through the huge speakers. The coloured lights flashed manically. Sheila grabbed Charlie's hand and dragged him up to dance. Andrea spun the ice around in her empty glass.

'Let me get you another.'

She nodded. I had the terrible feeling that when I came back she would be dancing with someone else. That we would have to pick it up where we had left it off as if our life since then had come to a standstill. But as I made my way back I saw her still sitting there spinning the ice. Her hair was shorter than I remembered and lighter in colour, more fair than brown. Her figure was fuller, suited her frame more. Before she had been a little gangly. But her high cheekbones still gave her that eternally happy look. That was what had attracted me to her in the first place. It was just as attractive all over again. I only wished I knew where she fitted in at this moment in time.

'I thought you mightn't come back,' she said taking her glass from me, shouting over the music.

'I thought you mightn't be here.'

We both seemed resigned to the fact that we were.

'This was not a good idea, you know that?'

'I can't hear you,' I shouted back.

She laughed and looked down at Sheila and Charlie on the dance floor. I felt good all of a sudden. It was inexplicable really. It was like something big had dawned on me. Something I should have known all along. But in my heart of hearts I knew it was just the alcohol. Andrea said something which I couldn't catch. I moved in closer to her and asked her to repeat it.

'They're a good couple,' she said. 'They'll make it.'

'I don't know Sheila that well,' I said, 'but I like Charlie.'

'He's a sensitive sort.' She pushed her tongue into the side of her mouth and let her gaze wander towards nothing in particular as though considering if Charlie's sensitivity was a good or a bad thing. 'Come on.' She jumped up quickly and took my hand. 'Let's see if your dancing has improved any.'

We all ended up back in Charlie's flat next to the cinema in town. We drank tea and talked about how he lived with all that noise next door. Sheila said she envied him, envied how he had Russian trains passing by one moment and Amazonian waterfalls the next. Charlie looked at her as if she was crazy. Then moments later the two of them had disappeared. Charlie came back after a few minutes and threw a duvet on the living-room floor.

'It's the best I can offer.' He was gone again.

It was neither casual nor graceful, but Andrea and I climbed in beneath the cover to rediscover bodies we once had known.

By the time Charlie woke me the next day both Sheila and Andrea had left.

'She said to tell you she was going back to Dublin. And that she enjoyed herself very much.' Charlie made no effort to hide his grin.

I wondered how much more deeply I could possibly dig myself in.

CHAPTER TWENTY-FIVE

I rang the agent a few days later. I stalled as long as I could. The phone intimidated me. I feared its consequences. I passed it in my hallway and avoided it, dreaded its ring. I was wary too of what the agent might say, how he might easily dash my only real hope, but in the end I lifted the receiver, got his number from the phone book, and cautiously rang him.

His voice sounded abruptly after the first ring. 'Mullen. Yeah?'

I was taken by surprise by his sudden response and struggled for words.

'Mullen here,' he said impatiently.

I thought he might put the phone down as quickly as he had lifted it. There was no guarantee I would dial his number again.

'Jim Gallagher here, Mr. Mullen.' I heard the click of a keyboard the other end. I could see him in his office, the phone strangled beneath his chin, staring at a computer screen only halfways aware or interested in anything I might have to say.

'I don't know you,' he said. 'What's this about?'

I wondered how to proceed. I heard the sound of a door closing as though someone was entering or leaving his room, then the sound of muffled voices. I realized I didn't know the name of the man who had spoken on Frank's behalf. There might never have been any mention of me at all.

'Someone spoke to you about an Eskimo,' I went on. 'I'm the one who dragged him up in the nets. They said you might be able to help me.'

'What's that?' He spoke again to whoever was in the room with him. He didn't seem to be listening to me.

'I believe you might have some information about an Eskimo. I'd like to speak with you.' I spoke concisely as though this might somehow permeate the surrounding disinterest.

'What did you say your name was?'

'Jim Gallagher,' I repeated.

'Well Mr. Gallagher, what's it got to do with you?' He still sounded as though his attention was focused on something else, as though whatever I might have to say was of no real consequence.

'I found him. He came up in my nets. I was hoping you might be able to help me identify him.'

'I wonder.'

I didn't know what to make of this. I was unsure who ought to speak next.

'Let's see,' he said. I could still hear the keyboard clicking. 'It's Tuesday. Meet me here Thursday at six.' Then the phone went dead.

I needed to borrow Frances' car again. Maybe I'd have to ask her to come with me. I really didn't want to. Killybegs had led us nowhere. I didn't see the point in repeating the experience. Our whole lives had been spent repeating the same sorry experiences. It was time to learn from the past.

She was wiping down the tables when I called in to The Porthole. There was no one else in the bar. The radio was on low in the background, some agricultural programme discussing EC funding and policy. She looked up when I entered.

'Look what the cat dragged in,' she said. I hadn't seen her since the night of the row with Knucky.

I smiled. I nodded my head towards the harbour. 'I see Knucky's still at it.' He had been working on the *Lorna Doone* when I passed. I thought he might have seen me, but if he did, he didn't let on.

'Uh huh. There can't be much more left to do.' She went over behind the counter to wash out the cloth and empty the ashtrays she had gathered.

'I would have thought he'd be finished by now.' I sat up on a high stool.

'I suppose she needed a good overhaul.'

'Don't we all?' I resisted ordering a pint. I told her instead about the agent, about my meeting with him. Frances listened attentively.

'What do you think he might know?' she asked. The tap ran in the sink beside her. The water poured down the drain.

'Everything or nothing. I don't want to get my hopes up.'

She washed the filthy ashtrays under the flowing water and turned them up on the draining rack. 'You'll be needing the car, I suppose?'

'That's why I came.'

'Of course,' she said. I thanked her. She turned the tap off firmly. 'That's my afternoon off.'

It was not what I wanted to hear. Frances waited on my response. It was an obvious test, but I had no way of telling what reply she was expecting. There was no easy way around this.

'It'd probably be best if I went alone. Don't you think?'

She looked disappointed, like I would never learn. She reached behind her and switched the radio off sharply with her wet hand. Drops of water dripped from the dial.

'Yes,' she said. 'You're probably right.' She meant it too, but I knew she was bitterly disappointed.

I picked the car up on Thursday afternoon. I had thought about ringing Therese and asking her to go with me, but I was afraid of Frances finding out, of what that might do to us. And I was afraid that Therese would refuse. So I drove alone.

I was apprehensive about the meeting but glad to be out on the open road again. I took the back roads to Letterkenny and headed north up the coast of the Fanad Peninsula. I wondered if they felt as hemmed in there as I did across the way.

The day was grey and cold. A mist formed continually on the windscreen. The fields and the hills disappeared behind it. The roads narrowed and slipped between rows of hedges then emerged again. The muggy sky swept evenly to the horizon. I missed the company of someone else. I recalled being on my own in Alaska. At times I revelled in my own company, at other times I despaired.

I remembered the prostitutes at Prudhoe Bay. Women as lonely for company as the men they attended to. A number of Eskimo women among them offering an exotic attraction. I thanked God now I had never yielded. I had enough on my conscience as it was. There were far-fetched stories about the Eskimo women's abilities in bed. Their cultural deviances. Their sexual peculiarities. But nothing of their desires and their love.

I got Mullen's address from the phone book before leaving. I drove down through the town of Ramelton looking for his office. I turned left past the pier. A splash of seagull-dropping splattered across the front windscreen. The waves curled in noisily to the shore. A row of small narrow houses and shops lined the left-hand side of the street. His office was somewhere amongst these. A small whitewashed alleyway divided the buildings. I looked down the alley and made out his name on a chipped wooden sign on the side of the wall. It was only quarter past five. I still had three quarters of an hour to kill. I parked the car just past the alleyway and got out. A fine drizzle fell. I took my reefer jacket from the back, glad now that I had brought it along, and walked towards the water. The waves crashed against the headland. A dour, heavy mist shrouded the horizon. Except for the red spherical buoys dotting the surface the near waters were empty. A row of seagulls dithered at the end of the pier.

Off to my left a Guinness sign hung below the guttering on a short terrace of buildings. I pushed my hands deep into my jacket pocket and thought about it. Sooner or later I'd have to make a decision and stick to it. But right now did not seem the time. I walked through the drizzle into the bar.

An elderly lady sat behind the counter watching television, a rural soap opera. Two middle-aged men sat on barstools at the far end of the counter. They glanced over when I came in and then turned back to themselves. The lady nodded and said something about the weather. It was bad, I agreed, and ordered a pint. On consideration I asked for a whiskey as well. A green clock on the wall advertising Major cigarettes showed that it was almost half-past five. I sat watching the clock and the television while waiting for my drinks.

The lady brought me over the whiskey and placed it in front of me. A cold breeze blew through the gap in the door causing me to shiver. Burn marks from cigarette butts smudged the yellow tiled floor. I was nervous. Nervous of Mullen. Nervous of what he knew and what he didn't know. Nervous of myself. The pint arrived. I paid the lady, drank back the whiskey, and started on the Guinness.

The lady did not say a word. She turned her attention to the soap opera. The two men kept to themselves. The sharp warmth of the whiskey pinched my chest. I drank slowly and watched the clock until five minutes to six. I swirled the remains of my pint around the bottom of the glass and drank them down. I said a quick goodbye which was ignored by all and left.

The sky had darkened considerably. I turned up my collar into the water-laden breeze and walked back towards Mullen's office. Gulls wheeled above me in the dulled sky. Two cars passed slowly, their wipers wiping the light rain off the glass. I turned up the alleyway and saw stairs like a fire-escape leading up into a loft. Another faded sign identical to the one on the wall was attached to a blue wooden door. This was it, I thought, one of the few real moments of truth in my life. A cat mewed at the end of the alley. Its wet scraggy fur washed down in clumps against its scrawny body. We eyed each other up for a moment, then it tottered off. I blessed myself and made my way up the stairs.

I knocked hard on the door, determined not to show any sign of weakness. I heard a gruff *yeah* and opened the door inwards. A tall stocky man sat behind a desk, covered in paperwork, talking on the phone. The computer screen scrolled repeatedly. He nodded for me to sit down.

'Get it,' he ordered down the line. 'Then ring me back.' He replaced the receiver in the cradle and looked at me much as the cat had done. 'You Gallagher?'

I nodded. 'And you must be David Mullen?'

'You're clever,' he said, *tsk*ing twice as though calling a dog. He leaned over to the computer and turned it off.

He looked to be in his late fifties. He swept his fingers through his curly mess of greying hair. His chunky face was stubbled with a day's growth. I wondered if he was dangerous if you got on his wrong side. It was too soon to tell.

Boxes of overflowing paperwork were strewn around the office. A large overcoat lay crumpled across a wooden chair. An uneven row of out of date calendars with pictures of busty women in swimsuits was tacked to the wall. The green paint had flaked where the tacks were driven in. He saw me looking at them and winked.

'It's my harem,' he said. 'Not bad for an old guy, huh?' I was unable to respond. Mullen coughed then sniffed the air. 'Aha! You've already imbibed.' He looked pleased with himself. He opened the top drawer in his desk and pulled out a half-empty bottle of Jameson whiskey. 'You won't mind if I do a bit of catching up then.' He took out a single glass and poured himself a drink. He didn't offer me any. 'So Gallagher,' he snapped after a quick taste, 'what's your story?'

The office was poorly lit. A sky-light in the roof proved almost useless with the darkness of evening. A pale bulb no more than forty watts hung from the ceiling. Mullen held his glass and waited on my reply. Where could I begin? It was a question I had never been able to answer. It was perhaps the only answer I had ever been looking for.

'My story begins with finding an Eskimo snared in my fishing nets,' I told him. I watched his face carefully. His expression did not change. 'I want to find out who he is.' I waited. Mullen took a drink of whiskey and sucked in his lips.

'It's an old story,' he said. He put his glass down and folded his arms on the desk in front of him.

'What's important,' I reminded him, 'is who's telling it. And the difference this time is that my life depends on it.'

Mullen *tsk*ed again. 'It's interesting, isn't it, how curtailed our stories really are?'

'How much more do you want to hear?' I pulled my chair in closer to the desk.

He shrugged his shoulders. 'That's up to you.'

'I could use a drink,' I said nodding towards the bottle.

Mullen pulled another glass from the open drawer. 'You only have to ask.'

I wanted to tell Mullen everything. He seemed to possess that air of criminality that I had so much relished when breaking in to the harbour masters' offices. It was as if, apart from Father Jack – maybe even more than Father Jack – he was the only real person I could trust, ludicrous as this might have seemed. I wanted to tell him all those things I could not tell Frances or Knucky about my relationships with them. About my need to get away from Donegal and my need to return. About Therese, how much I felt for her and how little I showed it. What I told him instead were the details of my finding the Eskimo, how no one in authority seemed capable of tracking him down. I told him all that I knew from Charlie, Dr Brennan, George Fleming, the porter, everyone. It was like when I had spread out across my table at home all of the information I had gleaned in the hope that something relevant, something absolute, would reveal itself.

Mullen listened throughout, filling our glasses as required. 'So, that's it,' he said when I finished.

'That's it.'

He brought his glass to his lips, spoke from beneath it. 'What do you want me to do about it?'

'Frank Bonnar told me he had asked someone to speak to you about it. He said you might know something.'

'Is that a fact?' Mullen asked.

'That's how I heard it?'

Mullen considered what to say next. The phone rang. He picked it up. I sat back so as not to appear to be listening in although I could not avoid hearing all that he said.

'I told you to get it,' he shouted down the line. 'For fuck's sake!' He looked up at me. I turned my gaze away. He continued to stare, then he turned his attention back to the phone. 'Don't go fucking me over. Just don't do that.' He listened to the response. He didn't seem satisfied with it. 'Well who the hell else will?' His voice was still raised angrily. He slammed down the phone. He breathed out heavily and looked over at me again. 'You can't depend on anyone these days. Take that to heart.'

I did.

'Now you.' His anger was transferred to me. As if I was someone else he had to take care of. 'Gary McElhenny.'

He clearly expected me to respond to this. I had never heard the name before.

He looked exasperated. 'McElhenny spoke to me.' I nodded. It had to be him. 'I'm telling you what I told him, something about an Eskimo rings a bell. I heard about that one you fished out of the water. To tell the truth, I didn't think twice about it until McElhenny started asking. There was something a few years ago, but I'll be damned if I know what.' He narrowed his eyes. 'That's it,' he said.

That wasn't enough. That couldn't be all. 'Can't you remember what it was?'

Mullen *tsk*ed. 'My memory, what I make of it, is my business.

You want to do business with me?'

I heard a light scratching at the door. Then a loud mew. Mullen got up and went over to open the door. The bedraggled cat strolled in and jumped up on the overcoat lying on the chair. Mullen banged the door shut. The light above the desk flickered on and off.

'How can we best arrange it?' I asked.

Mullen took out a handkerchief and blew his nose. He pointed at the boxes around the room. 'There,' he said. 'That was it before this machine took over.' He ran his hand, still clutching his handkerchief, across the computer monitor. 'Two and a half grand's worth of intelligence. I have only had it six months, but already I don't know how I ever managed.' He took his seat again. He looked at the almost empty bottle. The cat stretched and extended its sharp claws. Mullen placed his hands on the desk. 'I keep good paperwork. What you're looking for lies in there,' he swept his hand towards the boxes again, 'and in here.' He tapped the side of his head. 'What I'm looking for lies in there.' He stabbed his finger repeatedly in the direction of my heart. 'Spondulicks.'

He was after my wallet. 'How much?' I asked.

'How much is your life worth?'

It was a fair but frightening question. I had no idea what information Mullen had. Whether it related to my Eskimo or not. Whether it would have any relevance at all. I told him this.

He was unperturbed. 'That's the gamble.' He smiled, rubbed his fingers across his teeth. 'Let me tell you something. There are ships coming and going on these waters every day of the week. The schedules can tell you that.' He looked at his fingernails. They were chipped and dirty. 'The men in customs could tell you something else. The pilots would have their side of it. But people like me, we know the inside story.' He spread his mouth as if to say that was the truth of it.

The whiskey was beginning to numb my senses.

'The gamble is this,' he continued. 'Five hundred quid.'

I had the money to pay him, I just wondered about the sense of it.

'The inside story,' he repeated for effect.

'Okay. It's a bet.'

What else could I do? I had already come this far, I could see no other way of proceeding any further.

He spat in the palm of his hand and held it out for me to shake. I grasped it firmly. I felt his saliva in my palm like mucus. He held me there a moment. 'One other thing. This is between you and I now. You remember that.' He gave a short, meaningless laugh.

He said to contact him again in a week's time. He'd tell me how he was getting on. Then he let me show myself to the door. I drove back home in the dark. My headlights swept across the night revealing parts of an unlit world. This was my business now, shining lights on elements of my life. I had no idea what I was getting into with Mullen. It could be something harmless, but it could be anything else, something much worse. I felt drunk. I should not have been driving.

CHAPTER TWENTY-SIX

I dropped the car off at Frances' and walked home, then went straight to bed and fell asleep. All night long Therese and the Eskimo wandered in and out of my dreams. Several times I awoke, but each time I fell back asleep the dreams returned. I rang Therese first thing in the morning. There was no reply.

Between the dreams and the drink the night before my head was clogged up. I went out for a walk to clear it. I joined up with the coastal path and walked into town. The fresh breeze felt good. A few boats fished the lough. I felt in need of a coffee so I turned up towards the hotel stopping in at a newsagents to buy the local paper. The front page was taken up with news of the cruise ship that was soon to include the lough in her itinerary. The first time in twenty-five years a passenger ship would have sailed these waters. The last time one sailed it was taking people away for a new start in America. Never to be seen again.

I remembered the last morning I had woken up in Valdez with a godalmighty hangover and the stale smell of vomit suffocating the room, with little memory of what had gone on the night before, knowing that it would have been no different than any other time. Without any real conscious decision I showered, packed my belongings, and went down to take the ferry to Whittier. I boarded it and as it started up I took a last look at the bleak factories, the dark waters, and the long low supertankers docked at the Alyeska Terminal in the port. As we turned into the Narrows into the Valdez Arm and out into the Prince William Sound I tried not to think about where I was going to or where I was coming from.

I watched the seals and the porpoise loping through the waters as if they hadn't got a care in the world. I got off at Whittier and took the train to Anchorage. We rocked our way through the blackness of the tunnel, blasted through the heart of the mountains during the war, and back out into the light. I caught the bus to the airport and took the next plane home. We took the short route over the North Pole. It was that easy now. That uncomplicated.

The next time I saw Valdez and the Prince William Sound after that was on the television during the oil spill. In the beginning I couldn't tear myself away from the news reports, the oil soaked beaches, the birds' lives dripping away in thick black gunge, the inadequate boons unable to contain the darkest drowning sea, but shortly afterwards I stopped watching altogether. Frances was consumed by it too. Although she had never been there herself, she said she felt as if a part of her had never been anywhere else. At one time she even discussed us all going out there to help, but I told her we'd be more of a hindrance than anything else. The truth was I couldn't have stomached it. And maybe that more than anything else was what would keep me from ever going back.

Even yet a shiver ran through me as I thought about it. I paid for the paper and went up the main street to the hotel. I was looking forward to a coffee and a quiet read. I opened the doors into the foyer and almost left again. Father Jack and Hal were sitting together at a table by the fire. They both looked up as I entered, and there was no going back.

'Ah, Jim. Talk of the devil.' Father Jack grinned over at me.

'Father Jack.' I smiled and clutched the paper under my arm more tightly.

'You'll join us.' He pulled a chair out for me to sit on.

Hal gathered up some loose papers and closed over a file he had open in front of them. He kept his head down as though he were intensely busy.

'You'll have some coffee.' Father Jack shouted across the foyer to the receptionist to bring another cup. 'We were just talking about you.'

'Nothing bad I hope.' It didn't sound as humorous to me as I had intended. I put the paper down on the table beside me.

'You know Hal of course.' Hal was forced to look up. He nodded. He looked uncomfortable. It was not a look I would have associated with him.

'We were talking about islands. Remote islands. People buy them

221

it seems. Use them like holiday homes, visiting a couple of times a year for a week or two at a time, bringing enough provisions for an army for a year.' Father Jack laughed at his repetition of someone else's small joke. 'I'd like to do that for when I retire. But I haven't the money or the character. It'd take a very special person to live on a remote island. Someone who could take the lack of habitation. The singular solitariness of it all. I was saying the only person I could think of was yourself. Any man that survived Alaska the way you did.'

'That was different.' Although I didn't say it, I would have thought that Father Jack's profession, if you could put it that way, would have prepared him more than anyone for that way of life.

Hal ran his fingers along the edge of the file as if testing its boundaries. He looked everywhere but at me. Father Jack kept talking. Keeping the conversation moving along swiftly. He looked pleased with himself. Ebullient.

'I bet Jim here could put you in touch with quite a few uninhabited islands up in the northern hemisphere. You two could strike a deal on it.' He grinned first at me and then at Hal. 'Hal here could take you on as an agent. A scout of sorts. I tell you if you two pulled together, you'd have it made. Jim running around the outer reaches of our world picking up these forgotten islands and Hal passing them on. What do you say men? You going to shake hands on it?' He was thoroughly enjoying himself. Practically rubbing his hands with glee.

'I don't think so,' I said. 'I hate to put a damper on your plans, but I'm not sure I've seen an island yet that wasn't in its proper place. That didn't have as much habitation as it already needed.'

Hal's mouth and eyes wrinkled at their corners. It was impossible to say if he was smiling or grimacing. He cleared his throat as if about to speak, but said nothing. I looked beyond him to the large clock above the fireplace. A half-grandfather clock. A long brass pendulum swung behind a glass door beneath the full smoky face. A fine line of inlay ran along the length of the mahogany casing. Father Jack saw me looking at it.

'It's a beauty, isn't it? I've had my eyes on it for over thirty years. Never lost a minute that I've noticed in all that time.'

Hal looked back over his shoulder at it. He didn't seem to know what to make of it. The door of the hotel opened, and he looked away from the clock towards it. We all turned around. An elderly couple came in, stood in the foyer for a few moments, and walked out again. Father Jack looked keen to get the conversation moving again. If he had seen me in the bushes the week before, he gave no indication of it. But I needed to know where he fitted into this.

'So Hal, how's Therese's business coming along?' The suddenness and content of my question surprised even myself.

Hal placed both palms on the front of the file. He spread his fingers and stared at the spaces between them as if the answer he was looking for lay somewhere in there. 'These things take time,' he said. He glanced up at me as if I knew all of this already.

The receptionist came over carrying a tray with a single cup and saucer. 'I'm sorry for the delay. There was no one in the kitchen. I had to get it myself in the end.'

Father Jack thanked her graciously. He began to pour me a cup.

'What about you Father, do you know Therese Doherty at all?' I could scarcely believe I was asking these questions. It was as if someone or something else had taken control of my tongue. My heart raced. I sought to keep my body steady. I was certain that the stream of coffee Father Jack was pouring dipped in its trajectory momentarily.

'I believe I do. I knew some of her family way back.' He topped up his own cup and asked Hal if he wanted more. Hal shook his head. Father Jack placed the coffee pot down in the centre of the table, then poured a spoonful of sugar into his cup. 'One of my vices,' he said. He looked me right in the eye.

He had answered truthfully, nevertheless there was a certain evasiveness to his response it seemed. But what was I expecting, that he would answer that yes, he did know her, that he had dinner with her in fact, had embraced and kissed her on the cheek?

'I hear you found a body.' I was as ill-prepared for Hal's statement as I had been for my questions. He was clearly seeking to level the playing field.

'I don't like to talk about it,' I said. Hal suppressed a smile, but let it be known that he was suppressing one. I wondered about his islands, if any of them were lost in international waters uncertain who they belonged to if anyone. Yet it seemed to me that this was what we were all striving for, a place where no one could make claims upon us, where we could be ourselves and nothing more.

Father Jack leaned in towards me and spoke in a low voice suggesting privacy, but not low enough that Hal could not hear.

'If you ever do want to talk about it.' He let the rest remain unsaid. He drained off his coffee and stood up. 'Now I'd really better be getting off. There's a world of sinners out there ready to teach me a thing or two.' He threw a few pound coins onto the table to pay the bill, checked his watch against the clock, and began to leave. He turned back at the door and spoke over to Hal. 'Keep me informed.' And then he was gone.

I took a drink of coffee and watched Hal. I waited for him to look at me. I smiled over at him when I finally caught his eye.

'What do you say, Hal, why don't we go and get drunk, just you and me together?'

Hal picked up his file and pushed back his chair from the table. 'Another time, perhaps.' He got up and walked out.

I have no idea what had come over me.

There was an occasion in Anchorage when 1 was camping in the middle of the city in someone's front garden for a few dollars a night. It must have been one in the morning, or more, and the sun had still not set. I sat outside my tent reading a newspaper someone had left behind when a taxi pulled up and two men got out. The driver opened the trunk, and they lugged out two huge backpacks and three large canvas hold-alls. One of the men was in his late thirties, slim but strongly built, with a straggly brown beard, looking like the mountaineer he most certainly was. The other was in his mid-fifties with a white beard and white hair. A big stocky man wearing a khaki jacket and trousers with two large belts criss-crossing his chest. He looked unreal. Like someone out of a Hollywood jungle adventure.

'Howya doing?' He boomed across at me. He walked over and stuck out his large calloused hand. 'Paddy's the name.' A thick Irish accent broke through the stillness of the night. I didn't want to reply, afraid of what was certain to happen next. But I couldn't see any way out of it.

'Jim,' I said and took his hand.

'Well what do you know,' he roared looking over at his companion who was paying the taxi driver. 'A fellow Irish man. Another one from the Old Sod. We're proliferating, that's what we're doing.' He threw his backpack and hold-all onto the ground beside me. 'Just back in from the Brookes Range.' He continued shouting as though there still might be one person somewhere out there unable to hear him. 'Led a party through a section of mountain never crossed by humans before. Bloody dangerous occupation.'

He began to spill the contents of his hold-all out onto the ground. 'Are you hungry?' he roared. 'We'll fire up the old stove. Get a bit of a stew going.' He rifled through packages of freeze dried pasta and zip-lock bags with all sorts inside. 'Here. You may as well have these.' He began to stack mounds of teabags and plastic bags of pink lemonade powder in front of me. 'No need for these in the Sunshine State.' He was on his way back to California he told me. Had lived there for over twenty-five years. Originally from Dublin. Out near Churchtown. But had never gone back. 'I'd be afraid to,' he said. 'Afraid of what I might find there.' The man he had come with had his tent up now and bid us goodnight as he got in.

'Are you off?' Paddy roared. 'Will you not have a bite of an old stew?' He turned back to me. 'Think I'll sleep out in the open myself. One last night beneath the stars.'

Another taxi pulled up and someone stumbled out after a hard night on the town. Paddy called into the driver shamelessly and asked him if he knew the times of the buses to the airport in the morning. He said he didn't, but he'd ring in and see if he could find out.

'Good man yourself,' Paddy said when he told him the times. 'Are you hungry? I'll fire up the old stove.' The driver wisely refused and drove off.

Paddy finally got the stove on and put some potatoes and carrots and meat into a small pot with some water. As it cooked he told me how they had found a crashed plane up in the mountains. 'It could have been there forever,' he said. 'No one might ever have known about it if we hadn't gone in.' He told me how he had found a body in it. The skeleton of a man crumpled over the wheel. 'Brought him into the tent with me that night. Laid him down beside me.' He took a big spoonful of stew from the pot and pushed it into his mouth. A soupy mixture dribbled down his beard. He wiped it with the back of his hand. 'Now I'll tell you this, Jim. I'm not a man to scare easily, but I didn't sleep a wink that night.'

'What did you do it for?' I asked. 'Why didn't you just leave him where it was?'

'I couldn't bear to. I couldn't bear to leave him lying out there alone in the cold for one more night.'

Then he told me he had radioed in with details of the plane when they got back and discovered it had been missing for twenty-eight years.

'Missing even before I had left the Old Sod. What do you think about that?'

I didn't know what to think or what to believe. But I heard him tell the same story again the next morning, in front of his companion, to the lady who owned the house. The lady was enthralled with him, wouldn't let him take the bus but insisted on driving him to the airport herself.

For reasons I couldn't explain I knew it was Father Jack who had brought back the memory of Paddy, of his outrageous persona and the humanity behind it. I thought of the human remains mysteriously scattered in unknown locations. And despite sitting in the warmth of the lobby, the fresh chill of the Alaskan air settled on my goose-bumped skin.

CHAPTER TWENTY-SEVEN

Knucky continued to work on his boat every day. I'd see him from time to time carrying tools and parts down to it or up on deck doing one thing or another. I kept out of his way. I hoped he was working his anger out of him. Frances kept her distance from him also. She had heard about Andrea and I being together at The White Strand from someone down at The Porthole, and between that and my decision to go to Ramelton alone she was keeping a distance of sorts from me too. We were isolating ourselves in ways we could never have contemplated. Whatever it was that was happening now it was a dreadful thing, but we had to keep on working our way through it in the hope that there was a way out.

I kept stumbling along in the dark, being driven by instinct. An instinct I had no assurance I could depend on. I finally plucked up the courage to ring Therese again. One last desperate act. There was no reply. It was as if she had opted out of this world. No longer existed. Yet her life persisted within me.

The Eskimo returned to my dreams. Dreams that had apparent-ly nothing to do with him whatsoever. He made appearances in the most unexpected places as if he had somehow slipped out of his own dream and couldn't find his way back. His rotting body seemed to deteriorate with each encounter. I woke from the middle of one such dream and heard a loud mournful groaning in the pitch dark of my room. As I gripped the sheets and listened I realized I was hearing the pathetic sound of my own body.

The following morning I decided to partially take Father Jack up on his offer to talk to him. I went to early mass. It had been years since I had gone to mass other than on a Sunday morning. Not since I was at school. I sat in at the back. About twenty people were spread around the church. Mainly elderly men and women praying to themselves. A young boy, no more than ten years old, sat by himself a few seats in front of me. I didn't know what I was doing there. I wondered if any of them did. A couple of short coughs interrupted the stony silence. Then the echo of feet tapping on the tiled floor as someone else entered. An old man made his way right to the top. His frail footsteps resounded importantly the whole way up. I looked around at the Stations of the Cross hanging on the walls. The cold carved stone figure of a pained Christ making the arduous journey to His death. Then I looked at the crucifix hanging above the altar. The lonely down-turned head of a wronged man, and the outstretched bloody hands.

Another set of footsteps echoed. Frances walked up the aisle past me. She stopped about halfways up, genuflected, and moved into the long wooden pew. She knelt down and blessed herself. I was completely taken aback. She had told me herself she wished she could believe more. But hearing her say this was one thing, watching her pray at early morning mass was another. Before I could contemplate it further the sacristy door clicked open, and Father Jack walked out on the altar. He stood in the centre in his long white surplice and soutane, the crucifix high above his head, his hands held aloft. Powerful and glorious. The blessing began.

I felt faint. As though all the air was being sucked from the church. I held onto the seat in front of me and steadied myself. The wave of weakness passed over. I breathed in deeply, the words I knew so well trundled out of their own accord. A ray of early morning sunlight beamed through one of the long thin windows and spread across the centre of the aisle. Flecks of dust flittered like midges in its light. I listened to Father Jack's deep voice. As intricately a part of the church as the wood and the stained glass. Its sonorous chant swept me through the ritual without any conscious knowledge of time. Moving and reciting at will.

I watched him kiss the chalice and thought of those same lips on Therese's flesh. I could taste the rich red wine pouring over his tongue and down his throat. At Communion I waited until Frances got up, then I got out of my seat and followed up the aisle after her.

'Body of Christ,' Father Jack placed the communion host on her upturned palm.

She seemed to hold it there a moment, testing its weight, then said, 'Amen,' and placed it on her tongue. She gave no sign of recognition as she turned past me. Nor did Father Jack when I stepped forward. It was as if we were in another world. One where none of us recognized each other. Where individual identities ceased to exist.

'Body of Christ.'

I murmured, 'Amen,' closed my eyes, and extended my tongue. I felt the thin wafer cling to its surface, contract across it. I withdrew it into my mouth and opened my eyes. I saw the angels painted on the high dome ceiling fly in circles above me, then lose their momentum and crash to the earth as the world was plunged into darkness.

Frances sat with me outside on the cold steps of the church. The early morning traffic passed by the gates. The boats moved slowly down the lough towards the bay.

'Are you all right?' She peered up into my face, her own twisted with concern.

I felt my head shrink and expand. The flesh beneath my chin leading to my throat tingled. 'I'm sorry,' I apologized. 'I'm beginning to make a habit of this.'

Frances squeezed my hand. 'As long as you're okay.'

The crystals embedded in the stone steps sparkled beneath me. 'I'm fine. Really,' I said. I felt as if I might faint again at any moment. I tried to stand up, but my legs wobbled, and I slunk back down.

'Take your time,' Frances helped lower me back down like I was an invalid. Someone who had lost control of their own body.

'You're an angel,' I told her before I remembered how they had soared and fallen.

'And you're an unwell man.' Frances rubbed her thumb along the veins in my hand. Following their paths. 'I should never have moved out. Perhaps I should never have moved in.'

'Help me up will you? Before everyone starts coming out.'

Frances put her arm around my waist and her other hand in under my arm. I stood up and rested on her support. I waited for my head to clear then walked down the steps.

'Here, put your arm around my shoulder.' Frances lifted it around the back of her neck.

'What will anyone think who sees us,' I said, 'coming out of the church with our arms around each other?'

Frances gripped me tighter and laughed. 'They'll be queuing up tomorrow. Father Jack won't know what's hit him.'

We went across the road and sat down on one of the benches on the green. There was no one else around.

'How are you feeling now?'

'A lot better. Really.' I joined my hands behind my head. I felt cold and shivery. Frances folded her arms across her stomach. 'Do you go often?' I asked. 'To early mass I mean.'

'Most mornings recently.' She sat back upright on the bench. She ran the sole of her shoe lightly across the blades of grass.

'I didn't know,' I said.

'I don't tell you everything.' She seemed as disappointed by this as I was.

'Once you did.'

She shook her head. 'No. I never did. You just thought that.' She pushed her hands up her sleeves.

'Is it helping you? Going to mass?'

'It's something to do.' She squinted as though trying to settle her vision on a single distant point. 'I think I'm infatuated with Father Jack. That has something to do with it.'

She looked at me, her lips pushing upon one another, her forehead furrowed. She wanted me to explain something to her. She wanted me to understand what she was telling me, then to explain it to her.

'I'm sure it's nothing like that, ' I said. 'He certainly strikes an impressive figure up there on the altar. But that's as it should be.'

'No,' she said. 'It's more serious than that. It's more serious than you can imagine.'

A blur of consciousness rushed past the backs of my eyes. I shut them tightly and held the wooden seat. I was frightened of what was to come.

'Don't,' I said. I opened my eyes. Frances was staring out at the water.

'My own thoughts scare me,' she said. 'It's a terrible position when that happens, don't you think?'

'It's okay.' I took her arm in mine.

'Imagine making love to Christ,' she said. 'Imagine the grief of it.' She pulled hard against me.

'There's nothing wrong with thoughts,' I said. 'It's the actions that count.'

'No, that's where you're wrong, Jim. That's where we're all wrong.' She rubbed my arm with her hand. 'We're a doomed race, Jim. You and I.'

I heard the footsteps and chatter of the small congregation leaving the church. I looked back, across the road, and saw Father Jack at the door talking to one of the women. He laughed hard. Frances heard his laughter and looked around sharply.

'God help me,' she said. 'God help us all.'

CHAPTER TWENTY-EIGHT

I rested up for the next few days. Frances insisted on dropping by to prepare my meals. Neither of us knew what to do about it. I didn't want to accept her offer, but I couldn't refuse. I was badly in need of her assistance.

When my strength returned enough I contacted Mullen. He was as rough and offhand as ever. He wouldn't say anything on the phone.

'I'll see you Saturday,' he said. 'Same time.'

Once more there was no negotiating with him. Everything was on his terms.

Frances was firmly against my going. I had to tell her about it in order to borrow the car.

'You're not fit for it,' she said. 'Not just the journey. You need a break from this Eskimo for a while. Whatever he has to tell you can wait.'

'Don't you understand?' I asked. 'It's the lack of knowledge that's making me ill.'

'No,' she said. 'It's what you're doing with the lack of knowledge that's making you ill. Just take a couple more weeks, that's all I'm suggesting.'

'The ships will be back soon. The next season's only a few more weeks off. I don't have time.' This was the truth of it. In a few weeks the factory ships would be returning. It was possible, even probable, that the Eskimo's ship would be amongst them. It was on the tip of Frances' tongue, I knew, to suggest coming along with me, but she couldn't bear to be refused again.

'It's up to you,' she said.

On Saturday I borrowed the car and set off once more. I had withdrawn the five hundred pounds from the bank the day before. I placed it in my shirt pocket sealed in an envelope. I felt it there like Mullen's saliva on my palm. I truly felt part of a conspiracy now, and oddly it was very consoling.

The evening was overcast as usual. I got there a little early and had my whiskey and pint chaser in the same pub as before. The same lady was behind the counter. The same men were at the bar. Afterwards I walked up the alleyway and up the stairs. The cat was the only thing missing, but sure enough he was inside sitting on the overcoat when Mullen told me to come in.

'Well if it isn't my old friend,' he said. He looked at his watch. I observed his strong muscular arm. 'You keep good time. I'll give you that much.'

The dull office light cast murky shadows around the room. 'Next time I'll bring a brighter bulb along,' I said flicking my eyes upwards. 'Help throw some light on the situation.'

Mullin creased his eyes. He scratched at the inside of his ear. 'Your humour is not the most appealing thing about you,' he said.

'Tell me, what is?'

Mullen eyed the bulge in my shirt pocket. 'That is.'

'This is the stake,' I said. 'It's time for you to lay out the cards.'

'Money first.' He rested his elbows on a wad of papers piled on the desk in front of him. He joined his stout fingers together.

This is what it had come down to. Gambling all or nothing. I pulled the envelope from my pocket and threw it on the table. He lifted it up and squeezed it between his fingers. Then tore it open and flicked the notes with his thumb.

'It looks close enough,' he said.

'Five hundred even.' A tremor ran through my hands and arms. My head twitched involuntarily.

Mullen opened the drawer the whiskey had been in the time before. He threw the envelope into it, then closed it over. He sat there silently looking at me as though that was it, as though there was nothing more to come. He stared and *tsk*ed twice. I held my ground. On cue the phone rang. Mullen looked down at it and then back at me. I almost thought he was going to tell me to answer it.

233

'The bane of my life,' he said. It continued to ring loudly. He lifted the receiver. This time there was no verbal abuse. 'I see,' he said. He looked unconcerned. 'Be that as it may.' He fiddled with the flex of the phone. He looked over at me and rolled his eyes. 'Well that's it then.' He put the phone down. 'You win some, you lose some. But then you know that.'

I had still to find out. 'What have you got?' I asked.

Mullen got up and walked over to one of the boxes pushed against the wall. He pulled a bulging green file out from the top of it. 'It took me forever to find,' he said. He waved it in the air above his head. Papers slipped and appeared at its edges. He sat back down straightening them up. 'It's from five years back. Who would have thought? I was looking at those from three years ago. Then four. It slips us by, time.'

He didn't look the sort to get too philosophical. I just wanted to know what was in it.

'Before we begin,' he said opening the drawer again. He pulled out a new bottle of whiskey and two glasses. He broke the seal and poured out two stiff ones. He put his hand back into the drawer and ran his fingers across the envelope. 'To wishful thinking,' he said toasting me. He drank and wiped his thick lips with the back of his hand. 'What's this Eskimo to you?' he asked. He put his glass down on the chubby file.

'I found him. I told you.'

He *tsk*ed. 'There has to be more than that.'

'I feel responsible. That's all. I owe it to him to identify him.'

'You owe it to him or yourself?' He grinned oafishly.

'Who knows?' I tasted the whiskey on my lips, on the tip of my tongue. The cat stretched, dug its sharp claws into the back of the chair. The scratching sound caused Mullen to look over.

'Five hundred pounds could be considered a lot of money.' He continued to look at the cat. 'What would you have done if I had said a thousand?'

'I'm really not sure. I'm glad you didn't.'

He looked back to me, tapped the file with the bottom of his glass. 'Perhaps this is worth a thousand?'

'Perhaps not. Perhaps it's not worth anything at all.'

He took the glass off the file and flipped it open. 'What you need to understand,' he said, 'is that some of these fishermen don't exist. Not legally anyways. Some of what I do has to take that into account.'

He was telling me what I had failed to grasp all along. That one simple fact. My Eskimo could not be identified because he did not exist in the first place. I couldn't believe how foolish I had been to miss this. No doubt the guards and IMES were ahead of me on this. Another obstruction in their way.

'I take care of these ships. Cater for all their needs. You wouldn't believe?' He *tsk*ed and grinned that oafish grin again. He flicked through the papers in the file. Pulled out a receipt and pushed it across to me.

'Currency, supplies, all the paraphernalia. There is nothing I cannot or will not get for them. And that includes my confidence. My silence. That's why they come back to me. I'm going out on a limb for you in an effort to save your life.'

Mullen trusted his own words as little as I did. His concern did not stretch to my life. He was breaking confidence to earn a quick buck, nothing more, nothing less.

'What does this mean?' I asked him pointing to the receipt.

'Look down it. Surely a man like you can interpret the details. Form conclusions from a list of facts.'

I shook my head. 'You've got the wrong man, Mullen. That's why I've come calling on you.'

Mullen grinned pleased with himself. 'I'm indispensable, am I not?' He ran his finger down the list, stopped about halfways down. 'There.'

I was meant to recognize something. I looked at the item he was pointing to. Beef jerky.

'What about it?' I asked.

'We don't sell a lot of that around here,' Mullen said squinting up at me. 'Not for the Irish taste, it seems. I had to import it specially from an English supplier, came in over the border in the nick of time.'

'For the Eskimo?' It was making sense now.

Mullen winked. 'You're getting the hang of it,' he said. 'Deduction.' He tapped his forehead. 'It's what make us different from the primates. At least that's what we hope, is it not? What we've been counting on.'

'What was the name of this ship?'

'Right again,' Mullen said. 'Another distinction.' He wiped his mouth with his fingers. 'The *Balticskayaslava II*.'

The name rang a bell. I was sure it was on the list of ships I had. 'And you've never heard of another Eskimo on board any of the ships?'

'Never.' He shrugged. 'That doesn't say anything.'

But it must have said something. There couldn't be much that escaped Mullen. He shut the file over quickly. 'I've said too much already. I've stepped dangerously overboard.' He gave me a sinister look.

'I appreciate that,' I said.

Mullen stretched like the cat. 'I just hope you do.' He *tsk*ed again. He stood up and went over to replace the file. 'I'm going to tell you one last thing.' He kept his back turned as he spoke. 'The season starts up again soon.'

'I know that,' I said.

'I'm sure you do.' He was stooped over pushing the file back in to the box. 'I've started making arrangements.' He looked back over his shoulder. 'The *Skayaslava* is coming back. I have the dates.' He straightened up and grinned. 'But I think that might be worth another hundred. Wouldn't you agree?'

'Most certainly.' It was the easiest option.

'I can do business with you, Gallagher,' he said.

I wondered about going the whole way, making the most of his position. 'How much would the name be worth?'

Mullen looked serious. He shooed the cat off his overcoat and sat down in its place. 'You're missing it, aren't you?' he said.

'Missing what?'

'Something quite basic.' The cat slunk under the desk. 'I don't want to know about this Eskimo. I don't remember him from the first time. I didn't hear anything about a body. When those boats come back there's going to be enough of people asking questions. I'm not going to be one of them. A question like that could put me out of business for ever.' He put his hands on his knees and leaned forward. 'You would be wise to be very careful too.' It didn't sound like a warning more a matter of fact. He looked at me for a long time. 'Don't let me down, ' he said. He stood up as if to show me to the door.

'What about the schedule?' I said.

'What about the money?'

'I don't have it on me. But I'll get it.'

He smiled grimly. 'I don't have the schedule, but I'll get it.'

There was nothing I could do about it that night.

'There's no panic,' he said. 'Nothing's happening for a while. Send the money in. I'll ring you with the details.'

I wasn't sure I wanted him to have my number. But one way or another there was little I could do to prevent him. He only had to look in the phonebook. I wrote it down for him and left. The cat hurried out as soon as the door opened and disappeared into the dark.

I almost certainly had the ship I was looking for. This fact scared me more than anything had done so far. In a few weeks time I'd catch up with it. I didn't know what I'd do then. But this hadn't stopped me so far. When the time came I would act, and in return receive reactions.

CHAPTER TWENTY-NINE

I sent the money off to Mullen the next day. Five twenty-pound notes. I had checked my list. The *Balticskayaslava II* had docked at Mc Swynes Bay outside Killybegs last season when the Eskimo was found. She would have been in the waters returning home a few days before the body turned up. It was as I'd expected.

I could hardly function while waiting for Mullen's reply. I thought about contacting Therese, but I needed to hear from him first. Frances called over, but I pretended not to be in. The days were all cold and dull now. Autumn was well and truly on its way. I was already looking forward to a cold wet winter. I was still sleeping and rising at odd hours and had started listening incessantly to the radio. An important attachment connecting me to the world had gone missing. I was in no humour to look for it.

Mullen rang a few days later. 'Gallagher?' he asked when I answered.

'Yes.' I recognized his gruff tone.

'I got your correspondence,' he said by way of introduction. 'September the nineteenth. I thought you might like to know.'

It was only two weeks away.

'It seems early,' I said.

Mullin agreed. 'It's amongst the first to arrive. The season's started early. The fish are on the run.'

'Aren't we all?'

Mullen hung up.

I rang Therese. She had asked me to give her more time, I only hoped I had given her enough. She answered and did not seem entirely displeased to hear from me. I asked if we could meet.

'I could come over,' she said.

I realized she had never been in my house before. 'Do that,' I told her.

She said it would take a few hours, that she had business to take care of first. I wondered what sort of business it was but knew better than to ask.

I decided to make her that dinner I had promised before. She was due around seven. About the only thing I could make of any significance was pasta with a carbonara sauce. Frances had taught me how one time. 'You ought to be able to make one dish,' she said. 'That's the very least expected of you.'

I went down town to get the pasta, garlic and wine. They had a poor selection of wine in the supermarket which made my job a little easier. I looked to see if there were any I recalled from The Grapevine.

'Fit for the altar only,' someone murmured beside me. I turned around. Father Jack winked and laughed.

'What would you recommend?'

'Another off-license.' Father Jack cast his eyes over the range. 'What are you looking for? White or red?'

I thought to ask what Therese would appreciate. 'Maybe a white.'

'Dry or sweet.'

'Oh dry.' Sweet was not how I would define our relationship right now.

Father Jack reached up to the top shelf. 'There you go. A little on the pricey side but worth it.'

I looked at the label. It was Australian. Beyond that it didn't make much sense. I thanked him and went around to the counter to pay. When I left he was still perusing the shelves of wine.

Therese arrived on time. The pasta had just gone on. The sauce was simmering away. The pungent odour of garlic clung everywhere.

'Oh God, you haven't been cooking, have you?' She looked upset.

'It's not that bad, honestly.'

'Oh no, I didn't mean it like that,' she said. She sounded flustered. 'It's just that I've eaten. You didn't say anything about dinner.'

'I must have forgotten.' I thought it was a given. I assumed my previous offer still stood. I should have known better. 'Well maybe you could have a little.'

'I've literally just finished.'

'I see.' I wondered where she had eaten and who she had eaten with.

'You go ahead.'

'I will.' I was angry. Angry at her for having eaten. Angry at myself for not asking her first. I brought her into the living room where the table had been set.

'I'm really sorry,' she said. 'You should have asked. You should have said something. You shouldn't take these things for granted.' Now she sounded angry. Angry at me for taking her for granted.

'I forgot,' I repeated. 'It's as simple as that.' But both of us knew it wasn't.

She saw the wine glasses. 'I could have brought a bottle if I'd known.'

'There's one in the fridge,' I said going out to get it. I brought it back in and poured out a glass each. Things were not going well. 'To better times,' I said and held my glass out. She touched hers against it.

'That should be easy.' She tasted it. 'Mmm, that's good. I suppose you're not completely useless.'

I pulled out a chair for her at the table and sat down too. 'Father Jack's choice.' I couldn't help myself.

She stopped, her glass in mid-air. 'He chose this?'

I nodded. 'It is good, isn't it? He's a surprising individual.'

She brought her glass down to the table. 'Did you tell him about this? About us?' She looked concerned.

'Would it matter?' I asked.

'Of course it would matter,' she snapped. 'What did you say precisely?'

'Precisely, I asked him what he could recommend. No more, no less.'

'You didn't mention us?'

'No. I didn't mention us.'

She took another sip of wine, relieved with my response.

'Why would it matter?'

'You'd better eat your dinner,' she said, 'before it gets ruined.'

I wanted to tell her it was too late for that. Instead I went out and drained the pasta. Filled my plate and poured some sauce over it. I brought it back inside.

'It looks and smells great.'

'Are you sure?' I offered her my plate.

'I really couldn't.' She was tired of having to refuse.

'Why would it matter if I had told him?' I asked again, twirling long strings of spaghetti around my fork.

'It might give people the wrong idea.'

'What would the wrong idea be?'

'I don't know. Look, Jim, we don't know what's going on between us. I just think we should settle that before other people make up their minds.'

She was right of course. Irrespective of Father Jack.

'And what do you think is going on between us?'

'I wish to God I knew.' She looked past me towards the window as though the answer was not to be found in this room. 'We don't exactly bring out the best in each other, do we?'

'That depends on how you look at it,' I said.

'How do you look at it?' Her eyes settled back on me. Her stare weighed heavily.

'Well looking at it from here I know that I need you.' I put down my fork on the plate. Even to me the words rang true.

Therese rubbed at her cheek, its smooth skin. 'You have a strange way of showing it.'

'I'm not completely useless,' I reminded her. I got up and went to her. I stood behind her and placed my hands on her shoulders. I held them, felt the bones beneath her flesh. She looked straight ahead. I moved my hands and began to stroke her neck. It felt warm. I slipped one hand across the front of her chest at the opening of her white blouse. Therese caught it with her hand. Laid it gently upon mine. Halting it and holding it. Her fingers tapered softly across the back of my hand. She looked back at me over her shoulder. I placed my other hand on her cheek and turned her face to meet mine. I bent down and kissed her lips. She responded warmly then pulled away.

'Not now,' she said. 'I'm not ready yet.' She still held my hand.

I stayed where I was feeling the pulse beneath her fingers. The curtains blew lightly in an uncertain draught.

I told her what I had found out from Mullen although I didn't mention him by name, just that Frank had heard it all from someone.

'So you can trace him now,' she said.

'It may not be that simple, but I'm certainly more hopeful.'

She looked happy for me. 'I'm glad.' I knew she was thinking that maybe things could settle down then. I was thinking the same myself.

'Do you think something unnatural happened to him?'

We were sitting again at the table, the table I had spent all those nights at trying to piece the Eskimo's life together. 'I really don't know.'

'It could still be dangerous.' I was glad for her concern.

'I suppose.' I looked at the swelling of her chest as it rose then fell away. I felt saddened by her beauty.

'Is that important to you?'

'The danger?'

'Yes.' Her eyes darkened. She inhaled and held it.

'In a way,' I said.

'Then you've got what you've been seeking.'

'Not really. I wouldn't have put it that way at all.'

She poured the last of the wine between us. The silence seemed to grow.

'How's business?' I wanted to hear her speak about herself.

'It's too soon to say,' she said. She pulled at the ends of her black hair. 'It may work out yet.'

'If it doesn't?'

She looked at me as if I had asked a foolish question. 'I don't know.' She finished her wine. She looked at me harshly. A wisp of hair lay across the side of her face like a worry line. I thought I saw a weakness, not a flaw but something necessitating attention. 'I need dangers too in my life,' she said. 'Maybe that's why I've held out this far.'

She was talking about her work, her newfound home, and me. She may have been talking too about Hal and Father Jack and all those other people in her life I knew nothing about.

'And how far is this?' Specifically I wanted to know how far we had come, alone and together.

Her harsh countenance began to melt. 'Sometimes I think far enough.' A trace of a smile spread thinly across her lips.

'And other times?'

'Other times I think I need to go all the way down.' She held one hand in the other and looked at it like you would someone else's, someone you were unsure about. She dropped her hand suddenly and glanced about the room. 'So this is what you want me to work on.' She spoke rapidly.

I followed her eyes, tried to see the room as she might. The old faded armchairs and couch, the scratched table, the blue painted walls, the chipped floorboards, the wall plates, the picture of Our Lady above the door.

'A bit of a fiasco, huh?'

She arched her eyebrows. 'It has character. A lot more than many newer homes. But some new ideas wouldn't harm it all the same.'

'That's what I was thinking. I don't want to alter it completely. There are memories I need to preserve. It's just grown a bit stale.'

'Do you still want me to begin? After everything?' She rested her chin in her hand.

'More so than ever.'

'It's a business arrangement, nothing more. You understand that? This has nothing to do with you or I.'

I didn't believe that was possible any more than she did, but her intention was for the best.

'I understand that.'

The slight but firm muscles in her supporting arm flexed in a gentle ripple. I wanted her to stay. Now that she was in my home I didn't want her to leave.

'My mistake was getting the work done before I arrived.' She lifted her head. 'Nothing turned out the way I wanted it to. I knew it wouldn't. I know how these things are, how you have to be there yourself to fight your corner, to ensure what you ask for is what you get. But I wanted it to be ready to move into. I wanted everything to be set up. I spent a fortune in phone calls. At all God's unearthly hours to make up for the time difference. It was foolish, and I knew it was foolish.'

'I thought your place looked wonderful.'

'You don't know the half of it, ' she said. 'You don't know what it really is like beneath the veneer. The difficulties, the disillusions. What you see is not necessarily what you get.' She paused, wet her lips. 'But I've only got myself to blame.'

'We're here now. So surely the odds must be on this working out. We can make of it what we like.'

She momentarily closed her eyes. 'I hope you're right.'

Therese stayed a little while longer, then she said she must go. It would have been unhelpful to try to persuade her otherwise. She stepped outside and looked up at the starless sky. A haze of moon showed beneath the clouds. A dog barked continuously in the distance. A cool breeze blew in off the water.

'I'm glad I came,' she said.

I apologized about the dinner. She folded her arms. Nothing more would happen. She looked despondent. 'We need to discuss this further.'

'Yes,' I agreed.

'Then I can get started on the plans.' She was talking about the work again.

'We do need plans, don't we?' I was cold. A dampness hung in the air.

'Oh yes,' she said. 'Nothing else will do.' She whispered goodnight and walked in the direction of her car.

CHAPTER THIRTY

Therese rang back a few days later asking for the house plans to be sent on to her. I told her I couldn't be sure they still existed, but I'd look and see. I spent the rest of the day turning the house apart. Sifting through all the old papers hoarded beneath the stairs and in the attic. I hadn't done this since my parents had died. I hadn't been up to it. I was afraid of the feelings it might stir up.

I came upon old family photos, letters, receipts, bills, newspapers. I brought it all into the living room, piled it up on the table, and looked through everything. Photos of my parents before they were married, photos of me as a baby, as a child, receipts for the old stove, newspaper reports of local and world events, tide timetables from those early years, school reports, First Holy Communion prayer books, memoriam cards. Looking for plans of a different sort now, a detailed layout of lives. As if somehow, like the information I had gleaned about the Eskimo, this could add up to an understanding of a past, a comprehension of a present.

I found an old photo of Frances, Knucky and I, taken when we were about sixteen. The three of us were sitting at the pier, our legs dangling over the water, grinning broadly as though someone promised us something very special, a promise we knew would be kept.

Stuck between the pages of a photo album I found a yellowed envelope containing the cowl from my mother's birth, a membrane that sometimes covered a baby's head when they were born. I recalled her telling me about it when I was very young. How it was considered lucky by sailors and how she could have sold it for a lot of money. But she never parted with it. She preserved it within the pages of a photo album. I opened it out carefully. It was delicate and badly frayed.

Knucky could have done with it. The Eskimo could have done with it. Anyone of us could. I placed it gently on my head. Wore it like a newborn baby. Then I folded it over. Replaced it as I had found it.

I couldn't find the plans anywhere. I rang my parent's solicitor to see if he knew anything. He said he'd check into it. I rang Therese back the next day to tell her. She said not to worry. If they didn't show up, she'd manage. I suggested meeting again. For the purposes of discussing ideas about the house.

'For that only,' she said. 'For now.' I agreed with her. Against my best wishes.

I was happy to have something to occupy me. Happy to be thinking about the house instead of the Eskimo. I needed something to get me through to the nineteenth. It was barely over a week away now. I ought to have made contact with Frances or Knucky, see where things stood, but I was happy to keep it to Therese and I. We didn't mix well together.

Therese came over a couple of days later. She arrived mid-afternoon carrying colour charts, design catalogues, samples of wall and floor coverings, the works. She was taking this more seriously than I had up until then. She came in and piled them all on the table. I went out to the kitchen to make us coffee. She followed out after me.

'First things first,' she said leaning up against the sink. Her long paisley dress filled and then settled against her lithe body. Her long curly black hair gleamed as though freshly washed. 'How much can you afford?'

I recalled Mullen asking how much a life was worth. 'That depends,' I said. 'I have no idea of costs.'

'It adds up very quickly,' she said. 'Something big will be tens of thousands.'

This was already out of my league. 'And something small?' I poured the water in on top of the freshly ground beans. The grains swirled through the murky brown liquid like sand through water when the seabed is disturbed. 'I've got about five or six thousand. Is that too little?'

She shook her head. 'I can work with that.' She sucked in her bottom lip. 'Of course my fees will have to come out of that.' She sounded embarrassed.

'Of course,' I said. I didn't like to ask what she charged.

'It would normally come to about a thousand. But we can come to an arrangement.'

I shook my head firmly. 'Business, we agreed.' I plunged the coffee, compressed the grains back down to the bottom, then poured us each a mug.

We spent the next few hours discussing all the possibilities. I had never imagined there could be so many options, so many ways to change while maintaining the basic structure. Was this same capacity in all of us I wondered?

'Don't make any decisions today,' Therese said. 'Run the choices around in your head a while. You may have to live with your decision for a long time to come.' It sounded like a warning.

At one point our hands met turning over one of the charts. It was an inevitability. The unplanned touch of her flesh came almost as a shock. I pulled my hand away instinctively. Therese smiled at my action. Perhaps I was getting somewhere after all. But I could not be certain I had done the right thing.

At six she said she had to go. 'An appointment with Hal. He doesn't like to be kept waiting.'

I was tempted to say, how few of us do. Instead I thanked her for coming over, for sharing her knowledge.

'Get back to me, ' she said. 'Next week sometime. We can take it from there.'

This was all we could do now it seemed, take it from each stage.

CHAPTER THIRTY-ONE

The *Balticskayaslava II* was due in Killybegs the following day. I called on Frances and asked to borrow her car. It was the first time we had spoken for ages. She didn't ask me why I needed it. She just said that I had no need to ask and handed me the keys. I felt worse than ever. She looked tired, drawn.

'Are you okay?' I asked.

Frances nodded a yes.

I asked if she had seen Knucky recently. Although I had seen the *Lorna Doone* tied up in the harbour there had been no sign of him.

'Oh, he's still about,' she said. 'But that's about the height of it.'

I talked for a little while longer just to be polite then went back home.

I left it right to the last minute to ring Therese. It was the wrong time to ring, of course, and I truly hoped she wouldn't answer. But she did.

'It's me, Jim.' Lest there be a doubt.

'Hi,' she said. 'Made any decisions yet?'

'Decisions?' How could I tell her that nothing was being based on decision, that everything was happening according to the events that occurred, most of which were unplanned.

'About the house? I presume that's why you're ringing.'

It sounded like a statement of fact, as though there could be no other reason. I had been thinking about the house, all week. But whenever I did my thoughts ended up with Therese, her leaning against my sink, her dress settling against her body, the shocking touch of her hand. The nights we had spent together.

'No. It's not about the house. It has nothing to do with that.' Before ringing I had no idea what I would say, and now it was just coming out. 'What are you doing for the next few days?' I was being rushed headlong now into something bigger than I could handle. 'Come away with me for a few days.'

I could hear her breathing. Against the odds it was a soothing sound. She seemed to be wondering how to react. Trying to gauge her feelings as though they surprised her, were unpredictable and troublesome. 'Please, Therese. I have to go to Killybegs. I really have to. The ships are due. Come with me. It'll be all right.'

'We were talking about the house, Jim. We were talking about business.'

I heard a sharp snapping sound as if she was banging her front teeth together. I wanted to ask her there and then if there was anyone else in her life. To be straight with me. But I knew that would have finished us off for good.

'We were talking about trying again. Giving me another chance.'

'Jim, I don't like this.'

'Therese.' Rushing further and further in. Leaving everything else behind.

'Strictly business, Jim, we said that.'

'No, we never said that. We talked about time, a breathing space of sorts.' As time always was.

'I need more time.' She sounded exasperated. But not with me, with herself.

'How much more time? Therese, we're avoiding what cannot be avoided. Sooner or later we have to face up to that. Come with me. We can find out.'

Therese sighed. 'I can't, Jim. I can't just drop everything. You can't ask me to do that.'

But I already had done. 'I'm sorry,' I apologized.

The receiver was sweaty against my ear. I heard the clicking within my eardrums. Neither of us knew quite where to go from here. If there was anywhere left to go.

Therese's weak voice filtered down the line. 'How long are you going for?'

'I don't know. A few days. No more than that I hope.'

There were no answers I could give that could solve anything. We were being swept away, and there was nothing we could do about it.

'And you expect me to go on that?'

'No, I don't. The truth is, Therese, I don't expect that at all.'

The receiver shook in my hand. I wished she could see it. I wished she could see what I had been reduced to.

'When are you going?'

'Today. As soon as I put the phone down.'

'You don't give a person much time, do you?' She gave a tired laugh.

'I'm out of time. That's just about how it is.'

She breathed heavily. Unhappy with the strain of her life. 'I may live to regret this.'

'You'll come?'

'I may live to regret it.'

'Jesus, Therese.'

'I suppose you want me to pick you up?'

The weight of it had still to make its full impact.

'No. I've borrowed Frances' car. I'll pick you up.'

'In Frances' car?'

'Of course. What is it?' I thought she was going to back out.

'Nothing. You do that then.'

She put the phone down. She left me hanging.

I drove up her laneway an hour later and parked outside the cottage. The front door was open. She was inside in the hall talking on the phone. She looked out, holding the receiver between her chin and neck, and beckoned me with her hand to come in.

'I don't care,' she shouted into the receiver as I entered, 'that's just the way it is.' She cast her eyes upwards looking over at me. An overnight case stood next to the stairway. A strong smell of perfume clung to the air. A sweet musk. She took the receiver from her neck and gripped it until the whites of her knuckles showed. 'I know what I'm doing. Don't think I don't know that.' There was a pause. I felt embarrassed being where I was. Listening to this. I felt certain it had to do with me, that she had brought me in to hear this. 'Yes,' she said quietly. 'It is my decision.' She put the phone down. She wiped her brow. 'Hmm.' She looked at me accusingly. Then smiled. 'Ready?' As if I was holding everything up.

'Ready.'

'Good. Then let's get out of here.'

For the first mile or two of the journey she just sat there. She stared ahead as if keen to see the road passing beneath her. I sneaked glances across from time to time. She looked gorgeous. I inhaled and thought I could smell her hair. I badly wanted to touch it. From time to time she ran her forefinger along her left eyebrow as though she had an itch there that wouldn't go away. Her lips parted then closed again. Once I saw the tip of her tongue protrude and lick her top lip lightly. She smoothed her long white cotton skirt with the palm of her hand, running it along the length of her upper leg. Her fingernails were about a quarter of an inch long and perfectly manicured. I listened to the jingle of her metal earrings like a pair of small wind-chimes. She gave a short hushed cough when it seemed she was ready to speak. She drew one leg up under her and twisted around to me.

'Goddamn you,' she said. 'I could hit you or something.'

She didn't sound angry, more matter of fact.

'It's not an uncommon feeling,' I told her. The tall trees curved over the narrow road like a tunnel. We drove through their shade past the ripped open body of a badger. Its red insides bulged through its dark fur. Therese's nose wrinkled when she saw it.

'They're all over the place,' she said. 'I've yet to see a live one.'

I told her what I had heard from Frances. 'They're not all hit by cars, you know. Some have been involved in baiting. They throw their bodies on the sides of roads to make it look like an accident.' I pushed the car into a higher gear.

'Why did you have to go and tell me that?' She wrinkled her nose again and squinted her eyes. 'Don't you understand the simplest of things?'

'It was just conversation.' I lifted one hand off the wheel by way of excusing it.

'It's no wonder we do better not talking,' she said and pulled her leg back out from underneath her. Her skirt got caught up under her and exposed her leg to her knee.

'We certainly do,' I said looking overtly at it.

She freed her skirt and pulled it down over her. She closed her mouth hard.

'That was a joke,' I said. 'A poor attempt, I agree.' I stopped at the junction to the main road and waited for the traffic to pass. I put the car into neutral and revved the engine. She leaned over suddenly and kissed me on the cheek, her right hand on my shoulder for support.

'Don't go making too much of that,' she warned. But it was far too late for that. I felt a great sense of relief. Like finding a landmark you recognize after the panic of being lost. I indicated and pulled out. Frances' car roared with approval.

'What's all this about?' she asked. She was looking at the map Frances kept in the glove compartment. 'What's in Killybegs?'

'Good question,' I said. 'Let me know if you find the answer.'

She traced the route with her finger. Trailing it along the blue main roads and the brown secondary ones, occasionally veering off on the broken black lines of the dirt tracks.

'Really, Jim, what is it?'

'It's a long story.' I wondered how much of it I should tell her, if any.

'We've got a long journey.' She folded the map up, kept it on her knee.

'Well, let's see.' I pulled out to overtake a tractor and trailer. A large articulated lorry sped over the brow of the hill from out of nowhere. I stomped my foot down heavily on the brakes and pulled back in briskly. It roared past.

The road shook beneath us.

'Good God, Jim!' Therese was tossed to one side. The map slid off her knee.

'Sorry. He came out of nowhere.'

Therese looked shocked.

'It was nothing, honestly,' I told her. 'I was in control all along. He just came up on us too fast.' I put my hand over on her knee for reassurance. Then thought better of it and put it back on the wheel.

'I don't know, Jim. Will it ever be any other way for us?'

'Therese! It was nothing, I'm telling you.'

'Nothing! We could have been killed.'

This was getting out of hand again. We had never been in that type of danger at all. I barely crawled along at ten miles an hour now. I was afraid to pull out again. Afraid of what it might do to Therese and me. I followed behind the tractor for three or four miles. Neither of us speaking again. Every time I looked there seemed to be a hill in front of us or a bend in the road or oncoming traffic. I needed a long clear straight stretch. This simple act of passing out had proven to be a test. A test of my commitment. A test of our resolve. I dreaded to think what the whole journey would become. When I saw an opportunity I pulled out smoothly and passed without undue haste. Relaxing only when I was back on my own side of the road. Therese held on to the straps of her seat belt. She loosened her grip and made it seem as if her hands had just been resting there.

'Tell me something about yourself,' she said. 'Something non-threatening.'

'Like what?'

'Tell me something about yourself when we were both living here before.'

I was confused. I laughed. 'Have we had another life together I don't know about? Are we in another lifetime? Another incarnation?'

'Before my family moved away.'

For the first time it really dawned on me that we had lived here together before, that our paths had surely crossed, that our lives had in some way intermingled. It was like reincarnation, like getting a second chance to make amends, in a not altogether dissimilar way from how my life now, second time around with Frances and Knucky, contained the possibility of redemption.

'I hadn't thought of it like that before,' I told her. I felt reassured by it, as if finally a glimmer of light was visible through the northern fog. 'What age were you when you left?'

'Nine.'

I was only a couple of years older than her. We had discovered this in one of our earlier more honest conversations.

'Tell me something from this time,' she repeated. 'Tell me something innocent.'

It took me a while to think of anything. Then I remembered the true, but out of character, story of my parents waking me up one warm summer's night to go swimming together at White Strand beneath the glittering stars and the fullest of moons as the flickering lights of the trawlers were scattered about the horizon. They woke me to tell me they were going, and in a reversal of roles I stayed awake until they returned. And although they never said it to me I knew that when they were out there swimming in the ocean together, night-swimming, they had for that time forgotten all about me as though I did not exist within their lives.

We were approaching Frances' favourite part of the journey. Barnsmore Gap. Therese lowered her window a little. We had swapped stories of childhood over and back trying to pinpoint an occasion when we possibly would have met, but without success. Therese looked out at the mountains. She seemed to be considering all that we had said. I saw Biddy's Pub up ahead.

'Do you feel like a break? We could get a coffee.' I carefully avoided mentioning alcohol. I was determined not to abuse drink in any way in her company. I wondered if I should have avoided the pub altogether, but a part of me wanted her to see me in there not touching any drink at all.

'Yes,' she nodded.

I pulled up in the car park opposite. Therese got out and looked down to the river.

'Isn't it beautiful here?' I walked over to her.

She put her arm around my waist and held me to her. 'You'll be careful won't you?'

She may have been referring to the Eskimo, but she could just as easily have been talking about us.

'I know this means a lot to you. Just don't let it mean too much.'

I put my arm on her shoulder. I felt the curve of it in my palm.

She laughed. 'I don't know how we ended up here. There's really nothing you can do about anything, is there?'

The water gurgled over the rocks. A hare dashed through the thick grasses and disappeared. I could hear the birds chattering away.

'One way or another you end up going along with it.' She didn't seem bothered by this. Just bemused, as though it had never occurred to her before.

The light dulled behind the mountains with the approaching dark clouds. The bright oranges of the land dimmed to brown. She tugged at me.

'Let's keep going.'

I booked us in at the hotel. I thought I saw the receptionist smile to herself as she got the key to our room from the box behind her. I was certain she remembered me from the last time with Frances. Therese waited behind me while I signed the form. I booked the room for two nights to begin with. It was only when I got upstairs that I realized I had been given the same room as the last time. The receptionist must have done it on purpose. It was no wonder she smiled. Therese put her case on one of the beds. I dropped mine on the floor. The bathroom door was open. I thought of Frances asleep in the bath.

'What is it?' Therese looked at me oddly.

'What?'

'You're grinning to yourself.'

'Am I?'

'Yes, you are. What's so amusing?'

'I don't honestly know. I didn't realize I was grinning.'

'Well you were.'

It wasn't in the least bit funny. I went across to the window looking out onto the harbour. It had been opened to ventilate the room but let the strong smell of fish in instead. I closed it. I could feel Therese looking after me yet.

'Honestly, it was nothing. Sometimes I just grin. It's something you might learn about me.'

She didn't look convinced, but seemed content to give up on it.

The harbour was full of activity. Fishermen unfolded their nets across the ground, cranes loaded and unloaded the boats and trucks, sightseers tried not to get in the way. A group of gulls perched on the edge of a litter bin and scavenged viciously at its contents, tearing at plastic paper and empty cartons. One stabbed its beak through a polystyrene box and pulled at a half-eaten burger, scattering paper and an empty coke tin on the ground.

'So when are your ships due?' It was the first time she had asked me this obvious question as if up until now, until our arrival, they had been of little consequence.

'Tomorrow if all goes to schedule.'

'You mean to say they might be late, that we could be on some wild goose chase?' I had started to annoy her again. 'Couldn't you have checked before you left? Couldn't you have asked someone?'

I stepped back from the window, sat down on the edge of the bed. 'No, I couldn't. There really was no way.' This wasn't true. I should have rung Mullen, made sure there was no delay, but I didn't want to involve him any more than was necessary. It most probably would have cost me more in any number of ways.

Therese shook her head despairingly and unpacked her clothes. She hung them up in the wardrobe or put them away neatly in drawers.

'I've always wanted to do that,' I said. 'It just never seems worth it. I usually end up working from my bag.'

'This time it's going to be different,' she said forcefully.

I knew she needed to be right about this. So while she knelt down and pushed her empty case under the bed I unpacked my clothes. She stood up and put them away for me.

'So what now?' she asked after she finished.

'Whatever you want?'

'I'd like a walk. I could do with stretching my legs after the journey.'

'No sooner said than done.'

We took a walk through the town and down by the harbour.

'The smell of this place!' Therese wrinkled her face in pretend disgust.

'I know.'

The stench of fish living and dying hung heavily in the air like an invisible but dangerous cloud. I looked over at the window I had broken on the Harbour Master's office. It had yet to be replaced. A sheet of wood was boarded over it. We walked right down to the end of the pier. I scanned the water as if any moment now those factory ships would come charging into view the way that lorry had earlier in the morning. A long line of oyster catchers flew past in front of us. A heavy metallic banging clunked behind. Therese held on to the lapels of her jacket. Her face strained into the breeze. An off-white foamy sludge sloshed against the walls.

'Is this what you wanted?' she asked. She ran her toe along the edge of the pier.

'I'm just glad you're here.'

'I am too.' She let her shoulders drop in a vague gesture of hopelessness.

'What do you plan to do when the ships arrive?'

'I'm hoping that I can meet up with some of the crew and see if that leads me anywhere.'

'That's it. That's your plan?'

'I'm afraid so,' I said. 'That's as good as it gets.'

I had let her down again. I had revealed the worthlessness of my position.

'Have you thought about passing this information on to the guards. Telling them the name of the ship, seeing what they can come up with.'

I had thought about it many times. But I didn't trust them anymore. Not that they would not investigate it, but that I might never find out the results. It would also mean involving Mullen. The guards would want to know my source. I had promised to keep him out of it. Although he had said nothing directly I felt threatened by him, more threatened in fact than by any of the unknowns with the Eskimo.

'I want to try myself first. See what I come up with. I'm not sure how concerned the authorities really are.'

As Mullen had pointed out they may well be investigating the returning ships anyway. They might not be interested in anything I might have to say.

A bell sounded from one of the buildings across from us. It rang clearly across the water. Therese was right of course. I needed a better plan. I needed to ensure this opportunity did not slip by me. The ships would drop anchor at McSwyne's Bay outside of town. I still had to figure out how I would trace crew members of the *Balticskayaslava II*, what I would say to them if I was able to communicate at all. Some would come off board to drink, there was no doubt about that. But how was I to track them down?

Therese linked my arm and led me back down the pier. 'You're not cut out for subterfuge,' she said. She spoke as though she knew precisely what she was talking about.

I walked around the wrong side of a bollard and stepped over the thick rope. I wondered if she had seen me that night out at her cottage after all. Maybe from her upstairs window after Father Jack left. It was a frightening thought.

'Are you all right?' Therese watched me closely.

'I'm fine.' I tried to sound convincing.

'You look uneasy. As if you're unhappy here.'

'I'm enjoying this,' I told her. 'Despite all that's going on I like what we're doing. I want you to know that.'

What I was saying was true. Despite the Eskimo, despite our troubles, the fear, I was happy here in Therese's company.

'I know,' she said. 'Me too.' She squeezed my arm. 'Let's go back to the hotel. We could both do with a rest.'

I looked up at the greying sky. The strong odour of fish swept back up the street again and clogged in my nostrils. Perhaps, I thought, this was the best you could hope for. Perhaps, in the end, you had to settle for this.

Back in the room we took off our shoes and lay down clothed on separate beds. I closed my eyes and imagined Therese would do the same.

'Are you ever sorry you came back?'

The bed next to me creaked slightly as Therese shifted on it. 'Most of the time. And you?'

'Sometimes, I suppose. Sometimes I think it's for the better.' I heard a shower running in the room next to us. Therese's bed creaked again. 'One way or another, there's no right or wrong to it.' I looked into the blackness I had created, its red tinged glow. I was aware of the perilous nature of my questions and yet I persisted. 'Are you any closer to knowing why you did come back or shouldn't I ask?'

'You can ask.' It sounded as if she was moving herself into a different position as though my question had caused her to take stock. 'I came back to see what the alternative was.'

'Have you found out?'

'I don't know. It's too soon to say.'

'Do you think you will stay?' I tried to make it sound as if I had no more than a passing interest in her answer.

'That depends.'

I opened my eyes and looked over. I had been wrong about her. She wasn't sitting on her bed. She was standing in front of it looking down upon me. She looked stern as if deliberating the possibilities of her future, as if disappointed by what she saw.

I moved over on the bed, and she lay down beside me. I held her hand. 'There's a long way to go,' she said.

The shower was turned off next door. Somebody would dry themselves off. Walk naked into a room.

'We have no holds over each other. You can't expect that.'

She could have been referring to any number of other relationships in her life that I couldn't gauge. Her fingers pressed into the back of my hand. 'It was a good idea to get away.'

We lay there quietly until we both fell asleep.

Therese wanted us to have dinner together in the hotel. 'Like a normal couple,' she said.

'Is that what we are,' I asked, 'a couple?'

'I thought for a moment you were going to question our normality.'

'That's been in question for a long time,' I said. 'But a couple, are we a couple?'

'For now,' she said and began to undress.

It was like being back in the room with Frances all over again. She would remove her clothes and shower or take a bath in my presence. I couldn't stand it another time. I told her I'd go down to the dining room and reserve a table.

'All you have to do is ring,' she said. 'It's zero for reception.' She unzipped her skirt and stepped out of it.

'I don't think so. I don't trust those objects too much. They haven't exactly done me too many favours in the past.'

Therese grinned. If only she had known, it was that exact phone I had called her from. She began to unbutton her blouse. I really had to get out of there.

'Back in a minute,' I said quickly and left.

Down in the dining room a young man and woman moved around shaking out table cloths and setting the tables. The manager appeared from behind a pillar and approached. I asked to reserve a table for eight-thirty.

'No problem,' he said. 'Things are quiet tonight.'

I decided to play my hand. I asked him what he knew about the factory ships. He said he heard they'd be arriving the following afternoon. He didn't ask why I wanted to know, didn't seem concerned about it in the slightest. As if it was all part of the service. I felt relieved to hear the ships still weren't due until the next day. Although that was what was scheduled if conditions had been favourable, they could easily have dropped anchor by now. I would have thought that I would want them here as soon as possible, to find out whatever I could about the Eskimo. But faced with it now, I felt afraid. Afraid of what I might hear and afraid of what it might involve. I was pleased to be able to put it off. I could take the night as it came now. Try to relax and enjoy it.

I stopped outside the bar on the way back upstairs. I thought about having one drink, but wisdom got the better of me. All the same I was wary of going back to the room. Scared of finding Therese in the bath. I went up to the corridor and stopped outside the room. I listened with my ear close to the door as if I were spying on myself. I could hear nothing. I put my hand on the handle, felt the cold sheen of the brass. I pulled it away and walked on down the corridor. For the want of something to do I checked the positions of the fire exits. I made sure none of them were locked. I pushed open the emergency bar on the nearest exit to our room and looked down the metal staircase into the alley at the back of the hotel. A mound of filled black plastic bags gathered along the wall opposite. Looking at them I was reminded of a time when I had worked in the hospital during the school holidays as a temporary wardsman, filling in for those who were off on their holidays. I used to bring black bags out to the incinerator to be burned. I never really considered what was in them. But one time I picked one up containing a long rounded object that felt for all the world like a limb. Like an arm or a leg. And once I thought about this I could barely hold it in my hands. Its hardness weighed down on my palms. I could feel the softness of my own flesh deep in the pit of my stomach. The hollow feeling of revulsion and loss. Nothing I could fathom. I had only ever felt it one time since. When I had run over a cat as it ran across the road in front of me. The hard yet soft plop of its body beneath the wheel. Of course it could have been anything inside that bag. But I couldn't bring myself to look. I hadn't the courage to. So I had to live with that uncertainty forever. A fear worse than any reality. It took all the strength I could muster to cast it into the scorching flames.

I pulled the emergency door shut and leaned up against the wall. I looked up at the light embedded in the ceiling. Its silver underside. I had a sudden dread of Therese's cold flesh. Ridiculous as it was I seriously considered leaving through the fire escape and putting her behind me.

By the time I returned she was sitting on the edge of the bath in front of the mirror, fully dressed, applying make-up.

'I thought you'd got lost.' Her mouth twisted beneath a stick of lip gloss.

'Just took a walk around the hotel. Getting my bearings.'

'Getting the bearings of the bar, I'd guess.' She sounded neither pleased nor displeased.

'No. Although I have to admit I thought about it.'

I could see her looking at me in the mirror. Examining my demeanour.

'What about dinner?'

'Eight-thirty. Is that okay?'

'Perfect.' She widened her eyes into the mirror, looked deep into them. Wiped something away, some blemish, something she didn't want to see. 'How do I look?'

She stood up and did a half-twirl. She had changed into a long black dress and her hair was tied back, the first time I had seen it that way, revealing the fine lines of her face. She looked stunning. I told her so. She gave a small curtsey.

'Now you,' she said and pointed her finger at me.

For a moment I thought she was going to start undressing me, like I was a little boy in her care. But she went outside to the bedroom and left me to my privacy. I undressed and showered. Afterwards I had no option but to wrap myself in a towel to go back out for fresh clothes. She half sat up on the bed resting her head and shoulders against the headboard. She stared right at me. I felt very self-conscious. Although she had seen me naked before, it was like she was waiting to see me for the first time. Waiting to scrutinize my body. I wanted to take my clothes and go back to the bathroom. But it would have seemed foolish. I dropped the towel and dressed quickly without looking at her. I could feel her eyes on me all the time. I slipped on my shoes and tied the laces then turned to face her. She was lying back on the bed with her eyes shut. She could easily have been asleep.

We had a drink in the bar first. She suggested it. She ordered a Pina Colada with all the trimmings. She said she felt like something exotic, something from outside of this particular world.

'I'm happy where I am,' I told her, not convincingly, and ordered a pint of Guinness.

The bar was quiet. It was early yet. One man sat up at the counter by himself reading the paper. Two other couples sat at the tables.

'So how's Hal?' I asked. 'Are there any islands still left off our coast?'

Therese tilted her head. 'He's so-so. He's made one or two sales. Enough to cover his expenses he says.' She spread her lips as though she were smiling.

'Is he planning to stay much longer?' I wanted it to sound casual, not like I was calculating her response.

'He wants to see my business off the ground, he says. But that could take any length of time.'

The barman came over with our drinks. He carefully lowered Therese's Pina Colada to the table then put a fresh bar mat down beside me and placed my pint on it. I asked him to put it on our account.

The tone of the conversation seemed acceptable to her so far. I decided to press on.

'Well I got to hand it to him, he's no slouch. I even saw him the other day with Father Jack. Looked like he was trying to sell him a better version of Paradise.'

She pulled her umbrella out of her drink and closed it. 'Bad luck,' she said. She looked up at the clock behind the counter. It was twenty past. 'I'm starving. Why don't you see if our table's ready.'

Like the umbrella the subject was closed.

I went across to the dining room. The manager handed me the menus and wine list and told me to wait in the bar. He'd call us when they were ready. It seemed everybody wanted me in the vicinity of alcohol. Wanted to test my resolve.

'It's a start,' Therese said when I returned with the menus.

She read through hers with extreme care, going through each item one by one, reading the ingredients, considering their implication. I scanned for the steak. A ten ounce sirloin with pepper sauce. Therese finally decided on the Lemon Sole, with Deep Fried Camembert in Raspberry Sauce to start. I opted for the vegetable soup.

She went through the wine list with just as much care, then handed it over to me. 'You choose.'

I refused graciously. 'I've enough trouble telling a red from a white.'

'Which do you prefer?' she asked.

'I really don't mind.'

'Well I think we should choose a red in honour of your steak.'

'What about your fish? That requires a white doesn't it?' It was about the only thing I knew.

'It can live with a red,' she said. 'We all have to make do sometime.' She smiled sweetly at me as if she were joking.

She choose a Chilean. A *Reserva* from somewhere in the Maipo Valley. I told her it sounded like bandit country.

'You'll be on familiar ground then.' She assured me I would like the wine. 'It's good and bloody.'

A waitress came to take our order and show us to our table. I held out the chair for Therese like the last desperate act of a hopeless gentleman. I sat down opposite her. The flame from the candle flickered in the silver cutlery. Therese placed her hand on top of mine.

'You're not all bad,' she whispered.

'You don't know the half of it,' I warned.

'Isn't that the truth?' She took her hand away as the waitress came back with the wine. I let her do the tasting. She took a drink, held it in her mouth then let it slide down. She nodded her approval.

'To your new business,' I said holding up my glass. 'To your future.'

She tipped it gently with her glass. The fragility of what we held more evident than ever. 'To what follows on from the past.'

The wine was warm and rich. It seemed to cling to my palate and dry rather than wet the surface of my tongue.

'Good choice,' I said not knowing if it was or not.

I tasted her Camembert when it came. I bit through the crisp fried surface. The thick runny cheese poured into my mouth and down my throat. The sweet fullness of the raspberry sauce bore down on its sourness. I washed it all down with a mouthful of the *vino* as recommended by Therese. She waited on my response.

'Well?'

'Heavy,' I said when the cheese finally cleared from my mouth.

'But you liked it?'

'Getting to.'

'Good.' She looked pleased with herself. 'Wait until you get to the meat.'

Usually I ordered it well done, but she had insisted I try it medium to rare.

'I can't stand the sight of blood,' I told her to no avail.

'You'll love it,' she guaranteed.

I didn't go that far in my praises when it came. I was wary of the soft pink flesh inside. But I had to admit, it wasn't bad as long as you didn't look at it. Therese insisted on me 'mixing the juices. The blood of the meat, and the blood of the wine'.

'You're scaring me,' I told her.

'Proper order,' she replied.

Afterwards we had chocolate fudge cake and coffee. Then went back out to the bar for a nightcap both of us ordering brandies.

'Feeling good?'

She nodded. 'A little too good.'

'There's no such thing.' I took a drink and felt the deep warmth work its way down to my stomach.

'Let's finish these upstairs.'

I could see the brandy glow in her cheeks and behind the pupils of her eyes. There was no doubting what was to follow next. We went upstairs. I pushed the two single beds together.

I awoke in the early hours of the morning. I felt the warmth of Therese's flesh against mine. Her arm lay across my chest. Her stomach pressed into my hip, and her thigh bent over mine. My arm was numb beneath her. It prickled and tingled at the joints of my elbow and shoulder. The day was starting to break. The first light filtered through the curtains. My mouth tasted awful. I remembered the intensity of our pleasure and felt immensely sad. We had seen what we were capable of, and now that had to be lived with forever.

CHAPTER THIRTY-TWO

We ordered breakfast in bed the next morning. Coffee and croissants. I showered quickly afterwards and went out for a walk on my own. The streets were quiet. As ever the raw stench of fish hit back at me. I walked down the pier and looked at the boats tied up at the side. A group of three men unloaded cartons of food from one of the trawlers into the back of a small van. One man stopped to lift a half full bottle of whiskey from a box and poured a generous helping into three mugs resting beside him on top of a bollard. A voice crackled over the radio from the wheel room. Something splashed in the water to my side. I looked down but saw nothing. I heard someone laugh loudly further back up the pier. Someone else shouted in French. I felt wide open here. Exposed for all to see. I looked back down the pier at the hotel and up to our window. For all I knew Therese could be standing there watching me. I squinted my eyes into the glare of the sky. It would be good to get this over with.

Therese was still in bed when I got back. She was watching a bought-in American chat show on the television.

'Home from home,' she said.

I stopped by the door of the bathroom to look at it a while. A male presenter was talking to a mother and daughter about the mother's near decision to have an abortion when she discovered she was pregnant with her daughter. They sounded very serious and unreal for this time of the morning. The daughter was discussing forgiveness. I gave up on it. Another world I could not enter. A world where nothing, it seemed, was hidden, where too much was disclosed.

'Is this how you spend your time?'

'Some of it, you know.' Therese turned it off. She fixed a pillow beneath her head. 'I suppose I should get up. The tray with the remains of the breakfast lay on the ground beside her. 'What's the plan for today?'

'I was thinking maybe we should just take a trip in the car. Get out of here for a while. The ships ought to be here by the time we get back. Then I can get to work.'

Therese said she liked the sound of it.

The phone rang on the locker beside the bed. I jumped. I looked back at it as though it had behaved in a way it shouldn't have. Therese leaned over and lifted the receiver. She listened a moment then thanked whoever was on the line. It sounded like she was waiting for a call to be put through.

'Hello,' she said. 'Yes I am.'

She was obviously familiar with the caller. I felt a great intrusion in my life. Someone knew exactly where she could be contacted. Therese looked uncomfortable. She leaned away from me shielding the phone with her body as if that could diminish the effect of the call.

'I'll have to talk to you later,' she said. 'This is not a good time.' She rubbed at her upper arm. It was covered in goose bumps. 'No, no. Everything's fine.'

She listened for a while. Something was taking a long time to be told. I knew I should be moving around the room, giving some indication that I wasn't listening in. But I felt as if I had a right to. That whatever calls were made to this room could not exclude me.

'Yes. I told you I would.' She sounded impatient. She sat up in the bed and swung her legs over the edge. She was about to terminate the call. It was clearly annoying her. 'Now, I really have to go. I'll talk to you later.'

She hung up. She sat looking down at the floor with the sheet gathered around her waist. Then she stood up, stretched, and looked somewhere in my vicinity. 'I need a shower. I'll be with you in a moment.'

She still had a trace of annoyance in her voice. Almost as if it was my presence that annoyed her and not the voice the other end of the phone.

I sat up on the bed, turned the television on, and waited for her to come back out. She was going to ignore the call. Say nothing about it. Nothing about why anyone should ring our hotel bedroom. As if it was none of my business. I could ask her about it, but I was afraid of where that would leave me. Her decision to make no mention of it already left us precariously perched. I flicked through the channels without stopping. Then I turned it off altogether.

She came back out drying off her hair. I watched her. I wanted her to prove me wrong, to explain what that call was all about. She pulled the towel away from her head and shook her hair out. She smiled over.

'So where do you suggest we drive to?' Her nakedness made it worse.

'I hadn't really thought.'

'We could just drive up the coast. It's been years. It's been a lifetime.'

'Okay.' It was in her hands now. That was obviously the way she wanted it. And that's where I decided to leave it.

We followed the coast road up into the hills of Glencolmcille. Therese's humour had improved, and my own lightened in turn. The roads wound dangerously in and out along the edge.

'Don't take your eyes off it for a moment,' Therese urged. But the view was too striking to ignore.

'I'd forgotten how beautiful this country could be.' Therese gazed through the window. She lay back in the seat, kicked off her shoes, and rested her feet in the open area of the glove compartment. 'Do you know it?' she asked.

'Like yourself I keep forgetting.'

'Did it seem that way when you came back from Alaska?' She put a hand on the back of my seat. Barely a hair's breath away from my neck.

'What, like I kept forgetting?'

'No-o-h.' She drew the word out as though she loved the sound of it. 'Did it seem beautiful all over again when you returned?'

'I couldn't see it properly then. I couldn't tell.'

'And now?'

'I'm still not seeing it properly.'

She leaned in against the side window as though capable of seeing over the edge. Two shaggy sheep, yellow-fleeced, grazed at the side of the road. A few more climbed, without hesitation, on the steep grassy incline. The waves ran in long lines of white foam across the surface of the ocean.

'What do you want from here? What is it you're after?' She brushed the back of my neck with her fingers. It made me feel good for the first time since that phone call.

'God, Therese, you certainly ask all the big ones.'

She laughed and pushed her fingers up through my hair. 'You must want something.'

I felt the texture of the grainy leatherette steering wheel between my fingers. I kept my eye on the road. 'To tell you the truth, I think right now, if this doesn't sound corny, what I want is you.' I embarrassed myself saying it. But she asked, and it had to be said.

Her hand continued to massage my scalp. 'But you want this Eskimo more?'

'No. It's not like that. That's just unfinished business. It'll soon be taken care of.'

'And if not? If you don't find out what you want about him?' She took her hand away and clasped both of them over her knees.

'I'll have to take that as it comes.'

'This might never end, Jim. You know that.'

I slowed down to negotiate a steep bend. 'It has to end somewhere.'

'You know what I think?' She waited for me to respond. To look over. But I couldn't take my eyes off the road. She would have hated me if I had. This was the way it was with Therese. The way it was with everything. I couldn't win, no matter what I did. She gave up on me. 'I think you should try to forget all about it. I don't think you should go looking for him tonight.' It sounded like a plea.

'By tonight everything could be clear.'

'Just let it go. Let him go. Let him drop right back into the ocean. It's you, Jim, who's keeping him up on land.'

I didn't understand any of this. I felt so close to a conclusion. 'All I need is his name, an address, and he'll sink on his own accord.'

'Just think about it.' She stared back out the window down to the ocean and spoke almost to herself. 'It's a long way down.'

We stopped in the village for a sandwich, then drove on to the strand. Therese waded to her ankles in the water. A wave took her by surprise and splashed in across her, soaking her skirt to her thighs. She gave a look as though incredulous at the ocean's gall then burst out laughing.

I laughed hard too. I reached out and took her arm, pulling her to me, as if I was simply pulling her to safety. I twisted her arm gently behind her back and held her to me. A drop of salty sea water balanced on her lower lip.

She twisted her wrist in my grip. 'Do you think I'll run away?' She licked the drop away.

'Stranger things have happened.' A sudden swell of loneliness lurched in my chest. It felt like ages since I had seen Knucky and Frances. I was back in another unreachable part of the world. The reality of my nearness to them made it worse.

Therese ran her finger across my lips. 'What are you thinking?'

'You should know better than to ask.'

She held her finger upright on my lips to *shush* me, nodding her agreement. I should have kissed her, but I didn't. We stood there and waited. Then she put her mouth to mine. Over her shoulder the first of the ships came slowly into view.

'What happens now?'

I washed my hands in the bathroom. Therese stood at the door. It was almost six o'clock. We weren't long back. We had driven through Killybegs out to Mc Swynes Bay. The huge bulk of the factory ships loomed across the water. Despite their marine credentials they seemed out of place. Like the result of an unwarranted natural disaster, as though a shower of meteorites had crashed out of the sky and fallen to lodge in the shallow sea bed, protruding through the surface of the water.

When Therese and I saw them from the beach earlier in the afternoon an unexpected sense of doom descended as though something was about to end. Something neither of us might ever fully be aware of, but something we would have to bear the results of forever.

We sat in the car at the bay and watched. Neither of us spoke. Therese leaned across in her seat and lay against my shoulder. I tried to make out the names of the ships. I thought it possible that I could see the *Balticskayaslava II* but could not be certain. I could easily have fetched the binoculars in the trunk of the car, but I chose not to. Therese rubbed my hand. I waited a few moments more then started up the engine and drove back to the hotel.

I dried my hands and looked at Therese framed in the bathroom door. 'I'll head out again in a while. Try to meet up with some of the crew. It's their first night in town, their first chance to get off the ships in days.'

Therese came in and put her arms around my waist from behind. 'I'm worried.'

I watched her in the mirror. Her chin rested on my shoulder. Her cheek brushed up against mine. 'I can handle it,' I told her. At least she was worried. There was consolation in that.

'You don't know what you're getting into here.'

'Why should I be getting into anything?' Therese slipped her hand through the gap between the buttons in my shirt. 'What do you think I'm getting into?'

Her fingers rubbed my stomach above my navel.

'I don't know. That's why I don't like it.'

'It'll be okay.'

She kissed me behind my ear and pushed her hand up across my chest. 'Convince me of it.'

We ate from the bar menu. There was no mention of wine or alcohol of any sort although I could have done with a drink. Therese ate little. She looked agitated throughout. Afterwards she suggested getting some fresh air, after that she said she'd come back and leave me to it.

The evening light was pale in the sky. A faint glow of red dispersed along the horizon. A wan moon hung low. We both felt a chill and pulled into one another more. We crossed over the road and down into the harbour where some of the fishing boats were making their way back in. They slowly eased between one another, their engines chugging loudly or spluttering to a halt. Groups of men gathered along the pier talking and shouting at one another. Ropes were thrown from the boats and tied around the bollards and metal rings, cranes screeched as they winched crates of fish off the decks. Therese held her nose and made faces. A car drove past forcing us to walk right at the edge. Rainbow patches of oil streaked the surface of the choppy water. We stepped over ropes and netting. Family groups walked past in both directions. A line of people stood aimlessly at the end of the pier. I saw a number of small boats sail around the headland and felt a flutter of excitement; they would be coming to and from the factory ships collecting supplies, bringing the crew members whose shifts were over ashore.

I walked with Therese to the end of the pier and watched the boats. I explained to her what they were doing. She said nothing. She looked sad, as if the boats were coming to take one of us away.

'Come on,' I said and led her away.

We walked back to a bench halfways along the pier and sat down. I watched two young men, their heads kept low, standing on the deck of a boat dividing up fish into separate plastic crates. One whistled softly to himself. It could easily have been Knucky and me.

Therese saw me looking at them. 'Is this your life?' she asked.

'Was,' I corrected her. And then corrected myself. 'No. That was never my life. That's the problem, don't you think?'

'Whatever is.' Therese brushed back some strands of hair that had blown across her face. 'Does anyone ever really live their life?'

'I don't see how they can.'

Therese tried to laugh. 'We make a great couple, a regular bundle of laughs.'

I smiled. 'It could be worse.'

I put my arm around her shoulder. She leaned in against me. We sat in silence and watched the people passing up and down, listened to portions of their indecipherable conversations. Snatches of words cast adrift, at a loss for sense.

Suddenly the awkward sound of a foreign language cut sharply through the air. A group of eight or nine older women pushed through the other people walking on the pier. Their rough features were worn into their skin. All portly. They looked and sounded Russian. I turned to Therese and whispered, 'My ship's come in.'

She squeezed my hand. I felt nervous and very afraid. Three younger women followed behind the older ones. Taller and somewhat thinner but full-bodied nevertheless. They looked around and laughed loudly with confidence. The confidence that foreignness affords. Delighting in their being the centre of attention. Secure in the knowledge they could not be understood. One looked over her shoulder and shouted back something at a group of men now making their way through. A few responded together in a confusion of sounds, and the three girls laughed hilariously.

'Wouldn't it be great?' Therese said.

'What?' I asked.

'Anonymity.' She looked after the women who had passed. 'I told you about my island, didn't I, out in the Pacific? Someday I'll make it there.'

'What if you find it overrun with natives?' I asked watching after the women also.

'All the better.'

'I can just see you,' I said, 'lying beneath a palm tree drinking coconut milk, queen of some remote tribe.'

'Don't forget the part about me making demands of dark muscular men.'

'That too.' A small wave splashed in across the pier and sent people scuttling back. Therese was pressed in against me.

'We're all born to be rulers, don't you think? It's just a matter of discovering whatever it is we were meant to rule.'

'And have you?'

'Don't worry,' she said. 'I'm still looking.'

I wondered about the people that had passed, if it was possible they were off the *Balticskayaslava II*. What if I did meet up with some of the crew and Mullen's Eskimo was with them? What Eskimo would I chase after then?

The motor boats that had brought the Russians in cast off their ropes and headed back out around the headland. The dying evening light suffused with the yellow of the moon to tinge their darkened edges. Like the calm before a storm. The lights came on along the pier. The wet concrete beneath our feet reflected their sheen. I was impatient to be moving now. I had a busy night ahead of me.

We spoke very little on the way back. We stepped into the lobby. A group of people came out from the bar. The bland piped music played softly. The clink of glass resounded. Therese said she'd go back to the room, watch television a while, and make an early night of it. It occurred to me that I did not know what would happen when she went back to the room. What calls she would make or receive.

She stopped at the base of the stairs while I handed her the room key. She held it in her palm like she had held my hand only moments earlier.

'I have only been back a few months,' she said. ' It's hard to credit.'

'It's a mysterious world,' I said.

'It is that all right,' she said. She leaned up and kissed me on the cheek. 'Good night. I'll probably be asleep when you get back.'

She looked sad again. It was a sadness I felt too. It had something to with returning, being back where you started. More than anything I wanted to take her hand and walk up those stairs to our room with nothing else to do than be with one another. She turned away and walked up the stairs alone. I waited at the bottom until she had gone from sight. I stood for a moment and felt her absence, then I went to the bar and ordered a drink. I half-expected her to reappear, to come back down and find me. I drank my drink down quickly and went out to the car.

I drove out to a point on the headland overlooking the harbour and the bay. I parked on the side of the road, took the binoculars and walked across the wiry grasses to the edge of the cliff. Its sheer face dropped on all sides. The waves crashed over the rocks and splashed high in the air. The winds whipped around me. The massive ships glowed in the darkening evening. Their vast length, the towering wheelhouses and their high masts, the tall cranes hinged like the heads and necks of giant birds. The engines of the motorboats going to and from the ships hummed loudly. I trained the glasses on them and tried to hold them steady as I focused on the nearest ship. I followed along the rails from the trawl deck at the back where the huge drag nets were hauled on board. I remembered hearing about these nets in Alaska, at least a hundred feet wide and forty feet high, gigantic open mouths dragging through the waters, strip-mining the sea. I imagined a host of corpses pulled from the depths, dumped through the hatches to the factory below, processed and frozen. I moved the glasses down the thick steel side to where the name was painted, but all I could see was a blur. I refocused the binoculars. The large black lettering appeared in my vision with startling clarity as if it had always been that easy to see what was before me, the simple act of focusing, adjusting light in the right direction. *Geroiperikopa*. I scanned across the other ships focusing slowly each time. *General Radizefskiy*. *Vasileostovskiy*. *Frederyk Chopin*. Until finally I spotted it, half-hidden by the ships in front of it.

Balticskayaslava II. My heart pumped rapidly.

I observed people on deck moving to and fro. I watched them for a few minutes then searched the waters again. Motorboats moved amongst the immense ships appearing and disappearing. A low grating noise echoed through the air. Further behind I could see the reefers. The Klondykers that carried vast chunks of ice across the northern hemisphere. Gouging through economies and cultures. The return of an ice-age ordered by man.

I brought the glasses back to the *Balticskayaslava II* and examined every visible part. It must have been almost three hundred feet long. The crew would be large. It was entirely possible that some crew members would not be aware of the existence of others, particularly if they worked opposite shifts. I saw more activity further along the deck. Bodies descended the ladders towards the deep sea. I followed down with the binoculars until my view was blocked by the prow of another ship. They must have been boarding one of the small motorboats. I watched the waterline. Some time later the water churned white, and the boat came into view. I lost it again as it sailed between the ships. I spotted it again further up then lost it once more. A different boat wove around the anchored ships confusing me at first. The two boats cleared the fleet and headed across the open water. I identified the first one I had seen. It was lighter in colour and slightly bigger. I returned to the car and drove back into town.

It was the best I could think to do, to follow this boat and the people on it. God only knew where this would lead me. I parked by the harbour, positioned myself on the pier, and waited for the boats to come in. People continued to mill around. The taste of salt water coated my tongue. Pumped water gushed off a fishing boat back into the harbour. The boat from the *Balticskayaslava II* approached ahead of the other. It looked dangerously full. Someone shouted something incomprehensible across the water. I watched it all the way in. It pulled in by the steps. A crowd of about a dozen people climbed off. A mixture of men and women. They talked and laughed loudly. I thought of Therese and looked back at our hotel window. A light shone behind the curtains. A thick smell of cigarette smoke brought my attention back to the passing group. This was it. This was where I would follow them. Engage in duplicity.

I waited until they were well past then followed about twenty yards behind. They had split off into a number of smaller groups. I wondered which to go after if they went their separate ways. I was sorry now that I hadn't made some plans. Devised a better scheme. Once more I was fumbling my way forward unable to see what was right in front of my eyes.

They turned left at the harbour into town. A few stopped at a fast-food takeaway and peered through the window. The second group continued to walk ahead. Someone turned back, stopped, and said something. There was much talking between them before those at the takeaway went in. I crossed the road and watched from the other side. The other people carried on walking. I decided to stick with them. They seemed to know exactly where they were going. They walked up through the centre of the town and stopped outside a pub. Some words were exchanged. Two of the men and women waved and went on. The rest went inside. I waited by the edge of the pavement while a truck passed. Then I crossed over and entered also.

I saw them gathered in the corner and sat a few tables away. I ordered a drink and wondered what to do. I listened in to their conversation but couldn't understand a single word. I drank from my pint when it arrived and pretended to be watching television. Shortly afterwards another round of drinks was brought to their table. I finished my pint too and ordered another. I sat there unsure how to proceed. I could go over and say something, but what would I say and how much of it if any would they understand? The pointlessness of what I was doing had never felt greater.

Moments later they all stood up noisily. Two men banged their glasses together and drank down their drinks, vodkas I presumed. Then they all began to leave. I finished my drink, waited until they were outside, and followed them once more. I felt as though I were being led on some wild goose chase, where I would wind up down an alley beaten to a pulp.

They crossed the road and entered another bar about a hundred yards away. I crossed and went in after them. They stood by some tables at the back talking to some other people they seemed to know. I ordered a drink and sat down near to the door. I was drinking too fast, being forced along by their swift current. Already my eyes felt heavy.

They pulled in extra chairs and sat down with the others. One man went to the counter. I heard him order a round of drinks in broken English and felt a great relief. At least there was one person I might be able to communicate with. It was the first good sign. A few of the women laughed loudly. I looked down at them. One pushed at her dark hair. She caught me looking and smiled over. I lowered my gaze. I felt guilty as though I had been caught red-handed. I was further away than ever.

More drinks came and went. I needed to use the bathroom. I would have to pass their tables on the way. This was my opportunity, I decided. I would look towards the man who had spoken English at the bar, nod to him, say something in greeting, make his acquaintance no matter how slight. I awaited my moment, stood up uneasily and walked over. But by the time I got there he had turned away deep in conversation. The woman who had smiled over looked up at me instead. I knew I should say something. But she held the advantage, and I could think of nothing to say. I looked ahead as though I had not seen her and pushed the door of the toilets open. I stood at the sink and looked at myself in the mirror. My eyes blurred. I could scarcely recognize myself. I went to the urinal. I would have another chance on my way back out. I needed to make the most of it. But when I came out they were gone again.

I thought about going out onto the street after them one more time. Instead I sat back down to finish my drink. They could hardly be too far away. The town was not big enough to lose them in. Before I knew what I was doing I had called for another drink. Once more it had got the better of me.

I wandered from pub to pub afterwards drinking, looking out for them. There were plenty of foreign accents to be heard. Men and women in off any number of the ships swapping sleep for alcohol and relief, for the absence of fish, their ceaseless flow through hatches, the continuous movement of conveyor belts. More ships would arrive over the coming days, more people.

I approached many groups thinking I recognized some of them from those I had followed earlier. Maybe the man who had spoken English. Maybe the woman who had smiled over. But each time I got up close I was no longer so certain. Sometimes I tried to speak with them, but they didn't understand me. I barely understood myself. I should not have been drinking so much. I was wasting my opportunity with the Eskimo, wasting my opportunity with Therese.

But it didn't stop there.

I got back to the hotel sometime after one. I had talked to any number of foreigners, but I hadn't found the people off the ship. I hoped I hadn't been a nuisance. I hoped I hadn't said anything compromising.

Therese was sound asleep. I undressed and got into the other bed. I pulled the blankets up around me and sank into a viscous state of unconsciousness.

CHAPTER THIRTY-THREE

I awoke before Therese and opened the window to let out the stale smell of alcohol I had exhaled during the night. I reprimanded myself for another wasted opportunity. I looked at Therese sleeping. The rise and fall of her breathing. I would have to tell her something plausible.

I went for a short walk to clear my head. The day was overcast and humid. As ever I was drawn to the harbour. The activity continued unabated. Engines starting up, netting and lines being untangled. Gulls dived at the water breaking its surface with their beaks. Large refrigerated trucks rolled past. I watched a few men fishing off the side of the pier, walked a little further and then returned.

Therese was drinking coffee in the lobby. She greeted me and suggested we go in for breakfast. She asked about the night before.

'Not much to report, I'm afraid.' I told her about watching the boat and following the men and women into the pub. 'I didn't know how to approach them. I tried but to no avail. You were right. I should have planned it better.'

The waitress arrived with scrambled eggs and toast. 'What will you do now?' Therese asked.

I cut the egg and balanced it on the back of my fork. 'All I can think to do is try again.' I pushed it into my mouth.

Therese buttered her toast. 'Is that the best you can manage?'

'What else can I do?'

'It's your call,' she said. 'I'm only here for the break.'

'Tell me about it,' I said earnestly. I poured out a cup of coffee.

'What?' she asked. 'What do you want to know?'

I dipped my toast into the coffee and chewed on it. 'Why did you come?'

'You were worth another try.' She said it matter of factly.

'You believe that?'

'I have to. Otherwise...'

She left it there. As if she herself did not know how to finish it.

'Otherwise what?' This had to be resolved. For her and for me.

'Otherwise I won't make sense to myself anymore.' She twisted a strand of hair between her fingers. Looked away, down into herself. Her lips parted in a way that aroused me. 'I like you, Jim. This is what it comes down to ultimately.'

I felt a surge of pressure in my chest. It was the first time she had expressed her feelings so clearly with words. And they were clear. Even though it was so basic, and even though it was like and not love she had said it was as much as I could have hoped for.

'There are so many complications,' she went on. 'That's the difficult part. The simple act of caring is not enough. All around it are tangents and intersections. If you could only get down to that simple act and isolate it, then there might be something.'

'Buy it an island? Is that what you're saying?'

'No, that's not it at all. There you have the waters to contend with.' She laid her knife and fork down on her plate. 'Look.' She indicated over to a middle-aged couple by the window. 'What do you notice?'

'Tell me.'

'They're not talking. They're just sitting and eating. Pausing for silences.'

I looked over and thought about what she might be saying. I saw the couple look up from time to time and observe one another. But I did not know what their observations were, if they were even aware of them.

'It happens all the time,' Therese said. 'Couples. On holidays. Evenings out. Regular daily meals. Eating in silence as though they have nothing to say.' She ran her fingers along the edge of her plate, traced its contours. 'A priest told me one time that he thought this was terribly sad, how it came to this.'

I wondered if she meant Father Jack, if they had been out together making this observation.

'What do you think?' She looked to me as if she depended on my answer.

'Maybe they have no need to speak,' I suggested. 'Maybe that's all their silences are saying.'

She smiled and nodded. 'That's what I told him. It was another possibility, but it was not one he had considered.'

The waitress came back to clear away our plates. She asked if we wanted more coffee. We both said no.

'It's possible they have isolated something very simple,' she said. 'It's either that or isolate themselves.'

'And the priest? He must have been very isolated not to consider that other possibility.' I would gauge everything by her response.

Therese squeezed her throat between her fingers and thumb. She gazed past me. 'I believed so.'

She spoke in the past tense leaving the possibility that she no longer felt this way.

She looked back at me. Took in all of my face. She seemed capable of seeing deep inside of me in a way I could not manage myself. 'We are outside of each other's lives,' she said. 'We touch up against them every now and then, but that's all. The question is whether to alter this and to allow each other's lives to enter our own.' She smiled over. 'You see how seriously I am taking all of this.'

I reached across and placed my hand on hers. She began to withdraw it then let it rest. 'Maybe that's the only way to make sense of them.'

'Maybe it's the easy way out.'

'Was this a mistake, coming here?' I rubbed the backs of her fingers. She turned her hand around and held mine.

'There is no simple answer to that,' she said her fingers intertwining with mine. 'What is clear, however, is that we are not comfortable with silences yet.'

We got in the car and drove out of town again. I might have been better staying put. Some of the people from the night shift would be coming to shore. Some of those might have worked with him. But, it seemed to me, Therese and I needed to continue our investigation just as much. Besides I needed the dark of night. It was too easy to look in the wrong direction during daylight hours, too easy to be distracted. I only wished I could have believed this.

We drove up through Glenties towards Gweedore, the Irish speaking Gaeltacht region. Therese wanted to know if I could speak

Irish. I had enough trouble being understood in English, I told her. She didn't disagree. She told me that despite the years she had never forgotten the Irish she had learned. She had never consciously tried to remember it, she said, but that just like me it wouldn't go away. Could that be such a bad thing, I wondered? Therese smiled. 'There is no way of knowing,' she said.

The smell of turf drifted from the bungalows and thatched cottages. Like an indication of something hopeful the sun broke through.

We got back in around the same time as the day before. The day had gone well. We had enjoyed each other's company. Therese said she'd like a swim in the hotel pool, maybe a small workout in the gym. She looked serious.

'Are you coming?' she asked. 'It'd do you good.'

'I don't swim very well,' I told her.

She looked surprised 'I'll teach you. You can trust me with your life.'

'I didn't bring my trunks.'

'I'm sure something can be arranged.' Therese was not letting go.

'I'll watch. How about that?'

'That's cheating,' she said.

'I never claimed to be honest.' It was only meant as a joke but Therese looked upset. To take the emphasis off my honesty or lack of it, I relented.

They had a box of swimming trunks people had left behind by mistake. I sifted through them and found a pair to fit. Therese went back to the room for her swimsuit and for towels. We parted at the changing rooms. I changed and showered, then went on through to the pool. Apart from an older man swimming lengths purposefully it was empty. Therese came through at the same time. She wore a black sports swimsuit. It clung smoothly to the curves of her body. Her long hair was pushed back in under her white cap. Her face looked stark with the absence of hair. The thin angularity of her features were exposed, but her beauty was amplified by this not diminished. She had the graceful appearance of a bathing beauty from an early black and white movie.

'Come along,' she said taking my hand.

We walked together to the steps at the edge. She went down first and I followed after. The water rose above my feet and ankles, and with each further step higher up my calves, knees, thighs and waist. It came halfways up my chest as I stepped onto the bottom of the pool. I held onto the silver bar on the side. Therese pushed her arms out in front of her, ducked her head, kicked with her legs and was gone, propelled along the surface of the water. I was left alone.

She turned expertly at the far end and pushed off back up towards me. She didn't stop as I had expected but turned and set off again. I noticed the firm muscles in her calves and thighs, the splashes of water at her heels. I let go of the bar and splashed out with my arms and legs across the width of the pool. I didn't want to get out of my depth. I would not have been able to swim the length of it and back. I would have been stranded. The water that supported her so easily would have been my downfall.

Therese did ten lengths of the pool before stopping.

'That was impressive,' I said.

'That shows how little you know,' she laughed. Water streamed down her cheeks. She nodded down the pool with her head. 'Now you.'

'I couldn't.'

'Of course you could. I saw you swimming.'

'I'd never make it all the way.'

She looked cross. 'You didn't give up on the Eskimo so easily.'

'That's not the same,' I said. I was angry at her for bringing him up here and now.

'Yes it is,' she said. 'It's precisely the same.' She leaned back and floated beside me on her back. For a split second I imagined her dead. Her drowned body floating lifelessly. Then she bent her legs downwards and stood up again. 'Come on. I'm with you all the way.' She took my arm and pulled me along. I felt forced into doing something I wasn't comfortable with. I wanted to tell her it was unreasonable, but I understood there were certain expectations she had of me that I was obliged to live up to. I shook free of her grip and swam.

My feet were too high in the water, and I felt the heavy splashing and the slap of hard surface tension against the front of my feet. My arms moved sluggishly beneath the water, broke free and submerged too soon. I tried to keep my face out of the water unlike Therese, who pushed hers beneath it. The effort was strenuous. My arms and legs were tired and weak. I was short of breath. I swallowed a large mouthful of water through my throat down into my stomach. The insides of my nostrils burned. The taste of chlorine choked in my mouth. I spluttered out water losing all balance and momentum. The back of my body was pulled sharply downwards as though heavily weighted. My head went under. Before I closed my eyes a refractory smattering of light particles distorted my vision. I thought of Frances and our acid trip together. I felt her lips on mine kissing me as she kissed the Eskimo. A cold blue kiss of death. I swirled in the water, my body turning helplessly, effortlessly, as it sunk to the depths. My limbs floated easily, free of conscious movement. And my mind floated too, unrestrained by conscious thought. Waves of deep pleasure rippling through a world devoid of corporeal confinement. No longer a stranger but an intimate of everything natural.

And then the unwelcome surge from below, consciousness returning as my body arose from the depths to tear apart the frail surface, reaching for contact and gasping for air as some unwanted survival instinct resurrected itself from the recesses of my body. Gulping and spluttering, retching water from my lungs. I stretched out my arm and grasped the bar at the side of the pool to hold myself aloft. With my free hand I rubbed my eyes and sought out Therese. She was swimming at the far end of the pool oblivious to all that had occurred as a result of her encouragement. Unaware of my drowning, and worse than that unaware of my coming back to life.

We dressed after swimming and as with the evening before we had something light to eat before Therese retired for the night. I walked her to the room and stood with her just inside the doorway. I apologized that we could not spend more time together, but Therese said it was fine.

'It's as much as I can take of you,' she joked. She tiptoed up and kissed me on the lips. 'Really,' she said, 'this is good for now.' She stepped back, brushed at her hair with her right hand and folded her left arm across her stomach. 'I still would prefer if you did not do this,' she said, 'but I know I am being unfair.' She touched her lips lightly with the tips of her fingers. 'Just do me one favour, settle it tonight, do whatever needs to be done, not for my sake but yours.'

'I will,' I promised her. She was right, I could not afford another night like the previous one.

'Good,' she said as though she were placing all of her trust in me. 'Now go.'

It was not easy to move with the burden she had placed upon me, but I wished her goodnight and turned to go.

'If it is at all possible,' she said after me, 'have fun.'

I smiled and closed the door behind me.

I stood outside the entrance of the hotel and wondered what to do, if I should drive out to the headland again, follow the same procedure as the night before. But already that procedure had been broken, and for the better I hoped; I had by-passed the bar on the way outside.

I stood there absently looking towards the pier contemplating all of this without formulating thoughts with any real structure. I closed my eyes and breathed in the air. For a moment a feeling of absolute pleasure swept through me as it had done in the pool earlier when I had slipped beneath the water. I held my breath then exhaled deeply. It was then, with my breath escaping from me, my vision closed off, that I heard the swathe of voices, the harsh Russian accents. I opened my eyes and looked across. A group of men and women were passing on the other side of the road. I recognized some of them from the night before. This was it then. This was the way it was to be.

'Good fishermen do not follow the fish,' Knucky had told me once, 'they are ahead of them. It's in here.' He patted his chest. 'All you have to do is follow that. The rest is easy.'

I hoped he was right, that from here on in the rest would be easy.

I followed them down the street into one of the bars. The smell of alcohol washed through me as I entered. I was determined to go easy on it tonight.

I counted eight people in all. Five men and three women. They pulled two tables together and sat around them. I sat up at the counter and ordered a Guinness. Someone came up beside me and ordered a round of drinks in broken English. It was the same man I had wanted to speak to the night before. I held my Guinness in front of me and looked into the creamy sea of froth. Another ocean to drown in if I wasn't careful. I lifted it to my lips and poured a mouthful between them. I looked at the man standing beside me and listened to the noise from the tables behind me. I could speak to him right here and now if I wanted, but I decided to bide my time. It was too soon to interrupt. I needed to let their night grow on them some more, let the alcohol loosen their tongues and the tight integrity of their group. They were bound here by their differences, isolated like Therese's island, but in time their underlying plates would drift and our landmasses would merge. All it would take was aeons of patience and oodles of booze.

The barman placed a tray of drinks before him. The man paid and left. A quiz show played on the television above my head. I remembered then that this was the bar I had come into with Frances where the old man had complained about Alaska. I looked around to see if he was anywhere in sight, but I couldn't see him anywhere. I would like to have spoken more to him, to have found out what it was really like in the past, in its previous lifetime. I drank slowly keeping my glass at a safe distance.

Sitting there sober remembering the old man and my time here with Frances I began to feel uneasy. Both Tom Harte and Charlie had suggested they knew I had broken into the harbour master's office here. It was possible was it not that I was under surveillance by the guards while I was here? Right at this moment in fact. I even looked around to see if anyone was watching me, but no one seemed to be taking any interest in me at all, as though I was of no consequence whatsoever. But then that was the requirement of good surveillance, was it not. To give the appearance that you were not watching someone when in fact you were? Much as I was watching the group of Russians without them knowing it. Much as I had the investigation into the life and death of the Eskimo under surveillance too.

I nursed my pint and paranoia while the men and women drank their alcohol down hungrily, eating and swallowing their foreign conversation just as ravenously. Laughing loudly as though glad to see the back of their working day. The women smiled and flirted, the men placed their arms around them until they were brushed away. They raised their glasses and banged them together making a home from home for themselves. Singing songs that crossed oceans as treacherously as fishing ships, as frail as human beings, resurfacing in bars with strength and endurance. I wished Frances was here to see this.

I looked at the clock. It was almost ten. I finished the dregs of my pint and ordered another. I thought of Mullen alone in his office with his cat and his whiskey. Was that what I was doomed to become, a lonely man lost in misplaced subterfuge? A man shrouded in danger, the possibilities of violence. I wondered what numbers he had dialled when I left his office, who he was ringing and what he would reveal to suit his own ends. My visits, my requests were occasions of illicit commerce too no doubt, information to be traded for monetary gain.

The barman interrupted my thoughts. He placed a fresh pint on the beer mat in front of me. I thanked him and handed him the money. He remained where he was looking at me.

'I remember you,' he said lifting the coins into his hand. 'You were the one asking about the Eskimo. I had to throw you out in the end.'

I smiled wearily. I thought about denying it, but it would only have made matters worse. 'That's right,' I said, 'but I've learned my lesson. No Eskimos, no drinking after hours.'

The barman shook my money in his loose fist. He looked me over again. 'You look harmless,' he said after due deliberation.

'It's a look that suits me,' I told him. 'But don't go judging a book by its cover.'

He opened his fist and took out a coin. He flipped it in the air, caught it in his palm and turned it over onto the counter, covering it with his palm. 'Heads or tails?' he asked.

'Heads.'

He smiled and took his hand away. 'Tails,' he said. 'You know they found one in someone's nets?'

I nodded and took a drink.

'You know the guards have been asking around?'

I nodded again.

'That's what I thought, ' he said. He placed the coin on its edge and flicked it with his thumb so that it spun on the counter top like a globe. 'The way it is,' he continued, 'we don't pay much heed around here. These people they come and go, keep us in business. I wouldn't know a fucking Eskimo if he hit me in the face.'

'Way I hear it,' I said, 'this one would do precisely that.'

The barman grinned like he already knew. 'They come, they go, they come back.' he said. 'It's our business.'

'Except this one isn't coming back.'

'Not him exactly, that's true, but someone else will take his place.' He grabbed the spinning globe put an end to its revolution. 'What's your interest?' he asked.

'He hit me in the face, in a manner of speaking,' I replied.

'It's like I say, you look harmless.' He looked down at my pint. For a moment I thought he was going to drink it on me. 'My advice to you is to play dead. It's your best chance for survival.'

He left with my money. I returned to my pint. I listened to the unintelligible drunken babble from behind me. We were all a long way from home. I thought of Therese tucked up in a strange bed in the hotel. I thought of her dark red lipstick on the pale white flesh of Father Jack's body like the scars of a crucified man and the purple bruises on the Eskimo's body.

The same Russian man came to the counter to order again. He pushed in beside me. His broken English kept him in this position no doubt, speaking for others. I felt ready for him now. I turned to him and said hello. He looked at me with confusion, then grunted something back and repeated his order to the barman. They were drinking vodka. The barman filled eight glasses and placed them on a tray for him. As he headed back down to this table he looked at me momentarily, nodded and carried on.

At least some contact had been made no matter how insignificant, like a faint beam from a lighthouse someplace in the distance. I drank until my pint was almost finished. The barman asked if I wanted another. I shook my head, 'Not yet.' Then before he left I made a snap decision. 'Buy them a round on me, ' I said indicating the tables they sat at.

The barman looked at me as if I was overstepping boundaries. Then he shrugged, 'It's your call. Your funeral.'

He reached for a new bottle of vodka, broke the seal and took it to their tables. He filled their glasses and said something to them. Then he nodded over to me. The man I had spoken to at the bar looked over. He raised his glass then waved for me to join them. I hesitated although this was the moment I had waited for. The man waved again. I slipped down off my stool and brought my drink with me.

The man held his glass up. 'Why?' he asked in English.

'To welcome you back to Donegal,' I said.

He looked at me strangely as though he had no understanding of what I had just said. A moment later he burst out laughing with a loud raucous roar, the meaning finally having sunk in.

'Sit,' he ordered making room.

I pulled up a chair and joined them. Now it was I who were a stranger in their midst, but I was there where I had wanted to be. I could hardly believe how easy it had turned out.

The man wagged his finger over and back. 'We speak little English here.' It sounded like a warning of sorts.

The rest of the group continued to shout and talk as though I wasn't present. Thick chunks of smoke were blown from their cigarettes, and the heavy fumes of alcohol hung above the table. Coarse coughing and laughing and shouting rasped all around. One of the women handed me a large glass of vodka and raised her glass in a toast. It was the woman who had caught me looking over the night before. I wondered if she remembered me. I drank the vodka down too quickly. My head felt light. A man could slip away into the midst of this and never be missed nor found.

'Yuri.' The man beside me held out his large hand.

'Jim.' I surrendered my hand to his. He wrung it hard.

'Jim.' He repeated my name but in his deep accent.

'Yuri.' I repeated his for good measure. He growled with laughter and banged the table with his empty glass.

'The Irish like to drink, no?'

'We have our moments,' I said. Despite my best intentions the alcohol was creeping up on me.

Another round of drinks arrived at our table. I was included amongst them. Yuri handed me my glass. He rubbed at his forehead hard then banged his glass against mine. '*Slainte*.' He roared laughing again delighted with his solitary word of Irish.

'*Slainte*,' I repeated, and we drank to each others' health. Then he rejoined the conversation going on around me. I was left floundering at the edges. I hung in there. More drinks appeared from out of nowhere. The woman who gave me the vodka leaned across and said something I could not understand. She waited as though expecting a response. I realized she had spoken in English. I raised my hands. 'I am sorry,' I apologized. 'I do not understand.' I asked her to repeat it, but this time she did not seem to understand me. She gave up, smiled and shook her head. Then she turned to the woman beside her and said something which made them both laugh hard.

Moments later the loud rattle of the shutters came down hard on the counter like a lift door closing. My stomach heaved, and I felt myself begin to descend.

Somebody slapped my back and laughed into my face. I laughed just as heartily and said something which prompted more laughter. I discovered another glass of vodka in my hand. My Guinness from earlier was nowhere to be seen. I spoke to anyone who would listen. Then we were all surging through the bar in a wave, spilling out through the door and into the street. The woman who had tried to speak to me slipped one arm around my waist and the other around Yuri's. She sang at the top of her voice. Others began to accompany her. I picked up on a few sounds from the chorus and shouted them out loudly. She looked down at me and dug her fingers into my ribs.

'You sing good Russian,' she laughed.

I smiled stupidly just happy to hear her speak good English.

We turned up street after street as though someone knew exactly where we were going. At one point Yuri turned to the woman and shouted out my name. He seemed to be making introductions. The woman nodded and told me hers. I grinned and immediately forgot it. Then we were turning into the gateway of someone's house, and up the driveway, and in the open front door. I stood in the hallway at the bottom of the stairs. A crowd of men sat in a circle in the room opposite me playing cards and drinking from open bottles. A man and woman sat halfways up the stairs kissing and clawing at one another. People pushed past me in both directions. Someone pressed a glass into my hand. Yuri and the woman were gone. I walked down the end of the hallway into the kitchen. It was crowded. The fridge door was wide open. A carton of milk and a half pound of butter were the only things left inside. A few six packs were torn open on the sink, and cans full and empty littered the counter tops. I saw Yuri in the corner talking with three other men. A blur of languages and accents collided in the smoke-filled air. I was strangely disappointed to hear the clear strain of English being spoken naturally and to recognize distinctive Irish features mingling with the strangers. Something in the back of my mind told me it was for the better, that it would protect me, make my inquiries when they came less threatening. But there was something about being alone too, about standing out, that appealed to me. It upped the ante. Ensured better returns. Yuri waved over at me. I pushed through the people passing by, but when I got to his corner he was gone.

A doorway led into another room. It was only partially lit. People stood around in the shadows, some sat in chairs, and a few lay out on the ground. A voice sang out from the dark in Russian. A lonesome dirge. A man and woman danced slowly together. He held the back of her head with his hand, the red glow of a cigarette between his fingers like a neon indicator of something illicit about to unfold. I leaned back against the wall. My head spun. The slow song ended and something boisterous took its place. People cheered and clapped. I imagined a man crouched down to the floor with his hands on his hips kicking his legs out in time to the music. I pushed myself up off the wall, forced my way out into the hall and up the stairs, brushing past the amorous couple. Despite the chaos in my head I knew I needed to do something about the situation. I needed to redeem the night.

The bathroom was locked when I got there. I knocked on the door loudly. And knocked again. I waited a moment and knocked a third time. A toilet flushed, the lock turned and a man and woman came out. She had her arms about his neck. She blew me a kiss, whispered something to the man, then stumbled off down the stairs. I went in and locked the door after me. A shower attachment was fixed to the wall above the bath. I turned it on to cold and plunged my head under. The water streamed over my face, into my eyes and ears and mouth. My head shook with the bitter shock of it. I pulled my head out, wiped the water from my face with my hands, then stuck it under again. I did this two or three times more then turned off the water and dried myself with a towel. The front of my jumper was drenched. I wrung it out over the bath without taking it off and looked at myself in the mirror. I looked like I had just come up from out of the sea.

I went back downstairs and found Yuri in the front room watching the men playing cards. He seemed to be shouting instructions to everyone.

He smiled when he saw me and put his arm around my shoulder.

'My friend,' he said. 'My Irish friend.'

'Yuri, can I ask you something?' I put my arm around his shoulder also and tugged at him to follow me. I felt a little more sober. Yuri mumbled something I couldn't understand but came with me nevertheless. I brought him out into the front garden. We sat down on the doorstep. We were high up on a hill at the back of town. The lights shone brightly below us.

'Look,' Yuri said, 'home.'

Off in the distance, right at the edge of the darkness, a geometric line of lights from the factory ships lit up the sky like a constellation.

'Do you miss your real home?' I asked. Yuri didn't seem to understand. 'Russia. Where you live. It is a long way.'

'Yes, ' he said. 'A long way. ' A woman squealed behind us, and Yuri laughed.

'Do you miss it? Would you like to be back there?'

Yuri put his glass down on the step. He shrugged. 'I am here.' He put his hands on his knees. 'Do you understand that?'

'I think so.' I tried to remember what question I had asked him but was unable to.

Yuri began to sing. A man stepped between us and walked over to the wall. We could hear him retching. Yuri stopped singing. I pushed my head into my hands and rubbed my eyes and temples. Although the cold shower water had helped I needed to get my mind more in order. I had to find out if Yuri knew the Eskimo. With Yuri drunk it would be easier to ask. There would be fewer recriminations.

I waited until he paused in his singing then I spoke. 'Yuri, a friend of mine, George Fleming, mentioned an Eskimo he used to drink with sometimes when the ships were in. Perhaps you have met George.'

Yuri shook his head. 'I meet many people.' He started to sing again. His song was taking him somewhere out of here, somewhere he wanted to be.

I put my hand on his arm. Yuri stopped. 'George has something for the Eskimo. He asked me to watch out for him while I was here.' Yuri did not react, as though he had not heard me in the first place. 'Do you know him, the Eskimo? Can you help me?'

Yuri breathed deeply. 'What is it you are asking?' He looked like he was wondering where he was and what he was doing here with me.

'I need to find the Eskimo. George has something for him.'

'Who is George?'

'George Fleming. He used to drink with the Eskimo here. He has something for him.'

'I do not know him, this George Fleming.'

'Do you know the Eskimo?'

'What Eskimo?'

Yuri was taking none of this in. So I told him again about George drinking with an Eskimo and the lie about George having something for him.

'I am wondering if you might know this Eskimo, that's all.'

Yuri crossed his hands behind his head. He closed his eyes. 'I do not know,' he said.

'Have you ever heard of an Eskimo on board one of the ships?' I did not want him to know that I knew there had been one on his.

Yuri looked like he might fall asleep. He breathed heavily. Finally he spoke. 'There was an Eskimo on board the ship I am from. But I did not know him. There are many people on board.' He opened his eyes and looked up at me. 'This may not be the same Eskimo. There is more than one Eskimo, yes?'

'Maybe.'

'I think so.'

He closed his eyes again. I was afraid he would really fall asleep on me. I shook his shoulder until he looked up. 'Yuri this is very important. Is the Eskimo still on board? Is he here?'

Yuri sighed. 'It is too late. This Eskimo. It is too late now.'

'What do you mean?'

Yuri hummed to himself. Then he sat up and threw back what was left of his drink. He stood up quickly. He kicked his glass off the step into the grass. I could not tell if it was by accident or on purpose. His foot slipped down off the step, and he almost fell. He climbed back up to go back into the house. He turned around at the door. 'Fucking Eskimo. That's what you say, no?' I seemed to have heard nothing else. 'Ask Zoya, she will know.'

That was her name. Zoya. The name Yuri had shouted to me as we walked down the road together. Yuri said something else in Russian and went inside. I stayed outside for a long time looking at the lights of the ships. It seemed I might have found my Eskimo. In one way or another I felt more in control now. More capable of determining my immediate future. I went back in to look for Zoya.

I glanced into the front room on passing. Yuri was arguing with another man. The card game continued on the floor. The amorous couple were gone from the stairs. I went into the kitchen. It was still packed with people. I couldn't see Zoya anywhere. I pushed through into the room where the singing had come from. More couples were dancing haphazardly to an Irish traditional tune playing on a tape recorder. An Irish girl danced a jig by herself. A few people watched her. The rest danced or talked around her as though they had lost interest.

It was hard to make anyone out in the darkness. I walked around the edges of the room looking for her. A number of men and women were sprawled across the floor. It was impossible to see their faces. She could have been any one of them. She could possibly be upstairs. I stepped over legs and stood by the table trying to decide what to do next.

A pair of arms encircled my waist from the back surprising me, and a woman's voice spoke softly into my ear in Russian. I half-turned in her grip. Zoya smiled.

'Zoya,' I said grateful to have found her or for her to have found me.

'Jem.' It sounded good the way she said it. Her face was tipped to one side, and her dark hair spread behind her. She was very drunk. My head spun from time to time, but my thoughts managed to keep a semblance of order. 'You are here.'

Although she had spoken some English before it came as a great relief to hear her speak it again.

'Here I am, ' I said. I leaned back against the table her hands still wrapped around my waist.

'I am happy,' she said. 'Very, very happy.'

'That's good.' Everything seemed to be falling into place, but I was unsure what to do about it. Zoya was drunkenly holding onto me. She possessed information I needed about an Eskimo, but I had not yet deserted Therese. Every time I looked at Zoya I thought of Therese. Zoya's features were plain, her build fuller and bigger than Therese's, her accent harsher. She was attractive, but Therese's presence held sway. Zoya stepped forward and fell against me. The weight of her body pushed against mine. I helped straighten her up.

'I must thank you,' she said. 'I am too drunk.' She looked like she might laugh. 'Please dance.'

She tried to pull me out onto the floor. An Irish reel was playing. It was against my nature and both of our conditions, but it seemed the only thing to do. Within seconds Zoya stumbled beneath my legs. She lay prone on the ground laughing hard. I bent down to help her up. She took my arm and pulled me down on top of her. I spun in a swirl of faces as I fell. Zoya wrapped her arms around me. She whispered in my ear. Something in Russian. It sounded dangerous and erotic. But it could have meant anything. I was aware of an audience looking down on us. I tried to get up, but Zoya wouldn't let me. Every time I moved away she pulled me back down on top of her. Then she began to kiss me passionately. I tasted salt on her lips. Salt which I imagined had risen from the depths of the Siberian salt mines. I heard a roar of approval from above. An incomprehensible chant began. I got my arms under her shoulders and finally managed to pull her into a sitting position. I forcefully disengaged myself and lifted her up. The crowd began to clap.

'Let's go,' I whispered and led her out by her arm. We walked out into the front garden. Zoya pointed at something in the sky then pulled in close to me. We walked down the path and out through the gate. I turned us to the left down the hill in the direction of town. I needed to get her away from the party. For us to be alone.

'Where do you stay?' Zoya nuzzled against my cheek.

'At the hotel.' I followed along the avenue unsure which way to turn.

'We go there.' She looked very pleased.

'No.'

Her lips dropped in mock disappointment. 'We must,' she said.

'We must not.'

'You don't like me?' She smiled as she said this, disbelieving it herself.

'I like you.' I kissed her for good measure. 'Let's walk a little first.'

We walked down the hill through a small housing estate. We seemed to be lost, getting nowhere, walking around in circles. It was not the way we had come, but I didn't mind. It would do us both good. Give us time to sober up a little. Zoya leaned in against me willing to go wherever it was I was taking her. I watched the lights in the houses snap on and off. Angry voices screeched from behind a window. Dogs barked. A car alarm rang continuously a few streets away. I saw a taxi pull up at the end of the street and four drunken teenagers got out laughing and talking louder than was necessary. One young boy pulled a can of beer from under his jacket and drank it down. Zoya hummed quietly.

'Where are you from? What is the name of your town or city?' I asked. I wanted to hear her say Khatanga or Anadyr. Names I had heard mentioned in Alaska. Places high above the Arctic Circle bordering its icy ocean.

'Kalinin,' she sang it low. 'It is near Moscow.'

I saw a Give Way sign at the bottom of the street to our left. It seemed to lead back onto the main road. I turned us down towards it.

'How did you end up working on a fishing boat?'

'It is my penance, is it not?' A door banged, and a man came running out onto the street in front of us. He got into a car and drove off.

'Is it?' I asked.

Zoya shivered. 'It is as cold here as home.' She pulled me closer. 'It was a man,' she explained. She exhaled in despair. 'The work is okay. I think I like it.'

We came out on the main road leading down into town.

'Look,' she said pointing to the lights in the sky from the flotilla of ships.

'I see it,' I told her. The rumble of an articulated lorry reverberated through the stillness. I could feel her shivering. I took off my jacket and threw it across her shoulders. The wild drunkenness of the party had diffused into a quiet inebriation. She almost looked sad as though a great unhappiness lay just beyond the horizon which we could come upon at any moment. The questions I was about to ask could easily precipitate it, but I could see no alternative.

I rubbed my hand along her upper arm for comfort. 'The last time your ship was here a friend of mine met an Eskimo. I need to find him. Yuri said you might help.'

She pulled her head back and looked up. 'Yuri said so?'

I nodded. Zoya slowed her pace. She pulled back from me. I tried to keep in step with her. She brushed her hair from her face. She seemed to listen to the sound of our footsteps.

'I have something for him from my friend,' I lied.

'Yuri said so?' she repeated. She stopped walking. She folded her arms and stood in the middle of the pavement. She looked as if she was considering all that Yuri had ever done. She pushed her folded arms upwards and pulled at the lapels of my jacket. 'I have little interest in your Eskimo,' she said. Then continued walking. I followed alongside and put my arm around her. She let it rest there. I kissed her neck.

'Please Zoya, I need to know.'

'What do you need to know?' She looked at me as though she despised my existence.

'I need to know who he is.' She breathed hard as though her breathing was becoming more difficult. I stroked her cheek. 'Please, Zoya.'

Zoya put her hand on mine and held it there. A light drizzle began to fall. It swept lightly across our faces. 'What do you have for him?' She wiped the rain from her eyelids.

'Hope,' I said.

'What do you mean by hope?' She was angry, as if her English had finally let her down at a point when she most needed it.

'I wish I knew the Russian word for it,' I told her.

Zoya began to sob. Small cries choked in her throat. Her shoulders hunched up and down. We came back out on the main street of town. The lights of the hotel were visible ahead. The streets were deserted. Although the rain was light it soaked through our clothes. I stopped and pulled her in to me. I felt the dampness all around her and the heat of her body beneath it. Her wet hair covered the side of my face. She sniffled and tried to control her crying.

'What do you know of the Eskimo?' she asked.

'Nothing,' I said.

'That is it,' she said. She stepped back and wiped her eyes with her fingers. Then she ran her knuckles below her nose. 'Now. Zoya and Jem. What will we do?'

This was as much as she was going to tell me for now. I trailed the toe of my shoe along the ground in front of her as though drawing a line between us. 'I don't know.'

She pushed her hands into the pockets of my jacket. 'A boat will come. You will come with me to the ship.' She nodded her assent.

'Is that permitted?'

Zoya laughed sharply. 'It will happen,' she said.

I looked back up to the hotel where Therese was waiting for me, then out at the halo of lights reflected in the sky. I didn't want anything to happen between myself and Zoya, but I needed to know more about the Eskimo's world. I needed his presence. He had been on Knucky's boat with me. It seemed the least I could do to go out on his. I wanted to feel the firmness of his ground beneath my feet.

'How will I get back?'

Zoya smiled. 'A boat will come.'

'This requires a lot of trust in boats,' I said. But Zoya did not seem to hear.

She pushed my wet hair back behind my ears with her hands. She kept her hands on the sides of my head. She looked up into my face, and then down to the ground.

'The Eskimo is dead. Whatever you have for him, it is not good now.' She glanced back to see my reaction. A light trickle of rainwater ran down her forehead along the bridge of her nose.

'What happened?'

She breathed loudly through her nose, moved her hands down to cup my face. 'Nothing.' She looked down to the harbour. 'You will come?'

I covered her hands with mine. They felt wet and cold.

'Yes.'

'Good.' She reached up and kissed me on the lips. She quickly pushed her arm through mine and began walking.

I looked back up at the hotel as we turned down onto the harbour. The lights in our room were out. Ahead of us three men stumbled along in silence. The tall masts of the boats bobbed and swayed. We walked down to the end of the pier. The men sat with their feet over the edge. Zoya and I sat to the side on an empty bench. I began to say something, but the sound of my voice carrying in the night stopped me. I put my arm around Zoya.

'When will the boat come?' I whispered.

'I do not know,' Zoya said. She sat huddled in my jacket beneath my arm. I listened to the clinking of metal off the boats. It reminded me of the bells at the beginning of 'Harbour Lights', an old song from the fifties my parents had liked to play. I felt happy and lonesome at once.

A short while later we heard shouting from out on the street. A group of men and women turned down into the harbour. Over the next three quarters of an hour more arrived in dribs and drabs. A few hoarse voices continued to sing, and squeals of laughter occasionally erupted. One man and woman disappeared into the darkness behind the toilets. No one took any notice of me. Zoya looked up from time to time but barely spoke. I had the feeling of being in the wrong place at the wrong time. Another fifteen or twenty minutes passed. Then the three men on the edge of the pier began talking loudly and pointing out in front of them. I heard the muffled roar of the motor boat. I saw its light. Everyone stood up and began to gather at the steps leading down off the pier. Zoya yawned and stretched. She smiled and stood up then sat down again.

'It is not going to our ship. We must wait.'

The boat filled and pulled away. We continued to sit in silence. More people arrived. Two more boats came and went. Zoya leaned in against my chest. I put my arm around her. She looked to be asleep. I heard the sound of another boat approaching. I wondered if I should say something to her, but Zoya stirred and looked up.

'Now,' she said in a low voice and stood up. She held out her hand to me. I took it and stood with her behind the others. There were a lot of people gathered now, and I wasn't sure there would be room for all of us. But when the boat docked Zoya spoke out and pushed her way forward. I helped her down then climbed in after her. I waited for someone to point out that I shouldn't be there, but again no one said anything. The boat filled up, then the engine started, and it pulled away. Those left on the pier waved and shouted what sounded like obscenities. Zoya whispered something I couldn't catch and clung onto my arm. I watched us leave dry land.

The journey out of the harbour and around the headland was quiet and calm. It would have been the perfect night to spend alone on the water. Knucky would have gone down after the pub closed, untied the ropes, and started off.

A few people spoke on board, but most just sat there silently. Some closed their eyes, dozing off. One man at the back snored loudly. I held Zoya close. I felt like a refugee. Someone escaping an intolerable régime. I heard the heavy scratch of a match as a man behind lit up a cigarette. I smelt the sulphur on the air. We sailed further along the coast and then rounded the headland into the bay. The large ships glowered before us. The loud sucking sound of water slurped against their huge sides and slipped through the great chains that rooted them to the seabed. An involuntary shiver rippled through my spinal column. My wet shirt clung to my arms and back. I missed the extra warmth of my jacket. The boat chugged in between their hulking mass. It seemed as though we were lost, wandering aimlessly through a vast watery scrapyard. The engine died as we pulled in alongside one of the ships. I saw the large black letters spelling out the *Balticskayaslava II*. One man stepped to the front and held tight to the steel frame of the ladder. People began to stand up. We stepped out and climbed up the ladder one by one. Zoya's firm legs moved ahead of me. The cold steel of the handrail cut through my palms to the bone as I moved slowly upwards. My legs felt dead, and the pull on the rail required more effort than I thought I possessed. My arm muscles clamped tight and ached. The hand of the person beneath me caught against my foot. I had a sudden fear of falling back into the surging sea. I held my breath and concentrated on each individual rung. Plates of dark steel passed before my eyes. The sound of a large door, like the heavy door of an ice room, smacked shut above us. A motor laboured ponderously as though pulling against something stiff. Footsteps echoed on metal floor panelling. It continued to drizzle.

I finally made it to the top and stepped on board. Across the deck the enormous wheelhouse soared above me, its large door tightly shut, a tall metal stairway leading upwards, while high above, lights glared from the surrounding observation windows like an eerie revolving restaurant. An array of masts and aerials pointed high in the air seeking contact, communication with the invisible. Zoya reached back and took my hand again. We walked along the large deck. People scattered in all directions. I heard the boat setting off back across the water. I looked at the huge rusted winches and the thick coils of rope, the tall metal scaffold like a monstrous gallows. The treacherous waves of netting.

We passed the sweeping arms of the cranes, the highly perched life boats, the rigging, the block and tackle. The loud cranking and rumbling of machinery. The overwhelming nausea of fish odour.

Zoya led me down a flight of stairs. The noise of the factory grew in volume.

'Do you want to see it?' she asked.

I nodded. She brought me down a narrow corridor and pulled open a metal door. I peered in. It was as if I had been transported back to Alaska. Lanes of conveyor belts carried endless quantities of fish. Dozens of people lined the belts and tables all dressed in rain gear pulling the unwanted fish off the belts or grabbing the sorted ones and placing them in trays moving swiftly past them. They had to work fast. Two fish or more a second. From there the trays went to the filleting machines. From there to the processors, one person to straighten the fillets and one to check for bones and worms. Those passed on would be frozen and packed into cardboard boxes transported to the strapping machine and finally to the ship's freezer hold. The pace was hectic and demanded keen concentration.

I asked Zoya what she worked at. She pointed to the people putting the fish in trays. I did not envy her. She worked twelve-hour shifts she said. It was not easy.

She pulled me along, pointing out the spray-down hoses to wash the fish scales off the raingear. We passed a small TV room. A few people sat in chairs quietly watching the flickering screen, some looked to be asleep. Then she led me in through a cabin door. It was pitch dark inside. She strode ahead assuredly. I walked behind trailing one hand against the wall for security. We climbed down another small set of stairs and in through another door. She put her hand on the wall behind the door and turned the light on. We were in a small bunk house. Two bunk beds were placed against the walls. All four beds were unoccupied. Zoya closed the door behind her. The ground vibrated beneath our feet.

The beds were all perfectly made. The room neat. Zoya went over to a locker and took out a towel. She handed me one also. I wiped my face in it and ran it through my hair. She bent her head over. Her wet hair hung straight down. She dried it with the towel then swung her hair back over her head and brushed it flat. She slipped my jacket off and hung it on the corner of the bed. We were both soaked through. Zoya opened another door at the side which led into a small bathroom.

She stopped at the door, the towel still in her hand, and turned back to me.

'Do you like it?' she asked

I did not know what specifically she was referring to.

'This.' She cast her hand around the room.

'Yes,' I said. 'It's nice.'

She put the towel down on the toilet lid and pulled off her jumper. She dropped it on the floor. She unbuttoned her blouse and dropped it beside her jumper. Her white bra straps strained across her broad back. A fold of flesh was trapped beneath them. I didn't want to be there. Her friends could come back at any moment. I didn't want to see any more of her body. I wanted to find out about the Eskimo.

She started to unzip her skirt. I went in and held her shoulders from behind. They were warm and soft. A few light freckles dotted her pale skin. She turned and smiled. I pushed gently and sat her down on the toilet. I stooped down in front of her. My head hurt. I felt the cold loss of my drunkenness receding.

'Zoya, you must tell me about the Eskimo. I have to know.' I tried to say it in a tone that would imply the seriousness of this.

Zoya clasped her hands together and placed them on her knees. 'What can I tell?'

'How did he die? What did he die of?' A sound like steam escaping came from somewhere outside. Zoya's shoulders drooped. 'He died of himself,' she said.

'What do you mean?' I was unsure if she was suggesting suicide or not. She wiped at her eyes and brushed a tear from the side of her face. 'Tell me.' I held her arms. I could hear footsteps above us.

Zoya wet her lips as though she had suddenly found that they were dry. I heard more footsteps from the corridor outside. Zoya stood up. 'You do not want to sleep with me.' It was a simple statement. One without doubt.

'I'm sorry,' I said.

'I will bring you back to the boat.' Zoya went out and got some dry clothes from the locker. She dressed. I waited in the doorway of the bathroom and listened to the approaching footsteps. I heard voices, and then the door opened. Three women came in together. I recalled two of them from the bar earlier. They went quiet when they saw me there. They smiled at me, and one of them said something to Zoya. Zoya shook her head. She finished dressing and nodded for me to follow her. I took my jacket, said goodbye to them, and went out after her. They were laughing as the door shut behind us.

I wondered what would have happened if we had slept together, if we would have had to share the room with the others. It was entirely possible. I doubted that I could have gone through with it. We walked back up the stairs into the dark corridor. I decided to come clean with Zoya. I needed to shift the balance of the Eskimo's weight between us.

'I found his body in my fishing nets.' I told her this in the darkness.

She kept on walking as though she had not heard. We climbed back up the stairs out onto the deck. A light mist had come down making it almost impossible to see beyond the lights of the other ships. Zoya walked to the edge of the ship and leaned against it.

'You found him?' she asked.

'Yes. His body got caught in the nets, and I pulled him up.'

'I did not hear.'

'You would have been on your way back home by then,' I explained. I looked at her standing against the railing. The darkness of the night seemed to cling to the edges of her body. A clamour of voices came from further up the deck. Another boat had arrived. I saw the shapes and shadows of people moving in and out through the weak beams of the ship's lights. A yellow haze of mist wavering before the dull bulbs.

'Where is his body?' she asked. She looked unwell.

'He was buried. Somewhere near Malin Head. Do you know this place?'

Zoya nodded. 'Yes, we have sailed past it.' She paused as if to think. 'Yuri, does he know? Did you tell him this?'

'No.' I sat down on one of the steel bollards the ropes were winched around. I felt the slight sway of the ship. The sky was clouded over. I could not see a single star.

'Zoya, what did you mean when you said he died of himself? Do you mean he killed himself?'

Zoya folded her arms in front of her. 'Yes. You are right. In the end he killed himself.' Zoya seemed to be reasoning with herself. She stared up at me. Defiantly. The mist trailing about her. 'He has done terrible things.'

She shook as she cried. She turned away. Faced the sea. I should have gone to her, but I did not. Instead I sat on the cold bollard and felt the undulations of its uneven surface under my fingers. I listened to the water beat through the throb of the engines. I had no right being where I was, yet I felt in control, as though I were the captain of the ship and not a stowaway. For one moment I felt as though nothing could ever touch me again, as if we were so far out at sea we could never be reached. Not docked off the northwest coast of Ireland but in the middle of the freezing Chukchi Sea. And as I looked into the darkened waters I imagined the massive bodies of the humpbacked whales waiting to surface from out of the depths.

'All the time he fights. We do not go near him.' Zoya's voice trembled. 'Sometimes he says things in words we do not know, but still we understand.'

She looked at me to see if this made sense. I nodded to let her know it did. It is the words we are most familiar with that make the least sense.

'He looks at us. Us women. We are afraid.'

Though the drizzle had stopped, a mild dampness seeped off the mist. I heard a loud splash of water like someone or something had fallen overboard. The deck creaked loudly. I wanted to tell Zoya had sorry I was, how somehow I felt responsible for a part of this. I wanted to take the guilt the Eskimo should have felt upon myself.

'What happened?'

Zoya looked at me, then looked out into the dark night. She turned back. Her hair was coated in a sheen of moisture.

'What happened, Zoya? Did he do something to you?'

She shook her head. 'No.' She gripped the railing hard. 'My friend Nina.' Again she turned away. Spoke no longer to me alone. 'She is by herself on deck, smoking. It is night time. Then he is there, beside her. From out of the darkness. Then words, his words. She is scared and tries to leave, but he holds her arm. He does not let go. She is very frightened. He is looking at her body. She tries to pull away but still he holds her, still he continues to stare. She hears his breathing. Then he puts his other hand on her, here.' Zoya pointed to her chest.

She was crying, struggling to speak above her tears. I wanted to go to her and comfort her, but I could not. In a moment such as this, any touch, no matter how tender, seemed to me another possible act of violence.

'Did he hurt her?'

'She pulls away again, and he lets her go. But yes, she came to harm.' Zoya turned around. 'She has a boyfriend on this ship. She must tell him. Do you understand? He must know. So she tells him.' Zoya stopped. She wiped at her eyes. 'This is your Eskimo.' Her voice had quietened, was hard to hear. 'She does not work this time, does not come with us. My friend. Nina.'

'And your friend's boyfriend, what did he do?'

We were here now, here at the moment of the Eskimo's death, on this ship where I sat on cold metal with deep water churning all around. This movable floating island of steel.

Zoya tossed her hand up in the air. 'It is not important. No.'

'Yes,' I pleaded, 'it is.'

Zoya looked puzzled as though truly she had expected a different response. 'I do not know you,' she said.

'It is important for me.'

Zoya sighed. She placed her hand on her forehead 'There is a fight. Here.' She looked around the deck, the edge of the ship. 'I do not know.' She shrugged. 'He is in the water. It is too dark to see him. He cannot be saved.'

'Was it an accident?'

'What do you call an accident?' She shook her head. 'He kills himself, do you see? Who else can you blame?'

The engine of a motor boat rasped and started up. I looked out to the side and saw it set off back across the water. The white line of its spray was visible through the mist like a lit fuse burning its way to an explosive substance. A few men approached. Their boots clunked on the deck, reverberated across its length. They talked together solemnly.

'It is Yuri.' Zoya spoke aloud to herself.

She called out his name and walked towards their shadows. I stood up beside the bollard. Alert. I heard her talking with him, and I could see them stopped by a towering mound of cable. The other men carried on walking. They passed me by. They looked at me, but didn't say anything. I nodded half-heartedly towards them. I saw Yuri put his arms around Zoya and hold her to him. The steps leading down below deck rattled beneath the weight of the men. Yuri looked over in my direction suddenly as though Zoya had just informed him of my presence. Then they both began to walk towards me. And for the first time that night I felt the fear borne out of my actions.

Yuri's large body moved menacingly in the dark. It was completely unexpected. A fear that seemed to surface from out of nowhere. Containing nothing of the excitement of breaking into the offices at the harbours. As though it had been accumulating from the outset, from the first moment I set eyes on the Eskimo's decomposed body, festering inside of me, until it finally broke through. I stood next to the bollard shaking. I felt physically sick. The sway of the boat seemed to amplify throughout the structure of my body. I was in danger of falling over. And yet I had spoken to Yuri before and felt I could trust him. But it was as if the other side of trust was now exposed. What I had to fear from him I didn't know. I had done nothing deliberately to harm anyone. My bladder hurt. My muscles contracted to prevent urination. My whole body tightened towards my groin. I looked at Yuri no more than twenty paces away and saw a protector and avenger at once. Father Jack upon the altar.

Yuri came closer. I saw the backwards swing of his large arm, the forward movement of his fist, and I felt the blinding pain from within, the collapse of my body, stumbling back across the deck, hitting the bars of the metal railing, falling over the edge of the ship. The thump of the steel structure against my shoulder, the passage of air across my cooling flesh, the hard crack of the water's surface as its molecules tensed together before tearing apart, the whisking currents of the ocean sucking me inwards, forcing the mass of my body into its own irregular motion. I felt my flesh transform, disintegrate into its separate component parts, merging with the one vast ocean.

I looked up. Zoya and Yuri stood before me. Staring at me. Neither of them moved. Then Yuri spoke.

'Zoya has said you found the body of the Eskimo.'

I was shaking hard. They could not fail to miss it. I nodded a yes.

'You are okay?' Zoya sounded concerned. 'You are too wet.'

'She has said he is now buried.'

'Yes.' The sound of my voice was reassuring to me.

'And the police, what did they say?' Yuri spoke slowly, concisely.

My fear subsided. Moved back down inside me. Yuri was not going to harm me. 'They believe he died of natural causes and was buried at sea. They could find out nothing about him.'

'They are finished with him?'

'Yes. For them it is over.'

Yuri nodded. 'And for you?'

I wrapped my arms around me, still shivering badly. I could hear no other human presence than ours. I listened to the internal workings of the ship and the wash of the sea.

'Who was he? Where did he come from?'

Yuri shook his head. 'Mush. We called him Mush. It is not his proper name. I do not know where he came from.' He made a futile gesture with his hands.

'This is true,' Zoya said.

'Somebody on board must know,' I insisted.

'He could speak to no one,' Yuri held Zoya again, supported her. 'He did not understand us. And we did not understand him. He had his language only. It kept him from us, his temper too.'

'But he was seen drinking with some people.'

'Sometimes. But always he would fight. He could pull fish good. That is enough.'

'So who will tell his family he is dead?'

Yuri and Zoya looked at one another. 'There is no one to tell,' Zoya said. 'He was there on the ship. That is all.'

Yuri looked at me sternly. 'The boat will soon be back. You will go.'

He was right, I would. There was little else I could do. No one on board knew him. Mullen already told me he would have no papers. The Eskimo was just there, and then he was there no more.

I turned to Zoya.

'I am sorry about your friend.'

Zoya squeezed Yuri's arm and said something. He walked away. 'I will take you to the boat,' she said.

We walked back up the deck. I listened for the noise of the motor boat. I heard it approaching. The tall angular shapes of the ship stood firm. We walked side by side. We stopped by the steel ladder leading down the side of the ship and waited. The lights from the other ships wavered in the dark. Noise filtered over and back.

'What happened to Nina's boyfriend? Is he still on this ship?'

Zoya shook her head. 'You must forget him.' She nuzzled up against me. The touch of her body ran through me. She took my hand and held it behind her back. Her palm felt warm yet.

I looked down at the dark water and thought of the Eskimo disappearing beneath it. His place on the line would have to be filled. His trays could not pass empty. Some people would have to increase their shifts, work sixteen hour days. But no one would say anything. Their jobs depended on their silence.

I listened to the increasing volume of the noise from the boat's engine. Measuring the passage of time. I thought of Father Jack's clocks, how he listened for eternity. I looked back into the mist. I saw the blurred edges of the boat but nothing else other than a few hazy lights. The boat came in closer and Zoya looked down to it. It pulled in beside the ladder. The engine cut. A man started to get out. Zoya shouted down to him. He shouted back. He appeared to be protesting. Zoya shouted something else. He swatted his hand in front of his face as if knocking away a fly. Then arguing with himself he started the engine up again.

'You should go now,' Zoya said. She reached up and kissed me on the lips. She held it for a few moments then took her mouth away. 'What we have missed,' she said. She let go my hand.

I turned and began the slow climb down the ladder.

Neither of us spoke on the way over. Before getting out I emptied my pockets of all the money I had. About eight pounds in all. I gave it to the boatman. He grunted. I stepped out onto the stone steps of the pier. I heard him pull away. Head back into the mist. I walked back up the pier, and across the road to the hotel. I rang the night bell. The porter came to the door and opened it with his keys. I thanked him and went to my room. I was afraid it might be locked, but Therese had left it open. She was sound asleep, curled away from me on the far side of the bed. I took my wet clothes off and got in beside her. Soon it would be dawn. I felt the softness of the pillow and nothing else.

CHAPTER THIRTY-FOUR

It was noon by the time I woke. I was alone. For a moment I thought Therese might have left without me. It would not have been unreasonable. But her belongings were still there. I had a piercing headache and felt shaky all over. Like the worst kind of hangover. I lay looking up at the white ceiling, examined its blemishes. I couldn't allow myself to think about the night before. That would come later. Despite my condition I felt at ease. I was looking forward to seeing Therese again.

She came in some time later. I had dozed off again, but I heard the door open and was aware of her entrance. I forced my eyes open.

'Welcome back,' she said. She stood at the end of the bed as though she didn't know where best to position herself. My eyes took time to focus. She faded in and out. The room spun away from me. Light vanished.

When I looked up again Therese was sitting on the edge of the bed. She held a damp facecloth to my forehead. Its moisture mingled with my sweat.

'How are you feeling now?' she asked.

I opened my mouth to speak, but its searing dryness prevented me. I put my hand to my throat. I would have loved for Therese to wring the facecloth across my lips. I was reminded of Jesus looking for gall. I concentrated my efforts on creating saliva within my mouth. Then swallowed hard. I managed to ask for a drink. Therese went to the bathroom and brought back a glass of water. She held it to my mouth and tipped it up.

'I feel fine.' Finally answering her question.

'Is everything okay?' She took the facecloth from my forehead and dabbed at my cheeks.

'Yes.'

'Good.' She seemed content with that level of response. 'You can tell me all later.' She lay on the bed beside me. I closed my eyes and fell asleep again.

It was a quarter to three by the time I finally got up. I still felt frail, but my headache had cleared.

'I really ought to be getting back,' Therese said. She looked genuinely unhappy about this. 'Do you need to stay longer?'

I shook my head. 'We can leave whenever you like.'

We started to pack. Afterwards we went down to the desk to settle up. Therese insisted on paying the bill.

'I invited you,' I reminded her.

She handed across her credit card and said we could fight about it later. I was happy there was going to be a later. We got in the car and drove back. She didn't ask me about the night before. That would all come out in its own good time.

I dropped her off at her cottage.

'Give me a call,' she said. 'Can I trust you on that?'

'Rest assured,' I told her.

She gave me a quick kiss on the cheek and went inside. I was feeling tired again. I drove home and went straight to bed.

CHAPTER THIRTY-FIVE

I slept right through until the following morning. I made breakfast then dropped the car back to Frances. She would have to be told everything. Including all about Therese. I wondered if she would view my not telling her before as a deception, a slight on our friendship. I had a lot to apologize for.

I drove past the harbour and parked in front of The Porthole. The winds were picking up. Waves gathered in the lough and the water sloshed noisily within the harbour. The *Lorna Doone* was gone. For Knucky's sake I hoped the winds would not get much worse. I walked around to the back entrance of the pub and up the stairs. Frances' door was open. She stood in the kitchen eating toast. When she saw me she ran over and hugged me tightly as if I had been away for years. I held her and started to cry. I couldn't explain it. Frances didn't ask me to.

'I want to tell you everything,' I said wiping my eyes and cheeks. 'On the way to his grave.'

Frances smiled. She went over to the cupboard by the fridge and took out a map. She shook it at me. 'It's all in here,' she said. She finished her toast, drank down her tea, and put the mug on the table. 'Come on.'

Frances practically ran down the stairs. She had the car running by the time I got there. As we drove up the hill to town I looked back to where the *Lorna Doone* had been tied up. Frances saw me looking but continued to stare ahead.

The Eskimo's burial was an official act by the state which meant he would have been buried in a graveyard. I knew it was somewhere out near Malin Head, so it shouldn't have been too hard to find, but Frances was intent on using her map.

'I told you, I've worked it out already.' She wanted to prove herself right. Convince herself of the power of those energy lines. It would be like dying and finding that heaven did exist after all. I didn't want to spoil anything for her. All I wanted to do was find his grave and be there with him. I was ready for that now.

I told Frances all about the trip to Killybegs but left Therese out of it for now. I told her about the bar and the party, going over to the ship. Frances loved the sound of the name Zoya. She kept repeating it to herself in a deep, sensuous voice. She told me she admired my dedication when she heard that nothing had happened between us. I knew I should have told her about Therese then, but still I didn't.

'Who would have believed it?' she asked when I finished.

'I have to,' I told her. 'I have nothing else.'

Frances drove slowly. Remotely. 'Do you think it was an accident?' she asked.

I looked at the familiar fields and hills falling away behind us. The trees blew sideways in the winds. 'Can it be permissible to think anything else?'

A car beeped and overtook quickly. Someone waved. I looked in time to see the blue gloved hand of Father Jack heading off for his golf.

'There's my man,' Frances said and laughed. I watched his car disappear around the corner. Frances smiled after his fleeting image.

'Would you sleep with him?' I asked and fiddled with the cuffs of my shirt.

'Father Jack?' Frances paused as though she needed more time to think. 'It would be like death, wouldn't it?' she said.

'I don't know.'

'It would. It would be like death. It would be heaven.' A sheepdog ran out of a laneway and along the grassy edge of the road. An old man on a bicycle came out after him. He waved, and Frances and I waved back. Frances pulled out to give him room. 'I would,' she said. 'That's the terrible thing about it.' She tapped her thumbs on the steering wheel. 'Does that shock you?'

'I've been forewarned,' I told her.

'I'd like to seduce him. I'd like it to be all my doing. God help me.'

I sat for a few minutes saying nothing. Then I took the plunge. 'I didn't go to Killybegs on my own.'

Frances pulled a loose strand of hair from her eyes. 'I know that,' she said.

'How?'

She tapped her thumbs again. 'Ah now, Jim.' She looked idly out the side window. 'I suppose you think you love her.' It wasn't said in a mean way but out of real concern. Out of her own disbelief in love.

'I think I do.'

'She's very beautiful.'

'It's not just that,' I said.

'I know.' A light mist of rainwater fell on the windscreen. 'Knucky's gone again.'

'I saw that. When?'

'The boat was gone this morning when I got up. He had it looking very well. Like new.'

'Maybe he's just gone fishing.'

Frances sighed at me impatiently. I didn't believe it either.

'I hope it doesn't get any worse out there,' I said.

'You don't have to worry about Knucky. He's been through worse than this. He'll just batten down the hatches if need be.'

She was right about this. We drove over the brow of the hill. The estuary came into view.

'How long can this go on for?' I asked.

'You know Knucky.' Frances let down the window. The wind blew in across her face. 'Can you feel the Eskimo yet?' She closed her eyes briefly and grinned. 'We're closing in on him.'

I didn't feel anything.

'My bones are tingling,' she said. 'We're approaching his world.'

We drove around by the Five Finger Strand. In the same direction as Therese's.

'Did you ever find out his name?'

'No, I didn't.' It didn't matter anymore. If my search taught me anything, it taught me that names told you nothing. They were just distractions to be spoken as a way of avoiding the truth. Sometimes in deep, sensuous voices.

'What about his family?'

'We are it.'

Frances smiled to herself, happy for that. She slowed down and stopped the car. She got out and brought the map with her. She spread it out on the bonnet of the car. It flapped wildly like a flag. She held it down and called to me.

'Run your fingers across it,' she said. 'Let them go where they have to.'

The light rain settled on the paper. Frances really wanted me to do this. So I tried. For her sake. But I could feel nothing. I was lost.

Frances looked disappointed. 'Close your eyes,' she said. 'Try again. Really concentrate this time.'

I did as she told me, but still nothing happened. 'You just don't make the effort,' she snapped. Then she closed her eyes and ran her fingers along the surface of the map. Guiding them perfectly along the marking for the road we were on. Turning at every turn as though she could see them clearly beneath her closed lids. She opened her eyes, folded up the map and got back in. She drove without speaking.

Further along she took a right turn away from the coast up a bog road. We drove over hills, bumping along the rutted dirt surface. Blue plastic fertilizer bags littered the sides of the road, and sinewy turns of spaghetti turf were heaped everywhere. The deep mauve heather glistened with a fine mist of rainwater. A host of working tractors and trailers were deserted around the bog waiting to be used. I could just about make out the rough sea off to our left.

We hit a pothole. The car shook hard on its suspension. Frances kept going. She turned right again down another dirt road, grimacing at an old washing machine and kitchen table dumped along the side. I knew how much this indiscriminate littering must be hurting her.

A few minutes later she stopped again and got out with the map. I almost asked her if she knew where she was going but stopped myself in time. I stayed where I was, watching her through the front window trailing her hand once more across the fluttering paper surface. She could hardly hold the map steady. It looked like it would blow away. Where would that leave her then?

'We're almost there,' she shouted back. I couldn't tell if she was still angry or not. She got in, took a turn to the left and drove on about another mile. The sea came back into view. Frances pulled in yet another time. This time she remained sitting in the car. I watched the choppy waves tumbling in the distance.

'We'll have to do the rest on foot,' she said.

'That's fine.' All I could do was go along with her. We were far away from the site of any official graveyard here, far away from the Eskimo.

Frances put her hands on top of the steering wheel and rested her chin upon them. 'I'd like to be buried up here,' she said. Her gaze swept along the wiry bog land back out to the water. 'Promise me.'

'There's laws against it,' I told her.

'Jesus, Jim, if they can bury the Eskimo here, they can bury anyone. And that was the law. There are ways around everything.'

She really believed he was there. Buried beneath the surface. An absolute faith in a hidden source. One she had tapped into. In time Frances would learn of her mistake. What would she choose to believe in then?

'Promise me.'

'I promise.' It was a terrible thing to have done. It was not a promise I believed I would carry out. But it was all I could manage to do at that moment in time.

'Good.' She lifted her chin and slapped the wheel sharply. 'That's settled then. Let's go.' She opened the door and stood out on the road.

'Here, you'll need this.' I brought the map out to her.

But Frances refused it. 'I'll let the earth speak directly to me now.' She stepped out onto the bog and stood amongst the heathers, closed her eyes and held her arms out in front of her as though she was sleepwalking. The increasing winds blew about her. A chink of light broke through the clouded sky. Watching Frances standing there I could almost have believed she was sinking into the ground. She turned about twenty degrees to her left and began walking. She took an irregular path into the centre of the bog. The ground was uneven and full of depressions filled with dark bog water. She could easily fall and hurt herself. But I didn't dare interrupt. I followed carefully after her. The wind tussled at our clothing. The rain fell down harder. Frances never stumbled once.

We walked over a large section of cut bog. The smooth brown surface felt soft and secure beneath me. I understood why Frances would want to be buried here. Land like this would hold you close, give you comfort in your passing. We stepped back onto an uncut area. The small plants and heathers looked like miniature forests. It was like crossing over the line of latitude into the Arctic Circle for the first time.

We must have walked for a mile or more in the rain before Frances finally stopped. We were both wet through. Frances let her arms sink slowly to her sides. She stood there for a few moments then gradually opened her eyes. She smiled broadly. The water poured across her face. She clenched her fists and shook them as though she had scored a minor victory. Then her smile retreated into a cold expression of sadness.

'Sweet Jesus,' she said shivering. 'I'm standing right on top of him.'

I looked at her feet. The ground looked no different there than anywhere else. It hadn't been disturbed in recent times. For centuries perhaps, thousands of years. Frances must have known this. She crossed her arms on her chest both hands still clenched.

'I can feel the life that's drained out of him,' she said. 'It's ours for the taking.' She threw her head back to the sky. Her long wet hair trailed behind her. She looked immaculate. Beatified.

'Make love to me here,' she whispered. She could have been talking to the Eskimo or to God Himself. For a moment the whole world was silent. I listened, but I couldn't hear a single sound. Frances lowered her head and looked right at me. 'Make love to me, Jim.'

She would never forgive me if I didn't. I stood there motionless. Frances waited, held my gaze. I did not know what to do. She waited then let her arms drop from her chest and began the long walk back to the car.

CHAPTER THIRTY-SIX

Frances didn't speak on the journey home. Something irreconcilable had taken place between us. She dropped me off at my house. I said a quiet goodbye as though it were my last. Frances acknowledged it with a slight shrug of her shoulders and drove away.

Was this the way it was? Always slipping out of someone's life into someone else's, as the Eskimo had slipped from his, as he had slipped into mine?

I went into the living room, lit a fire and lay back on my parents' old sofa. Was my plan to change the house a way of killing off their past? Yet what was the alternative, to live with the knowledge of all you could not undo? Had the details I had learned about the Eskimo revealed anything about him at all or anything about myself? The more I thought about it the more confused I became. The answer it seemed was not to think at all but just to continue living your life without question hoping that in the end everything would somehow fall into place.

The heat from the fire embraced me like a narcotic. I closed my eyes in front of it and fell fast asleep.

The phone woke me later. I rubbed my eyes and reoriented myself, arose from the armchair and went to answer it. I heard the winds howl outside, the rains lash against the windows. I lifted the receiver.

'Yes,' I said still adjusting to a waking state. I seemed to be spending as much time now in sleep as I had previously done in a drunken stupor.

'Gallagher.'

I knew the voice but could not place it.

'Just ringing to see you got your money's worth.'

It was Mullen. That was all I needed. He had my number now. He was privy to a part of my life nobody else was and could invade my privacy any time he wanted. Despite the financial repayment I was indebted to him. It would always be that way. The moment you ask a question of anyone, seek out the knowledge they hold, you are doomed to a lifetime of indebtedness. The only safe knowledge worth possessing is that which you discover for yourself.

'Please don't ring me, ' I said. I meant it as a firm request, but I knew it sounded as if I was pleading with him. This was not the way to deal with a man like Mullen.

'What the fuck's up with you?' he asked angrily. 'I just wanted to see if you got your man.'

'I got him,' I said. 'As best as I could hope to. Your information was good.' If this was what he wanted to know, now he did.

Mullen laughed. 'My information is always good.'

'What do you really want?' This was the way to deal with Mullen.

'That's what I like about you, Gallagher,' he said, 'no pussyfooting around.' I thought it just possible that Mullen did in fact like me much as I, against my better wishes, could not help liking him. 'You're not a man of grace are you?'

'Coming from you that's rich.' I was treading on dangerous ground speaking to Mullen in this way. I did not know what he was capable of. He could be quite harmless underneath everything or he could be as unsavoury an individual as ever existed. If the circumstances were just so, could Mullen harm me? It was entirely plausible, and yet here I was throwing caution to the wind. Nevertheless I continued. 'I asked you, what is it you want?'

Mullen snorted as if unable to clear his nose. 'What do you know?' he asked.

'About what?'

'The fucking Eskimo of course. What did you find out?'

'Why do you need to know this?'

'The truth is,' Mullen said, 'I don't need to know. I don't even care what happened to him.'

'What is it you need to know then?'

'I need to know that whatever you learned you will keep to yourself. I don't want to be dragged into this. These ships are my business, hiding dead Eskimos is theirs. Do you understand?'

'I understand.' I did. Mullen's greed for money had led me to one of his ships, to its murkier recesses, and had compromised him in return.

'I hope for your sake you do.' Mullen snorted again.

'You don't need to worry,' I assured him, 'there's nothing to tell.'

'There's always something to tell. The trick Gallagher is not to tell it. Whatever you heard, you haven't heard the half of it.'

'Then like I say, there's no need to worry.' I heard the cat mewing in the background.

'I need your word on this. You've taken liberties with my kind nature.'

'It's a virtue,' I said. 'Listen, Mullen, everything I found out was for myself.'

'Just make sure you keep it that way.'

'Don't concern yourself about me, Mullen.'

'It's not you I'm concerned about, Gallagher, it's me. You could roast in hell.'

'I probably will,' I told him.

Mullen ignored me. 'You know what bothers me most. I short-changed myself. I should have charged you twice as much.'

'Three times,' I said. 'Never mind, what's done is done.'

'You don't believe that any more than I do. Just take care you don't end up like the Eskimo, an unknown entity set adrift.'

Mullen put the phone down. He was an unknown quantity. I did not know if I was being threatened or not. In some ways he sounded as worried as I was, as though he too felt out of control of his situation, but in other ways Mullen was clearly in charge. For the moment I held the upper hand. Everything was dependent on me. I wondered if that was the way it always was, if the underdog was in fact top-dog, if it was not the Eskimo who was the one in charge around here, directing operations, controlling our lives.

I put the receiver down and leaned up against the wall. What was to become of Knucky, Frances and me? Had we gone as far as we could go?

I felt drained from the conversation. I closed the curtains and went back to bed.

I rang Charlie the next morning and asked if we could meet. He said he'd be glad to and suggested meeting, as before, on the dunes beside the golf course. He said he could be there in twenty minutes.

I showered, dressed and set out walking. The winds were getting stronger, but this was what I needed, to be replenished by the fresh air through my body.

I passed the golf course and walked down the small road to where I had arranged to meet Charlie. I saw him standing on top of a wiry dune, the wind blowing through his hair. Charlie, who one day might become the sergeant around here, who was seeking out the difference between what was lawful and what was not, who was finding his way inside the restricted zones.

He saw me and waved over. I walked up the sandy path towards him. I felt a need for confession, absolution, but I did not know how much I could tell him. Like everything else this far I had rung him on a whim with no thought for the outcome.

For once the artillery was quiet on the other side of the lough. The whitecaps rolled over. Gulls swooped in for food. Rich pickings.

The last time I had seen Charlie was in his flat after the nightclub in Buncrana. I hoped there would be no mention of that today. We said hello to one another as Charlie stepped down off the dune and walked with me towards the shore. Water carrying discoloured froth lapped in over his black leather shoes.

'Welcome back,' he said.

He obviously knew I had been out of town, but did he also know where I had gone? It was not just possible, it was likely.

'Where do I stand, Charlie?' I asked.

Charlie looked to his shoes. 'There,' he said, 'right at the edge with dirt washing in on you.'

'But I feel cleansed.'

'There's just no telling, is there?' He moved back from the water. 'Mullen's a bad type,' he said. 'He's not the sort I'd trust. We've been watching him for quite some time, but it's hard to pin him down.'

'I see.' So Charlie knew about him and me. 'I'm done with him,' I said.

Charlie watched a boat out on the lough. 'Can you be sure about that?' he asked.

'I guess we can never be really sure of anything.'

'That's so. You see, Jim, we are not really sure that you broke into the harbour master's office in Killybegs. We could have dusted for fingerprints, but would it have been worth it even if we had

319

been successful? As the sergeant said, it would have been a waste of resources, not worth the result. You're like the Eskimo in that way, Jim, there is only so far we can go.'

The glare from the sun broke through a gap in the grey clouds. Charlie and I squinted our eyes. I heard a tractor pass on the road. Charlie instinctively turned to look. Then he turned back to me.

'Associating with Mullen puts you in danger, and not just from him. You become worthy of resources then. Don't get me wrong, Jim, but you're not worth it. You're not worth the resources. Don't go forcing us to waste them because then they have to be justified. Then the result is everything. You and all of us come out the worse for that.'

I was fortunate to have Charlie on my side. I told him this.

'There are no sides.' he said. 'Sometimes it works for you and sometimes against. Tell me you are going to drop it. That's what I need to hear.'

'You have my word,' I assured him.

Charlie looked relieved. 'Did you find out what you needed to?'

'The truth is, Charlie, I didn't need to hear about any of this at all.'

Charlie scuffed the toe of his shoe against the sand. He seemed to think about my response. 'I don't believe that,' he said. 'Despite everything, maybe it was just what you needed.'

I laughed gently. 'You may be right. I don't know yet what it is I found out. Maybe I never will. It was not what I expected.'

Charlie dug his hands deep in his trouser pockets. 'What would be the point in finding out what you expected, learning what you already know? That's the one thing this job of mine has taught me, nothing is as you expect it.'

I pushed my foot hard into the sand, removed it and watched the print fill with water. It seemed to rise from nowhere. 'Tell me, Charlie, do you not want to know what I found out? See if there's something yourself and the sergeant did not discover for yourselves.'

'Are you asking to be called in for interview?'

'No, I would prefer I wasn't.'

'Well then.'

'So it's finished for you too.'

'It has to finish sometime.'

'And you personally, do *you* not want to know?'

'Maybe I do.' He looked across at me. 'Don't think I find it easy. Don't presume that I don't think about him.' He cast his eyes downwards, rubbed his hand across the back of his neck. 'I was once called out to a barn to cut a young boy, eighteen, down from a rope he had hung himself with.' I saw his head shake involuntarily. 'It doesn't get much worse than that.' He looked up at me again. 'Maybe I do want to know, Jim, but, the truth is, I can't be told. I'm not involved in this anymore.'

'Why did you get into this, Charlie?' I asked. 'Why not a fisherman like the rest of us? Your father fished, didn't he?'

'And my grandfather. I don't know. I just didn't like fishing. I couldn't even tell you what it was I didn't like about it. I just knew I didn't want to do it. Entering the guards was something to do, that's about it. I wish I could say it was a lifelong passion, a need to protect the community, an undying belief in right and wrong, but it's just an occupation. A way of passing time in this time-filled world.'

'But you're good at your job.'

Charlie shrugged. 'Maybe, maybe not. I'll stick with it though. I have no real desire to do anything else. And you?'

'God only knows. I'm through with Knucky, it seems. I don't think he'll be wanting me back again.'

'I'm sure you've said that before.'

'Many times, but this time, Charlie, it feels different. Too much has occurred.' I nodded towards the mouth of the lough. 'He's out there somewhere on another of his voyages.'

Together Charlie and I looked out beyond the lough at the rough waves.

'Rather him than me.'

Charlie offered me a lift back in the garda car. I thanked him but told him I'd prefer to walk. I couldn't get enough of this fresh air.

I didn't stop at my house but decided to continue on into town. I could be headed for the harbour, The Porthole, Annie's, my own downfall. I got as far as the church and stopped. I wondered about the factory ships, travelling for months on end, huge numbers of people on board, did they have a place of prayer? A chaplain even? Maybe that would suit Father Jack, preaching amongst the conveyor belts, the long lines of gutted fish. I turned in without thinking and began to climb the steps upwards to the large ornate wooden doors.

I turned the handle and entered. A hinge creaked. My footsteps echoed on the tiled floor. I stood holding the handle and stared in at the empty church. The long pews seemed pained by absence. I remembered sitting in them with my parents at the top of the church as a young boy. Although I did not feel unwelcome now, I did not think I could go any further.

Suddenly a door to one of the confessional boxes opened. I looked across. Father Jack stuck his head out and smiled.

'Ah, Jim, I was about to give up hope.'

I was startled by his sudden presence and for moments could not speak. Then I heard myself tell him that I could not afford for him to give up hope on me.

'Not you, Jim,' he said. 'I was just about to give up hope that anyone would ever come. I've been waiting in here for over twenty minutes. I suppose I should have used the time to pray. The truth is I've been very bored.' He smiled again, but it was as much a smile of loss as pleasure.

'I'm sorry to disappoint you,' I said, 'but I'm here more by accident than by design. I didn't come for confession.'

It struck me that I hadn't been to confession in almost twenty years. It was a disturbing and fearful thought.

Father Jack shrugged. 'While you're here...'

I shook my head. 'Not now, Father. I'm not ready for it yet.' My talk with Charlie was enough for one day.

Father Jack nodded. He disappeared back into the confessional then moments later walked out, dressed in his white robes and closed the door behind him. 'I may as well shut up shop. I don't think there'll be anymore customers today.'

I was afraid he was disappointed with me, but if he was he gave no indication. He walked down the aisle towards me but stopped about halfways down and sat in one of the empty pews.

He looked over his shoulder. 'Won't you join me?' I hesitated. 'It's all right,' he assured me, 'I'm off duty.' He loosened the collar around his neck. 'Close the door behind you and turn the key.'

'Do you often lock the church?' I asked him, having joined him in the pew.

He nodded. 'When it's not being used.'

His answer came as a surprise. 'I thought the church was always open, twenty-four hours a day.'

'The Church is,' he smiled, 'the building unfortunately is not. Can't be too careful these days. Desecration of the altar, poor-boxes being stolen.'

'I find it hard to believe.'

'In Christ? Just joking.' Father Jack looked in his element. 'I know,' he said more seriously, 'it wasn't like that before, but things have changed.' He stretched his legs in front of him and placed his arms behind his head. 'It's peaceful here, isn't it?'

I had to agree.

'Sometimes I lock up, take the newspaper and just sit here reading under God's watchful eye.' He sighed with pleasure. He turned his head towards me. 'Seeing the day that's in it,' he said, 'I have to confess to you that once I dropped off. Fell fast asleep here in one of the seats. I must have slept for over two hours.'

I laughed softly. 'You've found your home,' I said.

'I still think there's got to be better, but for now it's the best I've come up with.' He turned his head back, appeared to stare straight ahead at the angels on the domed ceiling. 'Do you ever think about marriage?' He continued to stare at the angels as though the question was posed to them and not to me.

'Often.'

'Me too.' He paused. 'Does that surprise you?'

'Yes. Although I know it shouldn't.'

'What do you think it would be like?' Sudden spears of light shone through the stained glass windows illuminating them like magic lanterns.

'I have no real idea, odd as that might sound. My parent's marriage seemed to work well for them. They seemed very content.'

'Content,' Father Jack repeated. 'Would that be enough?'

'It would be an improvement,' I answered honestly.

'That bad?'

'It's getting better.'

'Are you still bothered about that Eskimo?'

'Not so much. I tracked him down.'

Father Jack took his hands from behind his head and sat upright. 'Did you really?'

I nodded yes. 'I still don't know who he was or where exactly he came from, but I learned a little of his life and a little of how he died. It seems enough for now.'

'Troubled?'

This is how he had described the Eskimo that night I had visited in his house, a troubled soul. 'Yes. You were right. A troubled soul.'

He joined his hands in his lap. He seemed pleased that he had been right. Frances, I knew, would have been pleased for him too, how he had been able to sense this simply by praying over him. They were kindred spirits, two of a kind.

'Don't tell me any more,' he said. 'It's between him and his Maker.' He stretched back in his seat again. 'I'm glad for you. I'm glad it worked out.'

'Can I ask...?'

'Go ahead.'

'Would you really like to give all this up and marry?'

'Like yourself, Jim, I've no real idea.' He laughed. 'Don't worry, I'm not going anywhere. I'm a bit long in the tooth for that, don't you think? I'll still be here ready to officiate at your wedding when the day arrives.'

I followed the fourteen stations of the cross with my eyes, images of a death and resurrection.

'What about that Miss Docherty?' His question slipping as easily off his lips as a prayer. I felt my heart flutter. 'She'd make a grand wife, don't you think?'

I saw him watch my face, watch for my response.

'For me or for you?' Another easy prayer.

Father Jack roared. His laughed echoed in the hollowness of the church. 'For you, of course.' He continued to laugh. 'I knew her father well. I was a couple of years behind him at school, but we were good friends. Played football together, went to dances, that sort of thing before I entered the seminary. And, well, maybe a few times after also, but all above board. I was sorry when he decided to move away. But for some people leaving is the only option. I was glad when Therese came back. It was almost as if he had returned in a way.' He pulled at his sleeve. 'She likes you I gather.'

I felt myself blush liked a young boy. 'You seem to know as much as I do,' I told him.

He laughed again. 'She confided in me. Maybe I was not supposed to tell. That's the problem with being a priest, it's never easy to know what it is you are being told. It's hard to distinguish between conversation and confidence. And it's hard to open your bloody mouth when people put too much faith in your words.' He coughed. 'I suppose you know about Hal.'

'What should I know?' I asked him.

'He's gone back.'

Once more I should not have been surprised, but I was. 'I didn't know.'

'Yes. A few days ago. Ah, it's for the best.'

Father Jack gave me a slight sideways look. He knew something more that I didn't. Something about Therese and Hal. Something he knew I knew nothing about. Something he was now going to tell me.

'Do you think so?' I asked.

'I do. Well, hadn't Therese already decided before moving here that they should not get married, that it would be better for them to go their separate ways? Oh I know Hal would say that he had no intention of getting her to change her mind, that he had only come over to help her settle in, but, you'd probably agree, he was hoping she'd discover she had made a mistake, that she should stay in New York after all, marry him, keep her successful career, be close to her family.'

'I suppose so,' I said.

'You've got to hand it to her, it was not an easy decision to make. Some would say she had it all, everything you could wish for. I know her father would say that for sure, would be unable to understand how she could turn her back on it. It takes a lot of courage, heading out into the unknown. You see, Jim, you have that in common.' He nodded his own agreement. 'Of course, her father should realize that he has that in common with her too, that she's only doing what he himself did all those years ago. As you know both he and Therese's mother have been ringing frequently to try and get her to come home, arguing pointlessly with her on the phone. Ah, we're a strange race sometimes, Jim, totally inexplicable.'

Father Jack was deliberately telling me these things, providing me with information he knew I was missing. In this way he too was heading into the unknown, breaking confidences for what he no doubt deemed the better good.

He looked at his watch and stood up. 'I'd better be off,' he said. 'I'm due on the first tee in less than an hour.'

'Thank you for your conversation,' I said.

'That's it, Jim, a casual conversation.'

I walked home with no thoughts of Annie's, no thoughts of The Porthole, thinking only of Therese. She had clearly spoken to Father Jack about me. I remembered her being angry when she thought I might have told him about her the time he helped me choose the wine for our doomed meal together. We had come a long way indeed.

Those mystery phone calls almost certainly being made to or by her parents, Hal gone back, Therese here to stay for a while at least, my Eskimo back on dry land. This is what we had arrived at. This is where we could now set out from.

CHAPTER THIRTY-SEVEN

Frances' call came early the next morning. 'It's Knucky,' she simply said.

I knew it was bad. 'What is it?'

'His boat was found adrift off Malin Head. There was no sign of him aboard.'

A sharp jab of pain stabbed deep within my skull. My legs shook violently. I felt dizzy and weak. I reached out and held onto the phone table for support. 'What's happening now?'

'A search is underway. Tom Harte is leading it.' She sounded calm, but nothing, I knew, could be further from the truth. 'Can I come over?' she asked.

'Of course.'

I opened the door to her twenty minutes later. Frances looked lost, as lost as I had ever seen her. I put my arms around her and hugged her. We stood there in the doorway holding one another, afraid to move.

'Let's go in,' I finally said.

We walked inside the house to the kitchen. I asked Frances if she would like a cup of tea.

'Don't you have anything stronger?' she asked.

I shook my head. 'I have nothing left of any strength anymore.'

Frances closed her eyes. 'God help us, Jim.' She opened them again and looked at me. 'I am so tired,' she said. 'I need to join the search for him, but first I need to sleep.' She extended her hand. I would take it, I knew, but I did not want anything to happen between us.

'I mean it,' she said, 'I want to sleep, that's all.'

I took her hand and led her to the bedroom.

Frances clung to me and finally cried, tragically and pitifully. I held her in my arms and rubbed her like a child until gradually her cries subsided. Like a storm ending I heard the deep soothing sounds of her breathing as she drifted to sleep. I lay awake beside her thinking of Knucky, wondering if there was any way he could have survived, beaten the odds as he had beaten the odds on his heart for so long. Perhaps he had just deserted his boat, it was not an impossibility. Maybe he had walked away from it and all of us. After all it was what we had been threatening to do all along, what we had urged each other to do.

I kissed Frances as she slept, full on the lips. I tasted her salt as I had tasted Zoya's. 'We all go down,' I whispered to her, 'but few of us ever come back up.'

Later when Frances awoke we drove out and joined in the search of the coastline. Frances said she did not want to be with a group but to look for him with me alone. We drove out to secluded areas where no one else was searching and walked the beaches, crossing over the rocks into small inlets, expecting at any turn to find his body floating on the tides, caught amongst the rocks. We saw the boats in the distance slowly, painstakingly, making their way around the coast.

I never realized before how little I knew of the landscape I lived in. We walked beaches I had barely known existed, stood on prominents I had never stood on previously. I scoured the water for a glimpse of something that could be a human body and recognized, perhaps for the first time, the water's ever changing nature.

'Shape-changing,' Frances said, 'a normal consequence of a physical world. Which one of us ever knows who we really are?'

Frances never once suggested that she would know where to find him using her maps and energy lines. I would have been disappointed if she had. Although Frances believed in those lines, I knew she believed in Knucky more.

We searched until dark, relieved to have discovered nothing.

'We could stay out here all night,' Frances suggested. 'Just you, me and Knucky.' She even suggested going back for our tents. 'It'd be like the old days,' she said. 'It would be as if they had never ended.'

Although she said it, we both knew she did not mean this. Instead we walked back across the fields to her car and drove to my house unable to think of a single thing to say to one another.

Therese rang about an hour after we got in. Frances and I were already in bed. I held her cold body in my arms and wondered whether to answer the phone or not. I could just lie there and let it ring out, but in the end I answered it in case it was news about Knucky.

Therese's voice sounded warm. I was glad to hear it. She said she had been ringing all evening since she found out about Knucky. I told her we had been out searching, and she said she had assumed this. Then she told me she was there if I needed her. I told her I did. I said I'd call when it was all over. I put the phone down and went back to Frances. I lay next to her, wrapped her in my arms once more. It did not seem unnatural or wrong in any fashion. I wished I could have told Therese about it in such a way that she would understand, but how many of us are willing to understand intimacy in all its peculiar forms?

Each day we walked together hand in hand, holding out our foolish hope, and each night we slept in each other's arms with the same pointless aspirations. Maybe Knucky, Frances and I had always been beyond redemption. Maybe everyone was if you considered it enough.

Knucky's body never did surface. The rescue services were withdrawn after four days, and the search was officially called off. Charlie rang to let us know. The news came as a relief.

'I will almost certainly go on searching for the rest of my life,' Frances said when she heard. 'Endure the fruitless possibility, but I am still glad the official search has come to an end. Everything must finally. I am just not brave enough to make that decision.' We sat by the fire in my mother and father's armchairs like an old married couple. 'Knucky always said when the time came he would opt out, take the difficult route. I wished I had it in me.'

'Don't ever go, Frances,' I pleaded, 'without you where would I be?'

Frances leaned across and squeezed my hand. 'You have already left me, don't ever forget that.'

That night we went for a walk along the coastal path. A quarter moon hung in the sky, and the stars flickered big and low as if within our grasp. The yellow and red lights of the returning boats swayed like a line of festive bulbs. People were preparing small bonfires at regular intervals along the path to act as welcoming beacons for the cruise ship when it would arrive the following week. Some stopped us to say how sorry they were to hear about Knucky and that maybe there was hope yet.

We walked on past the houses and down onto the beach. Frances stopped by a small dune that the three of us used to come to some evenings after school. The spotlights of the prison beamed brightly in the sky with false promise. We sat down on the dune. I put my arm around Frances' shoulder and held her. I knew that she would not come back to my house that night. We had moved beyond this now, something else to be relieved about.

'How do you feel?' she asked.

'I don't know,' I said. 'I'm not sure if I feel anything.'

'I feel happy.' She pushed in against me. 'It has been a long time since I felt this good about Knucky.'

'Do you think he could turn up yet?' I wished I had the heart to believe it.

'Knucky's not gone anywhere,' Frances said. 'Of all of us he's the least likely to leave.' She lifted up a handful of sand and shuffled the grains in her fist. Then she stood up, walked to the edge of the sea and cast them outwards high into the air. They dispersed, flickered in the prison lights and fell across the surface of the water.

Frances came back to me, and we lay there on the dune until the early hours of the morning.

A service was held for Knucky the following Sunday in the church. Before going I went up to the attic and took my mother's cowl from the photo album and placed it carefully in my jacket pocket.

Father Jack spoke of Knucky's generous spirit. He spoke of the great loss and of the comfort that was to be found in it. Afterwards he came over to shake our hands. He took Frances' hand between both of his and held it lovingly. I thanked him, and I left them talking together. I had seen Therese at the back of the church during the service. I looked for her now but could not find her anywhere. Charlie Doherty came over. He shook my hand.

'I'm really sorry,' he said. 'We needed him around here.'

I told him what Frances had said about Knucky, how he wasn't gone anywhere and Charlie said that she, if anyone, would know. I looked across from the church and saw Therese's car parked on the other side of the road. I could see her sitting in the front seat.

She seemed to be waiting.

'Listen, Charlie,' I said, 'I want you to know that I really am through with the Eskimo. I mean it. I've taken it as far as I can. I want to thank you for all you've done. I'm not sure I'd have made it without it.'

'So, are we all in the clear then?' Charlie asked and laughed. He looked embarrassed at my gratitude.

'There's none of us in the clear,' I said. 'Unfortunately we don't get away that lightly.' I looked back down to where Therese was parked. I was afraid the car would be gone, but it was parked there yet. I excused myself from Charlie and walked down the steps and across the road to her.

Therese leaned over and opened the passenger door. I sat in, closed it gently behind me and looked out at the lough. I thought of Mullen. I no longer felt afraid of him. Yes, it was possible he might do something to harm me, but he would only harm himself more. I knew this now. All of our actions are selfish however we portray them. No matter how much we intend to hurt others all we can ever do is hurt ourselves more.

Therese reached over and took my hand. 'I am so sorry about Knucky,' she said.

'Yes, I know you are.'

A pilot boat led a coal ship through the lough's safe waters. A lone fishing boat headed towards the open sea.

Therese let go my hand and started the engine. 'Hal's gone back,' she said. Her words were an offering.

'I heard that,' I told her. I said it gently, with care. I looked back at the church. Father Jack and Frances were still talking. He was still holding her hand.

'Where to?' Therese asked.

I put my hand in my pocket and felt my mother's cowl. I should have given it to Knucky long before now, but it was not too late. I would go down to the coast with Therese later and drop the cowl into the sea. He would need it wherever he was travelling to.

'I'd like to go home,' I said, 'if that is possible.'

Therese put the car into gear and indicated to pull out onto the road. 'I'll do the best I can,' she promised.

And no one, I thought, could possibly ask for more than that.